Nasty Pasty

By

Jon Cleave

Paperback ISBN – 978-1-910256-25-1
.epub ISBN – 978-1-910256-23-7
.mobi ISBN – 978-1-910256-24-4

'For Caroline - A woman of Kernow.'

'The Cornish; protected minority
or endangered species?'

Contents

Chapter One
Into the Fiery Furnace

It was good for the Cornish,
It was good for the Cornish,
It was good for the Cornish,
And it's good enough for me.

The last verse of 'That Old Time Religion' *(trad),*
when all present raise their glasses and drink a toast to
the dear old county and its people.

The Sloggetts were a Cornish family, though locally it was agreed that they were more like a herd. Like cattle, their heads dipped and bobbed whenever they moved en masse, and their eyes would pop and bulge and stare with a bovine inquisitiveness. Apart from the fact that they walked upright on two legs, it was only the absence of swishing tails that truly distinguished the family from heifers and steers.

There had always been the unkind rumour that those swishing tails might, in fact, be cleverly hidden beneath their undergarments, but this had yet to be substantiated. The unkindness was in all likelihood borne from the fact that, as with cattle, some people were wary or even a little scared of the Sloggetts and kept their distance, lest they be at best jostled, or even charged and trampled underfoot, or worse still, gored. Others said 'They're all right. They won't hurt you. Just don't run away from them, that's all; they're just curious.'

Curious? They most certainly were a little curious, the Sloggetts.

*

Vi Sloggett scooped a few pasty crumbs off the surface of the shop counter into the palm of her hand, and then brushed them into a bin. The family portrait on the wall was at its usual jaunty angle, and she corrected it, as she did every day of her life. She remembered how surprised she'd been that against all odds, Jean Couch (family photographer, pet portraits a speciality) had managed to capture what appeared to be a millisecond of family joy during the entirety of what had been a rather stressed and strained morning twenty years ago.

Reflectively, she ran her index finger across the top of the frame, and twiddled for non-existent dust between her finger and thumb. The family were all there, frozen in time at the front of their shop. They were posed so unnaturally beneath the 'Mother's Pasties' sign that you could be forgiven for believing them to be the work of a Victorian taxidermist, a stuffed tableau one might find fading in a glass case in some long forgotten corner of the county museum.

Vi was cradling Cheel, never the easiest of babies, who moments earlier had managed a projectile up-throwing of violent frothiness; a pink cocktail of formula and Calpol all over her pristine christening robes and, never being one for half measures, splattering the lay preacher to boot.

Vi could recognise the strain in her own forced smile, made worse by the fact that Oggy was grasping Mervin's hand harder than he should have done, for the little boy had been whimpering to be let on the beach and was bored.

Behind the proud parents and their two kids, Oggy's father stood, just a few months before he choked on the crust of what turned out to be his ultimate pasty, and next to him rosy old apple-cheeked Uncle Clar, who at least looked as properly cheerful back then as he still did today.

And then there was Mother herself, glaring hard out of the portrait and right down the lens. Mother, whose helpful child-rearing advice on the day of Cheel's christening had not exactly helped ease the frisson of tension.

Mother, Vi's own, dear mother-in-law
Mother, Nan to Cheel and Mervin.
Mother, of Mother's Pasties.
Mother, she-wolf of the Sloggetts.
The Mother of discontent.

Some things never changed. Oggy grunted and grumbled out from the kitchen behind, and joined Vi at the counter.

'Hellfire and bloody brimstone missus,' he muttered. 'We can't run a business like this. Every time I says we should try something new, Mother threatens to curl up in bed and die.'

Vi squeezed his arm. 'Shh, now,' she said. 'Don't bite.'

Mother was earwigging from the kitchen. 'Your father would turn in his grave, boy!' she cursed at him loudly, from behind the door.

'Nothing wrong with her hearing,' he hissed. 'Christ, she got ears like radar.'

'I heard that too!'

'And don't call me boy, Mother, I'm bloody sixty!' he shouted over his shoulder. 'Did you hear that all right?'

'Hush now. Come look at this,' said Vi. She pointed and Oggy focused smiling on the portrait. 'How small she was.'

'Aww, dear little maid. Never no trouble, that Cheel,' said Oggy gently.

'Remember her tiny little fingers?'

'Yes, tiny. And Mervin's too. Look at his little smile. Dear little fella,' said Oggy.

'That ain't a smile. You was squeezing his hand.'

'I never was.'

'What was that?' demanded Mother, her head poked around the kitchen door.

'Nothing to do with you Mother. Get back in the kitchen or you'll frighten the customers. Get to bed!'

'I might too. You're bringing on me bilious again. I can hardly breathe. Hear me gurgling? I'm gurgling! Tell him Uncle Clar.'

'She is gurgling, Oggy,' confirmed Uncle Clar.

'Whatever, Mother. Go up and close the bedroom door behind you and then we shan't be able to hear it!'

By the time their first customer came in, around half an hour later, Mother had indeed gurgled on up to her bed, and Vi had soothed and calmed Oggy so sufficiently that he was cheerfully and big heartedly singing away to himself while he racked up the pasties. He sang old songs and new songs, choir songs and songs that he sang in the pub with his mates, songs from the shows (except Andrew Lloyd Webber songs which he loathed), religious songs as long as they were from the Sankey hymnal, and Cornish songs.

He particularly liked the revivalist medley that Jeff, musical director of the Tredogend Fisherman's Male Voice Choir, had arranged, a medley that merged what could be a dirgy, rather dreary 'My Grandfather's Clock' into the hearty 'That Old Time Religion'. Oggy's natural vibrato echoed around the artexed ceiling and a customer, rather intrigued, appeared at the counter and listened politely as he sang out like a lark ascending.

> '...Give me some of that old time religion,
> And it's good enough for me.
> And it will save you from the fiery furnace,
> It will save you from the fiery furnace,
> It will save you from the fiery furnace and ....'

The lady complimented Vi on her husband's fine bass baritone, and Vi thanked her very much whilst she attended to her pasty order with an easy, naturally pleasant patience. She called the order out aloud to Oggy, who creaked open the heavy metal door of what was his own personal fiery furnace, the antique Treleaven Pasty oven. Embroiled in the swirling, steamy, savoury fog of baking pasties, he momentarily stopped singing, and in a movement that appeared at first suicidal, put his head and shoulders right inside the cooker and reached for the scalding lip of the pasty-covered baking tray, and gingerly slid it out.

Gingerly was the way in which Oggy had to do everything. He had no option, for his thatch was neither merely sandy nor reddish, nor even strawberry blonde. It was proper in your face, carrot-topped, Day-Glo ginger.

The Cornish generally regard themselves as a dark and swarthy race, a genetic melting pot of dark and swarthy Celtic stock with perhaps a dozen or so dark and swarthy survivors of the Spanish armada, those who had managed to loop storm-blown up around the north of Scotland and then down past the west of Ireland, until on the final leg of their return journey to Torremolinos they were unluckily shipwrecked on the unforgiving jagged rocks of North Cornwall.

Finding that, back then, the locals were quite tolerant and welcoming of incomers, especially dark and swarthy ones, and that the climate was equable if just a *poco* wet and windy, they shacked up with willing Cornish maids in places like Chapel Amble, Scredda and Talskiddy, and had dark and swarthy families.

In striking contrast to the dark swarthiness there are, however, enclaves of Cornish gingerness, notably in St Just, parts of Redruth (funnily enough) and up on the north coast in the small fishing port of Tredogend, where Oggy Sloggett was very much a little ginger enclave all to himself.

He swore blind that his temper was not as short-fused as it might once have been, and opined that anyone would be likely to fly off the handle under a constant barrage of not-so-gentle teasing involving carrots, orang-utans and Jaffa cakes, and he was probably right. We must conclude that it is the unforgiving world around the ginger that unfairly sets them all up as filthy-tempered buggers.

Vi had seen the hair go through a bewildering array of style manifestations since she had first arrived in Tredogend. She had first encountered the young man sweating beneath the untidy ginger straggle over a bottle of dry natch, up at Deli Disco in the Poldark Inn at Delabole in the early nineteen-seventies. She had witnessed his wildly alarming interpretation of the Status Quo classic 'Caroline', thumbs firmly hooked in his belt loops and his hair flailing around and around in a frenzied anti-clockwise whirl. It was a quite dizzying display of something that was not really dancing as such, but was clearly very popular down in Cornwall, and he had won her heart.

She had seen the hair metamorphose over the ensuing years, and it marked Oggy's rites of passage from callow youth through to the remnants of the fine man she knew and loved today. From that lank, disorganised mop of early Deli Disco days to a glam Slade feather cut and then a rebellious spiky crop, there came and went a mercifully brief curly perm (complemented by a droopy Mexicano moustache), a rather too sophisticated eighties bouffon and, when the rigours of backcombing became too much for him, an unpleasant flirtation with the mullet. Styles came and went, but the ginger stubbornly remained.

Oggy's acceptance of the onset of middle age, when to have any hair at all could be regarded as a blessing, was severlcy compromised by the ill-advised comb-over that he proudly swept, swished and swooshed slick into position at the sink every morning. But at least it did not constitute a mid-life crisis; though Vi understood that the ginger/comb-over combo would probably never capture the coveted 'Golden Scissors' for the outstanding student of the tonsorial arts at St Austell College, she could see that Oggy at least seemed happy with it. She was content with the thought that it was better than him splashing out on any flash red sports car that he couldn't afford, or blundering into a torrid and ultimately doomed affair with some flash, red-dressed spinster of the parish. Not that there were too many of those, mind you.

Oggy's skin was pale and freckled, and his complexion flushed and blushed scarlety crimson with alarming speed whenever anger or embarrassment called, or whenever he had occasion to put his head in the oven. The vivid, livid colouring was augmented by the big and bushy ginger sideburns he had farmed since he first discovered the joys of facial hair back in his mid-teens. He wore his old bugger grips with pride.

At two hundred degrees in the Treleaven Pasty oven, both his comb-over and grips were as usual beginning to dampen and bead with sweat. Strands of hair began to hang dangled and straggly over his ever-reddening face. It was a dilemma, for though he was finding it hard to breathe, the aromatic temptation of the pasties was seductive in the extreme.

'Aaah, hell! How many Mother's Traditional, missus?' he panted from within the deeply delicious recesses of his pasty shelves.

'One,' said Vi.

'Aaaay!? I can't hear you, I got perforation running right into me ears,' he shouted. The lady waiting at the counter looked a little bemused. Vi smiled reassuringly.

'He means perspiration, madam. Won't be a moment. Fresh batch,' she said quietly. The lady nodded.

Vi bent to repeat the order to her sizzled, frizzled, crackling-hot husband, whose entire head was by now beginning to cook very nicely indeed. She chuckled to herself. Shove an apple in his gob, she mused, and garnish his lughole with a sprig of rosemary and stick him on a spit, and he'd have made the ultimate Cornish hog roast.

Vi was not a native of Cornwall, and not for one single moment had she lost the accent she'd brought all the way to Tredogend from London in 1972. She'd started work as a waitress serving cream teas in a café on the harbour front, and before long Oggy had swept her off her feet with all his rustic-cidered charm and freestyle creative dance routines, and she'd gone to work with him and his family in Mother's pasty shop.

Vi still chattered with a twang that rang like Bow Bells, a voice that in truth would have been better suited to flogging jellied eels and pie, mash and liquor from a barrow somewhere down the Old Kent Road, but it was a voice that nonetheless lent a deliciously incongruous touch to the most delicious pasty shop in Cornwall.

'A Mother's Traditional, three Cornish Pixie pasties for the kids, and a Cornish Giant. Are you bleedin' Mutt and Jeff, darlin'?' she hissed.

Oggy straightened up and cracked the top of his head on the hot frame of the fiery furnace, the blow somewhat cushioned by the comb-over.

'Ouch, bugger!' grumbled Oggy. 'Jeff? What does Jeff want? Is practice off? We got a concert up at Bolventor Methodist Chapel on Sunday.'

Still partially deafened by the trickling perspiration, he rubbed his bonce. He slid and scraped and scratched and screeched the scalding pasty trays in and out, and then out and in of the oven, over and over again.

'Hellfire, that's hot!' he cursed, and gingerly handed Vi a tray of pasties.

'No, not *that* Jeff. I'll have to get you lessons in rhyming slang darlin',' she said, and began to bag up the pasties for the lady at the counter.

She glanced over her shoulder. 'Bolventor? That's up on the moors ain't it, love? They eat their young up there. Anyway, I'm still one pasty short. Where's me Cornish Giant?'

'They ain't done yet. They need longer than the others cos there's more filling in them,' said Oggy, as he creaked and tweaked, and twinged and whinged stiffly back to his feet. He rubbed himself down with the tea towel, paying particular attention to his sweaty, wet old bugger grips.

'Now madam, I'm so sorry,' said Vi in a rather faux posh voice. 'I'm afraid the Cornish Giants are not quite done yet. Mr Sloggett says they require longer baking than the others, don't you darlin'? There's more in them, you see. I can let you have another Mother's Traditional to be going along with, maybe two?'

'Perfect,' said the customer.

Oggy Sloggett began a deep down grumble, and his neck bulged and his shoulders hunched in a tense, knotted muscularity as he contemplated bending to the fiery furnace door once again. And as he grumbled and rumbled, the vibration seemed to resonate deep down through him into the slate slabbed floor beneath, and for a moment it seemed as if the fabric of the building around them was beginning to shudder and crack.

'Stop it, for gawds sake, you're making the whole bleedin' place shake,' said Vi. 'You're like an earthquake you are.'

'It isn't me missus, it's Mother's old deep freeze out in the pantry you can hear. I told her it's buggered. Just like my knees!'

Slowly Oggy re-opened the heavy old oven door, took out the pasties and handed then up to Vi, who dextrously placed each into it's own 'Mother's Traditional Cornish Pasties' paper bag, and then handed them across the counter to the customer.

'That'll be ten pounds fifty madam, thank you,' she said.

'Perfect. Do you take a card?' asked the lady, who with the lightest of touches fingered through the vast array of plastic lined up in her chintzy, floral Cath Kidston purse.

Oggy growled again.

'I'm afraid not madam, sorry about that,' said Vi hurriedly to the lady, who smiled kindly and handed her the cash.

'Thank you. Enjoy them madam,' said Vi.

'Oh we shall, thank you so much,' said the customer, and turned for the door and opened it, tinkling the shop bell in the process.

'Thank you, goodbye,' called Vi.

'Thank *you*,' said the customer smilingly, and closed the door, so tinkling the shop bell again, and they watched together as she turned left across the shop front and off towards the harbour.

'Card my ass,' cursed Oggy. 'Cash is king.'

'Aww, she was nice,' said Vi.

'Bollocks,' said Oggy. 'Course she was nice. We're too cheap, that's why.'

Chapter Two
The Birds

Pray leave me alone, I have hands of my own,
And along with you I'll not go.
You will hear the fond tale, of the sweet nightingale,
As she sings in the valley below,
As she sings in the valley below.

'The Sweet Nightingale' - *Traditional Cornish Folk Song*.

Emma clutched the warm pasty bags to her breast. She tripped lightly towards the harbour side, pretty in her white pedal pushers and Breton striped matelot top; with her bobbed, dark hair and big, bright eyes, and vivid flash of her cherry red lipstick, she was a picture.

Huge was waiting for her, bored, his legs dangling over the harbour wall which he kicked with the heels of his unstrapped yellow Wellington boots. He glanced up and caught Emma through the corner of his sly eye. He preferred blondes.

It all felt a bit too late for that now, with their three kids arrayed amongst the pebbles and little rock pools below.

'Look Daddy, I've caught a big fish!' called out the eldest Quenelle, his little sister's head netted and dripping in sandy seaweed. One might have expected such a tiny person to squeal and cry, but no, Julienne pulled the net off and snatched it from him, and threw it as a javelin across the rocks and into the foamy, frothy, weedy, plastic and crisp packet soup of the incoming tide. Quenelle squealed and cried.

Youngest brother Goujon didn't even look up, perched cross-legged atop a smoothed comfy boulder, and just carried on reading *Collin's Guide to The British Seashore*, a chapter about bivalves and their filtration systems. Always a worrying trend in a six year old.

'Careful darling, that's Quenelle's,' shouted Huge, clearly unwilling to jeopardise quality family time with anything like a proper parental intervention, or worse still an admonition.

Julienne shoved Quenelle into the rock pool and called him a loser in a spitty, hissy, poisonous little viper voice. He began to splash and cry and flounder around and Emma, still clutching the bags, began to run along the harbour side in panic.

'Stop them Huge!' she screamed. 'She'll drown him for heaven's sake!'

Huge grabbed a bag from her and waved it in the air, and called 'pasties' to the children, who as one turned and stopped what they were doing and ran back up the slipway and over to their Mum and Dad, and dived into their bags and grabbed the Mother's Traditional pasties.

'Oh no,' said Emma. 'Those are for Daddy and me. Here, yours are the Little Pixie pasties, with the Cornish pixie on the bag. Can you see his pointy hat?'

'Yuck, swizz,' said Quenelle shiveringly. 'I wanted a big one!'

'And me!' said Julienne. Goujon looked at the pointy-hatted pixie on his bag and just munched.

Huge was still delving. 'Where's my Cornish Giant darling?'

'They're not ready yet. They require more baking, you see there's more in them darling,' said Emma. 'Have a Mother's Traditional. I've got you an extra one.'

They all said 'Yummy,' and sat like a happy family eating their delicious Mother's pasties by the harbour side at Tredogend. They held them with the paper bags half-folded back to save their hands from the heat of the pastry. Other families promenaded up and down the street behind them doing the same thing. There was a general murmuring of approval and nodding and lip-licking and yum-yumming at the sheer uncomplicated loveliness of this traditional Cornish feast.

'Mmm,' said Goujon. 'I love the potato.'

'I love the meat,' said Julienne.

'What about you, Daddy?' asked Emma.

'I love the swede,' he said.

Truth was, he loved everything about the pasty, the ingredients, the pastry, the perfect seasoning. He loved its indefinable magic. It was truly wonderful.

Above, a beaked-banditry of opportunistic seagulls and jackdaws leered down with Hitchcockian menace from the parapets and guttering of the rooftops. Like feathered hoodies they eyeballed every pasty that was paraded past them, and waited for the merest slip where they could dive in and snatch a piece of crust or potato or meat from the ground.

Or worse.

Julienne had seen a small, jaunty bird dipping and scratching its living along the margins of the harbour wall, pecking at the weeds that clung between the granite blocks.

'That's a sweet little sparrow,' she said. 'Cute.'

'It's a pied wagtail,' muttered Goujon, his pasty in one hand and book in the other.

'I'm going to call him Mr Waggy,' said Julienne. 'Here, Mr Waggy.'

In kindness, she tossed it the tiniest piece of potato, a signal for the gigantic posse of gulls to squarrel down in a screaming, shrieking, screeching gullaballoo and mug the wagtail in a most supreme display of hooligullism.

'Don't be so stupid Jules!' shouted Quenelle.

Huge leapt to his feet and stumbled clumsily, and dropped what was left of his pasty. He squashed it with his own ghastly yellow wellie, and the innards shot out and spewed across the tarmac. He kicked and thrashed about to scare the marauding birds off and Quenelle, who liked to copy his Dad, did the same. This seemed to be the signal for a particularly bold gull to divebomb in; narrowly it missed the boy's left ear, audaciously snatched his Cornish Pixie pasty and then fly up and away with the lunch lodged firmly in its thieving beak.

All the other gulls now lost interest in the original miserly scrap of potato. They launched up and off in a squawking squadron and chased and mobbed the mugger until it dropped the pasty splash into the harbour, whereupon they all dived in to grab what they could of the floating fragments of pasty shrapnel. All in all, it had not been a very satisfactory demonstration of the art of sharing, but they were gulls and that was very much what they did.

Delightful little Mr Waggy meanwhile hopped back and swallowed the scrap of potato that had sparked off the whole drama. Julienne smiled at it. Goujon carried on munching.

Quenelle was distraught and in tears for the second time, and was being cuddled and consoled by Emma by way of Huge's second Mother's Traditional pasty, to make up for the one that had been bandited away by the gulls.

'Oh charming,' said Huge. 'And what do *I* get to eat?'

Emma gave him a look. He was bored on holiday. He had trodden on his own pasty, which was now firmly embedded in the tread of his size elevens. His eldest son was eating his other pasty. His younger son was just, strange. His daughter did exactly what she wanted. His wife was a brunette. And he was covered in seagull shit.

Emma passed him a Kleenex. Huge pulled on his shades. 'I'll be back in a minute,' he said.

He strode off through the throng of pasty chomping tourists and away from the harbour front. He wiped himself down as he passed the newsagents with their faded red and yellow buckets and spades and racks of dog-eared postcards hanging dusty outside; past the ubiquitous surf shop next door with it's funkily hibiscused flip-flops and surf dude t-shirts and boogie boards and beads; on around the corner past Dead Dog Wong's mock-Tudor Chinese Restaurant, and towards the dilapidated Wesleyan Chapel and it's forlorn 'For Sale' sign at the top end of the street. Just before that, on the left, stood Mother's Pasty shop.

From his secret stool between the pasty oven and a partition wall, Oggy sat with his mind very much in neutral, still just about cheerful enough to hum 'Pull for the Shore Sailor' to himself, tenor and bass, while he waited for his next customers.

The telephone rang, and he picked up the receiver and answered.

'Mother's,' he said jovially. There was a slight delay with the reply.

'Good morning sir. May I be speaking to the person who is in charge of the business please?'

'Yes.'

'May I ask your name please, sir?'

'Oggy Sloggett.'

'Good morning, Mr Oggy. My name is Colin. I am calling from Business Solutions for You. We are offering debit and credit card facilities. How are you today sir?'

'Could be busier I suppose.'

'Mr Oggy, I think we can offer you the opportunity for busy business, sir. Our customised service which incorporates the latest, cutting-edge, high tech, high-spec equipment ensures an instant link to your personal account and online banking set-up, with full technical backing-up by our expert team, instant replacment in the event of malfunction, and supplying of any sundry items required, both within twenty four hours. May I ask if this is of interest to you Mr Oggy?'

'What was your name again?'

'Colin, Mr Oggy.'

'You don't sound much like no Colin. Where's the catch then? What do you get out of it?'

'I am being paid for every business I get to sign-up for Business Solutions for You, sir.'

'Where be you ringing from then?'

'Delhi.'

'Oh, up Delabole. Proper job. I met the missus up there at Deli Disco, in the Poldark Inn? Do you ever go?'

'No…I don't think so Mr Oggy.'

'Don't go to the Poldark? Best disco in North Cornwall that used to be.'

'No, Mr Oggy I…'

Mr Oggy heard the loud ringing of the shop bell and the bang of the door opening with some considerable force as a large figure burst in.

'I gotta go Colin,' said Oggy. 'I got paying customers. You'll have to call back, sorry.'

'Shop!' called Huge, and seeing no one around he reached back and vigorously rang the shop bell again with his hand. 'Shop!' he shouted. 'Anyone at home? Hello!'

The deeply unimpressed Oggy replaced the telephone and got slowly to his feet. The man with the huge floppy fringe and huge shades came towards his counter. He looked Oggy up and down, and regarded him with a hugely superior and supercilious expression. Oggy looked right past and over the man's shoulder as a couple came in behind him, followed by a teenaged boy, and then two men with small children, a man in a wheelchair and then some others. The shop bell tinkled continuously and suddenly before he knew it, Oggy had a rush on.

Everything about Huge was huge. He had a huge mouth and lips from which came a hugely nauseating voice, he wore huge yellow Wellington boots, hugely flowery shirts and hugely garish trousers, and he had a huge house in the Cotswolds and a huge 4x4 car with huge tyres (that he had loudly christened 'the beast-cruiser') to take him to his huge apartment overlooking Chiswick Eyot to conduct his huge TV career as the hugest of all the celebrity chefs.

Then, of course, there was his huger than huge ego.

He had in reality been christened plain old Hugo Strutt. It was only as '*Huge in the Kitchen*' took off and swelled to such huge proportions that he took on his screen persona nickname 'Huge' with relish and gusto, so that as far as he and the rest of the world were concerned he was now, indeed, plain Huge.

Celebrity chef.

Huge in the Kitchen.

Huge. With a capital 'H'.

Huge was about to buy his pasty at the counter, when a man and a woman, on holiday from Smethick, stepped up beside him.

'Excuse me,' said the man, who was called Doug. 'I think you missed a bit.'

'What?' he snapped.

'The seagull mess, look,' he said. He wiped a bit from Huge's shoulder.

'Oh, yea, thanks,' muttered Huge, begrudgingly.

'It's good luck, mate,' said Doug. He plucked up courage. 'It is you, ain't it? Are you that Huge?'

A woman, rather impatiently, came from behind them in the queue and went around them and up to the counter where Oggy was leaning, waiting to serve and quite frankly looking rather mystified at all the goings-on with Huge and Doug and his good lady wife from Smethick.

'Who is it?' he asked the woman.

'Him off the telly. That chef. I can't stick him. Can I have a Mother's Traditional please?'

Oggy popped one in a bag and took the money. The woman left.

'It is him,' said the man Doug to his wife. 'You *are* him, ain't ya?'

'We love your show,' said his wife. 'Love it!'

'Huge in the Kitchen, eh? I always say to the wife, is he huge anywhere else?'

'Doug, don't. He's on holiday, aren't you love?' But you're our favourite,' she said.

'Next please,' called Oggy.

A man stepped around Huge and Smethick Doug and his wife, and up to the counter. Then the man in the wheelchair followed suite, and then a woman. They all bought several pasties each. Huge, though, was still trapped by the grinning Doug and his missus.

'Thought you might like to do one called '*Huge in the Bedroom*, what d'ya reckon? Get it?' asked Doug. He stepped to one side to let yet another customer past him and to the counter. 'Oh sorry mate, I'm in the way, was you trying to get a pasty? Pardon me, but we love him, we do. It's that Huge,' he said, pointing at the chef.

Huge was now well and truly distracted. Doug's wife managed to lead him away past Huge and over to the counter to get their own pasties. 'Keep it up mate,' he called over his shoulder, and then to the intrigued onlookers, 'He's that Huge in the Kitchen, he is. It is him, you know!'

So now a little crowd of fans mobbed like gulls around Huge in the shop, with pens and bits of paper and pasty bags to sign, which he did with the complete absence of a glad heart and with a very forced and very false smile. More folk peered in through the shop window and seeing that it was indeed him, came in and waited their turn for their signatures. When Huge finally came to the last one, a teenaged boy with livid spots around his mouth who had no pasty bag or piece of paper to sign on, he folded the brown streaked, gull-smeared Kleenex tissue over and over, making it into a kind of guano fajita and signed that instead, and squelched it shittily into the grateful boy's hand.

He'd only come in for a pasty, and was quite relieved when all those dreadful people had gone. Being a TV superchef was not easy; if people only knew what celebrities like him had to suffer. It wasn't all roses, the continual adulation. Sometimes he wished that for a minute or so he could just be, well, plain and ordinary like everyone else, and not always have to be this magnetically charismatic and charming superstar of the kitchenista.

Anyway, he was now the only customer remaining, and there was but one Cornish Giant pasty left in the tray. Thanks to the rush there were no other pasties at all in the shop. Huge reached back to the door and rang the shop bell again.

'Shop!' he shouted, for the assistant seemed to have vanished.

Oggy got up wearily from his secret stool and came to the counter with an order pad and sullen expression. 'What can I do for you?' he said. 'We open at ten tomorrow. How many would you like to order?'

'I'll take that one,' said Huge.

He snapped his fingers dismissively in the direction of the gigantic, beautiful Cornish Giant pasty, the only remaining morsel in the shop. Oggy didn't move. Huge clicked his fingers again, like castanets.

'The...Cornish...Giant....please....thank...you,' he said in an unpleasantly staccato voice.

'There isn't one for sale,' growled Oggy.

'Oh, really? Let's see now, shall we just take a peep? Oh look! Forgive me if I'm wrong, or isn't that one there right in front of us? That pastry thingy, shaped like a pasty?' said Huge, not used to being denied anything at all. He almost prodded it with his index finger. 'I'll take that one, shall I?'

'No you shan't,' said Oggy. 'That's Digory's.'

'Digory? Digory? What's Digory for heaven's sake?' demanded Huge.

'Digory Hicks has a Cornish Giant everyday, he do. That's reversed especially for him. That's why I put a pastry 'D' on it,' said Oggy, pointing.

'It doesn't look like a 'D'. It looks more like a 'P', or an 'O',' said Huge.

'It depends how you looks at it,' growled Oggy.

'What?'

'From this side of the counter 'tis a 'D'.'

'Oh this is bloody absurd,' snapped Huge. 'Do you have any idea who I am?'

'I know who Digory Hicks is,' said Oggy, who had remained surprisingly calm, but now felt the merest hint, just a soupçon, of the mythological ginger mist descending. It was rapidly degenerating into a bit of a standoff.

The door opened behind him. Vi had finished her lunch break, just a quick pasty and a cup of tea, and breezed in behind the shop counter with her husband. She could quite clearly smell the cordite of conflict.

'Ah, a person,' sighed Huge, feigning relief. 'Do you think we could get this pasty in the bag? Then I could maybe give you some money? It's a funny system I know, but it seems to work quite well elsewhere.'

'I know who you are,' said Vi excitedly. 'You're that "Huge" geezer off the telly, ain't ya'?'

'Perhaps you could tell numbnuts here who I am, then I can get my lunch and we can all move on, for Christ's sake,' snarled Huge.

Vi didn't hear. 'It's that "Huge",' she said to Oggy. 'You know him, love, that one Mother loves, we watched him the other night.'

'I don't give a tuppenny turd who he is,' growled Oggy, even more deeply than before. 'I don't care if he's the bloody pope.'

'That's cos you're a Methodist, darlin', said Vi. 'What can we get you today?' she asked Huge politely.

'I'd like that Cornish Giant, or whatever the thing's called…' said Huge. He stared at Oggy and did not look at Vi at all. 'Please…thank you…very much.'

'Certainly sir,' she said, and lifted it with the ancient pasty tongs and placed it in the Cornish Giant paper bag.

Oggy hissed into Vi's ear. ''Tis Digory's,' he said.

Huge held out his Coutts and Co Visa card in his flabby palm.

The shop doorbell rang and the door opened and a dapper little man walked in, and a stray, mangy lurcher with protruding ribs and a walleye loped in close behind him. Oggy reached over to Vi and gently took the bag from her.

'Thank you Violet,' he said with a slow and deliberate satisfaction. 'Good afternoon Digory, here is your pasty with the 'D' on it. Like what I makes and saves for you every day? Like what I done for the past thirty years?'

He smirked at Huge in triumph.

'Oh,' said Digory. 'Cheers Oggy, but I shan't be needing it today dear. I had a cheese sandwich on a drop off down Newquay airport. That's what I came in to tell you.'

It wasn't quite what Oggy had wanted to hear in the circumstances.

'Are you sure you wouldn't like to take it home and have it dreckly, Digory?' asked Oggy in the same deliberate tone.

'No, thank you.'

'Positive?' asked Oggy. ''Tis no trouble.'

For once, Digory wasn't picking up the signals. Huge thrust his floppy-fringe forward. 'So, I'll take it then, shall I?' he said, and thwacked his Coutts and Co card hard down on the counter.

Oggy glared, but did not move. 'Pity,' he said. 'Us don't do cards.'

Huge huffed and jiggled deep in his pocket for cash. It was hard to tell whether Oggy Sloggett dropped the bag accidentally, or accidentally on purpose, and Vi had her suspicions. Whatever, the pasty popped out and fell on the floor and the mangy, rangy lurcher slavered down on it in a flash, and shook it as if it were a coursed hare, and devoured it greedily in one mouthful. Huge stepped back and just stood there aghast, open-mouthed and utterly furious. The dog scarpered.

Oggy looked right at Huge. 'Aww, that naughty old dog just had your pasty mate,' he said. '*And* t'was the very last one too.'

Huge turned on his heels and strutted angrily for the door.

'What a terrible shame that was. Would you care to order one for tomorrow sir?' Oggy asked coyly, tentatively fingering his order pad.

'Bloody impertinence, I've *never* been so insulted...' cursed the enraged chef, and added something else very unpleasant about bloody inbred backwaters. The glass shuddered, and the 'open/closed' sign fell to the floor as he slammed the door shut behind him with an almighty bang, and left the premises.

'You ought to get out more then!' Oggy shouted after him.

'Who *was* that, dear?' asked Digory, quite bemused by what had unfurled in front of him. Oggy chuckled.

'Nobody,' he said.

Chapter Three
Dreckly Never Comes

Dreckly – *a period of time somewhere in the (possibly distant) future. Imagine 'manana', only without the sense of urgency. There is no direct English translation of this word.*

Huge barely slept that night. If it were not bad enough that he hadn't got his own way with the pasty, it seemed that the man didn't even know who he was. Surely that ginger buffoon *must* have heard of him. Surely. His wife evidently had, so why not him? Huge tossed and turned for what had seemed hours, and then he finally got off at three-ish, only to wake up in the cold sweat of a nightmare in which all of a sudden his fame and celebrity had deserted him and he had been left, well, just plain ordinary. The scenario was utterly unthinkable.

Morning came. Emma knew Huge well enough to know that he would still be desperate to have the pasty, and gave Quenelle some money for an errand to pop to Mother's pasty shop as soon as it opened. The little boy had gone in, all on his own, and bought a Cornish pasty each for all the family.

'Please may I have three little Pixie pasties, a Mother's Traditional pasty and a Cornish Giant pasty, please?' he said.

'Yes my darlin',' said Vi. 'What a little poppet, ain't he?'

'Proper little chap,' said Oggy. 'Very polite. Credit to his parents.'

Mother popped her head around the kitchen door and scowled with curiosity.

'No Mother, get back,' snapped Oggy. 'You'll give the poor little boy nightmares.'

'But I only…'

'Back!' he said, and kicked the door shut.

'There you are, lovey,' said Vi. 'Down on holiday, are ya?'

'Yes thank you. We're playing on the beach, me and my brother and sister. And Mummy too.'

'Oh, where's Daddy then, darlin'?'

'Daddy's a bit grumpy. He's sitting by the harbour. This is to cheer him up.'

'Good boy,' said Vi. 'Bye darlin'.'

'Bye bye, my ansom,' said Oggy.

Huge sat astride an old granite mooring post that had been sunk into the top of the harbour wall, and Quenelle took his pasty over to him and then ran off to play. From the post he could see across to the opposite side of the harbour, where the kids were building dams on the beach again, and Emma relaxing on the smooth-worn rocks of the tide line. He sniffed the air to take in the fresh, salty ozone scent of Tredogend bay. He was overwhelmed by the teasing, swirling burlesque of the aromatic pasty steam that danced beguilingly from the bag in his hand. At last, he was able to eat his pasty in peace.

Huge peeled back the paper from around the top half of the Cornish Giant pasty, leaving an end exposed. He studied the drawing on the bag, a depiction of giant John Payne, the terrifying standard bearer striding at the vanguard of Sir Bevil Grenville's victorious royalist army at the Battle of Stratton. Huge mantled his pasty to ward off Tredogend's squadron of flying bandits, for this time he was not going to be thwarted. He bit into it for the first time. Never before had he tasted such a magnificent thing.

An impudent one-legged gull hopped over and cocked its head to one side and squawked cheekily at the celebrity chef. Huge ignored the bird, and chomped and slavered his way through the pasty with all the savage relish of a starving lion tearing up a tender wildebeest calf on the Serengeti. In a flash, the pasty was gone. It had been so much like the best sex he'd ever had, even down to the obscene climactic grunts he'd made as he finished it off.

He stared, transfixed, at the bag. 'Yes, of course,' he said, and laughed aloud.

He folded the bag neatly and put it in his pocket. 'Yes, that's it. I've got it!'

Huge had to admit it, even by his own standards it was an idea of pure genius.

The gull stared quizzically. 'And you can fuck off too, you filthy feathered Cornish freak. There won't be as much as a crumb in it for you.'

He popped the final nub of pastry into his fleshy mouth, jumped to his feet, and with a spring in his step for the first time in days, made his way back around the harbour side to Emma.

The little widower Digory Hicks was Oggy Sloggett's oldest mate. They'd started school together on the same day in the autumn of 1953, in hobnail boots and long shorts, and sat next to one another in class and played together, grown up together, and grown middle-aged together in and around the little port of Tredogend.

Digory Hicks represented the finest Cornish tradition; never a Jacker of all trades, he was always very much the Renaissance man. In a poor county where it was tricky to make ends meet, it was as well to have several strings to your bow, and that was Digory all over. Several strings to his bow, and several quivers full of arrows.

Since Doreen's passing, on his small holding Dordigor Farm (lovingly named after them both) sprawled way up in the moorland heights above Tredogend, he had started a small rare breeds programme for endangered Cornish livestock. In addition he was a driver for his own taxi company (DigsCabs), and fancied himself, not without good reason, to be a bit of a herbalist and forager and all round countryman.

He'd had a pretty good day of it so far. To start with he'd picked up a commodities broker from an obscenely oversized house down at Rock and dropped him at Newquay airport. During the journey Digory had shared with him wisdom on an eclectic array of subjects, from the infuriating fluctuation of the price of lobster to the relative efficiency of wind farms and solar farms, and even the comparative merits of the castrato as opposed to the counter tenor in early eighteenth century Italianate cantata, most of which he'd made up. At the terminal, the bewildered broker had thanked Digory, but politely declined the opportunity to subscribe to his new website.

For Digory Hicks was also moving forward as founder and proprietor of the lonelyfarmersheartsclub. com, a sort of bucolic online knocking shop for those ruddy-faced, soil-toiling sons of Kernow who found mainstream socialising just too much of a challenge.

When he got back to Dordigor Farm, he'd found time to check the website and answer queries from his valued lonelyfarmersheartsclub.com clients. The clientele was generally, but not exclusively, of the agricultured persuasion: wind and sun farmers, wave and tide farmers, grant and granny farmers, grandad and subsidy farmers, organic farmers, a few gentleman farmers and quite a few more beastly old farmers who invariably seemed to wear cord trousers held up precariously with orange bailer twine.

Except, of course, when in lay-bys.

He fixed up an organic alpaca farmer from Zennor with a hot hotelier from Newquay, down a lane near the Roche rock (funnily enough a former leper colony, though who would care if it turned out to be a love match).

Once he had established that Bill Bottallick from London Apprentice (fibre glass slurry pit linings) had taken the carefully prescribed intake of River Camel oysters to, shall we say, stiffen his resolve, Digory then played e-cupid and set him up with a racy date with spicy mother of six, Sharon Smith of Stenalees. Sharon had no real agricultural connections at all, save a passing resemblance to a Percheron mare.

But Sharon was a fine, comfy great maid, and Digory'd had to assure Bill, using furniture manufacturer's parlance, that she was both built like a three-piece suite and that her skin had the corresponding allure of velour. Her long face was somewhat less appealing, but Bill was not over worried by aesthetics, and they met down a highly recommended clay pit maintenance road next to the Eden Project, with 'a nice view over the domes' as Digory had euphemistically confided.

The web-based business was going from strength to strength, though latterly the inclusion of the so-called Beast of Bodmin, Constable 696 Carthew Carew (former slaughter man and bouncer, and part time security 'consultant'), had as yet generated few enquiries from any interested ladies. This was despite the fact that in his online 'About Me!' précis, he had confided how much he'd enjoyed all the noise and smell of the slaughterhouse, or 'the buzz' as he called it, presumably partly in reference to his over enthusiastic use of his electric cattle prod, 'old sparky'.

No matter how he racked his brains and tried to conjure up a lady with a compatible profile, Digory was finding Carew a hard one to match, and this probably reflected well on the ladies of the dear old county. Though he wasn't strictly as agricultured as the majority of the clientele, Digory kept the officer's profile online at lonelyfarmersheartsclub.com for the time being, as it was always handy to have the law on your side, and the beast's knowledge of the little local highways and byways was impressive, as had been evidenced by Sharon and Bill's liaison.

The online love-matching concluded for another day, Digory turned his attention to the cobbled-together paddock in his yard, where his efforts to carnally cajole, persuade and inspire his St Piran Cross longhorn bull, Trelawney, into some sort of libidinous performance were thus far proving rather less than successful.

He couldn't fathom it, for Trelawney was such a magnificent specimen in *all* the required departments. It seemed to be very much a case of 'all the gear, no idea'.

The would-be covers, the so far rather coy inamoratas Pam and Brenda (of the same rare breed), evidently found the bull's black straggly moorland coat a little unkempt for their taste, and as for his horns, they *were* of an alarming length. Both would have been indifferent to any sort of advance had Trelawney actually made one, but they really had no need to worry.

Digory watched, Pam and Brenda stood their distance, and the bored bull ruminated on sweet, steaming silage that seemed to have no aphrodisiac qualities whatsoever.

Digory's mobile vibrated. Still forlornly encouraging the two cows to, so to speak, take the bull by the horn and help pro-create for the breed's jeopardised future, he put it to his ear.

'Go on, girls, fill yer boots,' he said, and then continued in the same breath, 'Lonelyfarmersheartsclub. com, may I help you?'

It was Oggy. 'What was that, Digory? Who've you got up there?' he said.

'Oh, 'tis you dear. Nobody, I haven't had time to swing a cat today, what's on dear?' he said.

'Are you coming to choir practice? Vi said Jeff rung,' said Oggy.

'Yes. All being well.'

'I'll pick you up six thirty. See you dreckly,' said Oggy.

'Dreckly,' said Digory.

But, as is often the case in dear old Cornwall, dreckly never came.

Huge had to search for a signal. He eventually found one in front of the public conveniences, next to an overstuffed and overflowing public bin policed by aggressive seagulls, on an unkempt triangular patch of grass regularly frequented by what must have been rather large dogs, like the one that had pinched his pasty the previous day. By standing on one leg on the top plank of the backrest of yet another bench to the dead, dedicated by a brass plaque that read, 'Malcolm - he loved this place', (dog shit and all presumably) he balanced and precariously made his call.

'So Nigel, when can I see you?...Tomorrow morning at the studio fine, nine thirty? Cool. It's the best yet, I can't tell you...She's fine, they're all fine. It's okay, she can keep the 4x4 down here, I'll get a flight... Will Ingrid be there? I need a researcher...Yea, yea, whatever, Inga, okay. This is going to be huge! Huge! Laters!'

He jumped down onto the seat of the bench to the dead and did a jolly, rather disrespectful little jig, with no regard to Malcolm (who loved the place) whatsoever. He jogged over to Emma and explained that he had to get back up to town to pitch his brilliant idea to Nigel, and that she could keep the beast-cruiser for her and the kids until he got back in a day or so, and that he had had catharsis over a giant pasty, and that they could change their lives forever. Forever!

Quenelle ran up the slipway.

'Daddy, I want the toilet,' he said.

'Over there darling,' he pointed.

Quenelle ran over to find the entrance blocked with a nailed up sheet of ply, and a sign that read 'Closed. Your nearest alternative is Priory Park, Bodmin'. Which was ten miles away. Quenelle danced the wee wee dance, clutching his flies with both hands.

'So Em. Are you okay with that?' asked Huge.

'Mummy, Mummy, it's shut,' screamed a desperate Quenelle.

'Go around the back against the wall darling. No one will see,' she called.

'Em?'

Emma looked him in the eye. 'Oh just go, Hugo. Do what you have to do. We'll be all right.'

She blinked as he kissed her pretty cheek. He kissed the children and told them to be good, and strode off and away from the harbour and his family.

*

When Oggy pulled into the yard at Dordigor Farm, Trelawney was still dispassionately chewing silage at his end of the enclosure and Pam and Brenda thwacking away evening flies with their black tails. After a quick look around, he ascertained that with the car gone, Digory and DigsCabs had obviously been called out on a job at short notice, and so went off to choir practice alone, joyously singing 'Cornish Lads are Fishermen', bass and baritone, melody and harmony, at the very top of his voice all the way there.

As the cab bumped and swerved around the high-hedged lanes, Huge tried to keep the mobile to his ear as best he could. He had no idea where he was at all. He had no idea either that the driver and the man who had come into the pasty shop after him the previous day were one and the same, for Digory was now disguised in his driver's cap and glasses.

During the course of the journey, Digory heard him book his return flight from Newquay to Stanstead, sort a cab to his apartment at the other end and ring some bloke called Nigel to confirm a meeting in the morning. Something about Tredogend and potential and pasties. Then he heard him ring some woman called Ingrid, or Inga, who it sounded like was out having dinner, just to make sure that she would be there in the morning. That seemed to be a *most* important element of his agenda.

Huge finished his call, and settled back into his seat. His stomach rumbled.

Digory glanced in the mirror. Huge looked out of the taxi window. His stomach rumbled again, loudly. He shifted uncomfortably.

'Fennel's good for that,' said Digory.

'What?'

'Tummy,' said Digory. 'My Gloucester Old Spots get it all the time dear – rich food and that. Afraid the window's jammed back there. Shall I open mine?'

'What! Just drive will you,' snapped Huge.

DigsCabs pulled up at the terminal, and Huge grabbed his overnight bag, jumped out and threw some money into the cab, and rushed into departures and checked in. He sighed and prepared himself for what is reputedly the most over- zealous rubber gloving in the entire aviation network.

On his way back home to Dordigor Farm, Digory Hicks called his old mate and told him about the famous passenger that he had recognised from Mother's the day before, though professional driver's etiquette had of course prevented him from asking for Huge's autograph. He was a miserable 'so and so' anyway, said Digory, and he told Oggy all about the telephone conversations he had 'accidentally' overheard.

'And he was farting like a chimney, I'm sure he squashed one under his leg. I had to open the window dear,' said Digory.

Oggy was just lining up alongside the basses and being prepared for vocal warm ups and breathing exercises, all prior to learning a new piece. He couldn't speak for long. Jeff was looking impatient

'Don't like his sort down here. I wonder what he's on upon,' he said in a low voice. 'I'm curious Dig. Very curious.'

He was right about that. Oggy Sloggett was very curious indeed.

Chapter Four
The Pasty

pasty – *a round of pastry folded over a filling of meat, vegetables etc: occasionally referred to in the vernacular as an 'oggy' - Collins Dictionary.*

Sorry *Collins Dictionary*, but it ain't as simple as that. Please may we be certain of one thing. A pasty is not just a round of pastry folded over a filling of meat, vegetables etc.

Let us, to begin with, take the 'etc:' and whatever that alludes to. In a proper pasty there is no room for manoeuvre. It follows that there is no room for 'etc'. There is no pork or lamb or venison or game. There is no fish or cheese or poultry. There are no peas, cauliflower, brocoli, beans and most especially, there are no carrots.

The punishments for the inclusion of such ingredients were clearly laid down in a statute passed by the Stannary Parliament in 1767. It stated that for a single pea, the offender should be sent to Coventry for a week. For several peas, the offender could be banished into silence for anything up to a year. For any vegetables other than those prescribed, i.e. potatoes, onions or swede, the punishment was to fit the crime, and the offender put in the stocks and pelted with the very same rogue vegetable with which he or, in those days mostly she, had offended. It was a sort of early doors five-a-day, before we *really* understood nutrition.

For those who used anything other than skirt beef, say topside or rump, or worse still cuts of pork or lamb or other meat of dubious provenance, there was the ducking stool.

The most strenuous and exacting punishments were reserved for the carrot, the inclusion of which was rightly regarded as a heinous cultural crime. The offender would have his/her right ear cut off, and he/she would be forced to bake it in an 'ear pasty', and then publicly eat the whole affair in front of a baying mob. To this day, there are scratched drawings made by condemned pasty cooks on the cell walls of the old Bodmin gaol depicting many such hideous and upsetting scenes.

And for unrepentant recidivists, there was transportation to the colonies, where they could stick what they liked in their pasties, and very often did.

Such is the history of the pasty. Not just a mere snack. Not just a meal. Not just some frippery to be fiddled and trifled with.

The pasty is iconic.

The pasty is magnificent.

The pasty has DNA.

The pasty is the Cornish.

The pasty is *Cornwall*.

For a pasty, the pastry is vital. Hot hands are no good for pasty pastry, and Mother's hands were as cold as charity. She used strong flour and a mix of shards of margarine and lard, with a bit of salt and, of course, water, 'special water', and she worked it, never overworked it, with her cold, floury fingers until it became elastic enough to hold all the bits and pieces of the filling, and popped it into the fridge for a couple or three hours to help with the rolling. She knew by instinct when it was right.

Each Sloggett had an old wooden rolling pin, and would take a pug of Mother's magical pastry, drop it onto the floured table surface, and roll out a roughly circular shape, neither too thick nor too thin, the circumference varying depending on whether they were engaged with Cornish Pixie pasty, Mother's Traditional pasty or Cornish Giant pasty duty.

The Sloggett's motto, 'slice don't dice', holds true for the preparation of the potato and the sweet, orangey coloured swede, cut laboriously into thin slices with sharp bladed knives, which made their thumbs scarred and unnaturally hard and leathery due to the incessant encounters from an early age with the unforgiving steel.

And then the onions. The Sloggett's had evolved as a sub-species apparently free of the encumbrance of tear ducts, for they could peel and chop and slice onions all day and night long with not a tear in sight.

Not only did they not cry, the Sloggett's, they could not.

They added small chunks of skirt beef, about the same amount weight-wise as the potato, in strategic places along the top of the filling thus far made, and then they topped it off again with a covering of more potato. They firmed and plumped up the filling, and spread and smeared a nub of Cornish butter across the top, and then liberally seasoned the whole mix with salt and ground white pepper.

The pasty was now ready for the final stage of construction, which encases the pile of ingredients into what is in effect it's own mini clome oven, and gave each pasty its own individual character.

The crimp.

The pastry, dampened by a little milk brushed around the outside edge, is folded up across and over the ingredients giving the whole thing a half-moon shape. The two edges are then dextrously sealed together and the pasty turned, with the seal now at the top. This is the point at which it becomes evident whether or not your pastry is elasticated enough to withstand the handling. The Sloggett's pasties always were.

The left end is folded in and held by the left hand's thumb and forefinger, and then the right thumb and forefinger fold the edge in towards the crimper, right along the join until the right end is folded inwards.

To watch the Sloggetts in action was to witness the stuff of legend, for the whole Sloggett herd, sorry family, were right at the top of their game. Their fingers worked with an innate dexterity at the speed of light, and had over years evolved to crimp with mesmeric and metronomic perfection, sealing the pasties as if with a combination of an industrial stapler and a tube of superglue. With a small steam hole prodded into the top by the insertion of a knife, the pasty is laid on a tray ready to be shoved into the old Treleaven oven at 200 degrees for baking, and is then taken out and allowed to cool, and finally eaten.

Would it be that it were so simple, for this was far from the whole story. Mother's pasties were possessed of something otherworldly, an enchantment, a secret magic conjoured up through the mists of time, and imbued by the touch of a sorceress, an alchemist, a necromancer.

Mother herself, custodian of the secret.

The secret buried deep, deep within her heart.

Special water.

Chapter Five
A Nice Cup of Tay

tay – *the Cornish vernacular pronunciation for the drink 'tea'; this is commonplace and is a result of transposing the 'e' sound and the 'a' sound. It is also evident in the Cornish pronunciation of sea, which becomes 'say', and meat which becomes 'mate'. There is a similarity in Irish dialect, notably in the title of the play by Sean O'Casey, 'Juno and the Paycock'.*

Mother's Pasty shop was tucked along Fore Street in Tredogend, just up from Dead Dog Wong's mock-Tudor takeaway and just down from the decaying shell of the old Wesleyan chapel, and it had been 'improved'.

It had been tastefully improved by Oggy Sloggett with the help of some skilled local tradesmen. At least, that had been the idea when Oggy had said that there was nothing for it, they *had* to carry out 'improvements' if they were to stay at the top. Dead Dog had sent a warning salvo across their bows ten years previously, when he had removed the final vestiges of anything that made his premises look remotely like they belonged in a small Cornish fishing village. He had given it the mock-Tudor makeover, complete with leaded windows, a Tudor rose in white plaster and a Tudor script for his sign.

It had all panicked Oggy a tad, and in fear of a Chinese take-over as opposed to a Chinese take-away, he'd at once gone into the DIY superstore in Bodmin and priced up a covering of reconstituted Cotswold stone cladding for the lower half of his own shop frontage. The top half was saved for one of Oggy's secret fetishes.

Pebbledash.

Not ordinary pebbledash, mind you, Oggy insisted on the very latest trend in the stuff; pink, beige and mauve chippings that from a distance gave an overall pucey, pukey effect. It was a matter of opinion how well all this sat among the old white-washed and stone built cottages of Tredogend, but certainly Dead Dog's evocation of the reign of Good Queen Bess was very 'heritage' by comparison.

Oggy had big plans to 'improve' Mother's even more. He'd seen a lot of nice stuff in that DIY superstore in Bodmin, not least of which were the imitation asbestos roof tiles that you could now get to replace all those nasty old-fashioned Delabole slates; all the lifestyle sophistication and style of asbestos without the attendant asbestosis. What was not to like?

But most exciting of all were the aluminium framed windows that would require no painting whatsoever, ever, forever, and had been made in such a way as to resemble from the outside the tiny paned windows of some of the older cottages of Tredogend, and on the inside some of the condemned cells of Bodmin Gaol.

Thus far, the original shop sign had survived Oggy's crusade of improvements to the shop front. It was not that Oggy had overlooked or forgotten it, for he'd decided long ago to replace it with a nice new plastic one; it was just that as with the new windows and the roof tiles, he'd run out of money.

The old sign was screwed up above and across the top of the shop window and doorway, a rather charming rectangular, golden-yellow painted wooden affair, with a narrow raised frame and black lettering that read, simply but perhaps not over-imaginatively, 'Mother's Pasties'.

Other survivors of the 'improvements were on the inside of the shop door, where a hand written open/closed sign hung on a rough piece of twine beneath the tinkling shop bell. Inside the shop window, the Sloggetts displayed row upon row of their fabulous fresh pasties, slid in on baking trays and tilted up at the back. Above these hung a giant three-foot long plaster pasty (made c1956) suspended almost invisibly by catgut, with 'The Cornish Giant' proudly painted thereon.

The rest of the inside of Mother's had not, however, escaped Oggy's improvements, for like many Cornishmen of his generation, he suffered from a severe psychological flaw when it came to decorating.

Mother's had been under the artexer's knife.

Mother herself had been fortunate to escape the scalloping, for the ceilings and walls were all smeared and suffocated by the sweeping repetition of the pattern that at one time threatened to cover the entire county, from the dizzy moorland heights of Brown Willy smearing down to the towering cliffs of the Penwith peninsula. Such was Oggy's obsession with this dubious art form, he would have had the floors scalloped too (the builders had mercifully advised against this), for he couldn't wait to be rid of all those dreadful, big, cold, old fashioned slate slabs.

No surface had been safe.

It had all cost a small fortune, even without the new windows and roof tiles that he so desperately wanted, and the loan that he'd secretly taken out with the bank to pay for it all had been secured against the value of Mother's itself. Ironically, the more improvements Oggy carried out, the more the property's value seemed to diminish.

Behind the shop counter (artexed on the front), Oggy and Vi shared the space with a giant old Cornish pasty oven, a beautiful thing cast for Granfer Sloggett by Thomas Treleaven down at St Just. Later, it had been converted to electric, and with eighteen shelves it was taller than Oggy himself, black and still with the original handles and controls.

There was nothing on the artexed walls save the family portrait, and two notices. One read, from top to bottom, 'Mother's Pasties – Mother's Traditional £2, Cornish Pixie Pasty £1.50, Cornish Giant £3' (there did not appear to be a vegetarian option), and beneath that the other notice, carelessly pinned up with rusty drawing pins, read 'In Concert – Bolventor Chapel – Sunday 25th June 7pm – Tredogend Fisherman's Choir. Admission £1, OAPs and children 50p.'

There was not expected to be an overwhelming demand for tickets.

The door behind the counter in the pasty shop was a portal to a forgotten world, for behind the door behind the counter in the pasty shop was the kitchen where Mother's Pasties were made. A secret kitchen, an inner sanctum into which only the curious Sloggetts were permitted access, a kitchen that had barely changed for nigh on a hundred years. The kitchen where Mother lurked.

Lurked with her brother, Uncle Clar.

It was curious that the jolly, rosy-cheeked face on the Mother's Traditional pasty paper bag looked exactly like Uncle Clar in an ill fitting curly wig, and not at all like Mother herself. She had more the look of an elderly Red Indian squaw of the great Hollywood westerns, all high cheekbones and cruel, narrow eyes and careworn, leathery skin that was deeply lined with rivulets of disapproval, and then a scowling mouth, the sort that you were left with if you hadn't smiled enough during your life.

It was certainly not a face with which to sell pasties; it was a face like a bag of spanners, which may well have worked had they run a hardware shop. But they had a pasty shop, and they had always had the sense to keep Mother back in the kitchen and well away from those paying customers who may have been of a nervous disposition.

Uncle Clar, on the other hand, was a joy who had never bothered to come out of the closet. He did not, probably could not, think in metaphors at all. He often wondered in his quieter moments why anyone could possibly want to go into a closet in the first place, as his own was still full of musty, dusty, sneezy old Utility garments that reeked strongly of mothballs and the sourness of old sweat. As for the soft piece of furniture that he used to put his feet up on in the evenings, he never gave its popular name a second thought.

He'd spent his entire life at his sister's side, striving always to keep her as sweet as she'd allow, and she in turn credited him with a depth of wisdom that he never really possessed, lovely old thing that he was, and this had filtered down through the Sloggett generations so that now he was held in rather higher regard than the Dalai Lama himself.

It was no mean feat to sustain an entire family with the proceeds from one pasty shop in one Cornish village, and yet the Sloggetts had managed to do so for many years. There was an ebb and flow between kitchen and shop counter, and Oggy, Vi, Uncle Clar, Mother, along with Cheel and Mervin when they were there, worked in harmonious unison (when they were not shouting and screaming and niggling at bitter loggerheads with one another) to produce the daily avalanche of homemade pasties. It was a family business in the true accepted sense, where decisions and pasties were made in equal measure around the grand old kitchen table (which had mercifully escaped the artex, save the odd accidental splash).

Oggy had not been singing so much of late, for uneasy was the head that wore the King Crimper crown. Vi knew that something was amiss when he had gathered them all round the table so early, not just a bee in his bonnet, but an angry, irritable swarm of them. Times were tight. He wanted changes. Improvements. With the bags for starters.

Mother, though, was not for turning.

'We got our own paper bags with them lovely pictures that your father had drawn, God rest his dear soul. The Little Pixies, the old Cornish Giant, people love them bags. And anyway, plastic makes the pasties sweat! Cheap isn't everything,' said Mother, and thumped the table for effect.

Oggy Sloggett growled. How he wished he'd had her artexed, or even pebble dashed, however sparingly. Uncle Clar looked a little alarmed, and Mother touched him on the arm reassuringly.

'Sorry Uncle Clar,' she said, and wagged her finger at Oggy. 'But he won't even let me out front to the shop counter to serve, neither.'

'You made a toddler scritch and cry, that's why!'

'I only smiled at him a bit. Don't you try to bully-rag me, boy.'

'Some smile! Christ! 'Twas enough to curdle milk. And don't call me boy Mother, I'm bloody near sixty years old,' ranted Oggy. 'Plain and cheap plastic carriers is the way ahead. Who cares if their pasties sweat if we got their money in the till?'

'The children love them pictures,' said Mother. 'Tell him Vi.'

'Don't drag me into it, Mother. I can't tell him anything, he's in a cussed mood he is. '

'And we got to put the prices up. We're too cheap,' said Oggy.

'Plastic bags. It's disrespectful to father's memory,' muttered Mother.

'And we put too much meat in them. Pascoe only just delivered Monday and it's gone already. And that freezer's knackered.'

'Nothing wrong with that freezer. He's nearly new. We got him from Trago.'

'In 1974 Mother! There's nothing in the bugger anyway.'

'Seventy five it was. Your father and I got it for our anniversary,' she said, choking a little for effect. 'We'll get it repaired. We got to have a freezer. Everybody else got one.'

'Have a look in the pantry and see for yourself! Heave it out, Mother!' said Oggy.

'No I shan't, and I ain't going in no pantry neither. There's something funny in there. Something's queer, amiss,' said Mother.

'Look, you tell me who's going to pay for our dear Cheel to get her cap and gown at that Universery down Falmouth. If she's to be the first Sloggett to granulate, we got to put less meat in the pasties and more cash in the till.'

'Something amiss,' persisted Mother. 'You mark my words.'

'I'll tell you what's amiss, Mother! Cash to pay for this lot!' and Oggy slammed down a grocer's and a butcher's bill on the table. And an electricity bill. And a council tax bill. And a telephone bill. Wisely, he did not slam down the demand from the bank for the interest payment on the loan that they did not know anything about.

So, as was usual, Mother played her trump card, the sage Uncle Clar.

'Uncle Clar?'

'I should dearly like a cup of tay,' he said.

'So should I. Put the kettle on Vi,' said Mother. 'He's bringing on one of me gasping turns, he is.'

'What, again Mother?' taunted Oggy. 'Must be coming up to twelve months since you last snuffed it!'

'Now Oggy,' Uncle Clar said kindly. 'Those drawings on the bags been there for years now. People *do* love them, and we've always had them.'

'Thank you, Uncle Clar,' said Mother.

'And we haven't had the freezer *that* long...'

'What about these?' demanded Oggy, and he shoved the bills towards Uncle Clar and Mother. 'Shall we pay them in pasties?'

'Rich Tea biscuit, Uncle Clar?' said Vi.

'Oh yes please Vi. Rich Tea, yes,' said Uncle Clar, and looked at the bills.

'Less meat,' said Oggy.

'No,' said Mother.

Uncle Clar bit into his biscuit.

'Smaller chunks then,' said Oggy.

'No,' said Mother.

Uncle Clar read the electricity bill, and choked on a Rich Tea crumb. Mother patted his back.

'Uncle Clar?' said Oggy.

Uncle Clar glanced at the other bills and coughed and nodded. 'Just a little bit smaller, Mother. Just for now.'

'All right,' said Mother, and then under her breath, 'Smaller chunks, but more of 'em.'

'And keep yer mug out of the shop, Mother. People don't like it!' said Oggy.

'Smaller chunks,' she said, not taking his bait. 'Thank you Uncle Clar, you're a marvel. Say thank you Uncle Clar, boy.'

'Thank you Uncle Clar, and don't call me boy, Mother,' said Oggy.

'Was there another Rich Tea, Vi?' asked Uncle Clar.

And amidst all the usual carnage of the family discussion, Oggy had seen the change in Uncle Clar's countenance when presented with a simple biscuit, and he wondered whether if the old man had became more suggestible with just a Rich Tea, what might be achieved with a Chocolate Bourbon, or dare he suggest it, a Jammy Dodger.

Maybe, just maybe, with a Hob Nob or two he could blow Uncle Clar's mind.

There was a big table up at ZeeTV too, but no dusting of flour or lardy smears on it, or gouges and scratches from years of artisan toil. It was rather polished and chunkily functional, with chairs to match. In the middle was a tray with bottles of still and sparkling Highland Spring water and glasses, and another with a cafetière and white china mugs, a bowl of those large brown sugar crystals that never seemed to dissolve but looked nice, and a jug of watery skimmed milk.

From the corner of his eye, Huge scanned an attractive young intern. She was a size ten at most he thought. Just on the normal side of emaciated, unusually for London. Her blonde hair was heaped up in a picturesque disorder, and she asked if anyone would like a cup of tea instead. She had raspberry, mint, lemon and ginger, lapsang souchong or red bush.

'Do you have English Breakfast?' enquired Huge, all smiles and smarm.

'Yes, and for me also. Love English Breakfast,' added the altogether more voluptuous Inga, and caught his eye, just for a beat. The young girl scurried off, and shortly returned with a small pot for two and two teacups and saucers and, ever the gentleman, Huge poured.

There were no biscuits.

'So Huge,' said Nigel. 'We're all ears.'

Huge sat back, interlocked the ends of his fingers and began his pitch. By the time he had finished, all were leaning forward eagerly.

'Oh my god, Huge, that's huuuge!' enthused Nigel.

A man called Tom nodded in agreement. 'Huge,' he agreed.

Barney Sanchez-DeVille, director of ZeeTV, got to his feet.

'Great Huge. Nigel, I'm leaving this one with you. Top idea, man,' he said, and shook Huge's huge flabby hand vigorously, before leaving the classy, glassy walled room for his cab.

Inga smiled like a cat, and pulled her fingers through her long blonde hair and tossed it back over her head, and as she looked down at her iPad, strands fell in an apparently careless fashion, one at a time, over her face. She was an ambitious, keen to get on kind of girl. She put her iPen to her lips.

'So Huge, just where is Tredogend and what's it like?' she asked.

'Well, it's on the North Cornish coast, not far from a town called Wadebridge. It's very unspoilt, but I guess quite down at heel. It doesn't look as if anything has changed there for years. There are lots of places up for sale, properties vacated, the council has closed the loos, the post office is closed, that sort of thing. But it has an undeniable charm, you know?'

'Oh yes, I know exactly,' she said, glancing up at him. 'I'd be very keen to get involved.' Huge shifted in his seat.

'So how exactly would the prog work, Huge?' asked Nigel.

'Well, I see it as a sort of fusion of *DIY 999* with *SupaChef* and *SOS-SaveOurShop*, the daytime one with that bloody irritating woman with the lisp and fat ass! You know, fly on the wall, drama doc job with loads of cooking pasties. Pasties, pasties and more pasties! And heritage, that's huge too. Heritage, heritage, heritage! Chuck it all in together and bake it up and see what comes out. Bound to be a winner Nige.'

'Wow. Sounds great. Where can we do it? Are there premises?'

'There's an old chapel for sale in the main street. Wesleyan Methodist or something. Falling down almost. We'll get the DIY boys in and give it a makeover. Barney'll pay. It's perfect. There's even an old kitchen in the back we can convert. We're going to call it *Huge in Cornwall*!'

Inga looked across at Tom, and they nodded to one another earnestly.

'And think of the follow-up series options. *Huge in Italy*, *Huge in India*, *Huge in the States*! *Huge in....* *Bruges*!'

'Brilliant! Brilliant,' Nigel said, and sat back. 'Only one thing though.'

'What's that Nige?'

'Pasties, Huge. Can you cook pasties?'

'Nige, dude, you're joshing, right? This is Huge, man! Huge! TV superchef extraordinaire, baby. If some half-witted inbred down in bloody Cornwall can make them, of course I can! And we're not just talking a fusion programme here, Nige. We're talking fusion pasties as well, man. Chicken tikka masala pasty, Sichuan chilli beef pasty, salmon and samphire pasty, wild foraged seashore pasty, game pasty, bush meat pasty, anything you want in a bloody pasty pasty, Nige. Oh…and I'm going to become part of the community. We can do it all! It's *Huge in Cornwall* baby!'

It had not been the most modest pitch that Nigel had ever heard; modesty was hardly Huge's forte, but he had a good track record and he *did* have the go ahead from Barney. Nigel rocked back in the chair, palms open.

'I'm all yours. When do we start?'

They chatted around the table for ten minutes or more, and discussed some of the initial issues that needed to be sorted, and as they began to make their way towards the door and shook hands with one another enthusiastically, Huge found Inga holding on to his just a little longer than the others, and as they double kissed she reached up and whispered quietly into his ear, 'I'd kinda like to see if you're "Huge in London", too.'

Meanwhile back down in Cornwall, at the other table in question, the Sloggett herd was stampeding around and making up for the time they had lost during the rather futile big bag debate. There were four pasty construction stations today, two at each end and two either side of the battered and scarred kitchen table. In the centre of the table, five big old Cornish blue striped bowls contained in turn pastry, potato, swede, onion and beef, there was salt and white pepper, and butter in a Cornish blue striped dish.

They worked perfectly in tandem. Mother sorcered up the pastry with her cold, white old fingers, her small bowl of chilled, special water in front of her. Vi and Uncle Clar rolled out and filled, and Oggy seasoned and crimped and finished them off, and when dreckly came and they were all baked and ready and good to go (at ten past ten on this day), Vi flipped the sign to 'open', and they began to dispense the glorious pasties in their signature paper bags. They sold them until the last one was gone, at twenty three minutes past four, then flipped the sign back to 'closed', and went back into the old kitchen to help Uncle Clar and Mother clean and tidy, and hung up their rolling pins until the next time, the following day.

And then the day after that, and so on and on and on.

This was what they did.

It had been a long night. Huge was awoken not by the alarm on his mobile, or by the light through the blinds he had forgotten to close, or even by the incessant screeching of seagulls that woke him when he was down in Cornwall. He was woken by Inga's persuasive touch.

She lifted the sheet and peeped.

'Hmmm, so you *are* Huge in London. Still huge….'

'Would you like a little breakfast?' he asked. 'What about the Full English?'

'Oh,' she said. 'I thought that we'd maybe start with a little Continental….'

Above Mother's pasty shop in Tredogend, Oggy Sloggett and Vi sat up in bed drinking tea. She called it their 'tea and reflection session'. Oggy drank tea, whilst Vi reflected on his usually questionable behaviour over the previous day or so.

'Are you any happier today then? Still want to cut down on the meat?' she teased.

'Do you?' said Oggy.

'Drink your tea, you dirty old sod,' she giggled.

'You mean drink your 'tay'.'

'Tay then.'

'You been living down here long enough to know that now, maid,' said Oggy.

'Well, Mother says it's only *just* forty bleedin' years. You ain't Cornish yet, she says.'

'You may not be a Cornish woman, but you *are* a woman of Cornwall, and an ansom one at that.'

'What are you after?'

'Nothing. Don't take no notice of Mother. Got enough trouble with her and that freezer,' said Oggy.

'You should tell her and Uncle Clar it's haunted,' laughed Vi.

'Ha! Do you remember when the kids were small and we told them it was, to stop them climbing in and playing in it?' said Oggy.

'Goes too quick,' said Vi.

'When is Cheel back then?' said Oggy. 'We could do with her nimble little fingers in the shop. It's getting busy now.'

'Sunday. She got two more shifts in Starbucks, then she's home,' said Vi.

'I hope it ain't affecting her studying.'

'You know her darlin'. She's full on with it all. They been short staffed, so they've trained her up to be a barista now.'

'Never! A barrister too? And I thought she was just doing dancing and drama and that,' said Oggy, puffed up with pride. 'A lawyer in the family, my God. Who'd have thought it? Our little Cornish maid.'

'Cornish my eye, that's the bleedin' cockney in her,' laughed Vi. 'Anyway, she makes a lovely cappuccino now.'

'Eh?' said Oggy, a little puzzled.

'Never mind.'

'Anyway, where's that boy of ours?'

'He's happy where he is darlin'. He likes all that surfing and stuff. He's fine.'

Oggy grunted. 'More tay?' he asked.

'Go on then.'

Oggy creaked down to the kitchen and put the kettle to boil, and popped a tea bag into each mug. Whilst they slowly brewed, he folded all the bills together, and slipped them behind the tea caddy. He looked at the utensils on the shelf, and the six brass hooks screwed below, each hung with its own labelled rolling pin, *Oggy*, *Vi*, *Uncle Clar*, *Cheel* and *Mervin*, and *Mother*. He counted his blessings and hummed to himself and stirred the tea bag in the mugs, splashed in a little milk, and carried them back up to the bedroom.

Huge was in a panic. The breakfast sitting had run on longer than he had anticipated, and over several sordid courses, he had missed his flight. He had always had a huge appetite for pneumatic blondes with libidinous, lusty and liberated tendencies, especially Scandinavian ones with their faintly quaint Americanised grasp of the English language. Huge was beginning to like 'the Swede' almost as much as he liked swede.

He took the tube to Paddington, and got a first class single to Bodmin Parkway. Barney would pay. He would have to. If Barney wanted genius at his fingertips he had no option. He settled into his leather seat, free from the common proletariat distractions of cattle class, and slurped on his macchiato.

He texted Emma. It was not, of course, that he felt guilty. Far from it. Had she not, after all, trapped him into the marriage and three kids just when he'd started to become stellar famous? Anyway, it was most unlikely that he could contact her down in Tredogend because of the intolerable backwoods signal issue. Far better just to text, that it might pop-up on her screen as she moved into an area that did have a signal, and that way she wouldn't be able to clock any guilty intonation in his voice.

'Hi M on train b back 4ish.gd meeting v excite. Start look 4 hse H xx'

Emma hadn't even bothered to take her phone to Porzeath beach. She wasn't really that bothered if he called, for he was up in London and she had her suspicions.

The kids stood in a row in front of the surf shack, beside the yellow surfboards, all kitted out in their hired wet suits.

'Smile Goujon, Julienne!' she called, camera at the ready. She waved her hand at the deeply tanned and dreadlocked young instructor. 'Come on, you get in too Mervin!'

'Hey, cool Mum, he's got shades,' shouted Quenelle. 'We're going surfing with a real beach dude!'

Emma sat in the dunes, hands around her knees, and as they ran down the beach towards the surf, she closed her eyes; all she could hear was the roar and crash of the waves, and the laughter of her children.

Chapter Six
The Reason Why

cheel – *Cornish derivation of the word 'child', often used as a term of affection.*

High up above Tredogend lay Dordigor Farm, on an open heath pricked with wind-crippled thorn bushes and gaudy thickets of yellow-heavy gorse, crumbled as Sunday School saffron cake and heady-scented with the exotic coconut temptations of a South Sea Island.

But there were no parakeets among fronded palms here, nor tropical beauties swaying dusky in grass skirts, just a parliament of magpies chittering and chattering from mayblossom to elder tree and back again. Rising high up above them, mewing buzzards wheeled and soared on swirling thermals, their sharp eyes focused hungry on the unwary rabbits that bob-tailed and gambolled on the closely-nibbled, grass-poor pasture land below.

The decaying farm sprawled wide in its untidiness, a supreme testament to the art of bodging and making-do. Alongside an abandoned combine harvester, the skeleton of an engineless Massey Ferguson stood rust-welded to its trailer, both jungled by Japanese knotweed and stinging nettles, spiteful brambles and giant cream umbrellas of stinking hogweed.

The subterranean web of the wretched weeds reached far and wide underground, popping up unexpectedly here and there through tarmac, piles of rubble or stacks of railway sleepers, and bursting through the cement base of the farmyard itself; strangulation even threatened a defiant allotment of potatoes that had learned, since time immemorial, to quietly fend for themselves. Now nothing seemed safe from the murderous finger grasp of the choking roots.

The galvanised, colander-leaky roof of Bovril the boar's old sty was held down, somewhat precariously, by an old colour TV (cumbersomely cabineted with a once-upon-a-time sought after finish in 'teak'), two and a half broken breeze blocks and a Baby Belling cooker in enamel (two Bakelite knobs missing, no grill element and the plug removed). With the cracked floor within now carpeted sticky with drying pools of emerald slimed stink-mud, and wiggling alive with the wriggling larvae of mosquito, the bristly boar and his hog harem had voted with their trotters and re-located to a caravan.

Digory's mould-freckled two-berth made a nice shelter, and Bovril had even welcomed the semi-naked, moulting chicken in with him and the girls, and kindly allowed them to share the accommodation. When it still had wheels, it had been used just the once by Digory and Doreen, a brief adventurous spree in 1977 that got them as far as a lay-by on the Tredogend side of Delabole. It was there that Doreen had decided that life on the road really wasn't for them, what with no proper toilet or teak-cabineted telly; the tay tasted funny with the water from the silly little kettle that took so long to boil, and as for the long life milk, she couldn't be doing with that muck. The final nail in the coffin had been the fact that she was such a fine great woman, she could barely turn around at all inside the 'Openroader Compact 75'.

They'd turned for home and given their brief dreams of a carefree traveller's life all up to Bovril and his concubine sows and the scrawny, flea-bitten hens;

all was brambled together now in a wanton macramé of neglect, and infused by the sickly-sweet steam of silage, piled unkempt in a corner of the yard.

Doreen would never have put up with it.

Oggy pulled up there early on the Sunday evening, ginger-slicked and blue-blazered, badged and flannelled as close up to the nines as Vi could manage to make him, and he found the jaunty little widower Digory Hicks awaiting. Digory, snappily-dappered, properly scrubbed up and shinily resplendent in choir attire, was the very antithesis of his own tumbledown farm.

He leaned, deep in thought, over his wind-rattled and paletted lash-up of a corral fence, while he carelessly splashed water into a leaky trough from a hose. Pam and Brenda were standing impassively side-by-side, rump-to-rump, sirloin-to-sirloin, their tails swishing in perfect unison. At the opposite end stood Trelawney, who ignored them with a studied disdain, his long black fringe dangled over his eyes as he clumped and chawed on some deliciously aromatic steaming silage. There had been no 'action' to speak of, just a moo and a passing warble fly.

Digory sighed, turned off the yard tap and chucked the hose down. 'I don't know the reason why, Oggy dear,' he said. 'Nothing wrong with them two cows there. Lovely ain't they?'

'Lovely,' agreed Oggy.

'Fine great rumps. It's all there on a plate for him,' said Digory. 'I suppose love will find its way.'

'I hates that Andrew Lloyd Webster bollocks,' mused Oggy. 'Why does Jeff make us sing that?'

Digory sighed. 'No, no, dear. I just meant that love will find its way, that's all.'

They stood there, shoulder-to-shoulder, and studied the indifferent cattle in a puzzled and rather uneasy silence.

'Digory, there's no easy way of saying this,' ventured Oggy eventually. 'Do you think that he's all he should be?'

Trelawney looked up from his silage, possibly a little offended, though the facial expressions of cattle, especially those with long fringes, are notably inscrutable. His magnificent long horns were like that of an auroch, those giant wild cattle from quite another age.

Digory was a little irritated. 'What do you mean?' he demanded tetchily.

'Well,' said Oggy. 'Do you think he's quite.... right?'

'What, with horns like that? Course he is!'

'It might be them two, then,' mused Oggy, pointing to Pam and Brenda. 'They might be...the other way inclined, do you think?'

'What, you mean...?'

'Yes.'

'Well I haven't seen any signs,' said Digory.

'Well, you wouldn't, would you? Not with cows.'

They turned towards the car.

'How's Mother?' said Digory.

'Keeps poking her nose into the shop,' said Oggy. 'Not easy.'

'Never was, dear,' said Digory. 'Artful as a bag of ferrets.'

'She says to tell you that she needs more of your special water.'

'Right on,' said Digory. 'I'll see what I can do.'

*

There were two choughs. One soared majestically upwards and the other swooped, the bright scarlet of their legs and curved beaks contrasting dramatically with their sleekly shiny black plumage. An oddly charismatic bird, the chough had long been extinct in Cornwall, and it was a desperate, crying shame for it was still an integral part of the coat of arms, a symbol of the dear old county's pride.

There had been an intensive breeding and release programme to return the species to it's rightful spiritual home, with stock brought in from the west of both Wales and Ireland where it still thrived out on the wild rocky extremities. Surprisingly, in lieu of the success of this enterprise, the introduced birds interbred with migrant birds that had found their way across the Irish Sea and Bristol Channel quite independently, and the new colonies were beginning to thrive.

Uncle Clar looked at the birds closely, and sipped his tay.

'I haven't seen one for years,' he slurped. 'Not since we took you and Mervin to Newquay zoo.'

Cheel smiled. She had not the features of her mother Vi, rather those of her Nan, of Mother herself, of the proud and haughty squaw, and indeed Cheel's entire appearance was now distinctly tribal, her once beautifully long dark hair now cropped short and dyed jet black, with the ends of the fringe tinged with a golden-yellow.

She was petite in stature, her arms and legs slim but well toned and defined. She wore black jeans and a designer T-shirt that she had created for herself. She had can-sprayed a St Piran's flag across the chest, consisting of just a simple black disc with a white cross sprayed on top of that.

Some believed the white cross of St Piran represented the bright lightness of good that shone out against the dark forces of evil, the light of God over the devil. Others maintained it to be the glint of a crossed seam of tin that gleamed out from the blackness of the bowels of the deepest, most hellish undersea tin mine.

Or maybe it was white-wash crossed on top of pitch, which was all the Cornish could afford for their homes in years gone by, before the dear old county had been well and truly Farrowed and Ballsed up with all the subtle greys and tonal sea-greens of those who now painted designer Cornwall, the Corniche Nouveau.

Cheel had had piercings galore, a nose stud and lip ring, and multiple gold earrings arranged around one ear in descending sizes, and in her left lobe a large ring that you could see right through. There were probably more still in addition to those that met the eye, and Uncle Clar was trying hard not to appear too alarmed at the dramatic change in his niece's appearance, but his cup was nonetheless rattling in its saucer.

'I remembers that visit to the zoo, Uncle Clar,' said Cheel. 'Father complained about his pasty to the woman in the cafe. Told her that she should be ashamed for selling factory-made filth.'

'Yes, filth, yes. He did say that, your old father,' said Uncle Clar. 'Did it hurt your dear neck when they did they choughs?'

Cheel fingered the still tender tattooed bird on the left side of her neck. 'This one's a bit sore, but the other's all right.'

'Well you're a very brave little maid. Yes, brave yes,' said Uncle Clar. 'What'll Mum and father say about it all, my ansom bird?'

'Mum'll be all right. I don't know about him,' said Cheel. 'Do you want to see me others?'

In addition to the choughs on either side of her neck, Cheel had spent a considerable portion of her first year's student loan on even more body art. She had barely left herself enough money to subsist. On her right bicep was a pair of crossed St Piran's flags, and on her left forearm the epithet 'Kernow Bys Vycken', in words and barcode, and on top of her left breast was a heart with an arrow and 'Kernewek' in scripted style within.

'Lovely that is, yes,' said Uncle Clar, and pointed to the left forearm. 'What do that mean?'

' "Cornwall for ever", Uncle Clar,' said Cheel. ''Tis the Cornish language. And this is a pair of St Piran's flags.'

'Well it's very nice, yes. Very nice. I don't know what your father will say, I'm sure.'

'I ain't decided what to put on me right forearm yet.'

'No, well, I'm sure you'll think of something though, won't you my dear maid.'

'And this is Kernewek, my Cornish heart,' she said, indicating the heart on her breast. 'Do you want to see the ones on me back?'

Uncle Clar coughed and gurgled as some tay went down the wrong way.

'More is there? My word, you have had a very busy time,' he said.

She turned her back to him and pulled up her t-shirt. Between her shoulder blades was a large tattooed pasty, with the word 'NASTY' across it in gothic lettering. Beneath that was a shield emblazoned with the fifteen golden bezants of the Cornish arms, five in the top row, four in the second and so on, down to just one at the base of her spine, just above the waistline of the back of her jeans.

'And I got "One and All" right across me ass,' she said laughing. 'Wanna see that, Uncle Clar?'

'Dreckly my lovely,' spluttered Uncle Clar. 'I think I'd better go up to bed now.'

Bolventor Chapel was hardly packed for the performance of the Tredogend Fisherman's Choir. Maybe word had got out that there were no fishermen in their ranks. Or that no one in it was under fifty. Or that no one was not wearing glasses. Whatever the reason, the thirty-odd strong choir walked into the chapel with a strictly choreographed military precision, top tenors, second tenors, then baritones then basses, and at the space in front of the pulpit they in turn spread to the right and left, until they were all aligned perfectly, in three ranks and facing the audience.

They all wore navy choir blazers, emblazoned on the breast pocket with the T.F.C. woven badge in red and gold and navy thread, depicting two fish and a trawler and a treble clef. They wore white shirts and choir ties in navy, red and gold, and grey flannels and black shoes.

One or two had limped into position with sticks, and one had a shiny new Zimmer frame. Four of them had hearing aids, one of which was whistling shrill and loud, but could still not be heard by the person who was wearing it, a gentle old man of eighty-three whose once friendly face had been contorted by a stroke into a grotesque perma-grin. But he still loved to sing. They all loved to sing.

Jeff, the musical director, came in last of all, and stood facing his choir from the centre, then slowly and deliberately raised the palms of his hands, and as one the choir members proudly lifted their black ring binders of music in front of them.

He turned on his heels and faced the audience, which consisted of two widows and a strange and rather stagnant old spinster with scarecrow hair, who trundled in late riding her pavement warrior and was clearly only there for the food. Then of course, there was the lay preacher himself, an earnest young man who thought that religion should be fun, and who in his spare time enjoyed juggling and riding a unicycle whilst wearing a red nose. This had not helped to swell the numbers in the congregation.

What had, initially anyway, was the post-op transsexual pianist Lavinia, who played organ and piano quite beautifully despite still having builder's hands and fingers. The novelty factor of having a six foot four brickie in twin set and pearls had been too much for some, and for several weeks the pews were filled to capacity with what were admittedly the curious rather than the devout. Although the 'tranny effect' had worn off and tonight things were back to what they had been pre-op and pre-Lavinia ('breeze block' Barry in his previous life, in fact), the young preacher took it as a victory of sorts. Even Wesley had had to start somewhere.

Lavinia sat at the little organ filing her nails with an emery board. Oggy nudged Digory, remembering the splendid job she'd done on his pebble dash and cladding, and they began to chuckle as only naughty schoolboys should. The musical director smiled to the audience and began.

'Ladies and gentlemen…gentleman….'

It was really too much for the old chums. They looked at the floor, their shoulders shaking with mirth, and even tried to think of loved ones who had died to stem the outpouring of hysteria.

They recovered sufficiently to commence the repertoire, starting as usual with a rousing rendition of 'Will your Anchor Hold?' and going down through the Cornish male voice choir staples, 'The Rose', 'The White Rose', 'Mighty like a Rose' (they liked roses), 'Simple Pleasures', 'The Sweet Nightingale', 'Harry's Song for Cornwall', 'The Cadgwith Anthem' and others, and finally as was traditional, the Cornish National anthem, 'Trelawney'.

Oggy Sloggett was filled with a joy that only singing could bring him. He held the black ring binder of music up in his right hand as all the others did, but looked right over the top of it and straight at the musical director, for he did not need to refer to it at all. He had sung these songs for as long as he could remember, as his father had before him, and he knew every bit of harmony and melody, every cadence and diminuendo, every a tempo and crescendo, every colla parte and colla voce of every word of every verse and chorus of every song in the choir's repertoire.

The applause would have been rapturous, had dear old Mrs Beswetherick not rather missed the preacher's cue, for first she had to gather together and put down the scarf she was knitting. Mrs Gupta (now a fully naturalised woman of Cornwall and known locally, without as much as a blink of an eye, as Mrs Tregupter, dear) had arthritis so bad that she could barely clap at all. Still, Lavinia had helpfully joined in, minding her nails, which were now drying nicely and these days free of dried artex and cement.

The stale, stinky and stagnant old spinster was not bothering with any of the niceties. She didn't like singing much, and had performed the sort of sharp handbrake-turn type manoeuvre beloved of boy racers. Before the choir had even finished the rousingly patriotic crescendo of the anthem Trelawney, *'Here's twenty thousand Cornishmen will know the reason why...',* she had jammed her pavement warrior under the trestle table in the ante room and was attacking the chicken drumsticks, egg and bacon pie, mini pasties and splits, jam and clotted cream as if there was no tomorrow.

But it was a Methodist tea, and unlike the stingy C of E ones that you occasionally got when performing in churches and church rooms for wealthy farmers or retired gentlefolk from St Albans, it was more than generous, and as the choir filed in and filled their boots, it was evident that the evening had been a proper success.

As they sped mostly downhill from Bolventor back towards Dordigor Farm and from there on to Tredogend, the two old friends ruminated over the evening.

'Tenors were as flat as a fart,' ventured Oggy.

'No doubt. Hellish.'

'They're too busy with their noses in their music Digory. They don't look up at Jeff. No point in him standing there and conducting if they don't look,' he continued.

'Anyway dear,' said Digory. 'I'm pleased to hear that your Cheel is doing so well down Falmouth. A barrister now, you say.'

'Yes, barrister, yes. She's back home today, for the summer.'

'Clever girl, she ain't been down there long.'

'She's learning it part-time in that Starbucks, help make ends meet.'

'Good money barristers. I thought she was doing drama and that.'

'Yes, that too.'

'Are they a Falmouth firm then?'

'I suppose they be. Anyway, we could do with a bit extra coming in. She makes lovely coffee now mind, and sandwiches and cakes and that.'

'Never heard of 'em before. Must have moved down from London. Nice bit of egg and bacon pie there tonight Oggy, and them little pasties too,' mused Digory.

'Proper. Don't know how that Mrs Tregupter makes pastry like that given the state of *her* fingers. Fair play,' agreed Oggy.

'Talking about fingers, what about that Lavinia with his nails? Queer as a newt if you ask me,' said Digory.

'Did you see his bloody great feet, in them red stilettos?' said Oggy. 'Least they matched her varnish, I suppose.'

'Will you have her to do your roof?'

'I ain't sure if he goes up ladders any more, being ambidextrous and that. Might be a bit dangerous in a dress,' mused Oggy. 'Shouldn't really allow it in a chapel either. I don't know what God would think, I'm sure, but there you go. I suppose he got other more pressing stuff to worry about.'

'Good pianist mind, Oggy.'

'I couldn't see it where I was standing,' chortled Oggy.

They pulled into the yard at Dordigor Farm, and the yard lights flickered on. There stood Trelawney in the dim glow, still chewing the silage, still with his back to Pam and Brenda.

'And you might as well have his chopped off too, for all the fun them cows are getting out of it,' said Oggy.

'He'll be all right. He's just a bit confused. Goodnight boy.'

'Cheers and gone,' called Oggy. 'And don't forget Mother's water for God's sake!'

Off he went, headed home down the road to Tredogend, and when he arrived he sneaked in the back door to avoid waking everyone up with the tinkling shop bell, and made his way along the downstairs hallway to the kitchen. Everyone, it seemed, was in bed as he had suspected. He knew that at ten thirty five, every night without fail, Uncle Clar sneaked downstairs for another cup of tay, and raided the pantry for a Rich Tea or two whilst always keeping up the pretence that he had no idea where they were kept.

Now was his moment. Oggy had to move fast.

He slipped into the pantry and lifted the lid of the deep freeze. The inside light, at least, was still working. He clumsily clambered in, and pulled it shut on himself, and there he waited.

Before long, Oggy heard Uncle Clar come creaking down the stairs and down into the kitchen, and put the kettle to boil. He could hear him rooting around for his favourite biscuits that Vi always kept in stock.

From inside the freezer, Oggy heard the click of the latch of the old planked pantry door. He heard Uncle Clar turn the light on, and then rustling and shuffling about for biscuits, just outside of the freezer.

Uncle Clar peeped among the ranks of bags of flour and catering tubs of margarine, the packs and slabs of lard and salt and white pepper on the shelves, large hessian sacks of potatoes and stringed bags of onions, and loosely piled swedes all around the slate slabbed floor. Where had Vi hidden the packet?

Oggy began to slowly and rhythmically rock, to and fro, inside the big old freezer, and it began to shake. Uncle Clar could feel the floor vibrating and shuddering beneath his feet, and Oggy began to shake the thing more vigorously. It began to rock violently from side to side.

The shelves all around the pantry began to vibrate too. Flour bags wobbled. A stray onion rolled off a shelf and a sack of potatoes toppled over onto the floor, the earthy contents spilling out.

Oggy began to moan and wail, quietly at first, then louder and louder and louder, from within the very depths of the freezer.

Uncle Clar was terrified. He lunged and grasped and grabbed and tried desperately to cling on to the shelves either side of the pantry, like a man caught swaying in a violent earthquake. He clutched at the wall and the pantry light flickered, and then went out altogether, and a metal meat tray clanged down onto the stone floor in a clattering crescendo.

Uncle Clar cried out for help.

Then, Oggy lay still and as suddenly as the commotion had begun, the noise and the vibration stopped.

The pantry light came on again.

All was quiet.

Uncle Clar reached out with his bony old right hand. Shaking with fear, he stepped bravely towards the freezer and grasped the handle and began to slowly lift the lid. A shaft of yellow light shone out from within.

Oggy lay inside as motionless as he could, hardly daring to breathe. But as Uncle Clar lifted the lid just a little more, Oggy knew that it was past the point of no return. His cover was about to be blown.

There was nothing for it. He let out a blood curdling, Hammer House of Horror banshee scream.

Uncle Clar dropped the lid of the freezer and ran out of the pantry, out of the kitchen and skittered up the stairs at a speed that belied his years, and burst into his bedroom and slammed the door behind him. He dived into his bed and pulled the sheets up over his head, and lay there in terror of what he had just witnessed.

Mother had said there was something funny in that pantry.

Oggy Sloggett chuckled away mischievously to himself at the successful haunting of the redundant freezer, and made a nice cup of tay in the kitchen. It was with joy that he saw Cheel's coat hanging behind the door, for in all the excitement of his paranormal activity he'd almost forgotten that she was due home. So he left his tay and ascended the narrow stairs and hurriedly skipped along the landing to welcome his dear little maid back home for the summer break.

He knocked on her bedroom door. There was no reply. He listened at the door to hear if she might still be awake. He could hear her chanting quietly to herself, 'On my honour and the honour of my country, I swear...' Probably revising from them law books of hers, he thought to himself. What a hard working little maid she was.

He went in. The room was dark, but the light from the hallway partially illuminated the girl that at first he did not recognise as his daughter at all, sitting cross legged on her bed in knickers and T-shirt, toning her biceps with a set of dumbbells, and chanting from a sheet of paper spread on the bed in front of her.

He switched the bedroom light on. She startled and gathered the sheet up quickly.

'Father!' she squealed. The weights dropped with a thud on the floor.

'Oh, it is you. What have you done to all your lovely hair?' he asked.

' 'Tis a new style father, Cornish colours. Do you like it?' she said.

'It's like a boy's. What's all them rings and stuff?'

'I've changed courses too. I got fed up with drama and dancing and all that, 'tis too trivial and shallow and superficial father,' she said.

'Your mum told me you was doing some law thing or other. 'Tis a shame, you was a lovely little dancer.'

'Law thing? What you on about, father?'

Oggy looked into her eyes. 'You ain't on drugs are you?' he growled suspiciously.

'No! I'm doing Sociology and Cornish Studies now.'

'Same thing. What's that on your arm?' demanded her father.

'Kernow Bys Vycken.'

'What?!'

'Cornwall for ever father!! It's time we young stood up, and stopped cow-towing to the English oppressor. Free Cornwall!' she shouted.

'Free Cornwall? I'm too bloody busy baking pasties and trying to make a living for all that!' said Oggy, crossly.

'Look father, all them smirking tourists you sells pasties to are just the vanguard, that's all. Merely the harbingers of the Orpington jackboot. They are invading and you, me, Mam, Uncle Clar, Merv, Mother, we'll all end up in reservations up on the moors, you see if I ain't right!' shouted Cheel, pointing at her neck. 'We'll be more extinct than these choughs.'

'Who's telling you all this bollocks? Who's Kernewek? It isn't another woman is it?' demanded Oggy, staring at her breast.

'Kernewek? It means Cornish, father! I got a Cornish heart.'

'As long as you ain't confused, that's all. I'm just thinking of that Pam and Brenda,' he said.

'Who the fuck are Pam and Brenda?'

'Never mind!' said Oggy.

'Like whatever, get over yourself, this is the way it is,' she shouted, and jumped up on the bed and turned her back to her father, and she dropped her knickers and mooned her message at him. 'One and all! Can you see that all right, father?'

Oggy averted his gaze. 'Hellfire bloody corner,' he said to himself, well and truly staring defeat in the face. He shook his head and turned past the small chest of drawers beside the bedroom door, and he saw her pink My Little Pony still standing next to the lamp with its toy grooming brush, and the Glee poster behind it.

And next to the toy he saw a college file. It was decorated on the cover by a plastic car sticker of the Cornish flag of St Piran, and beneath that Oggy read the ominous title beneath the words 'Cheel Sloggett, year one dissertation'.

It said 'Bury My Heart at Indian Queens'.

He closed the door behind him, and walked quietly into his own bedroom, where he took off his blazer and flannels and hung them up. He examined his frayed and tay-stained choir tie, and fingered the rather raggedy badge on his blazer, and reflected that although he might soon have to invest in new versions of each, at least the singing was still free.

He crept into the bed and lay motionless next to Vi. He looked up at the artex scallops of the ceiling, and the nighttime angsts that so irrationally magnify the trivial into the terrible slowly began to cloud his tired, cluttered mind. It had not finished well, the day. He could barely afford a new badge for his blazer, the freezer was buggered and his pasties too cheap, the tenors were flat, the organist had no organ, and his daughter had been radicalised and tattooed from head to toe by a lesbian called Kernewek, and was now as sexually confused as Digory's cows.

Vi snuggled up to him, and half awake asked, 'All right tonight darlin'?'

'As flat as a fart,' he said.

Chapter Seven
The Corniche Nouveau

emmets – *Cornish word for crawling insects, such as you might see if you were to turn over a stone, e.g. ants, earwigs, and sow pigs (woodlice). Recently used as a generic derogatory term for incomers and 'blow-ins', or for holidaymakers in general. It is interesting to note that a Cornishman can never, ever be an emmet, no matter where he may be, though he could be a foreigner, visitor, 'blow-in' or a 'grockle'. N.B. 'grockle' is the Devonian equivalent of emmet, only devoid of the bitter and angry connotations of the latter.*

Emma had walked out for her early morning stroll, and now lay out on a downy duvet of tussocky grass, above the towering cliffs that rose beyond the ruins of Tredogend castle. The surprisingly powerful rays of the rising sun warmed her through, and lit up her face with a smile she had long forgotten. Her eyes feasted on the rich palette of colour that made up one of mother nature's most remarkable wild gardens, a carpet of pink blobs of thrift and of the yellowy orange and blood red varieties of vetch, of fine stemmed bladder campions and cornflower-blue devil's bit scabious, the purple knapweed with their attendant scarlet burnet moths, and the sticky sweetness of wild thyme.

Emma watched as a pretty little puffin scratched its way into its sandy shale burrow, and her thoughts drifted back to when she and Hugo Strutt, in the days before he became Huge, first used to meet at her organic vegetable stall at the Saturday morning Borough Market by Southwark, and she'd bring in the finest of her produce for him from the family small holding near Hastings so that the jovial, budding young chef could deliver his customers 'the very finest on offer'.

She remembered the time when he came to her stall with a wide and eager smile, excited with the news that television producer Barney Sanchez-DeVille had eaten at his restaurant and wanted him for a new TV chef programme his company was going to make. She and Hugo had gone for a Spanish breakfast together, just around the corner under the old redbrick railway arches, and he'd asked her out, and she'd gone and it all seemed so perfect.

So perfect that when he asked her, she had given up working at the small holding and moved to London to be with him, and to help do programme research. It quickly did well in the ratings, and they married and had kids, one, two, three in rapid succession, and she left the production team to look after them, and he got bigger and bigger and bigger, and then huge, huger, and then eventually 'Huge'.

And then he got himself some new research assistants. One after another.

And then it all started to go wrong.

Emma recounted the ghastly media affairs where she was so often left talking to some crusty old fart or another from the BBC, invariably with wild, frizzy grey hair and roundy, horn rimmed pre-war spectacles, or else to some desperately right-on Bohemian young thing, glancing continuously over her shoulders in turn, looking for someone more important to impress in the clamber up the slippery ladder.

She thought of Huge, as he had become, who was now without doubt that important person to impress. He loudly and immodestly held court in the centre of the room, booming and braying, monstrously over-hearty and apparently hilarious. The gravitational attraction of his hugeness drew in a flood tide of blonde hair tossing, back-biting, bimbette, Barbie bitches. They Facebooked him, E-mailed and G-mailed him, they flirted and flashed him their mobile numbers, they touched him and twittered him, and all teeth and tits and all over him like a rash, they double-kissed him. And how he bloody loved it.

'Aaaagh!' she screamed, and sighed angrily. The little puffin peeped out of its burrow and peered at her inquisitively, and she felt ashamed to harbour such bitterness in this loveliest of places.

Emma lay back and mulled over what she and Huge had talked about so earnestly into the previous night. Bringing the kids up here in Cornwall would be so special, he'd said. What a gift for them, he'd said, what an opportunity, none of the constraints of life back in London and the Home Counties, just running wild and swimming, catching fish, beachcombing and building dams and dens, going to the local school with all their new village friends and growing up part of a real community, as one with nature and as free as birds, how could she deny that to them?

It was rather hard to take issue with. The cottage they were renting was perfect, at least until they were able to find one to buy. They'd have to find a new cleaner, of course. Morwenna had quit a bit suddenly. She was a pretty, fair haired little girl, waiting to go off to Uni, and had seemed quite happy. Funny, but there you go.

Anyway, the cottage was so close to the beach, and there was no doubt that the kids had loved it there over the past week or so, crabbing in the rock pools and surfing, and to be honest Emma had to admit she rather liked it herself too. Particularly the surfing.

It was just that deep down inside she questioned Huge's real motives for the move. Was it really for her and the kids, for the family, or when he had finished this series would he have them up sticks again and drag them, as if they were merely his personal baggage, on to the next huge Huge project that tickled his ego? Would he suddenly decide that there were more important things than mere sea air?

Somewhat naively, she had been buoyed by the faithful promise that he made her just as she was dropping off to sleep, that he had left the grotesque media monster Huge back in the smoke, and was determined to make it all work for them down here in Cornwall.

Of course, there would have to be the occasional trip back up to London to the studios for 'research' and so forth, but he was sure that she understood that that could simply not be helped.

Oh dear.

Still in bed and resplendent in just his flabby, polka-dot Johnnie Boden boxers, Huge had finished twittering some early morning lies about the shimmering, iridescent fresh mackerel that he'd just hand-lined so sustainably into his punt, the 'Emma', and then with artisan love effortlessly thrown together in a gourmet breakfast for himself and Em and the kids, cast iron pan-fried with just a twist of sea salt and the subtle aniseed hint of wild fennel in the driftwood clinkered kitchen of Fisherman's Cottage, their Corniche Nouveau, smugly-salty seaside idyll.

One could taste the very sea itself, apparently.

Huge, meanwhile, ate a bowl of ValuCheap's own brand sugar puffs from the pink plastic breakfast bowl that Julienne refused to use, whilst she and her two siblings were hungrily watching the cartoon channel downstairs.

As he chewed on the sugar puffs, his mind wandered back to a few days previously. They did seem to be a bit sheltered, the Cornish girls. Young Morwenna was pretty all right, petite and fair, and oddly attractive even in her cleaner's overalls, scrubbing down the skirting boards outside the bathroom, and when he just happened to pop out of the shower rubbing down his bits and accidentally dropped his towel, she had not seemed to be overly alarmed, but had scuttled off when he'd remarked that she was a sight for sore eyes; nothing more, nothing less. She never came back to clean again.

Win some, lose some, he thought and began the sordid sexting of Inga from a tented area beneath his quilt, which to his great tingling excitement he had gleefully discovered to be one of the few mobile hotspots in Tredogend. It was a spot that glowed even hotter as he treated the lucky Swede to a texted narrative of his recipe for the full English, the Huge English, plus a saucy list of ingredients and a detailed resume of just how he intended to prepare and serve it up for her when they next met. He was so taken aback by the boldness of her reply that he spilt the remains of his soggy cereal and semi-skimmed all down his commodious undergarments, and very nearly forgot to press the delete button.

By the time Emma returned from her walk, he was down in the kitchen having a fag and making a cup of instant in his onesie, and shouting at the kids to stop squabbling or else he'd switch the telly off and make them go to the beach. When Emma timidly suggested that that was exactly what he should do anyway, he responded by telling her that he had to go and concentrate on his new blog, which was to be linked to the new 'Huge in Cornwall' website, coming on-line that very morning.

Huge sat with his laptop on his knee, and began to type.

'Hey – Huuuge! In Cornwall! I bet you're wondering what we're on upon, me and darling Emma Huge and the little Huges? Well, here we are down in Cornwall in a really beautiful fishing village, re-locating and making it our new home. I'm going to become a part of this great Cornish community, I'm going to take one of Cornwall's most iconic symbols, the humble pasty, and give it a Huge! 21st century makeover! Yes guys, the pasty is going to be Huuuuuge-mongous!

Over the next months I'm going to develop my own community pasty bakery and shop, using only the finest sustainable organic ingredients of local provenance, and with the help of the community we'll give the pasty the status that it's always warranted.

The wild Atlantic coast is spectacularly beautiful, and the people here are just great. My children, Quenelle nine, Julienne eight and little Goujon six, just love it so much. They're out and about enjoying the freedom that only Cornwall can offer – out swimming, surfing, crabbing in the rockpools and……'

Julienne punched Quenelle in the ear for having the temerity to flick over to the music channel to watch rappers Jwalker Streetdog and YoBrother Driveby Bloodclot. Quenelle started to screech. Julienne snatched the remote and flicked back to Family Guy. Goujon carried on reading about green algae blooms.

'Will you stop that noise Quenelle. Jules, you mustn't punch people in the ears when they're listening to music, it's dangerous. Especially when it's rap music. Why don't you go outside and play on the beach? Build some sandcastles or catch some shrimps or go for a swim or something. It's such a lovely day,' said Huge.

'I hate sandcastles!' said little Goujon.

'I hate shrimping,' shouted Quenelle.

'I hate you!' Julienne screamed at Quenelle.

Goujon flicked over a page, and engaged with the life cycle of the squat lobster.

Huge shook his head, and returned to his keyboard.

'......*I can tell that we're going to have three real outdoor children who we hardly ever see, but hey! That's Cornwall for you. Emma's in her element, just as I expected really, she's going back to her roots....*'

He didn't realise, but she was reading over his shoulder.

'What do you mean "back to my roots"? I was brought up near Hastings!' she protested.

'Oh no one will know, for God's sake. Hastings is by the sea, isn't it? And you've been here before.'

'That was a weekend in North Devon,' she said.

'Just over the border. That's close enough. Did you have a pasty?' he asked.

'How do I know? I was only seven.'

'Did you ever have a pasty before last week?' persisted Huge.

'Well, yes, at Paddington Station last year. It was disgusting,' she said.

'There you go then. Don't be so bloody picky Em. In my book that makes you virtually Cornish. What was your maiden name again?' he said.

'What?'

'Your maiden name. Leaven, wasn't it? We can change it back and put a 'Tre' in front of it. That'll work, Treleaven, no probs,' he said.

'Oh yeah, right. And I suppose we can change all the kids' names too – Trelawney, Denzil and bloody Demelza – why not?' said Emma sarcastically.

'I'll be bloody Demelza,' called out Quenelle.

'It's a girl's name, Quenelle,' said Emma. 'And nobody is going to change their names. It's just Daddy being silly.'

'You don't get it, do you darling? You've been out of the game too long. Nobody gives a shit,' he said, and shrugged his shoulders and blogged on regardless,

'*...back to her seaside roots, with memories of long summer holidays in the Cornish sun, making pasties with her Aunt....Demelza...with her Cornish cousins all around. I felt so inspired by her longing to return to this idyllic place, that I've brought her back to where she belongs. Emma Treleaven, are you going to show me how to bake pasties?*

Keep Crimping!

Huge x'

The tweets were flying in from his legions of followers, all telling him what they were having for their breakfasts and where they were eating them and who with. Of course he wasn't in the least bit interested in any of them, chiefly because they weren't about him. Apart from one that is, and that said simply '#ingaswinga – mmmm lovin the Full English prospect'.

Within the hour, Huge had Nigel on the phone from the production office at ZeeTV, with news about the lease he was negotiating for the old chapel.

'For Christ's sake Nige, get the freehold, Barney can afford it. He's bloody loaded man. We bang on in there, smack out all the bloody pews and the font and hymnbooks and all that guff, wang in something rustic that looks like a fisherman's kitchen, get a few of the local inbreds in to do the day to day donkey work, use the Huge factor to get it throbbing baby, and then at the end of the series flog the bloody lot as a going concern. Bish, bash, bosh! Job done, dude!' he paused, just momentarily, for breath. 'Oh, and at some point I suppose we'd better give Barney his dosh back…'

Nigel explained that it would be so much easier if Huge, with all his wealth of personal charm, celebrity and charisma, maybe conducted the negotiation himself and made the offer to the only surviving trustee of the chapel.

That personal touch, he said.

The estate agent had put Nigel on to a Mr Digory Hicks, and he had seemed a very nice guy over the telephone, and had said that he would be as happy as toast to show someone round the chapel, even when Nigel had politely declined the chance to enrol on his website amongst the agricultured lovelorn.

Nigel had certainly done his research thoroughly, and passed it all on to Huge. Mr Hicks was a trustee of the chapel in Tredogend. He was a local businessman apparently, with many strings to his bow, including the preservation of rare breeds of farm animals, and he foraged locally for wild edible and medicinal plants and herbs, something which would doubtless interest Huge. Amusingly, Nigel confided, as a sideline Mr Digory Hicks ran a lonely hearts web site for filthy, depraved old Cornish farmers, whose attractiveness to the opposite sex lay primarily in the massive girth of their subsidy cheques.

Oh, *and* Mr Hicks ran a taxi service too.

On the journey up to Dordigor Farm, Huge recalled his taxi ride to Newquay airport, and prayed that Mr Hicks wouldn't remember him, or recall how he'd made him gag with the eggy stink he had made in the back, when he was unable to wind down the window because it was jammed. He also prayed that Mr Hicks wouldn't recall how obnoxious and arrogantly dismissive his attitude had been when he had so helpfully suggested an organic cure for his condition.

It was one of the fundamental differences between London and Cornwall; up in the smoke you'd be very unlucky to get the same cabbie twice, so you could get away with most things, whereas down in Cornwall such transgressions were rarely without consequence. Indeed, Digory had extracted retribution on many people who had annoyed him in his taxi, often after many years had passed and when they had quite forgotten what they had ever done to him.

So it was for those flimsy cotton t-shirted Newquay clubbers, one week rude or maybe even merely indifferent to him at the home drop-off, the next week expelled in the early hours from the DigsCab, midway across the never-ending boggy badlands of the Goss Moor, blindly blundering into the cruel teeth of a howling gale and it's horizontal sheets of freezing rain. 'Tis a long road with no turnings, Digory would darkly remark.

Digory was too canny to let on that he had recognised the TV chef from the trip to the airport and from Mother's pasty shop, and told Huge that he had another man interested in buying the chapel at the full asking price, and that to consider any other offer would compromise his integrity. As such he was unable to assist any further at the present, but he would be able to include him on the lonelyfarmershearts web site, even though he was clearly not any sort of a farmer. After he had paid the subscription, that is.

Huge seethed, and thanked him through gritted teeth, and jumped back into the car and headed down towards Tredogend to re-think his strategy. Digory watched as the hideously oversized 4x4, off road and with dust and dirt on its wheels for the very first time, disappeared away into the distance.

Trelawney chewed. Pam and Brenda just stood. Digory shook his head. 'Thought you'd pull the wool over my head, did 'ee?' he chuckled to himself. 'You must think I was born tomorrow.'

He went indoors and rang Oggy, for he knew for sure that his dear old mate would be very, very interested in what had happened.

Chapter Eight
Sweet

Little Lize, I love you, honey,
Little Lize, I love you, honey,
I love you in the springtime and the fall,
Honey, honey, honey, honey.
'Little Lize.' - *Traditional Cornish folk song.*

Oggy had gone to bed early and slept well, and just before light the following morning, he and Vi were engaged in tay and reflection, propped up by plumped pillows lain back against the headboard. He took a noisy slurp, spilling a little tay down his chins and onto his striped cotton winceyette jim-jams.

'So what did Digory have to say last night?' he said.

'He said to tell you choir practice is Thursday darlin', and he'd had that chef geezer Huge from the telly up there yesterday, trying to buy the chapel. Said he didn't trust him, and that he was as sly as a badger,' said Vi.

'A badger, eh?' said Oggy, slurping some more and looking rather puzzled. 'What's he want the chapel for?'

'To live in I suppose. He's with his missus and kids down at that Fisherman's Cottage. You know, Turner's old place. It's tiny,' said Vi.

'Used to be nine of 'em lived in there. Ma and Pa Turner and seven snot nosed kids. Poor as piss they were.'

'It's done up nice.'

'Digory's right. He's an artful devil.'

'She's very nice though. Her and the kids have been surfing with our Mervin over Porzeath a bit. Anyway, Digory told him that he wouldn't sell it to him.'

'Why not?' asked Oggy.

'Because he horse and carted in Digory's cab last week. You know what a memory he's got for that sort of thing,' said Vi.

'He chucked Roger Retallick out by Dozmary Pool in the mist last February, for being sick in his taxi in June 1984,' chuckled Oggy. 'Never got home until April Fools Day. And he was wearing all his lodge gear.'

They laughed as the door opened and in walked a rather pre-occupied Cheel, brushing the pink mane of her My Little Pony, with her iPad under her arm. She sat on the end of their bed.

'All right, babe?' asked Vi. 'You used to come and cuddle in. Now look at ya.'

Cheel curled up her nose in disgust. 'Mum, father, something's going on here. One of my mates was looking at that chef bloke's blog, that Huge. She reckons him and his family are moving here full-time. Reckons he's going to start making pasties here and putting it all on telly. It's all over Facebook,' she said.

'She? Who's she? Not that Kernewek woman is it?' demanded Oggy.

'No father! He's twittering about it too, there's rumours all over,' she said. 'You can't just sit there and do nothing, so I got us online, all right? Facebook, blogs, twitter, a website.'

'I don't know all about this old twittering and twattering stuff, do you Vi? How's that gonna sell any pasties?'

Cheel rolled her eyes and passed her bemused looking Dad the iPad, and scrolled down the screen for him to squint at and read the falsified and fancifully fake blog of Huge's new and interesting salty, seaside culinary adventure.

'But he can't make pasties. There's more to it than he'll ever know,' growled Oggy.

'Look,' said Cheel. She flicked the screen. 'I've started us up a website, motherspasties.com. We can go on here and put stuff about the family and the business and all that.'

'I don't want the buggers to know nothing about me,' moaned Oggy.

'You can tell 'em when you're baking pasties. Show 'em how to crimp and stuff online. You could, like, tweet '*#opening Mothers full of delicious pasties mmm,*' that sort of thing.'

'Hellish! Your life ain't yer own, is it Vi?'

'You can get on to Facebook and talk with all your mates!'

'I only got Digory and he comes in every day anyway.'

'Look. I got you a Facebook account too. There, with that photo of you down at Newquay zoo when you told that woman in the cafe her pasty was filth.'

'Bloody hellfire, I ain't that ginger, am I Vi? What a awful picture, me jabbers is redder than a turkey cock's.'

'You got thirteen likes already, father. See? Digory sent one look.'

'I'd rather have thirteen quid in me till!'

'And he says "Good choir practice the other night boy", see how it works?'

'I know that, I was standing right next to the silly old bollocks. What's he want to tell me that for?'

'Oh for God's sake, we gotta repel the invading aggressor, father,' said Cheel, hand on her tattooed heart. 'Cornwall for the Cornish!'

'Hang on darlin',' protested Vi. 'You're half of me and I'm from Plaistow you know, not bleedin' Padstow!'

Cheel stood at the end of the bed, and pointed at her Mum. 'Mam,' she said. 'Never forget this. You are a woman of Kernow, and you must stand proud.'

Cheel punched her fist into the air, then turned and lifted her tee shirt, baring her back to her parents, a back upon which the word 'nasty' stood out against the pasty tattooed between her slim shoulder blades, and the fifteen golden bezants of old Kernow stood in diminishing lines, from five in the top row, down to the single bezant at the base of her spine.

She turned and looked her Mum and father with a burning intensity in her eyes, and she spoke quietly and deliberately. 'The struggle begins,' she said. She picked up her My Little Pony and the grooming comb, and went to her own bedroom, closing the door behind her.

'Struggle my ass, I'm struggling to get rid of that deep freeze, that's all I know,' said Oggy. He shook his head and sighed. 'She's a bloody hellcat, that one.'

'Have you told Uncle Clar that freezer's haunted yet?' asked Vi.

'Not exactly *told* him, no…'

'What?'

'I just got one thing to say to you,' he said, and tapped the side of his nose. 'Hamburger Hill.'

Huge had had to have a re-think overnight. It was time to use an entirely different approach, and the pure genius of his plan had come to him just as the gulls screeched in the first dim light of dawn. When he later went down to the kitchen and made himself a cup of instant and some toast with peanut butter and marmite, he sat at the table to plot the logistics of the day, and was pleased to note the sun was shining in through the window. It was just such a perfect day for Em to take the kids off surfing again, and when he primed them they seemed animated at the prospect of another lesson with Mervin, who was cool and wore shades and was fun to be with.

And when he broached the subject with Em, she'd initially indicated that she'd been thinking to spend the day at home, do all the washing and cleaning and housework, and then pot out some geraniums and nasturtiums and trim the fuchsia, and prop up the giant thistle-headed artichokes and tropical looking echiums with some canes. Oh go on, he said, take them to the beach. Life's too short. They love the surf. We'll get another cleaner in for all that. Put a card in the beach shop window to advertise.

It's what their new life was all about, after all, and they had to embrace it, to live it, and they had to make it work for the kids as well. It's what they all wanted, wasn't it? Free spirited, bronze-tanned kids, running bare foot, their footprints in the sand and riding the wild Atlantic surf with abandon.

She had to agree. Huge was so right. He even said he'd drop them off at Porzeath and pick them up at sixish, which was kind as he had *such* a busy schedule getting this new project of his off the ground. Emma got the towels and trunks and buckets and spades together, chucked them in the back of the beast-cruiser, and off they went.

The day's busy schedule had all been arranged earlier, and by the time Huge was waving them off at the beach, the operation was in full swing. The main thrust (if you will pardon the expression) of it all was Inga, who had caught the seven a.m. from Paddington, and was now trundling over Brunel's tubular bridge across the Tamar at Saltash, leaving England behind and snaking along the creeks and valleys that led down to Bodmin Parkway.

Inga had been surprised to get such an early text from Huge, and had quickly packed up a case and taken a black Addison Lee cab across town, and arrived at the platform with twenty minutes to spare. She had gazed with curiosity at the Cornish pasty shop adjacent to the waiting train. Emblazoned right across the shop window was a bristle bearded pirate chewing heartily on a pasty; having had no breakfast she'd gone in and in the interests of research bought herself one for the train journey, and chewed it all the way to Reading.

Huge was waiting in the beast-cruiser to ferry her to the B&B in Tredogend. He could have got DigsCab to taxi her of course, but he had some catching up and 'briefing' to do. He breathed deeply as the gorgeously curvaceous and fulsome-figured Inga alighted at Bodmin Parkway, and bent to pull out the long handles of her wheelie case. He watched in his mirror as she stepped along the platform towards the car park, in crisp white blouse and figure-hugging calf-length jeans. And, phwoarr, what a figure to hug, thought Huge, as he gazed transfixed at her long, swinging blonde hair, held back by a pair of diamante decorated sunglasses. Without doubt, Inga was an area of outstanding natural beauty in an area of outstanding natural beauty.

He leaned across and opened the passenger door for her, and breathlessly but elegantly she shimmied into the seat, and pecked him on the cheek.

'Hiii,' she said. 'So this is Cornwall. Cool.'

'Welcome to the beast-cruiser,' he said. 'Hey, have I got something to show you.'

'More research?' she said, raising her eyebrows playfully. 'I can't wait.'

Huge pressed the ignition button, and started the ludicrously over-powerful engine. It purred into life, and he began to break into a lustful sweat.

'It's a bit of a drive to Tredogend,' he said. 'We'll take the scenic route, along the lanes up on the moors.'

'Wow. I'm in your hands Huge,' she said.

Emma sat on the driftwood bench at the Surfside beach hut in conversation with the sun bleached and dreadlocked Mervin. He was in his early twenties, and as fit and lean as a butcher's dog. He wore salty sun-faded board shorts and a baggy old sweatshirt with 'Dreckly Man' across the chest. He had beads and bands and leather strips around his neck and wrists and ankles. He was seemingly sustained by a combination of ValuCheap cola that he swigged from a family sized plastic bottle, honey sandwiches, and roll-ups that he constantly seemed to be manufacturing on the lid of an old Golden Virginia tin.

Mervin was the epitome of laid back. Emma admired his open and easy-going nature, his seeming indifference to anything material, and she was intrigued by his lifestyle. Why would he need anything else, he'd said, for he had everything he wanted, the beach, the surf, the sun when it shone, a little blow now and then, and his freedom to come and go as he liked. He made enough to get by, and he had his 'pad' hidden deep in the dunes.

Mervin told Emma about his family, and Mother's Pasty shop that had been established for so long no one could remember when, and how proud he was of them all, but he couldn't work there himself because he loved the outside so much. Emma told him how she had bought the fabulous pasties from there for her family, and how they'd loved them. What was the secret, she asked? There must be one to make them taste so good. Mervin just laughed a kind laugh.

'I *could* tell you,' he said. 'But I'd have to…'

'Shoot me?' she giggled.

Mervin looked over his shoulder, then leaned forward and whispered in a deep, hushed tone. 'The county is full of the shallow graves of those who have tried to unearth the secrets of the pasty.'

Emma momentarily regarded him with a serious expression, until she saw the mischievous grin light up his face. They smiled out across the beach, to where they could see the kids happily playing in a sandy pool.

'Huge said they'd love it, and look at them. He's right,' said Emma.

'Best place to bring up kids. They're lucky. Not many get to grow up like this,' he said. 'Where are you living?'

'Fisherman's Cottage. In Tredogend,' she said.

'No way! I know it. Used to play there with Tom Turner and his brother, their old family house. His Mum and Dad sold up for nearly half a million a few years back,' said Mervin.

'Wow!'

'They're still bitter and twisted about it though,' laughed Mervin. 'That's the thing about us Cornish. You'd think that would be half a million reasons to cheer up, but no. We got to keep up the resentment. It's a pride thing.'

'Where do you live Mervin?' she said.

'You'll like this,' he said smiling. He pointed back over the marram grassed dunes. 'Hidden away back there. In an old ice cream van.'

'No. My God. What's it like?' asked Emma disbelievingly.

'Cold,' said Mervin.

'Oh I bet, in the winter especially….oh, I see. Yes, cold of course,' she said, and giggled and nodded and smiled a wide, warm smile, and so did he.

Up on the moors at Delphy Bridge, between the granite villages of Blisland and St Breward, the sturdy moorland ponies exercised their common grazing rights, nibbling on the sedgy, rushy ground that formed a smooth, natural lawn through which the De Lank River threaded crystal clear. Little brown trout darted in and out of the shimmering green eel grass that grew out of the gravely river bed, snaking along and around sou'westerly bent thickets of blackthorn bushes and shrivelled oaks. And in the midst of all this, hidden from the view of passing motorists, Huge's 4x4 was off road. Again.

'So Huge,' said Inga. 'What's this you have to show me?'

'Close your eyes and hold your hand out,' he said.

'I hope this is all in the course of research,' she said, and did as she was bid. She clasped her fingers around it, and was not disappointed.

'Oh my God,' she exclaimed. 'It's huge! And it's soooo hot! Huge!'

She could resist no longer, and bit right into it.

Huge bit into his pasty as well. It brought tears to his eyes, for Uncle Clar had put extra seasoning into the day's batch.

'Oh – my - God, they're the best yet. What do you think Ingrid?' he said, staring reverentially at the pasty.

'Inga,' she corrected him quickly. 'I've never tasted anything quite like it.'

Together they chomped and chobbled their way through the Cornish Giant pasties that Huge had brought along, all the time hoping against hope that they would have an aphrodisiac effect on his Scandinavian friend. He was not to be disappointed, and when they had finished their magnificent Cornish pasty treats in the bucolic bliss of the beautiful backwater, they reclined their seats, and brazenly bonked like beastly baboons in the back of the beast cruiser. It really was the ultimate off road experience.

Emma and the kids enjoyed their pasty picnic down on the beach. Good old Daddy, Emma said, paying for us all to have these lovely Cornish Pixie pasties. Delicious. They shared some of Mervin's cola, as he told them all about the origins of the names of the three different sized pasties. When they had finished, little Goujon, Quenelle and Julienne scampered off back to the shallow sandy pool left by the ebbing tide, under strict instructions not to go into the sea on their own.

'So why do you live in the van?' asked Emma.

'Well, it can be a bit intense at home. Mum's good, but Dad's a bit fiery,' he said laughing. 'Mother, that's my Nan, well she's just Mother. Then there's Uncle Clar, he's nice, and then my sister Cheel. She's away at Uni most of the time.'

'Couldn't you get a small place?'

'There's no way I could ever afford to buy anywhere round here, and I don't really want to go inland. This is where I belong. So the van it is, and it's not as bad as it sounds. I keep it tidy like, and I've built a deck around it and got some plants and stuff in. It still goes too, and because it's on wheels I don't need planning. I love it,' he said.

'Sounds great,' said Emma.

'You can have a gander if you want. It's only two minutes over there,' said Mervin.

'I shouldn't really. The kids,' she said.

'Well, I can keep my eye from the top of the dune there. If you like. Up to you,' he said.

Emma smiled. 'Go on then, lead the way,' she said.

They marched up the sinky, sandy path through the spiky marram grass, over one dune, down another and then up the other side, to where Mervin pointed down into a small sheltered dip.

'There she is,' he said. 'Home sweet home. Go and have a look round. I'll keep lookout for the kids.'

Emma ran down the slope and up to the driftwood planked deck that surrounded the old ice cream van. It was covered in interesting bits of flotsam and jetsam that he'd beachcombed and dragged up over the past couple of years, torn old bits of blue and green net, and pink, yellow and orange lobster pot buoys, twisted trunks of wood, a fisherman's glove, and a beach bucket full of seagull feathers.

Mervin had fashioned a marram grass thatch out over the deck, and hung a string of Christmas lights around the rim, and there was a rusted metal drum that he used for a barbeque at the side. He'd put a fig tree in an old pot at the bumper of the van, and on the deck at the front of the van there stood an old beehive. Emma stood back warily.

'Don't worry,' called Mervin. 'They won't hurt, they're too busy making honey for me.'

'Really?' said Emma, intrigued. 'Don't you ever get stung?'

'Nah. I blow a bit of smoke in there. That quietens them down. Especially skunk. Trouble is they don't make any honey for days after that,' he laughed.

In the midst of it all was the ice cream van itself. Mervin had removed the entire original interior except the driver's seat, and made a soft and comfy bed where the freezer had been. There were interior fairy lights as well, and he'd dotted nightlights around the curtained windows, and hung beads and paper lanterns and all sorts of dippy hippy accoutrements from the roof, and he'd painted a surfing mural around the walls, in an Imperial Japanese style with dolphins and sea monsters, and pony-tailed samurai surfers riding the breaking waves. Emma peered in through the windscreen. Inside, a hand stitched felt pasty on a string dangled from the interior mirror.

'Oh wow,' said Emma. 'A little pasty, that's sweet.'

'My little sis sewed it for me. Reminds me of home.'

'It's really lovely.'

'The loudspeaker still works too. It plays 'Jack and Jill' and 'Three Blind Mice', and I put a couple of Chilli Pepper numbers on it as well!' he laughed.

Emma laughed back. 'The dude from the dunes!' she called. 'Perfect.'

They heard the scream even from where they were, and Mervin could see Julienne running back up the beach towards the surf shack. 'Quick!' he shouted to Emma, and she ran back up the slope from the van and together they skittered down into the dip of the dune and up the other side, and back down through the marram grass to where they had come from, huffing and puffing back to the surf shack where Julienne was standing. Standing very upset. Standing very cross. Very cross indeed.

'Jules, darling…'

'Where were you, Mummy?' she cried. 'It's Quenelle! He's been bitten. His foot!'

They ran across the wide flat beach to the sandy pool, around which a crowd had now gathered. A lifeguard and another kindly man were attending to Quenelle, who was screaming in agony at the edge of the pool.

'The air ambulance is on its way to get him to Truro Hospital. It's only over at Trevose,' said the lifeguard.

'He stood on a weaver fish,' said little Goujon. No one was listening.

'Is there a doctor here? Oh my God,' wailed Emma.

'There's a St John's ambulance back up the beach,' said someone helpfully. 'Go fetch them.'

Someone was despatched. Quenelle screamed. Emma cried helplessly.

'It was only a weaver fish,' said Goujon, again ignored.

'Here comes the air ambulance, over Stepper Point,' said another bystander.

'Has anyone informed the coastguards? They could evacuate him up over the cliff with ropes and pulleys and stuff.'

'Why? There's a path just over there. And steps.'

'It would be a good practice for them,' suggested another.

'Should we launch the Padstow lifeboat? Just in case. It could standby just outside the surf.'

'And the police? Where are they when you need them? Typical.'

Some mischievous wag at the back of the melee nudged his mate and said that maybe they could set someone alight, then they could get the fire brigade involved as well. Just in case.

Poor Emma was distraught.

Goujon tugged at Mervin's shorts. 'It was a weaver fish,' he said. Mervin knelt down and looked at the tell-tale puncture marks on the soles of Quenelle's foot.

'Little one's right,' said Mervin. 'It was a weaver fish, that's all. It's painful, but he'll be fine.'

'Can't we do anything for him?' asked Emma, as the air ambulance chopper began to land, and kicked up a circular sandstorm and blew windbreaks, inflatable crocodiles and beach towels into the path of the St John's Ambulance which blared across the beach in a blur of flashing blue lights, very nearly adding to the list of casualties on route.

'I tell you what Julienne, run back to the surf shack and grab my honey sandwiches. Goujon, just think of all the cola you drunk, and then I want you to pee on Quenelle's foot for me,' said Mervin.

So he did, much to his own amusement, and slowly but surely the relief showed on both his and Quenelle's face, and the pain began to subside. Julienne came back with the sandwiches and unwrapped them, and Mervin took one and smeared the honey across the puncture marks. Emma cuddled him up in a beach towel and Quenelle stopped his crying.

The St John's and air ambulances departed the scene, emergency over, and people began to drift away. Goujon and Julienne splashed back into the sandy tide pool, and Mervin sat with Emma and Quenelle.

'Good stuff, that honey,' he said.

Emma smiled and nodded. 'Good stuff,' she agreed.

Julienne stopped splashing and stood motionless in the pool, and frowned across the water at her mother.

Up at Delphy Bridge, the filthy beasts had totally steamed up the inside of the beast cruiser, and when Huge at last sweatily sat up and wiped the windscreen, he was more than a little alarmed to be greeted by the familiar beaky face of the one-legged gull peering in at him from the bonnet of the car. It mockingly cocked its head from one side to the other. It had seen everything. *Everything.*

'What the hell are you doing up here on the moors?' cursed Huge. The gull turned and lifted its tail and shat on the glass, and flew up and off, away back to Tredogend.

Huge yanked his chinos back on, buttoned up his flowery shirt, got out of the 4x4 and wiped the windscreen with a pasty bag. Inga leaned out of her window.

'What's the matter? Aren't we going to have another, Huge?' she said huskily.

'Darling, I've got to get back. It'll look suspicious,' he said.

'I can eat it as we drive along,' she said.

'Oh, sorry yea, that. Right. There's one left in the glove compartment I think. Help yourself,' said Huge.

The wantonly dishevelled Swede devoured her first ever post-coital pasty, in total her third of the day, and moaned in ecstasy. 'Oooh. My god, that's so good.'

Huge looked smugly across at her. 'Yea, thanks,' he said.

Huge drove them back towards Tredogend. As he came off the moors and began the descent to the little fishing port, Inga dusted the flakes of pastry and pasty crumbs from down her front and re-buttoned and re-assembled her attire, and within seconds she looked every bit the area of outstanding natural beauty as she'd done when she'd stepped so elegantly off the train.

He stopped outside the B&B, and before she got out he explained to her what he needed her to do first up tomorrow, all in the interest of research and furthering her career of course.

His icky, sticky, tricky honey trap.

'Okay Ingrid, listen up,' he said.

'Inga,' she said.

'Yea, yea, yea! Inga. Right Inga, ring this Digory Hicks guy and make an appointment to get yourself on his dating website, lonelyfarmersheartsclub.com or something, it's a thing for dirty old farmers. Take some photos of yourself up for him, you know the sort of thing, and reel him in. Make him an offer for the chapel whilst he's drooling at you with his beastly tongue hanging out, he's bound to take it. No question, look at you. You're gorgeous. It's Barney's dosh, offer the old fool below the odds and we'll split the difference, it's all got to go through your account. Have you got all that?'

'I think so,' she said, nodding.

'Then once you've done with him, find out everything that you can about how they make the bloody things down in that pasty shop. Everything! Crack on down to Mother's and hack in there and friggin frack out all their nasty little pasty secrets.'

'Frack?'

'Yea honey, frack. Crack on, hack in and frack out! Do you get me Ingrid?'

'Inga!'

'Inga, yes Inga,' he said.

She jumped out and gave him a little wave through the side window. He smiled and waved back, and after he had ogled her disappearing into the B&B, he rubbed his hands together with glee.

'Phwoaar, sweet,' he chuckled to himself. 'What a saucy old fracker you are Huge!'

Huge left Inga to mull over his instructions, and drove from Tredogend along to Porzeath, and as he neared the strip at the top of the beach and saw his family waiting, he felt uneasy, somewhat remorseful, a pang or two of guilt, almost. He pulled over on the side of the road, where the dry sand had been wind-drifted into the gutter, and Emma and the kids rushed over and jumped in, and began to recount the whole terrifyingly nasty episode with the weaver fish and the spikes in the foot and the air ambulance and lifeguards. Huge listened and drove, and when they got back to Fisherman's cottage, they put the tired kids up to their beds, all quite exhausted by the day's excitement.

Huge and Emma sat at their kitchen table. She looked down and fingered the rim of her glass of Oyster Bay.

'So,' said Huge. 'What's all this Jules is saying? Where on earth were you in all the excitement?'

'We were…I was watching. From the dunes,' she said hesitantly.

'One of them could have bloody drowned for all the use you'd have been. For Christ's sake Em, what were you doing there?' he demanded.

'The surfer guy was showing me his shack. Where he lives, that's all. It's just off the beach a bit,' said Emma tearfully.

'What's he live in, the bloody freak, an upturned boat I suppose!'

'He's not a bloody freak, he's actually very gentle and nice,' she sniffed.

'Oh, here we go,' sneered Huge.

'It's not like that. He's from the family that make those lovely pasties. He can't afford his own house. He lives in an old ice cream van, poor man,' she said.

'Poor man! Oh give me strength!'

'You should meet him. You're not being fair,' she said.

'Not being fair, oh really? My wife's up in the dunes shagging Mr Whippy whilst I'm out trying to build us a new life and make us just a little bit of money, and the kids are abandoned and left in mortal danger on the beach, and I'm not being bloody fair! Do you know how many meetings and phone calls I've had to deal with today?' he demanded.

Emma shook her head and began to cry.

Huge calmed his fake anger, and now began to act like a reasonable man. He put his arm on her shoulder, and kissed her hair.

'I'm sorry,' he said quietly. 'The thing is Em, I can't do this thing on my own. I need you to help, darling. There are all sorts of things you can do to help me, but this…'

'I wasn't shagging Mr Whippy,' she said.

'I know darling, I was angry. But can you see what it makes me think? If we don't have trust, what do we have Em?' said Huge.

'Don't be cross with me,' she said.

'I'm not. I was just a bit disappointed, that's all,' he said.

Chapter Nine
Love at First Bite

ansom – *Cornish derivation of the word 'handsome', referring not just to a person's appearance, but to anyone or anything that is considered lovely and with affection e.g. what an ansom pasty, what ansom weather, he's an ansom boy or she's an ansom maid.*

On the Thursday morning, Oggy had kindly suggested to Mother and Uncle Clar that as they'd been working so hard of late, they might like to take the day off and go on one of them mysterious tours. So they'd gone off together in a coach with all the blue rinsers of the Golden Circle for lunch, down at Hamburger Hill on the A30, so there was not too much mystery involved because that was invariably the destination of choice. Even though Uncle Clar was the only man on the bus, a daytrip with all the other old dears of the village seemed to fit the bill, taking in as it did a panoramic tour of Roche, Indian Queens and Fraddon en-route, and a precipitous ride through the helter-skelter lanes of the china clay pits on the way home. What better way to spend a day?

Back in Tredogend, it did not take Inga too long to locate Mother's pasty shop. She just followed the delicious aroma that wafted seductively along the street. She had a meeting at ten at the old chapel, and thought that she would have a breakfast pasty down by the harbour, just so she could take in the ambience of the lovely village to which she had re-located, albeit temporarily.

The sign in Mother's shop door window was flipped from 'closed' to 'open', and in she stepped, tinkling the charming bell as she did so.

Vi came out from the depths of the kitchen. Today, team Sloggett consisted of her and Oggy and Cheel, and Mervin who had come over from Porzeath especially for the day to help out. Vi closed the kitchen door quickly, for there had been just the merest hint of swearing and cursing emanating from back there, and this was not altogether helpful to pasty sales.

She smiled at Inga from behind her shop counter, who smiled sweetly back. 'Morning love, what can I get you?' Vi asked.

'A pasty please,' said Inga.

'Mother's Traditional? Certainly,' said Vi, and reached into the oven with tongs and pulled one out.

'Oh,' said Inga. 'No, not that one…'

'Oh you want the little one. The Cornish Pixie. Of course, have to watch our figures.'

'No,' said Inga, pointing. 'The big one please.'

'Oh right, sorry love. You want the Cornish Giant, here we are.'

'Oh,' said Inga. 'Maybe I'll take two…no, three. Please.'

As Vi carefully placed the Cornish Giants into their bags, and then those bags into a carrier, the kitchen door burst open behind her and slammed against the wall with a crash and a bang, and out backed Oggy's ample backside to the accompaniment of a ripping, tearing sound as his trousers split asunder and exposed the unpleasant ginger hairiness of his plunging crack for all the world to see.

'Bloody hellfire and bollocks, Jeff's checking uniforms at choir tonight, now what am I going to wear?' he raged. 'Whoa!! Why are you pushing so hard, boy? Just lift the thing gently and ease it through, and mind the doorframe or I shall have to get that painted too. More expense!'

'Hang on Father. I can't see nothing,' said Mervin.

'You wanna get them headlock things cut.'

'They'm dreadlocks, father! All right?'

'You'm like that Trelawney! He can't see bugger all through his fringe, and can't stick it to Pam nor Brenda neither.'

Mervin put his end down. 'Eh?' he said, exasperated. 'Who's Trelawney when he's at home?'

'Digory's poofter bull, that's who.'

'What! You can't say that.'

He shook his head and tucked his shock of beach bleached and blonded locks back from his forehead and face, and into a baggy woollen hand knit.

Inga was peering behind them and into the inner sanctum, trying to see any clues to help in the quest set her by Huge. Vi smiled apologetically to her. 'Sorry love, they're just moving the old freezer out,' she said, as if the open-mouthed Swede could possibly have misunderstood all that was going on in front of her very eyes.

Oggy and his son, both totally oblivious of any customers, squeezed the rust-bitten old freezer out from the kitchen and dragged it screechily, scratchily, gratingly behind the pasty counter, and then Oggy, puffed with the exertion and flushed horridly florid, leaned his shredded butt against it and stood panting and sweating, strands of ginger comb-over dripping over his face.

Mervin gave his father time to recover, and pulled out his tobacco tin and began to roll one in the lid.

'And don't you start rolling up none of that canapiss here neither, boy. 'Tis dislegal,' said Oggy.

'Like, whatever father,' said Mervin, and walked out the front of the shop still licking and rolling. 'It's just a fag, all right?'

Inga's attention had wandered to the lovely old pasty oven, a pretty unique antique if ever she had seen one. She particularly liked the way that the name of the manufacturer, Thomas Treleaven of St Just, 1922, stood proudly embossed above the oven door, and the way in which the whole thing had clearly been in continuous use since it was made.

Oggy flicked the ginger strands back and wiped his brow.

'Whatever am I going to do with this thing? We got to get it gone before Mother gets home,' he said of the freezer.

'The council'll take it, darlin',' said Vi.

'No, they won't take nothing for free no more, the thieving buggers. We can't afford it, and that's that!' he cursed. 'Makes you wonder why you pays your council tax.'

'You haven't paid it,' said Vi.

'That's besides the point missus,' he said, and shook his head despairingly. 'And I haven't even got another pair of trousers to cover up the hole in me ass.'

It dawned on Inga that now was probably an apposite juncture at which to slip out, and she picked up her bag. She looked at Vi and then at the forlorn Oggy who was staring miserably downcast at the slate slabbed floor, dripping sweat, cursing, groaning and bemoaning his lot, his bum hanging out of his filthy crimplene trousers, a picture of abject wretchedness. She politely smiled once more, and slipped out the door with her pasties.

'Thanks love,' said Vi. Mervin, who was on his way back into the shop, opened the door for her with a merry tinkle, and wished her a good morning, and she walked out and off in the direction of the harbour.

'What a pretty lady. Very nice too,' said Vi. 'And don't you worry about them trousers darlin', you can borrow a pair of Uncle Clar's.'

'That'll be nice,' groaned Oggy.

'Come on father,' cajoled Mervin. 'Let's get this thing out. I got to get back to the beach.'

Oggy looked at each in turn and nodded. At least they were getting rid.

'Sorry,' he said. 'And I didn't mean nothing about yer deadlocks, ansom boy.'

Inga made her way to the harbour side, to eat her pasty breakfast on a brand new hardwood addition to the dead bench mausoleum, 'Our Arthur - This was *His* view' on the shiny brass plaque, standing next to the now slightly tarnished 'Malcolm – he loved this place' one, and adjacent to the green triangle of unmowed, unloved, dog-shat-upon grass and weeds.

In front of the plywood-barricaded public toilets, the bins were overflowing, helped in no small measure by the usual posse of fearless gulls, who pulled and tore out the takeaway wrappers and trays and strewed them artistically around. There would be, Huge had said confidently, a signal of sorts there.

Inga, balancing one legged on Arthur's new bench, googled up the Treleaven oven on her iPhone, and then from there went to eBay where she found a similar one made for baking pies up north, and saw that the bidding was already up to a grand, with plenty of time still to go. It was clearly a piece of some value.

She sat down and nodded knowingly to herself, and chewed the Cornish Giant pasty with relish. A gull stood on the green, and when she had finished she tossed it the nub end of the crimped pastry. The gull immediately dropped the grease-congealed cheeseburger it had been struggling with, and swallowed the pastry nub whole. Even the gulls loved Mother's pasties above all else.

Inga glanced at her watch. There was still twenty minutes until her meeting with Mr Hicks at the chapel. She unwrapped another pasty and began to eat it. Why not? It was research. She had to get to know the product inside out. Huge had said. Maybe she could have the other one for lunch.

'Try them on,' said Vi, chucking Oggy an old pair of Uncle Clar's strides, a sort of baggy, beigy job, with turn-ups that were full of fluff and dust and pasty crumbs. Mercifully, Oggy found them to be much too tight around his tickle-tackle. Cheel looked on in mild amusement.

'That's a good look, father,' she said.

'Never mind, look I got to go into ValuCheaps in Bodmin for stuff. I'll stop off at Oxfam and see what they've got for you,' said Vi.

'Nothing over a fiver mind,' said Oggy. 'Dark grey if they got any. Choir tonight.'

'A fiver in Oxfam? You'll be bleedin' lucky,' said Vi. 'Leave it to me darlin'. You can't go to choir with scaffolder's crack now, can you? Anything you need Cheel?'

'Can I come in with you Mum? Got to get something in the DIY,' she said.

'All right darlin'', said Vi. She pecked Oggy on the cheek, and left him in sole charge at the helm of the counter.

Oggy sat on his stool and drummed his fingers. He looked out past the giant plaster pasty that hung in the shop window, out into the street and watched as Digory pulled up and jumped out of the DigsCab, and grabbed a large plastic container from his boot. He hurried into the shop.

'Can't stop, dear,' he said, and handed the container to his old friend. 'Mother's special water.'

'That should keep her quiet for a bit.'

'Got to get on! See you dreckly.'

'Dreckly,' said Oggy, and gave a wave as Digory left and closed the door behind him. 'Special water my ass, Mother.'

Inga finished the pasty. It had been as delicious as the first one. She walked back from the harbour side to the chapel, where she saw the DigsCab parked adjacent to the front of the building, and the man himself sitting in the driver's seat. The little widower Digory Hicks watched her approach, and as any man would be, he was struck by her beauty. He got out of the car and offered his hand.

She smiled, and dipped her head to one side, and shook his hand delicately. 'You must be Mr Hicks. So very nice to meet you. And this is the chapel?' she said.

Digory took the big old key from his pocket, and turned it in the lock of the heavy wooden door, and he opened the chapel up and stood back to allow Inga to step inside.

It had been over twelve months since he had been inside Tredogend Methodist Chapel for Doreen's funeral, a day when the proper old hard-assed pews had been packed to capacity for the very last time, and the

roof last raised by the melancholy strains of the White
Rose,

> 'Now I am alone, my sweet darling,
> I walk through the garden and weep.
> But spring will return with your presence,
> Oh lily white rose, mine to keep...'

The lusty singers of the great Cornish congregation had
emptied out in their shuffling, unspoken good order, and
filed black and blinking into the sun dappled, less than
merry morning of May; they processed respectfully
behind her wide and substantial coffin, draped as it was
with the flag of St Piran, and decorated by a small bunch
of cliff top cowslips and a single Mother's pasty on a
Cornish blue plate for the ferryman.

The pallbearers, all sturdy local men of robust
stature and led by Digory's oldest mate, worked in two
teams of six to bear Doreen to her resting place high
above the little port. While one team carried, the other
rested, and only the bearers and God himself knew how
much those breaks were needed. Especially with Doreen
on board.

They were headed by the undertaker who could
clearly hear the strained and wheezy whisperings of
the men, his black ribboned dignity intact beneath his
battered and faded velvet top hat.

'Hellfire,' said Oggy. 'She was a fine great woman
and no mistake.'

'I never knew how fine until now.'

Oggy's back bore testament to the fact. 'Does
anybody know one of they giropracters?' he wheezed.

'That's like a flying thing. You means a chiroscope,
Oggy.'

'That's what I said.'

And when his dear Doreen had been interred in the grey-green lichened graveyard above the village she loved so well, in a vast and voluminous grave with room for her dear little Digory to join her one day, he breathed a sigh of relief that mercifully and for all eternity, he would at last be on top.

Digory looked around. The space was virtually empty now, all the pews having been sold off. There was no ceiling, for the inside reached right up into the beamed eaves of the roof space. At one end was a balcony, tiered to accommodate five rows of pews, again all gone.

There was no lectern or pulpit or altar left, and just frosted glass windowpanes that were shaded by a shabbiness of paisley patterned, faded and dusty curtains.

There was a bible stand, but there were no bibles. There was no preaching and there were no sermons. There was no piano, no organ, no choir. There were no Sankey hymnbooks, and there were no hymns. The only sounds came from a scabby moulting pigeon that cooed up in one corner rafter, way up above a large pile of pigeon droppings full of corn and moulted, fluffy pigeon feathers, and a dead, desiccated squab.

Hanging crookedly on the back wall was a framed picture of Jesus, dressed in blue robes, pale-eyed and blonde, and with the palms of his hands opened benevolently to an assembled throng of tin miners, all standing in front of the engine house of a tin mine on an open Cornish heath.

It did not escape Digory's attention that this Jesus had the saddest countenance of any that he had seen before, and that on the day it looked even sadder still.

When you looked around the place, it was little wonder, he mused.

'Well,' said Digory. 'This is it Miss. I'm afraid it needs a lot doing.'

Inga spun around. 'It's perfect,' she said. 'A blank canvas. Would you take ninety-five Mr Hicks? That would leave me some to start renovation with.'

'Now to start with, it isn't Mr Hicks. You must call me Digory, dear,' he said.

She smiled glamorously. 'Digorydear…'

Mr Hicks, Digorydear, perked up. He explained that he would be minded to do such a deal; he'd had a nice gentleman in recently who was also very keen, but he'd like to get the chapel sold as soon as. He also suggested, if Inga was at all interested, that she might care to join his dating website (providing, of course, that she wasn't already attached in any way), lonelyfarmersheartsclub. com. It would enable her to get to know like-minded people in the vicinity, once she had paid the subscription via Paypal (or cash if she preferred). He had lots of interesting clients, many of them farmers, who would relish the opportunity to escort such a lovely young lady. She thanked him for the compliment, and said that she'd definitely think about it. As regard the chapel, she signed on the dotted line, and sealed the deal with a handshake. Contracts would be exchanged that very afternoon in Bodmin.

'Thank you, Miss,' said Digory.

'The pleasure's been all mine. Thank *you*, Digorydear' she said.

At Davidstow is a uniquely bleak moorland heath, an exposed and desolate plateau right at the outer edge of Bodmin moor. It has spectacular views across to the craggy, granite monoliths atop Rough Tor and Brown Willy, and it is bordered by darkly sterile post-war forestry plantations, and is close to the shivering vastness of the icy grey waters of Crowdy reservoir.

During the Second World War, the RAF built an aerodrome on the Davidstow plateau. Of course it was next to useless, as the place is perpetually shrouded in fog and mist and blowing a gale. So having constructed a vast, brutalist network of runways, corrugated Nissen huts, air raid shelters, practice ranges and other earthworks, and a massive concrete control tower, the RAF pulled out in 1945 and left everything behind.

So the resourceful farmers keep their tractors and animals and feed and stuff in them, and moorland ponies canter along the crumbling runways pretending to be Lancaster bombers. It was an outrage that the mutilated landscape had been left and not restored to its original natural beauty, but the Ministry of Defence worked on the theory that it was always foggy up there that you couldn't really see it anyway, and probably nobody would ever notice, so who'd care?

Huge realised this. His location manager, Tom, had found an old hangar deep in the midst of the forestry, at the end of runway two, screened off further from the outside world by a seemingly impenetrable square wall of tall and unyielding leylandii. Next to it stood an anonymous looking bungalow (sneaked up by the filthy old farmer without planning permission) with crumbling cement walls stained with rising damp, and guttering full of moss. Tom had arranged the rental of the lot, for it was key to the grand deception.

Tom had been busy. He had liased with the local constabulary and they had helpfully suggested a police liaison officer, Constable 696 Carthew Carew, though

Tom had been careful not to reveal the nature of the TV series itself to him; things were still very much on a 'need to know' basis and at the moment Carew, who seemed something rather less than a bright spark, didn't need to know.

It had been fortunate for Tom that during one of their somewhat limited conversations thus far, he had learnt of the plight of a party of eastern Europeans, probably Romanian, who'd run out of work picking daffodils down in the wild west of the dear old county in Penwith, and were being threatened with deportation. They were hanging out now on his patch, up here in the north, wandering around like sturdy beggars and hoping against hope to maybe get work picking caulis or broccoli for some dirty old lovelorn farmer, but it was still a bit too early in the season for that.

Carew was more than happy for them to disappear somewhere or another, as their continued presence threatened him with a most inconvenient paperwork overload, and he wasn't very good at paperwork, as it usually involved pens and paper and work, and writing and stringing a few words together in some sort of coherent order.

It was all a bit like the gulag archipelago up there on the old aerodrome, and thus Tom felt that the vibe would be quite perfect for them. They'd be cheap, and they'd be keen to keep everything quiet, and so he had the whole sorry array bussed in as his workforce. They would have to quickly learn the art of pasty making. Like Huge said, it couldn't be *that* hard.

Sitting in the porch at Fisherman's Cottage, Huge rubbed his flabby hands together in glee. It was all starting to go so swimmingly well.

Inga had rung and told him that she had secured the purchase of the old chapel in Tredogend, so he'd contacted Nigel and a team of builders and dressers was now on their way down from London to convert the chapel and set up the grand idea, complete with TV crew to record the whole thing for his new ratings buster, *Huge in Cornwall*. They'd be working 24/7. Huge's Cornish Pasty Emporium would be there within a matter of days.

There was, of course, the small matter of planning permission, and the local office had informed Inga that for six weeks 'change of use' there was no requirement for any at all. Huge had laughed, for once the Emporium was up and running and employing legions of locals *and* boosting the tourist industry beyond all expectations, the council would for certain feel obliged to grant them retrospective permission. And if they didn't, well, apart from all the hue and cry and great publicity, by the time they were closed down he'd have made some great TV and a small fortune to boot.

Huge had been in thrall to Inga with his vision of what amounted to a pasty theme park. There was to be a legion of ruddy-faced and plump, rustically rural-type ladies in striped aprons and mop caps, wielding rolling pins and rolling out pastry on old flour dusted kitchen tables. The pasties were to be filled with the freshest of fresh ingredients of undoubted local provenance, the potatoes, onions, and swede all overflowing from willow baskets haphazardly scattered across a beautifully renovated floor.

He would be bringing some pews back in from an architectural salvagers for people to sit on, and from those pews the punters were to sit and be amazed at Huge's own live demonstrations of the art of the pasty maker. Well, no, he'd confided, he hadn't made a pasty yet, but no matter. How hard can it be?

Visitors were to be enthralled at the visual displays, massive sepia print blow-ups of pasty makers from the very early days of photography, and a continuous rolling loop on a giant screen that demonstrated just how to make pasties the Huge way.

He told Inga of the interactive display of the pasty's historical and cultural significance to the county, telling of where Cornish miners had travelled around the world, taking their pasties with them; to Australia, South Africa, Canada, the States, Mexico, the West Indies, Chile and Bolivia and Argentina and beyond. Then, of course, he'd be able to go to all those countries and make pasty programmes there as well. He'd be *Huge all over the World*, and if she played her cards right, she might even be able to come along!

He rubbed his hands together again and cackled out loud. For the chapel was not going to be a shrine to the pasty. It was going to be a shrine to him. A Huge shrine where people could come and worship him in all his Hugeness.

Demand for his pasties would be very high, of course, and they wouldn't have a hope in hell of keeping up production in the chapel itself. So Tom had come up trumps and set up his secret pasty production plant in the secret confines of the hangar in the woods. It was to be from here that the mass production of cheap factory pasties would take place. From here where they would be sneaked out at the end of the night, and down into Huge's apparently artisan, organic, traditional, no food miles to speak of, sustainable pasty chapel in Tredogend, and no one, *no one*, would ever find out the truth.

Not from up there.

Not on the moors.

Then there had been the icing on Huge's cake. Inga had managed to get hold of a genuine pasty oven, that beautiful old oven that Huge had seen in Mother's, and now it could take centre stage in the emporium.

She told Huge that it was not long after she'd seen done the deal with Mr Digory Hicks up at the chapel that she'd managed to catch the pasty shop man on his own in his shop. She'd admired the oven earlier that morning, and offered him less than half what it was worth. Five hundred quid. Cash. And as a goodwill gesture she agreed to get the freezer taken away from the outside of his shop for him as well. He had apparently seemed quite desperate to get his hands on the fat wedge of notes.

The fact that the oven was cast with the name Treleaven had been such a bonus too. Now Huge just had to persuade Emma to change her name by deed poll back to her maiden name of Leaven, only to help the cause a bit by adding a 'Tre' as a prefix, which was a very Cornish thing to do after all. She'd be bound to do that, racked with guilt as she was over the Mr Whippy business. The Treleaven oven was going to be the centrepiece, and concrete proof of Huge's huge Cornish credentials.

So there was the master plan. Get the pasties made up in bulk in the hangar, as near as damned carbon copies of Mother's pasties as they could make them, sneak them down to the Emporium and shove 'em in the old pasty oven, so that it looked to all intents and purposes as if they were being made on the premises by the old ladies in aprons and mop caps, *and* by his Hugeness himself when the cameras were rolling. A deception ready made for TV and the great British public, and a production line of pasties to make him even more money. Bish, bash, bosh! Huge, man, Huuuge!

Oh, and Huge had been so pleased with Inga's work that he got Nigel to promote her from researcher to artistic director. He knew that she would be most keen to express her gratitude….

Before he closed Mother's Pasty shop early that day, Oggy had served one last customer who had jumped quickly out of a minibus that had pulled up outside. He was a tall, skinny bloke with slicked-back black hair and a funny German-sounding accent, and was wearing all dark clothes. He'd bought a Mother's Traditional, and left very quickly with barely a thank you. Oggy had served him, flipped the sign to 'closed', and then trousered his fat wodge of cash in his ripped and raggedy crimplenes, and was just heading for the door when the telephone rang.

He answered. There was a slight delay.

'Good morning. May I speak to Mr Oggy, please?'

'Oh, Colin. 'Tis you. Sorry, I'm about to go out. I gotta go Bodmin.'

'Thank you Mr Oggy. How are you today sir?'

'Proper, thank you. Look, I can't stop. What's the weather like up Deli? Foggy as usual I bet?'

'A bit of a smog today, actually, Mr Oggy. But it will warm up later sir. Maybe thirty degrees or more.'

'Really? Hellfire. How many have you signed up for your thing then, Colin?'

'In truth sir, none yet, so I am ringing to see if there is anything Business Solutions for You can do for you today, Mr Oggy?'

'Not unless you knows anybody what sells pasty ovens and deep freezers.'

'My uncle does electricals, Mr Oggy sir. If you go online to srinath.electricalsdelhi.com you can browse his selection.'

'I can't do none of that computer bollocks, Colin.'

'What is that, Mr Oggy?'

'Never you mind, boy…'

'Maybe it would be better if I rang when it might be more convenient for you sir? You can tell me all about… computer bollocks?'

'Yes Colin, try again dreckly. I can't say exactly when, just try and catch me here any time and I'll try and speak, unless I got cash customers.'

'I will try again…dreckly? On behalf of Business Solutions for You, thank you Mr Oggy, and goodbye.'

'Bye,' said Oggy, and replaced the receiver. 'What a proper boy he is. Pity there isn't more like him.'

Oggy left Mother's and went off to the second-hand catering equipment warehouse on Walker Lines industrial estate in Bodmin, having borrowed Pascoe the butcher's transit for the job, and had quite forgotten that the ginger-spiced flesh of the crack of his jacksie was exposed for all to see. Not that anyone would have chosen to peep, of course.

He bought a fairly tidy looking pasty oven, the same model that everybody else with a pasty shop had, with shiny steel handles and a smoky glass front, and a digital clock and control panel. He also found them a chest freezer without too much rust on it, and proudly peeled off the notes at the counter before getting the boy to help him load them into the back. He still had forty-odd quid left to pay towards the council tax bill, and dreckly to put towards some brand new choir flannels, and perhaps a new choir tie and badge for the breast pocket of his blazer. But his first priority was to stop off in Trebuggett Minor at the old post office, where he remembered they had an enticing selection of biscuits on display.

Back at the pasty shop, Oggy pulled up and parked outside, and he found Uncle Clar in there alone, drinking a cup of tay, and quite exhausted from his exciting and mysterious mystery tour.

'Did you have a good time with all the old ladies?' asked Oggy.

'By gar, what a day we've had. Up around the clay pits, Bugle, Goss Moor, Roche, Indian Queen's, Scredda, beautiful, all over we been.'

'That'll do you and Mother good.'

'And them burger things. Never tasted anything like them before. Ansom.'

'Proper job, them McDougals are.'

There was a little silence. Uncle Clar had something he needed to get off his chest. 'Oggy,' he said in a trembling voice. 'It *is* gone, isn't it?'

'Gone, Uncle Clar? What's gone?'

'That deep freeze. 'Tis gone from the pantry. I'm some glad you got rid of it, my darling boy.'

'Well, it was knackered Uncle Clar,' said Oggy disingenuously.

'Oh, my dear, it was more than that,' the old man said. He leaned forward and whispered. 'It was haunted you know. I had a proper queer turn with it the other night, it had to go.'

'Nooo!' said Oggy. 'No. Well I never. Haunted you say? You mean like a vibrating from inside, rocking to and fro…'

'Yes…!'

'Then like a moaning and a wailing…'

'Yes, yes, moaning and wailing. Exactly so…'

'Then, like…a terrible scream?'

'Yes, terrible, yes. Mother always said there was something funny in there.'

Oggy looked over one shoulder, then the other. 'It's not just the deep freeze or the pantry though. I had the same thing with the old pasty oven this afternoon, Uncle Clar. Moaning and wailing. I've had to get rid of that too,' he confided.

'No…me and Mother came in the back door. I never saw it was gone.'

'I don't know what Mother will say, I'm sure. You know what she's like,' said Oggy.

'She's gone to bed. Done too much today, the dear of her,' said Uncle Clar. 'But she'll be terrible upset.'

Oggy reached inside his jacket, and pulled out a cylindrical packet of biscuits, and opened the cellophane wrapper and offered them to Uncle Clar. He reached over and took one with his bony old hand, and bit into the chocolate biscuit with the velvety chocolate cream filling. He closed his eyes in apparent ecstasy.

'These are Gypsy Creams, Uncle Clar,' said Oggy and pushed the rest of the packet across the table to his uncle. 'They're for you.'

'Never you mind, Oggy. If that old oven was haunted too, then it had to go. I'll just have to tell her,' he said.

'Thank you Uncle Clar, it's for the best,' said Oggy. 'And tell her Digory brought her special water, that'll keep her happy.'

He made for the door. 'Oh, just one thing, my darling boy,' said Uncle Clar, still chewing. Oggy froze before he turned.

'Is the toaster all right? That's not…is it?'

'No, Uncle Clar, the toaster's fine.'

Relieved, Oggy rang Mervin to come over and give him a hand to unload the new oven and freezer from Pascoe's van, and then get them into position before the shop re-opened the following day.

Huge was still reflecting on all his marvellous developments and miraculous achievements as he and Tom made their inspection around the aerodrome site, darkly hemmed in by the tall bottle-green fir trees. He looked over at the stern, serious faced Romanians, standing all around the minibus, muttering and smoking.

'I suppose I'd better say hi,' muttered Huge. Tom nodded, and together they walked across to the swarthy men.

'Hi guys. Welcome to Cornwall. My name is Hugo, please call me Huge, everyone does. Now, we're going to be working together making Cornish pasties. On night shifts. Well, at least *you* will,' he said.

The Romanians just stared.

Huge turned his back on the men, and hissed in Tom's ear. 'They don't say much. Do they understand me? Do they know who I am even? Look how miserable they are.'

'When all is said and done, Carew says they're probably Romanian illegals Huge. Night shifts suit them fine. They'll sleep by day. They're too scared to go out anyway,' said Tom.

'Illegals! Oh for god's sake, what's he thinking of? And forgive me, but pasties are hardly a speciality of the Carpathians, Tom,' said Huge, perhaps a little too loudly.

A man stepped forward.

'I can make pasty. I am chef back in Bucharest. Learned to make zem vile vorking on farm down at

Zennor last years. Make wery good pasty. I show zem how to make.'

He was a tall, gaunt and unsmiling man, pale to the point of being transparent, with dark rings beneath his bloodshot eyes. His slicked-back, shiny black hair was flattened down with gel, or brilliantine, or tractor grease or something worse. He was wearing a black shirt, with the collar turned up.

Huge looked alarmed, and guided Tom away by his shoulder out of earshot, and whispered to him again. 'What? You expect Christopher fucking Lee there to teach them all to make pasties? I think not. No wonder they don't mind working at night, they'll be hanging around all day long up from the beams!'

'Well, they all seem very nice. Carew says they won't make any trouble...' ventured Tom.

The man, Krno, stepped forward one pace towards Huge and Tom, holding out a pasty in his hand. It was the one he'd bought from Mother's earlier that day.

'Zis is pasty I making earlier. Is good. You try,' he said.

Huge was suspicious. 'You get it, Tom,' he hissed. 'I'm not getting bloody bitten.'

Tom retrieved the pasty, and brought it to Huge, who split it in half and examined the contents. They appeared just right, potato, onion, swede and skirt beef, all in the right proportions, and good pastry too. The crimping looked fine. He bit into it and tasted it. The seasoning was perfect. In fact it was surprisingly delicious. Beautiful. As good as he had ever tasted.

'Well, that seems okay I suppose,' said Huge, handing it back to him via Tom. 'And you think you can teach your friends how to make them too?'

'Of course,' said Krno, still unsmiling. 'Very fast. No problem.'

Krno turned to his friends, and spoke to them in Romanian, nodding his head in Huge and Tom's direction. One of the men shouted back to Krno in Romanian, and they all began to laugh and guffaw loudly.

'What did they say?' said Huge. 'What's so funny?'

'Not funny,' said Krno. 'They say like make ansom pasties for you.'

'Ansom, Tom. What the fuck is ansom?' he said.

'Just go along with it, Huge. It's probably some gypsy thing.'

Huge nodded uneasily, still not entirely convinced at the Transylvanian translation, and neither should he have been.

Chapter Ten
The Asteroid Belt

Well, Cornish lads are fishermen,
Cornish lads are miners too.
But when the fish and tin are gone,
What are the Cornish boys to do?

'Cornish Lads' - *by Roger Bryant.*

Cheel pulled on a pair of tatty black skinny jeans and a black hoody, and sat on the edge of her bed. She angrily tugged the mane of her My Little Pony and bridled with indignation as she read the latest Huge blog. There was a pile of pink nylon mane on the carpet.

'*....all the crew are on their way down to Tredogend to create the Hugest Pasty Emporium the world has ever seen, right here in our beautiful old Methodist chapel. We're going to make the finest traditional pasties ever tasted anywhere, and create a whole new menu of delicious fusion and gourmet pasties for the discerning palate. We're going to make the pasty a global icon. Emma, the kids and I are loving it here in Cornwall, our new home. Oh, and guess what? To help integrate,I'm joining the local fisherman's choir. Hey! I know we've only been here a week or so, but we feel Cornish already, and I'm going to be a Huge part of this community...*'

'Whether we like it or not, by the sounds of it,' she said to herself. 'Well, if that's the way you want it.'

Uncle Clar happened to be walking past on the landing, and heard her dark mutterings through the bedroom door.

'Are you all right in there, my darling Cheel?' asked Uncle Clar, tapping from the outside.

'All right, Uncle Clar,' she called out airily. 'Just grooming my little pony.'

She hadn't the heart to tell her family what she had found out. She opened her small, black rucksack and put in two cans of spray paint, one black, and one white. She looked at her watch, and then out of her window, then lay back on her bed and began her wait for the evening and dusk to approach.

Huge was on the telephone in Fisherman's Cottage.

'So what time will they be there to set up, Nigel?.....Just one camera?...Seven o'clock is cool, singing practice starts at seven thirty....Yeah yeah, got all the uniform and gear and stuff. Helga got it for me.... Yeah Inga, that's what I said, Inga....Yeah, she knows my size all right....The pasties are all good, yeah, yeah, yeah, of course I've got the recipe and know how to make them.....Well, I will do soon. I need to get some more from those half-wits down the road to copy. I think I know how. Em will help...Look Nige, one more thing. The old branding business. ...I think I should become Huge with an exclamation mark after it. Huge exclamation mark, only the mark itself, not the words, do you get it?....Yeah, yeah, *Huge!* Can we do it? By deed poll?....Cool. The other thing? Oh, Emma's name, we need to get that done too....'

Emma peeped around the door.

'What's that, Huge?' she asked.

He covered the receiver.

'Just that prat Nigel. Sends his love,' he whispered, and then returned to Nigel. 'Okay Nige? Laters man, or as we Cornish say, dreckers dude.'

It was a still evening up at Dordigor Farm, and Digory was talking to his reluctant bull as he filled the trough with the hose.

'Come on dear,' he said. 'Just give her a little portion, you can do it. You don't even have to enjoy it; Christ knows I never did...'

Trelawney just stood and stared, in his accustomed trance-like state, blinded by his own straggling black fringe.

'What about you two then?' said Digory to Pam and Brenda. The cows stood motionless, facing one another, and then Pam licked Brenda's nose, and Brenda licked Pam's. Then they were still again.

Oggy pulled up to the yard in his car, wound down his window and shouted to his friend. 'What's on? Waiting for a bit of red hot action boy?'

'You're late,' said Digory.

'I been on the phone to that Colin, up Delabole.'

'Colin?'

'He works for Business something-or-other. Trying to get me to have one of they card things.'

Digory shook his head, and climbed into the passenger seat.

'I Facebooked you to say we needed to leave earlier, they're filming us tonight.'

'You did what?'

'Your Cheel told me you was online now.'

'I can't be assed with all that computer bollocks, Digory,' said Oggy, and shifted uncomfortably in the £9.95 Oxfam trousers, which were of a sufficiently vibrant check to make him feel rather like Mr Toad. They were held up with a brown leather belt.

'Jesus, what the hell have you got on?' said Digory.

'Thing is Dig, they're riding right up around me crack. I can't let the belt go, or they'll fall down. I'm in a awful precocious disposition and I'm sure they'll set off me asteroids again,' he said, lifting his bottom briefly from the plastic car seat to ease the pressure.

'Witch hazel or butcher's broom is what you wants for piles. It's a bit early for horse chestnut,' said Digory.

'Butcher's broom? Sounds painful whichever end you uses. I'd rather get a subscription from Dr Hoskin,' said Oggy.

'It's a plant,' said Digory. 'Grows up by Davidstow, in the forestry there.'

'I'll stick to me cream cheers, Dig. I ain't traipsing around up in that godforsaken place for nothing,' said Oggy, who with a wince and a groan and a twist of his buttock, drove them off towards the evening's practice of the Tredogend Fishermen's choir.

Huge washed and shaved and slapped on some aftershave. He put on his new shirt and choir tie. He got into the blazer and fingered the Tredogend Fisherman's Choir badge as he looked in the mirror. It all looked very clean and pristine and new. He came out of the bedroom, down the stairs and into the sitting room, where Quenelle, Goujon and Julienne were watching the music channel.

'So,' he said. 'What do you think?'

'Stupid,' said Julienne, without even looking up.

'Gay,' said Quenelle dismissively. Little Goujon just read his book.

Huge wandered out into the garden, where Emma was picking a bunch of lavender.

'It doesn't look gay, does it Em?' he asked.

'No, it's very nice, Huge.'

'Or stupid?'

'No, not at all. What's it all about?' she said.

'Oh, they're going to film me singing with all the pond life at their bloody silly choir thing. It goes with making pasties and being Cornish and all that,' said Huge.

'Well, you look very smart anyway. Come here,' she said, and straightened his tie for him.

'There,' she said cautiously. 'Look, are you sure you can make pasties? They have to be good, you know that.'

'Well,' said Huge. 'We both know who makes the very best; those dafty retards down at Mother's. But we daren't go in there and buy any to copy now. They're looking out for us. If only I could get their recipe, their secret, but I don't suppose…'

Emma looked down.

'I *could* ask…' she said.

'Look, if you could. I know there's nothing going on Em. Good God, how could there be, you with some hippy dippy surfer peasant when you've got me? Please! That's not going to happen, is it? Just ask and he'll be stupid enough to tell you anyway. I tell you what, here, give him this tenner, that'll do the trick. He can go out and buy himself a new wetsuit or some grass or whatever,' said Huge.

'Huge,' said Emma. 'Put the ten pounds away. I'll ask, ok.'

Inga sat alone in her room in the B&B. She felt a bit peckish, her last pasty having been consumed at one o'clock. Luckily, she'd had the foresight to go into Mother's and buy another Cornish Giant just after, and now it's time had come. She peeled back the paper and bit into it. It was her fourth of the day, and just as delicious as the first. Satiated, she lay across the bed and drifted off to sleep.

On her way out, Cheel came down into the kitchen to find Vi and Mother and Uncle Clar sitting at the table, drinking tay and talking about the oven.

'All right, darlin'? Where you off?' asked Vi.

'Out, Mum,' she said, a little defensively.

'What's in your rucksack, darlin'?'

'Stuff, that's all.'

'That's what you get, Uncle Clar. Stuff she says,' said Vi.

'Has father been checking his twitter account? Or his Facebook?'

'I don't think so, babe. He's gone to choir.'

'He should. He got over two hundred 'likes' for his pasties now,' said Cheel.

Mother stiffened. 'He ain't getting no 'likes' from me. Selling our old oven indeed.'

'It was haunted mind, Cheel. Haunted, and the deep freezer too,' said Uncle Clar.

'What?' said Cheel.

'He's only sold them. While we was down Hamburger Hill on a mysterious tour, if you will,' said Mother.

Mother scowled and shook her head. Cheel was frankly puzzled. She sighed, unable to keep it together any longer.

'Haunted oven? Haunted freezer? What *are* you on about? That's the least of our worries. We got enough on our plate with the chapel,' said Cheel.

'What chapel?' asked Vi.

'What plate?' said Mother.

'Was there any biscuits, Vi?' said Uncle Clar, who perked up at the mention of a plate.

'The old chapel up the road. Look I didn't want to tell you and worry you up, but here goes. That bloody chef off the telly's bought it! There!' she ranted.

Uncle Clar screwed up his face, confused.

'That Huge!' shouted Cheel. 'He's going to open a bloody great big pasty shop in there, right on our doorstep! Gourmet pasties, fusion pasties, proper pasties. Every ghastly, nasty bloody pasty you can think of, he's going to do it.'

'Oh dear,' said Uncle Clar. 'Would anybody else like a biscuit?'

'Shush a minute Uncle Clar,' said Vi. 'How do you know?'

'He's making a TV series here all about pasties. It's all over the internet; blogs, Facebook, twitter, his website, he'll ruin us, he will. I told father the other day that the vile oppressor was invading! He don't listen. Pasties is just the start. They won't be happy until they've taken over Cornwall, and we're nothing but exhibits in the county museum,' raged Cheel. 'Homo Sapiens Cornwallis. Stuffed and bloody mounted!'

'Homo what?' said Uncle Clar, with evident distaste.

'Stuffed and mounted Uncle Clar!'

'Oh dear…' said Uncle Clar. 'I ain't much for that kind of thing.'

'Anyway, who's father sold the old oven to?' said Cheel, as grim realisation dawned. 'Oh no. Tell me it's not true! Not him please!'

'I don't mind Rich Tea if there's no Gypsy Queens left,' said Uncle Clar.

'In the pantry, Uncle Clar, next to the new freezer,' said Vi.

'There's still something funny in there, I'm sure,' said Mother.

'Oh, wake up you three!' raged Cheel. 'We're talking extinction here! We are being exterminated.'

She stomped into the pantry and grabbed hold of a packet of biscuits and smashed it down in the middle of the table, and turned the biscuits to crumbs and dust.

'Look,' she said. 'You lot can do what you bloody well like but I ain't spending the rest of my life peeping out from behind the razor wire of no reservation!'

'Reservation?' said Mother.

'Razor wire?' said Vi.

'And I think these might be broken, my darling,' said Uncle Clar, fingering the packet. 'You'll have to take them back, Vi.'

Cheel shook her head and took a deep breath.

'We're all going to be broken, Uncle Clar,' she said quietly.

She got up and pulled on her rucksack, and left through the tinkling shop doorway, and walked off and away towards the cliffs.

As they sat around the kitchen table, Vi and Uncle Clar and Mother looked at one another in silence, and again felt the shaking vibration from the pantry, like they had felt so many times before. But the shaking was not from the old deep freezer, for that was in the back of someone's car, and it wasn't from the new deep freezer, because that didn't shake at all.

There was indeed something funny in the pantry.

It was around five miles from Dordigor Farm to the old hall where the choir practised. The hedges were high and narrowed by the lush early Cornish summer vegetation. As was their wont, Oggy and Digory spoke all the way of when they'd been boys and young men, in solemn and fond remembrance of those who had gone before them.

In memoriam that evening was Frankie Jacker the fish jowder, who kept his false teeth in his pocket and a sepia photo of his dear old mother in the other, and reeked in equal measure of sour man-sweat, salt fish and cheesy Cornish yarg. Frankie Jacker, engine oil slippery and stenched pungent like a slab of human lobster pot bait. Frankie Jacker, with his glasses so thick and clouded with mackerel scales that he could barely see through them at all. Frankie Jacker, the man with the vilest, filthiest mouth this side of the Tamar, and who pissed-up had tumbled into a tank full of live lobsters and drowned, so cruelly nipped off before his time.

They never found what was left of him for over a week.

It had all been hushed up though, and they still managed to sell the lobsters on at a good price, so it was a happy ending.

He'd have wanted it that way, old Frank.

They remembered Mazed Michael, poor old boy, as daft as a new broom said Digory. Aggie Richards, her with the biggest gob in the parish, had seen him being conceived over the bonnet of a Ford Corsair (F-Reg and full MOT) in a tryst between his mother-soon-to-be Renee and a washer-upper from the St Moritz Hotel at Daymer, whose name she never mentioned for the shame of it. A washer-upper indeed, it was a family disgrace; no one had ever married anything below a kitchen porter before.

Poor, poor Michael, cakey, flaky Michael, who ran everywhere with his hoop and stick, and used to race the Western National bus from Tredogend to Bodmin Road station like an Olympian in turned-down wellies. He could have won the marathon easy, they said, but instead he ended up in St Lawrence's, dribbling and rocking and scritching and crying, only to escape through an open window one day and, chasing his runaway hoop, ran into the road and got knocked over and killed. After all that care, too. Everyone awaiting the news had expected it to have been the Western National that did for him, but it was a Ford Corsair. It just had to have been one or the other in a life like that.

No one knew if it was his own father driving or not, and Renee still wouldn't say. For shame.

There was Maurice 'Bluff' Blake too, remember him? Adder catcher and master bluffer of the social security who never done a day's work or caught a bloody snake, save his spiteful wife of course, for nigh on sixty year. Sixty! How is it done? Cost the country a fortune, and for what? And Black Jack Berry the undertaker, as careful as a duck's ass, who undertook his own funeral arrangements to keep all his lovely, lovely money safe (and where did that get him?), and then Josiah Bodiah, barnacle scraper and brawler, hauler of other men's crab pots and mauler of other men's wives, the dirty old bastard that he was; the list was endless.

All remembered. Some more fondly than others.

Then they chuckled about all the naughty, naughty maids who'd done their little bit for the community over the years. Above all, the aptly named Glorious Gloria Cobbledick, who joined with her daughter to form an inexpensive al fresco tag-team for a brief yet golden era.

To the lusty, wicked young boys of Tredogend the mixed wrestling (or 'raslin' as it was known) was the spectator sport of choice, and from behind the drystone, herringbone Shillingstone wall, they watched the jowder, the adder catcher and the scraper and mauler sheepishly take their turns, their up and down asses white against the dark green skittery grass of the cliff tops.

And Peggy Parsons, with her webbed feet and extra finger and predilection for dancing the seven veils for Methodist lay preachers, whether Wesleyan or United Methodist, or occasionally even Lady Huntingdon's Connexion, and who used to hang behind for extracurricular moral guidance, post Sunday School, and usually got it.

We shall remember them.

'Somebody should write it all down before 'tis too late,' chuckled Oggy, momentarily forgetting the uncomfortably checked trousers. 'They don't make them like that any more, boy.'

'Thank Christ for that, Oggy,' said Digory. He looked across at his friend's choir badge. 'Your badge is looking a bit threadbare dear,' he said.

'It's brave and ancient now. It was Father's, and Granfer Sloggett's before him. He was a founder member, back when there *was* fishing.'

'I remember your Granfer, he was...Hell! What's that! Look out!' shouted Digory, lurching across and trying to grab the wheel.

Oggy swerved violently, and his car stalled to a halt as the giant beast-cruiser squeezed and roared past it at high speed, and forced them into the hedge, and kicked up dust and dirt and gravel all over them, and accelerated off up the lane and away into the distance.

Digory and Oggy sat stunned, bolt upright.

'That was the bloke what wanted to buy the chapel in that damn great thing,' said Digory.

'I don't trust the bugger,' said Oggy.

Digory looked at his friend and whispered, eyebrows raised. 'Nor me. I sold it this morning anyway. Lovely looking woman. Blonde. Going to get her on me website too. Saving her for somebody special.' He winked.

'I've seen her, I believe. She bought a load of pasties from Vi, and she bought me old oven,' said Oggy.

'What does she want *that* for?'

'Don't know.'

'Curious,' said Digory. 'Anyway, you can't teach a new broom old tricks.'

'That's true, Digory,' said Oggy, turning the ignition. 'Come on or they'll be started before we get there.'

Huge screeched into a lay-by, and tried to raise Inga on her mobile, but for some reason she wasn't answering. It was, of course, nothing to do with the signal. She was fast asleep, her tummy still frantically digesting the massive pasty intake of the day.

He jumped out and went to his boot and threw up the tailgate. He looked up the road. He looked down the road. He listened carefully, and could hear nothing. He grabbed the end of the rusty old freezer, and slid it out, and rocked it down into the lay-by, pushed it over and dragged and scraped it across the gravel, and shoved it into the hedge.

Huge turned hurriedly to get back into his vehicle for a quick getaway. On the roof stood the one-legged gull, head cocked to one side then the other, watching his every move inquisitively.

Huge ran towards it, and waved his arms wildly, and the gull took flight and flew up and up and up. He watched the bird as it circled overhead. He watched as it dipped lower. He watched as it dived, and he watched as it splat all over his brand new choir blazer, then turned a victory roll on its return flight back towards Tredogend.

Huge took out a handkerchief and wiped himself down. It was supposed to be good luck, but it didn't feel like it. He jumped back up into the beast-cruiser, and squealed off again, leaving the knackered old freezer far, far behind.

Oggy and Digory trundled up the lane.

'So this blonde party, dear. Is she an antique dealer?' asked Digory.

'Shouldn't think so. She took that old freezer too.'

'What'll she do with that?' asked Digory, as Oggy drove slowly past the lay-by.

'No idea, boy,' he said. 'Probably dump it in some lay-by, just like that one there. Look! Disgusting.' Oggy pointed.

'Dreadful,' said Digory. 'Should never be allowed.' They shook their heads in unison. Choir was about ten minutes away.

Oggy Sloggett and Mr Digory Hicks pulled up into the hall car park to find Huge's vehicle parked and apparently abandoned right across two spaces, and two other cars and a van with the ZeeTV logo on the side taking up all the rest of the room, and he was obliged to reverse out and park on the verge outside. They were a few minutes late.

When they got into the hall, they found all their fellow choir members in an excited knot, huddled around the over made-up Huge in his brand new smart choir uniform. A blonde make-up lady daubed the last vestiges of seagull splat from his lapel with a wet wipe, and he flirtily smirked at her. He was brightly lit up by powerful lamps, his every word being captured by the boom microphone and every move filmed by the camera. Oggy and Digory stood at the back of the hall and looked on. No one saw them come in. No one even saw them standing there.

'Okay Huge,' said the director. 'Let's do that again. And…rolling….'

'Hi, it's Huge. *Huge in Cornwall*, and these are all my old mates from the Tredogend Fisherman's Choir. Tonight, here at our practice, we're going to have a singsong, and then I'm going to show the guys how to make a pasty. Not any old pasty, but a Huge gourmet pasty. The Fisherman's Pasty, with smoked local haddock – probably caught by one of these guys - and oak smoked Gwennap gouda, sourced from my mates Will and Silas at Trebiffen Farm Smokery, and St Just leeks and capers, and a tartare sand. Garnished with the finest foraged River Camel samphire. Just delicious. But first, a song to whet all our appetites. What are we going to sing, Jeff?'

' "Cornish Lads"' Huge,' said Jeff.

Huge flashed his monstrously huge fleshy smile into the camera.

' "Cornish Lads"' he said. 'That's me.'

'And…cut. Thank you Huge. Okay, fishermen, can we line up for the song please.'

Oggy looked at Digory. 'What's he talking about? Show us how to make pasties. What's going on?' he growled under his breath.

'Oggy, Digory, over here please,' said Jeff. 'Normal positions men, thank you.'

'Do I do my solo bit, Jeff?' asked Oggy.

'Yes please, Oggy, yes' said Jeff.

They lined up, facing the camera, the boom overhead. Oggy prepared himself, for he loved this song and had sung the solo part for years.

Huge stood back with the director and they surveyed the line up.

'So Huge, where will you go? What do you think?' he asked.

'Oh, just about there,' said Huge quietly, pointing at Oggy. 'Right in the middle of the pond.'

'Jeff, can we move someone?' said the director quickly. Jeff nodded.

'You, yes you with the slacks, the trousers there... yes, ginger man, could you move?' he continued.

Oggy flushed. 'Me?' he said. 'Where to?'

The director gestured to the side. 'Anywhere over there. On the end, that'll do. In you get Huge.'

And as the disconsolate Oggy nudged his way side-on and crab-like along the middle rank and over to the side, Huge strode up from the front and levered himself over people's shoulders, and stepped through the front row and into the space that had been vacated.

Oggy stood on the very outside, next to the old boy with the whistling hearing aid and stroke-induced perma-smile.

'Okay, everyone. How are we all? Okay? Sound?'

'Picking up some whistling from over there,' said the soundman, nodding towards Oggy and the old boy with the squealing ear.

'Okay, can you two move out,' called the director to the two of them. 'Yes, you two. That's it. Right over there. Further. Go on. How's that now?'

'Great,' said the soundman.

'Just one thing,' said Jeff to the director. 'There is a solo bit in this song. Oggy normally does that.'

'Oh right. Did you hear that Huge? A solo bit. Are you up for it?'

'Yeah, yeah, yeah. Whatever. For sure. I don't have the music though,' he said.

Jeff piped up again. 'Oggy, could you pass your music over to Huge please? That's lovely, thanks.'

His file of music was passed along the middle rank of the choir to the man of the moment.

'Now, are the two surplus ones out of shot, Ken?'

'Yes,' said the cameraman.

'Huge?'

'Perfect,' he said.

'And…rolling.'

Oggy watched and listened as his choir sang 'Cornish Lads', and as Huge sang out the solo part of the verse, he felt his face flush and lip quiver, and he shook and stared at the man. He wasn't angry; he wasn't even just a little disappointed. Oggy was sad.

They did not cry, the Sloggetts, but he was sure that he could feel something like a real teardrop, trickling from the corner of his eye.

Cheel stole up and along the cliff path, rucksack on her back and black hoodie pulled up over her head, up to the ruins of the castle that overlooked their village. It was dusk, and there was no one around, though during daytime hordes of visitors would make the ascent, and wander around the ancient bits of wall and archway that the erosion of gales and storms had not worn completely away.

From up there it was possible to look down upon the cramped shantytown network of narrow streets and lanes, the courtyards and the drangs, the Delabole-slated rooftops and the spider-webbed pathways that enmeshed all together in a sticky, gossamer embrace, splashing along The Poor Court into Rat's Terrace, tripping along Donkey Patch and sideways through Squeeze Belly Alley into Dolphin Yard, and then panting breathless up to Captain Calloway's Folly.

Cheel could see the peeping and twitching curtains, the disapproving window eyes of the tiny-minded houses and cottages, the gaudy Day-Glo pink and orange of the surf shop and the lifeless, listless chapel. She could see the harbour strung in green-weedy mooring ropes and cramped abreast with the jolly blue boats that danced on the biller, and the fish-stinky fishy fish cellars, Dead Dog Wong's mock-Tudor Chinese take-away, and the aromatic, fragrant Mother's pasty shop of the Sloggetts.

All as a rock pool left by the ebbing tide, life darting to and fro, each undulation and overhang, every nook and cranny with its own tale to tell, a pool into which she had been born, and where she and her family had lived forever and ever and ever.

Apart from her Mum who'd let the side down and been born in Plaistow and not Padstow.

She began to read the history of the castle itself from the interpretive board attached to the entrance wall, a history that stretched right back and beyond the Stuart's improvements to the Tudor structure, which itself had been imposed on the Norman one, and then back further still to mounds and ditches of its early Iron Age foundations. It told of visitors in galleys from the Mediterranean and of Phoenician pottery excavated there, the remnants of goods reputedly traded for Cornwall's precious tin.

As she read she dreamed and wondered, and hoped beyond hope if any of the DNA of those early inhabitants of this beautiful spot was still present within her own. Maybe, just maybe, if she gave Dr Hoskin a swab he could send it off and get proof that she was truly a part of that Cornish aboriginal stock: pre-ice age, pre-Roman, pre-Saxon and pre-Norman, and pre-bloody Huge.

Beneath the written description and the drawn reconstruction of how Tredogend might once have looked, she shuddered at the nauseating depiction of the red English rose, and gagged as she read the words 'English Heritage', scripted in big, bold lettering.

Cheel's hand trembled as she undid the strap of her rucksack and reached for the two cans of spray paint, and placed them side-by-side on the tussocky grass. She stood up on a bit of low, ancient wall, and afforded herself an all round view. There was a hush, and lights were flickering on down in the village as the dusk gathered to gloom; there was no one around at all.

She looked up at the vast and endless array of stars twinkling above in a sky mercifully still free of light pollution. A shooting star flashed across the dark, and then down, down into the melting horizon.

Just a speck of dust, all the way from the asteroid belt.

Over her Cornwall.

She felt butterflies in her stomach, closed her eyes and made a wish.

She rolled up her sleeve and by the light from her iPhone, she read the tattoo on her arm.

Kernow bys Vycken.

Cheel shook the can of black spray paint vigorously, held it six inches in front of the English rose, and then sprayed a solid black circle the size of a large dinner plate right over the top of it, obliterating the offending symbol of English cultural repression from view.

She took the can of white spray paint, and shook that vigorously too, and with a deft cross motion of her hand, sprayed a white cross over the black circle. Still shaking, she stepped back to admire her work. She had done it. She felt liberated. It had been so easy.

St Piran. The flag. Tagged.

She fingered the still tender tattooed chough on her neck, and looked out over the vista below, and beyond to the silhouetted high cliffs and moorland hills of Cornwall.

'I done it,' she said breathlessly. 'I done it for you.'

The practice run was complete.

At the end of choir, Oggy had found his file of music discarded and left face down and open on the floor, a boot's tread mark across the cover, and the sheet music within creased, torn and dirty. He picked it up and dusted it off. He left the hall without speaking to anyone and waited in the dark of his driving seat for his mate, and when he came they drove away in silence, through the lanes and back towards Dordigor Farm.

'Come on then,' said Digory. 'What is it? What's the matter?'

'Well, everybody's telling me that matey boy's opening up a massive great pasty shop in the old chapel, and you're telling me you sold it to that blondie woman. What's going on?' said Oggy.

'I don't know Oggy,' said Digory.

'And did you taste that fish pasty? It was disgusting filth. It stunk like Frankie Jacker, *after* they pulled him out of the lobster tank.'

'Everybody said it was good. Jeff liked it,' said Digory.

'Don't talk to me about Jeff. Him and his uniform inspections. Said I looked like a clown in these things.'

'Well, they are a bit…'

'And he was having a go at Granfer's old choir badge. Bloody original that is,' said Oggy. 'He said I got to smarten up, or I shan't be allowed to do any concerts no more. I ain't havin' that.'

'How's your piles?' asked Digory, changing the subject.

Oggy screwed up his face, his features agonisingly contorted with discomfort, and he shifted his bum cheeks for relief.

'Hellish,' he said. 'Daggering right up me ring-piece.'

'Look,' said Digory. 'It's no odds to me. Pull over in the lay by and undo your belt, drop 'em a bit while you drive home. No one's to see. Give you a bit of relief.'

And so the wretched Oggy pulled over into the lay by, and switched on the internal light in order to find his buckle and his belt holes. All fingers and thumbs, he undid it all and began to pull the torturously ill-fitting Mr Toad trousers right down to his knees, and as he leaned forward in his struggle for liberation from the unsuitable garment, he accidentally bumped the light switch off with the top of his head. He reached up and tried to flick it on again, flicked it the wrong way, then the right way, then wrong, then right. It was all a bit of a kerfuffle.

It was an unfortunate coincidence that the Neanderthal-browed Beast of Bodmin was on late shift that evening. The nasty, brutish and tall Constable 696 Carthew Carew, had been on patrol in the Tredogend vicinity for an hour or so. He had hardly been overwhelmed with commitments that evening, and so relished the opportunity to investigate a clear-cut case of dogging; dealing with this sort of hateful, morally reprehensible perversion was right up his street, or in this case, right up his lane. He pulled into the lay-by and drew his patrol car alongside the suspect vehicle.

Recognising the Beast's fearsome profile from his gruesome online gallery at lonelyfarmershearts. com, little Digory Hicks slid down cowering from the passenger seat and curled up in the foot well into a foetal position, and hid his face from view.

Due to the positioning of the men's two bodies in the front of the car and their somewhat furtive behaviour, the constable's suspicions became aroused even further. It was his duty to immediately investigate what appeared to him to be an open and shut case of gross public indecency by two repulsive old doggers.

When he questioned the driver, a Mr Oggy Sloggett of Tredogend (the registered owner of the vehicle since 1989, with an address at Mother's Pasty Shop, Fore Street, Tredogend) whose trousers were inexplicably drawn down around his knees, and asked him about the switching on and off of lights in a lay-by, the man muttered that he was in a precocious disposition, and then blathered something about blessed relief and a belt and asteroids.

There had been a spate of such goings on in the vicinity of late, said Constable Carew, but usually involving persons (not always just two, it had to be said) of opposite sexes. And it was no use at all Mr Hicks crouching in the foot well like that, for he wasn't a police officer for nothing and could quite clearly see who it was.

It was he who had accepted the fifty quid subscription via PayPal for lonelyfarmershearts.com and then not come up with any 'crumpet or tarts whatsoever'. Most disappointing.

He wondered aloud whether Mr Hicks had perhaps met Mr Sloggett via his own website?

He wondered aloud, too, whether in fact he wanted to renew his own subscription to a website that apparently catered for such filthy old shirt-lifters.

Anyway, when the constable went and opened the lid of an apparently abandoned deep freezer, and in there found an empty Mother's Traditional bag with a picture of a cheery-looking drag queen in a curly wig on it, his suspicions were confirmed. If not a crime wave, this was certainly the start of a crime ripple.

'Well, well, well,' he said overbearingly, crouched at the driver's window. 'Seems like we got to have a little chat, don't it?'

'Chat?' said Oggy, trembling a little.

The beast screwed up his face.

'You disgust me,' he said.

He strode back to his patrol car, and with a shake of his head and a final stare of intimidation, crammed himself in and drove away.

All was quiet around the old chapel. Nervously, stealthily, the hooded insurgent Cheel emerged from the shadows, spray cans in her hands, and quickly tagged the St Piran's flag on the chapel door and on the two front chapel windows either side, and right across the estate agent's 'Sold' notice.

There was more to come.

It was to be 'Women of Kernow', sprayed large on the door, above the tag.

She held the spray can in position, and shook it hard, but it rattled and she realised to her horror that there was not much paint left. The legend would have to be abbreviated.

She sprayed it, took a pace back, and admired her artistry.

W.O.K.

Chapter Eleven
The Digital Age

Singing I do believe, I do believe,
Old Johnney Bugger was a gay old bugger,
And a gay old bugger was he.

'Old Johnney Bugger' – *Cornish Traditional folk song*

Inga woke early in the B&B, ready for the first day's filming up at the chapel. She showered and cleaned her perfect teeth, and lay on the bed to pull on her tight jeans, and giggled to herself when the top button pinged off and shot across the room like a bullet. She threw on her puffy, black North Face gilet, grabbed her artistic director's clipboard and her iPad, and made her way out to where the unit would be, up at the chapel.

Constable 696 Carthew Carew had never been a great fan of the quick turnaround shift; finishing at ten on a late and starting at six the next morning on an early was no fun. It felt a bit like jet-lag, only he hadn't been anywhere much to speak of.

But he had made the best of it and rose at four thirty, and when he got down into his kitchen he'd put on his 'Breakfast with Huge!' DVD and tied on his Huge apron and cooked himself something nice, following his favourite celebrity chef's screen instructions to the letter. He'd prepared eggs benedict, with oak smoked salmon rather than ham this time, and with a nice blob of spinach that he put on the side of the dish, because past experience had taught him that it could be a little watery.

He got up close and personal to the screen to see if his own hollandaise looked up to scratch in comparison to Huge's, and to check that it was hopefully of a similar sheen and colour.

'Looks good to me, Carthew boy,' he said to himself in congratulation, and held the saucepan up to the screen and gave it a little stir, right in front of Huge's televised face.

'What do you reckon, Huge? Nothing wrong with that, eh?' he asked the telly; it did not reply, but then it was *very* early.

With a nice pot of coffee, he breakfasted all alone, with only the over jolly on-screen banter from Huge and all his guffawing celeb pals for company, and Carew joined in and laughed along with all the matey in-jokes and added a few of his own rib ticklers, in his mind's eye backslapping with the very best of them.

He finished mopping up the hollandaise with a piece of granary bread at five ten exactly, stuffed it into his mouth and after bidding a chummy 'See you after lunch, Huge,' to the signed, framed photograph of the chef on the kitchen wall, he switched the DVD off, and selected a book from his collection on the shelf, *The Huge Cooking Pot*. He took old sparky from the hook behind the door and trousered it down his side truncheon pocket, and left for work at Bodmin nick, just about a mile away.

He had to visit Tredogend on a follow-up enquiry at Mother's Pasty Shop, for the distasteful task of cautioning the filthy, dirty old dogger there and getting to the bottom of the mystery of the dumped deep freeze. First, though, he resolved to take in the early morning ozone down by the harbour, look at a few glossy pictures in his book and maybe read a chapter or so (if the words were not too hard), and grab a fag if no one was around.

Police work was rarely on his agenda before eight a.m. Even if he had been called to attend an intruder alarm, it would invariably turn out to be some dickhead of a shopkeeper letting himself into his own giftshop (full of tawdry tourist tat that no self-respecting burglar would ever consider pinching anyway), and carelessly forgetting to punch his code in properly. So he figured they could all sod off; parked adjacent to the dog shitty grass triangle, in front of the boarded-up toilets and overlooked by the benches-to-the-dead, he sat in his car and puffed away contentedly, and tried to read the book.

So when Carew was approached at his open car window, with his clip-on tie congealed in egg yolk, drizzled with extra virgin olive oil (first press) and a suggestion of a splash of spinach juice, he would normally have given the person short shrift for having the effrontery to interrupt his routine.

But it was not to be the case at all that morning, for he was approached by the gorgeously glamorous, lusciously lovely Inga. She was a Cornish beauty spot if ever he'd seen one, though he later scribbled in his pocket notebook that even at this early hour of the day, she was already eating a large pasty.

He put the book down and stubbed out his dog end.

'Well, aren't you a sight for sore eyes, love?' he said, inappropriately scanning her up and down. 'What can I do you for, then?'

Inga tried as best she could to ignore his impertinence. Constable Carew was clearly an unsophisticated, unreconstructed brute, but she needed his help. She reported to him that the old chapel had been vandalised overnight, sprayed all over with graffiti. She couldn't say exactly what the graffiti meant, but it all looked a bit runic to her, or maybe even Masonic. It didn't overly matter, she explained, as the place was due for a makeover for a TV production at any moment, but she thought the officer should know, just in case.

Constable Carew licked his tie clean and then accompanied the lady to the site of desecration. He asked which TV programme it was, and when she'd told him that it was *Huge! in Cornwall*, Inga saw his primitive features light up.

Was there any chance at all that he could meet Huge, he asked. What was he really like? Was his food as delicious as it looked on the telly? Was he really, *really* as good a bloke as he seemed on the box? There were so many things he wanted to ask.

When they reached the chapel, he said to Inga that he'd seen the symbols before, and assured her that they were most definitely not Masonic; rather, they were evidence of a growing Cornish insurgency against the 'emmet', or to you and I love, the casual tourist, incomer or blow-in.

Or celebrity chef.

'Stand back, love,' he said to Inga. 'Police work.'

He ran his index finger across one of the spray-tagged circular black and white symbols. He examined his digit closely, and cleverly noted that it was clean, meaning the paint was dry. He sniffed it, and rapidly came to the conclusion that this was spray paint that had most likely been sprayed on, though he couldn't be sure, and probably the work of someone with at least two cans of the stuff. One black and the other, maybe, white. It would all have to be confirmed.

But when he looked closely at the abbreviation W.O.K., Carthew Carew began to wonder aloud whether this really *was* the work of a Cornish nationalist insurgent, or something altogether more sinister.

It was popular opinion amongst his contemporaries in the constabulary that although Constable 696 Carew was a vicious, intimidating bully of the highest order (which he took as quite a compliment), he was not by any means the sharpest knife in the drawer. In fact, it was popular opinion that he couldn't detect a fart in a phone box.

In addition to this, his diversity training had also evidently passed him by.

'WOK, love,' he said, and traced the outline of the letters with his finger. 'I think we're onto something here, but this ain't some Cornish nutter like what I thought, it's more serious. I reckons it's that Chinese bloke down the road, I don't trust him, never have. Sly eyes he got, and his special fried is crap. I seen films mind, dead sparrows on the doorstep and that. I reckons this is the work of them Triads.'

He turned. Inga smiled politely. You're the bloody nutter, she thought.

Down in Fisherman's Cottage, Huge was preparing to leave to commence filming of the chapel makeover, and gulped down his instant coffee. Emma was washing the breakfast dishes at the sink. He dropped his mug into the bowl with a soapy splash.

'Okay Em,' he said. 'Must get on. I'll probably be back late, so don't wake up for me. Are you taking the little bunny rabbits surfing?'

'I guess so,' she said. 'Later, when I've given the cottage a clean through. Can I bring them down to see their Daddy being filmed when we get back? They'd love that.'

Shit, he thought, that wasn't really on the agenda. 'Might be a bit tricky with health and safety on set, all the cables and equipment and all that malarkey darling. Maybe I could call you if it's pos?'

'Oh, that's a shame. Well, okay then, we'll leave it. Maybe another day.'

'And don't forget what we said about the secrets,' said Huge.

'Secrets?' she said.

'Of the pasty, darling. You know, you were going to find out for me,' he said.

'Oh,' said Emma, as he walked out the door. 'Well, I'll try.'

The Sloggett's kitchen at Mother's Pasty shop was, as usual, in full production. Mother was making pastry with her cold, old fingers, from which she flicked the special water from her bowl into the mix, and then rolled it out into circles. Vi was on ingredient duty and sliced but did not dice the vegetables, and chopped the skirt beef into the much smaller chewy pieces demanded by Oggy. Uncle Clar was today in the construction department, and he added those ingredients in perfect proportion and shape, and then seasoned them and passed them on to Oggy who crimped. Pasty after pasty after pasty.

'I could do with a bit of help over here boy,' said Mother.

'Don't call me boy, Mother,' said Oggy. 'Where's that Cheel to, Vi?'

'Still in bed. You know what they're like, these kids,' she said.

'She been up late studying hard I expect, the dear of her,' said Uncle Clar.

'I could do with her help,' said Mother, flicking. 'She got the touch.'

There was a rumbling noise from outside in the street, and Vi opened the kitchen door to investigate. She looked out into the shop, which was in complete darkness, because outside a massive lorry with ZeeTV written all over it was blocking the light from the windows. The lorry revved hard and loud, and rolled the front wheel on its passenger side up over the kerb. The unmistakeable stench of burning clutch mingled with diesel fumes began to creep through the crack of the tinkling door.

The Sloggetts heard a crash and Vi saw some masonry and dust and crumbled pebbledash drop from above the shop window, followed by the shop sign itself, which swung down across the glass and made the inside even darker still. The lorry had knocked the front of the shop, and the sign was hanging at an improbable angle, held on precariously by a single screw.

Oggy ran out into the street and blared like a bull and banged on the side of the lorry, and shouted at the driver and his mate to stop.

The driver's mate jumped out.

'All right, all right. Keep your bleedin' shredded wheat on, Ginger Rogers,' he said with an estuarine Essex squeal. He assessed the damage. 'It's just a screw mate, that's all. I'll get maintenance to do it. It ain't a problem.'

'Well, get 'em to get a hurry on. I got to open dreckly,' raged Oggy.

The man got back up into the cab.

'What's he say?' said the driver.

'He says he's got to open dreckly,' said his mate.

'When's that?'

'God knows mate.'

They manoeuvred off the narrow pavement, and set off up the street the short distance to the chapel.

Constable 696 Carthew Carew, despite being somewhat diverted by the lovely Inga, had come to town primarily to pay a follow up visit to Mr Oggy Sloggett in lieu of their unscheduled meeting in the lay-by the previous evening. Although in many parts of the country, an abandoned fridge and a flustered middle aged man with his trousers down in a car in a lay-be would not constitute a crisis, when Carew factored in the morning's graffiti incident as well, it began to feel like there was a complete breakdown of civilised society in Tredogend. His imagination was running riot, and he was swinging his mental truncheon and firing off his imaginary Taser in all directions at once.

Constable Carew followed up his less than inspired hunch, and now hammered on the back door of Dead Dog Wong's mock-Tudor Chinese take-away to continue his enquiries. Carew's suspicions were aroused even further when Dead Dog himself answered the door brandishing a wok in one hand and an impressive meat cleaver in the other.

Paying due regard to the cleaver, Carew asked whether he would be prefer to be addressed as Mr Wong or plain old Dead Dog. It was at this point that Mr Wong angrily recounted to him that Dead Dog was a nickname he had been unfairly saddled with since he had lost control of his car and ran over a pair of pooches, in flagrante delicto, in one hit some years before.

One had been a small, on-heat Jack Lussel he said, coupled end to end with a filthy old farmer's filthy old farm dog, and they'd been squashed together on the dog dirt squelchy grass down by the public toilets. The owner had been refused permission to put a small bench there in little Squeak's memory, and none of it had anything whatsoever to do with his menu, thank you very much.

Diversity training had never prepared him for so much detail, and Constable Carew was having trouble keeping up with it all in his pocket notebook, Mr Wong's Cornish/Cantonese accent and mispronunciations merely exacerbated the officer's own mild dyslexia and extra strong xenophobia, and he was about to confirm with Mr Wong whether in fact he meant a Jack *Russell*, and to ask if he had reported the accident (which had occurred in 1998) to any of his colleagues, when he was called up on his radio.

He held up the handset to show Mr Wong, and pointed at the small glowing screen.

'It's new, digital see. Control want me....696, go ahead over,' he said.

Carew was sagely advised by force control that although Mr Wong probably had any number of woks, they were in all likelihood used mainly for cooking stir-fly. He was not known for his Triad involvement, at least not here in North Cornwall, but he was a long-standing and respected Rotarian if that was any indication of complicity in any crimes.

Further, even if his fried rice was crap, his chilli beef Szechuan and Singapore noodles were to die for, and on ten to six night shifts he always gave twenty per cent police discount and a freebie bag of prawn crackers, plus he always generously dished out a handful of fortune cookies which came in handy for predicting crime patterns.

Carew was informed that Mr Wong was not in any way, shape or form a suspect, and that he had clearly been barking white up the wong twee. The radio room staff evidently found this all very amusing.

Diversity training had passed them by too.

It was all too much for Carew, who scratched the back of his head and warned Mr Wong that he was now definitely on his radar and should be wary of his future conduct, but that now he had to go on to Mother's pasty shop and interview the disgusting pervert that ran that particular establishment. Tredogend, he thought, was fast going to the dogs.

Emma and Quenelle, Julienne and little Goujon turned up at the beach hut with their picnic to find Mervin in his usual cheery mood, and he kitted them out with their favourite boards upon which he had painted their names and a cartoon of each of them, and their personalised wet suits too, and they ran off down the beach for a lesson with Mervin's helper for the summer, a man called Bread, if you can imagine such a person.

Emma and Mervin sat side-by-side on the driftwood bench next to the hut, and chatted and chatted. She was surprised how open he was when she asked him about things.

Even when she asked him about the pasties.

'I tell you what,' he said. 'We can make some up over in the van if you like. Then you can see for yourself. Bread'll see the kids are okay.'

Emma felt an uneasy sort of guilt.

'Are you sure?' she said.

'Yea, come on, no probs,' he said.

Emma looked out to where the kids were. It would be all right this time, for sure. And Huge *had* asked her to find things out, and Mervin seemed such a nice guy.

She smiled and nodded and they skipped up and over the dunes to the old ice cream van that made up Mervin's home.

Emma was amazed to discover that he had all the necessary utensils and ingredients that he seemed to need for pasty making. He told her how he sometimes made them up in there for all his mates and got them baked in the oven at the Porzeath Bakery, and then they took them off to Harlyn or Fistral or Tregardock or Trebarwith on surfing expeditions, wrapped up in their beach towels to keep them warm.

'Now,' he said. 'The secret of the pasty is simple. It must be made with love.'

She laughed. 'Right,' she said.

He passed her some sliced potato and swede and some onion to put on her circle of pastry.

'So,' he said, 'Your husband. What does he do?'

'Oh, he works in TV,' she said.

'No way,' said Mervin. 'Cool. What is he? A producer or something?'

'Yes,' she said, adding some small chunks of meat just as he showed her. 'A bit like that I suppose. It's hard to say what he does really.'

Mervin laughed. 'Oh right, like that is it? Look, add another layer of potato and then we'll crimp them.'

As Emma added the slices of potato, Mervin seasoned over the top, and put a nub of butter in the middle.

'Right,' he said. 'Crimping now. Watch and learn,'

Mervin demonstrated the crimp to Emma at top speed. She laughed again.

'Oh that looks *really* easy,' she said playfully.

'Ok,' he said. 'Take the left end between your thumb and forefinger and turn it in… that's right…now with your other hand crimp over…that's it…'

Emma missed a bit.

'Whoops,' said Mervin, and reached his floury hands across to help her, and brushed the top of her small hands with his, and then guided hers deliberately along the pasty crimp.

'There,' he said.

Emma turned, put her floury fingers to his cheek, and reached up and kissed him.

Mervin took his hands away and stared at her, his cheeks flushed bright red.

Emma took a small step back.

'I'm so sorry,' she said. 'I didn't mean it.'

'It's all right,' said Mervin, with a surprised smile. 'It didn't hurt.'

'It might though,' she said. 'I'm really sorry. I can't do this.'

She turned and jumped down out of the old ice cream van, and ran back across the dunes and down to the beach.

Mervin carried on crimping the remaining pasties.

'Make 'em with love,' he said, and shrugged his shoulders.

The pasties were all lined up in trays on the numerous shelves of the newly purchased pasty oven behind the still dark shop counter in Mother's. Oggy was putting the final tray of the first batch in, to be ready for opening at eleven am on the dot. He squinted up at the numbers on the green flashing digital control panel.

'Timer. That's the button what we want,' he said confidently.

Mother peeped around the kitchen door.

'I don't go much on that thing, boy,' she said. 'The old oven worked fine.'

'It was haunted Mother. Uncle Clar'll tell you. Now, get back in the kitchen.'

She did not move, but Oggy grinned inwardly. He pressed the timer button until it flashed 11.00 in green.

'There we are. Progress Mother. And the start button, yes,' he laughed and pinged it. 'What's the matter with that, Mother? Right, now you get back in there before somebody sees you and we'll have a nice cup of tay, then we'll do the next batch. Proper job.'

Mother shook her head and disappeared, and Oggy was about to join her and the others back out in the kitchen when he heard a knock on the shop door, and turned and saw Constable Carew shading his eyes with his hand and peering into the shop through the glass.

Up at the chapel it was an all action day, the DIY leg of the TV journey from dilapidated old chapel to pasty theme park. Everyone involved was wearing bright yellow overalls and baseball caps with 'Huge! In Cornwall!' printed across the back in red. They ripped out, chucked into skips, dragged things around, and swarmed all over the hastily erected scaffolding that encased the building and its walls and roof and doors and windows.

The street was rammed full of crowds of gawping people, tripping over cables and looking and pointing, and self-important runners with walkie-talkies in green fluorescent tabards trying to keep everyone back and shush them up, and there were cameras filming from every conceivable angle, and lamps and reflecting umbrellas and shiny reflector sheets, and long furry microphones on telescopic booms all around, like skewered Peruvian guinea pigs prepared for a spit roast. It was bedlam.

But then, to create the world's Pasty Emporium in under forty-eight hours, it was bound to be, wasn't it?

Cheel, tired after all her night manoeuvres, had been awoken by Constable 696 Carew's incessantly loud knocking on the shop door downstairs. Puzzled, she popped out of bed, knelt and peeped down cautiously through the net curtains of her bedroom window. She held her maneless, pink My Little Pony in a tight grip. She heard the tinkle of the shop bell as her father opened it and let the officer in. She peeled back the bedroom carpet and dusty carpet liner, and put her ear to the floorboard, as Red Indian scouts did in Hollywood, and she listened to the muffled conversation below.

'I can't afford no fixed penalty, Constable. I told you, that freezer isn't mine no more. I sold it,' she heard her father say.

'It's got your name in it, and that's good enough for me. Now, you either remove it from the lay-by and dispose of it in the right and proper manner, or you get the fine.'

'How much is it to dispose of properly?'

'Fifty quid.'

'How much is the fine then?'

'Fifty quid,' said the policeman. 'Plus another fifty for the proper disposal.'

'So that's a hundred quid.'

'Uhhh. Yes, it would be, yes. No, wait a minute… no, that's right. A hundred.'

'Well I'll have to move it, but it ain't fair. It ain't mine.'

'And we'll say no more about the trousers thing.'

'I was just adjusting! They was new.'

'Just consider this a caution, Mr Sloggett. A word of advice.'

'A precaution for what?'

'Look here,' whispered the officer with menace. 'We both know what you and your mate was up to in that lay-by.'

'No…'

'Yes, you dirty old doggers. What would your missus think?'

'It ain't right…'

'Filthy swine. If that got in the Morning News, you wouldn't sell so many pasties, now would you?' growled Carew with menace.

'Oh my God…'

'Now then,' continued the zealous Constable. 'On your way home from the lay-by last night, did you see anything suspicious?'

'Superstitious no. Nothing.'

'Does the word "wok" mean anything to you?'

'What?'

'No, not *what*. "Wok".'

'Eh?'

Cheel lifted her head from the floor. Her nerves began to tingle.

'Hooliganism, disgusting dirty doggery, filth and perversion, and now we got the bloody Triads. It's all rife here in Tredogend, Sloggett. Rife! This place needs a kick up the ass!'

'Like my shop sign there, eh?' bridled Oggy. 'That lorry up the road just ripped that down. That's hooligalism! What are you going to do about that?'

'Nothing. Ring it through to Traffic in Exeter, and they'll give you a reference number. That should do it. Now, I'm sure we can overlook the lay-by business this time…'

'Overlook?'

'Any chance of a pasty before I go, if you get my drift? You do wear latex sanitary gloves in the kitchen? Bearing in mind what you been up to, I wouldn't want any health issues.'

Oggy peeped through the smoked glass. They were still as yet unbaked.

'They ain't ready yet. Try again dreckly,' he said.

Cheel sat on the edge of her bed, still stroking the little toy pony. She had to make plans. Devise a strategy to further her cause.

Things were getting hot.

But not in the new pasty oven.

Huge was delighted and thrilled that Nigel had now got his name changed officially to Huge!, that is, Huge-exclamation mark, and Emma's had been changed to Treleaven, though of course there was no need to inform her of this detail just yet.

Being Huge! he clearly felt that it was beneath him to do any of the menial, manual tasks that the crews were undertaking, except of course if the cameras were rolling, when occasionally he might throw an old rotten piece of skirting board or a dusty pair of curtains into a skip with a big cheesy, floppy-haired smile and a preposterously loud guffaw.

Most of the time he stood back with Nigel and watched as the crew moved like worker ants over the dear old chapel and stripped it back ready for re-invention, and when he got bored with looking at that, he looked at Inga and plotted their next sordid little liaison.

Mervin had dropped the pasties that he'd made with Emma off at the Porzeath Bakery and they had obligingly baked them for him, and wrapped them in a tea towel ready for when he cheerfully arrived to collect them. He walked barefoot along the sand dusted road to the beach, and then down to the rocks where Emma was sitting, with the kids splashing about in a tidal pool.

'Hey,' he said. 'I've got your pasties. All baked off.'

Emma smiled. 'Oh Mervin, look, I'm sorry but I can't just take them. After all that effort you put in too.'

'Oh, why? That's a shame. Your husband should try one.'

'That's very sweet of you. Really, but I can't take them home. It wouldn't seem right.'

'Go on,' said Mervin. 'You could eat them now if you don't want to take them.'

The children saw Mervin and dashed wet out of the pool and jumped up and grasped and grabbed at thin air, as he swung the bag with the tea towel wrapped pasties teasingly over their heads.

'Hey, careful you lot,' said Emma, laughing. 'Thank you Mervin. What do you say guys?'

They chorused their thanks to him.

'It's okay,' he said. 'No problem.'

He handed her the bag by hooking it over her finger, and she passed them round to the children and took one for herself.

'Sorry…' she said.

'Look, it's cool,' he said. 'Enjoy.'

'There's a spare. Won't you have it with us?' she said.

'If you like,' he said, and they sat and chatted and laughed and ate, and when he walked away across the beach back to work in the surf shack, Emma just stared down at the lovely footprints he had left in the sand.

*

Oggy and the Sloggetts were at full throttle making the morning's second batch of pasties at the table in the kitchen, when Cheel slinked in, almost unnoticed and began to quietly help.

'Up late with your studying, my lovely Cheel?' asked Uncle Clar.

'Yes Uncle Clar.'

'You looks tired,' said Mother.

'Yes Nan. I been checking father's Facebook account for him. Everybody all wants to know why our pasties is so good.'

'Huh! We shan't be telling nobody that,' said Mother, nearly laughing, but not quite going the whole hog.

'Quite right Mother, tell 'em bollocks,' said Oggy. 'Pass the pastry brush Vi.'

'So what's the bleedin' Beast of Bodmin got to say for himself, darlin'?' asked Vi.

'He said that he's superstitious of me and is going to give me a precaution or something. And then he was blathering on about somebody who's pinched a wok or a tripod, I don't know which. 'Tis all Chinese to me.'

Cheel kept her head down. They heard the doorbell tinkle, and someone call out, 'Oi! Shop! Are they ready yet?'

Oggy dropped the brush.

'Hellfire. Here's PC bloody Plod again,' he muttered. 'All right Constable. Just on me way.'

Cheel scuttled unnoticed out of the kitchen, and Oggy went the other direction into the shop and opened the new pasty oven door, and prepared to be enveloped in delicious, scalding pasty steam.

But there was no steam, and there was no aroma. The pasties all sat on their shelves, row upon neat row like newborn babies, naked, perfect, and untainted by heat or cooking of any description. The green digital reading was the same as it had been fifty minutes before.

'What the hell's going on here?' said Oggy.

Ever the detective, Constable 696 Carew ventured an opinion.

'I don't think that your oven's been turned on. It's digital, like this thing,' he said, and pointed at his handset.

'Oh…'sighed Oggy.

The officer shook his head and glared.

'No pasty then, eh? That's a shame for you,' he sneered, and turned and strode out of the tinkling door, and with an ominous 'I'll be in touch,' he set off to resume his patrol.

Vi peeped out from the kitchen.

'What is it?' she said.

'It's the oven. He ain't bloody working,' sighed Oggy.

Mother peeped out too, half-hidden by her daughter-in-law.

'Well now,' she said. 'That's what you gets when you changes things, boy.'

'You've been told,' bridled Oggy. 'Out of the shop, Mother. Back off!'

'I ain't sure there hasn't been some shenanigans and skulduggery here,' she hissed darkly.

'Not both *surely* Mother!' said Oggy with a rather unconvincing indignation. 'How dare you, what do you take me for?'

He was shushed into silence by Cheel, who had first checked from her bedroom window that the officer had indeed left the premises, and had now come back down and squeezed past Mother and in behind the shop counter. She looked at the digital dial and reached up and began to press buttons.

'Right, now, see that li'l green dot father?'

'See Mother? Green dot. Nothing wrong with this oven,' said Oggy.

'Good job she knows what *she's* doing,' said Mother.

'It's digital, father,' said Cheel. 'You got to set the time first, then do the cooking timer.'

'See Mother. Time first, it's digical,' he said. 'It got to be set.'

'That little dot there means p.m. If there's no dot, it's a.m. Morning. Now this one's for the temperature. Two hundred degrees - there we go. When they're all done, it does a little bleep.'

'See that Mother. Little dots, there look. And a bleep. Listen out for that,' said Oggy pointing. 'Now, get back out of sight before you scares somebody of a nervous proposition.'

Mother turned, muttering to herself, and slunk back into the inner sanctum. Uncle Clar expressed his approval to Vi. 'See Vi, she's a clever little maid. That's what education does for you, by gar,' he said.

Cheel nodded and together with mum Vi and Uncle Clar herded back into the kitchen, while Oggy remained behind the counter and squinted at the numbers on the digital readout and the li'l green dot. He tentatively gave the temperature setting button a little prod, just to adjust the new oven only very slightly and to familiarise himself with its controls. He nodded in approval and grunted a little uncertainly, and then joined the others.

But he did not see the two hundred flick to two hundred and forty on the temperature setting.

Nor did he witness the li'l green dot disappear completely.

Inga was busy helping Nigel with the directing up at the chapel, and Huge! was busy watching and doing as little as possible. Nigel sidled up to him and suggested that very soon they should film a walkabout of Tredogend, taking in all the quaint streets and shops and boats and the harbour, and Huge! could do a sort of roving, rambling travelogue of the place in which he had chosen to film 'Huge! in Cornwall', and apparently come to live in and become an integral part of the community (whether anyone wanted it or not). Huge! agreed that it would be a great idea.

'Nige,' he said, and pointed at a patch of wall in the corner devoid of any plaster, and ringed with paint bubbles and damp stains. 'I just need to check this out with Inga. It needs filling in or covering up or whatever.'

'Okay Huge!,' said Nigel.

'Inga, can you take a look at this with me? There's plaster missing and stuff,' he said, and ushered her towards the corner with her iPad.

'Can we get this filled in and touched up a bit?' he said loudly, and then he turned away from Nigel and the crew, pointed at the corner and hissed conspiratorially under his breath, 'Can I come back to your's when we've finished the walkabout guff? For a little research? Maybe do some touching up ourselves darling?'

She entered into the subterfuge, held up the iPad and took a picture of the offending wall. 'No,' she whispered. 'It's too dangerous Huge! The landlady is a nosy old bag.'

'In the beast-cruiser then. I'll pick you up by the castle entrance.'

She nodded the slightest of nods. 'Okay,' she said quietly, her mouth barely open at all.

She showed Huge! the image of the wall on her screen. 'Yea, that should be fine, Huge!' she called. 'I'll get that seen to. I'll get it touched up. Any chippys about?'

'Anything else Huge! ?' asked Nigel.

'That's about it I think, Nige,' he nodded.

Huge rubbed his hands together, pleased to have got the itinerary for his evening's entertainment sorted and to have the prospect of being helped through his demanding day by lurid fantasies of the lovely Ingrid.

Sorry, Inga.

Chapter Twelve
A Nasty Smeech

smeech – *Cornish dialect for an unpleasant and rancorous odour, very often associated with, though not always from, the kitchen.*

The first swirly whirly wisps of smoke began to seep out from the new oven in Mother's Pasty Shop at about midday, and Mother with her sniffer dog nose was the first to pick up the whiff from the kitchen.

'What's that smeech?' she said.

'Relax Mother,' said Oggy. 'All is in hand. Just listen for the bleep, that's all you have to do.'

'We shan't hear it through that door, shall we? I'd rather have a bell. You can trust bells,' she said, and added, 'A bit more beef please, Uncle Clar.'

Uncle Clar passed her a bowl of meat chunks across the table.

'Trust me, you shall hear the bleep,' said Oggy. 'Now ease off on that beef, Mother.'

'I ain't sure I can trust you, boy,' said Mother with a scowl.

'Don't call me boy, Mother. I'm sixty and a grown up and I know what I'm doing. Pass me the rolling pin there please, Vi. And that's too much Mother. Back off with the beef. Smaller chunks please Uncle Clar.'

Mother sniffed the air again. 'You should go and check them pasties.'

'No one leaves the kitchen Mother. We wait for the bleep.'

*

Progress up at the chapel had been very swift that morning. The ripping and tearing out had just about been finished, and now the DIY bods and local volunteers were starting to makeover the old building. Carpenters, electricians, plumbers, fitters and technicians, all canaried up in their bright yellow 'Huge! in Cornwall' overalls, tripped over cameras and mikes and cables and over made-up make-up ladies and sound technicians and the army of omnipresent runners, all there to help record them building the massive demonstration kitchen and shop area.

To coincide with the opening of the Huge! Pasty Emporium, Nigel had confirmed with Tom that all was well in hand in the dark and secretive nerve centre of pasty production, hidden deep in the Davidstow forest plantation.

Indeed it was.

Over the previous couple of days, they had had a pasty production unit installed in the old hangar. All the ingredients had arrived and been safely stored away, and the hangar had been soundproofed and brightly lit to ensure the efficiency of its illegal nocturnal labour force.

There were rows of industrial stainless steel preparation benches and sinks, a pastry mixer, potato and swede peelers and slicing machines, onion choppers, meat choppers and every other conceivable kitchen utensil. There were templates and pastry rollers to ensure that each pasty was of a standard size, and a mechanical crimper to ensure that each pasty looked just the last, and there were fridges, freezers, and three giant pasty ovens.

All that was needed was the word from Huge! and Nigel to commence production, the labour force would be brought in, and the master plan would be in full swing.

Down in Tredogend at the chapel, Nigel was planning the next slice of action.

'Right, Huge!,' he said. 'Ready for your roving report on the good people of Tredogend?'

'I don't have to dress up like the custard tarts in those bloody silly overalls, do I?' said Huge!.

'No,' said Nigel. 'Wardrobe's got you a gansey sweater, with the Tredogend pattern knitted in, so you'll look like a real local.'

'What?' quipped Huge!, rather unkindly. 'Half-baked with an extra finger?'

'Very funny Huge!,' said Nigel. 'Are we all good to go, guys?'

Back in Mother's, everyone in the kitchen had now got a whiff of the smeech coming through from the oven on the shop side. Even Oggy.

'For God's sake boy, go and check,' said Mother.

'I haven't heard no bleep yet, have you?'

'Go on love, just have a little look,' said Vi.

'It *is* a bit of a smeech, Oggy,' said Uncle Clar.

Oggy went out through the kitchen door and was immediately overwhelmed by the choking fog of eye-watering burnt pasty fumes. He put a tea towel over his mouth, dropped to his knees and crawled on his belly across the floor, and reached up and opened the glass oven door, and the acrid smoke belched and billowed out into the shop. He frantically wafted the oven with the tea towel, and as the smoke began to clear from the interior, he discovered the grim, charred remains.

Row upon row of blackened, cremated pasties.

And as Oggy ran choking and coughing and spluttering back into the kitchen, the telephone started to ring, and he turned on his heels and ran out in panic to the counter again and reached towards the receiver. 'Where's Cheel? Cheeeaaald!' he yelled.

'She's gone to Plymouth darlin',' screeched Vi. 'Leave the bleedin' dog and bone and pull the oven plug at the mains!'

Oggy did as Vi had said, and he flung the tinkling shop door open to let the burnt pasty fumed pea-souper pour like a thundercloud out into the street, and he sprawled and spluttered, crimson faced and gasping and wheezing, ginger-headfirst onto the tarmac of the road.

'So,' said Huge! to camera. 'Let me show you guys at home what it's all about. This is Tredogend in Cornwall. My new home, and home to the world's first 'proper' Pasty Emporium.'

The camera panned back to take in a shot of the street beyond them, and Huge! grinned a huge, fleshy grin to camera, flopped his floppy hair back, and put his thumbs up.

'As we say down here in Cornwall, 'praper jab', he said. His mocking accent, a sort of cidered-up Bernard Matthews chewing an out of date turkey twizzler, bore little resemblance to a Cornish one.

The camera followed him down and along the narrow old street.

'It's a bit of a shame really,' he said. 'Some of these old fisherman's cottages have been left to virtually fall down, and some have even been condemned before folk like you and I came down here and bought them up. Rescued and restored them. Loved them up a bit. Look at this one now. Lovely pastel-hued paint, a sort of sea-grass colour, and this terracotta pot on the windowsill with the white geraniums. Gorgeous. But take a look at this, the brass doorknocker. A little brass Cornish pisky…'

Huge! pointed at the polished knocker. The camera took a close-up of the pisky's face. It wasn't a smiley one at all, rather more a grotesque and angry scowl. By a trick of the light, it seemed to glare angrily out at the celebrity super chef.

'Charming,' said Huge! with a little laugh.

He looked at a card that was displayed in the window. The camera panned in on his pointing finger. 'And this one's for rent… a London number,' he said.

The crew made their way down to the corner and began to film again, and this time Huge! stood by a rather dilapidated and plain looking cottage. An old lady bent out of the doorway and fed a grateful tabby.

'Contrast that with other parts of the village,' he said. 'And you begin to see why I want to come here and sprinkle a little Huge! pasty magic dust over Tredogend…'

The old lady did not hear him, and went back inside and closed the door.

'What's that smell?' said Nigel. 'Burning?'

A pall of smoke drifted up the street.

'Jesus,' said the cameraman.

Beyond him, and as yet out of focus, the scenario was rather frenetic. One by one the Sloggetts dived out into the street, choking and coughing, smoke still pouring from the doorway. Mother sat open-legged and panting on the windowsill, as if she was about to give birth for the first time in sixty years, and Vi put a comforting arm around her, while Uncle Clar limped out having rescued a packet of digestives and the tea caddy, and the telephone was still ringing.

Oggy dived in and out of the shop, each time emerging with a metal tray of perfect, miniature black and smoking pasties, and scraped them into a green wheelie bin. One after another, after another, after another…

Huge!, in a quieter voice, came closer to the camera and spoke candidly to his viewers.

'You see, this is what I mean. This is the old pasty shop in the village. It's *okay*, but it all looks a bit tired, a bit unloved. Indifferent if you like. Look at the shop sign, for instance. How long has that been hanging down like that? It only needs a screw, for heaven's sake. And now they've got a problem with what looks like a batch of burnt pasties. It all smacks of something that needs dragging up by the bootlaces and putting back into shape, do you know?'

Oggy had bent double, and with his hands on hips he huffed and puffed, the comb-over straggling his sweaty red face, having removed and thrown out the last tray of conflagrated pasties. The smoke now rose from the wheelie bin rather than from the shop itself, and Oggy flipped its lid shut and wafted the shop door to and fro to disperse the fumes.

'Oggy,' said Uncle Clar helpfully. 'I think the phone might still be ringing.'

Oggy sighed a heavy sigh, composed himself as best he could, and went in and picked up the receiver.

'Mother's,' he said.

There was a slight delay.

'Good morning, am I speaking to Mr Oggy please?'

'Oh, Colin, look…'

'Mr Oggy. Today I'm able to be offering you a wireless terminal set-up, equipment rent free, at 4.6% on the turnover and additionally twenty pence each per transaction. Just twenty pence, Mr Oggy. Business Solutions for You offers the best after sales service as I believe I have already been telling you previously Mr Oggy.'

'Colin, I'm sorry. I just had a small fire. All out now, but …'

'I'm sorry to hear that, Mr Oggy. I have an uncle who specialises in fire extinguishers…'

'Thank you Colin. You'll have to try again dreckly. Sorry.'

'Thank you Mr Oggy. You have a great day now…'

He went out and stood there facing Vi, Uncle Clar and Mother, and wiped his hands with a tea towel.

'There,' he said triumphantly, if rather breathlessly. 'All done.'

Mother looked up and glared at him with incredulity.

'All done? All done, boy? Is that all you got to say?'

'Don't call me boy, Mother.'

'Take me up to bed Vi,' she said quietly. 'I can feel it coming on again.'

The camera crew and Huge! tentatively edged a little closer down the street towards Mother's.

'Let's get some shots here, Nige,' said Huge!. The camera rolled. 'Here's a local. Excuse me sir. May I interrupt? What's been happening?'

Vi and Uncle Clar helped Mother back into the shop, and Oggy turned and looked up at Huge!.

'What does it bloody look like, mate? Me pasties have burnt, and your lot have pulled down me shop sign, and now dear old Mother's on her deathbed again, bless her heart,' cursed Oggy.

Head bowed and shoulders taut and hunched in anger, he snarled closer to the camera, and tugged at his old bugger grips in frustration, and grimaced directly at Huge!, who held out the microphone to him.

'So you're Mr?' Huge! asked, knowing full well that he was the rather uncouth man from the pasty shop.

'No odds to you who I be. Who the bloody hell be you? Coming down here with all your fancy ways and taking over and filming people's misery...'

'Who be I?' said Huge! condescendingly. 'Well, I be the man who thinks the village could do with a little makeover. It's a little down at heel, don't you think?'

'Down at heel? What are you casting nasturtiums about this little village for? How dare you!' raged Oggy.

'Just a little paint here and there? Straighten up a few signs?'

'Bollocks!' blared Oggy, and he turned on his heel and marched back into Mother's, and slammed the tinkling shop door behind him. From over the door, the shop sign creaked in the breeze, and the single rusty screw gave up its fight and the sign crashed heavily to the ground, and a cloud of dust drifted across the surface of the street.

'Well,' said Huge!, 'I wouldn't like to cast any nasturtiums, toss any tulips *or* lob any lobelias in our friend's direction...'

The crew laughed out loud off camera. Huge! grinned a wide supercilious smart-assed grin into the lens.

'A little resistance to change is always to be expected in circumstances such as this,' he said with a detached professional calmness. 'But, you know, I view this as a challenge, and maybe a journey that our friend over there might like to undertake with us....'

The camera panned across to the shop window of Mother's, where Oggy's face had contorted into a deranged and twistedly gargoyled gurney, and he gesticulated in no uncertain terms (with a bewildering semaphore of finger and hand signals) that he rather wished, if it were convenient, that they would all move away.

Huge! smiled wryly. 'I don't think we're too popular hereabouts at the moment. We'd better move on before he tries to *plant* one on me!'

More obsequious hoots and chortles from the crew; Huge! really was such a card. They moved on past Mother's pasty shop towards the harbour, stopping briefly on the way by the wheelie bin for Huge! to lift the lid, so they could take a shot of the stash of burnt pasties still smouldering in the bottom. The chef could not resist reaching in and pulling one out for a close-up.

'Let's hope mine don't turn out like *this*,' he said, and raised his eyebrows to the viewers. 'I tell you what. We'll give it the seagull test, shall we?'

Huge! carried the burnt Mother's pasty down to the harbour side, where he sat on dead Malcolm's bench and offered it to the gulls, whole and then in small pieces. The gulls gathered around in their usual greedy gullabaloo, and pecked and plucked and played with the blackened bits, but not one of them ate a single morsel.

'You see,' said Huge! 'They're very discerning customers, the seagulls here. Now you just wait until the Huge! Pasty Emporium is in full swing, and we'll soon see then how hungry they are. I think we can probably do a little better than this, don't you?'

He got to his feet and walked off along the harbour side until he heard the 'Cut! Great TV, Huge!', whereupon he stopped and waited for the crew to catch him up. He sat on a granite mooring post, and looked up at the parapets of the surrounding roofs.

On the finial at the end of a ridge, and standing on it's one and only leg, a gull stared down at him. Any ornithologist worth his salt would have recognised the barely disguised look of contempt.

Oggy sat alone at the kitchen table. He heard the rattle of his letter box, and went out into the still smeechy shop and recovered the day's post. It was half past two. He sat back down and slid his crimping finger into the envelope and ripped it open.

It was a final demand for Council Tax from the local authority, for £66.73p.

He threw it down on the table, and opened the next one.

It was a typed letter, headed with the crest of the Tredogend Fishermen's Choir.

It read -

Dear Oggy,

Further to our last practice evening, and the uniform inspection for future concert engagements, I noted the following.

Your choir tie was ragged and a little stained,

Your choir badge was somewhat frayed, and of the 'old' type,

Your trousers were not of the prescribed colour or description, (plain grey flannels preferred) as laid down by the choir committee (ref June 1997 minute 4). They also appeared to be rather on the tight side.

I trust that you will take note and remedy these observations in time for our next concert. I'm sure that you will understand that now we have our 'celebrity' on board, our profile is likely to be much higher than before.

Regretfully, if you are unable to comply with these requirements, we may have to suspend your membership until such time as you can.

Yours in Music,
Jeff Pengelly (Musical Director)

Oggy held up the letter and stared at it forlornly. Vi had come down from Mother's bedroom and breezed in and sat opposite him. He looked at her and offered her the piece of paper.

'That can wait,' she said. 'Your mother's dying again, and she says that this time she's serious.'

'I think I'll join her, Vi,' he said.

Cheel sat upright in the tattooist's chair, her right forearm resting across a cushion.

'What do you want then?' asked the boss-eyed greaser, his lank hair scraped back to form a nasty, slimy ponytail. He had his electric needle in his hand.

'Wok. W. O. K. right on this forearm, right along there.' She indicated to him the precise place she wanted the letters.

'Do you want small case?'

'Large.'

'What script?'

'Gothic. Plain black.'

'No colour?'

'Plain black.'

'Do you want a picture? I do a good bat.'

'No bats, just wok. The letters. W.O.K.'

'Lot's of people like bats. Some come back for more.'

Art is how we decorate space

Music is how we decorate time

n up the street
breath of fresh
stood opposite
med in front of
ed to the right of
alls was pinning
asty Emporium -
d Pasty Crimping

away,' said Oggy, confounded a. ⸺ ⸺s.

'See that darlin',' sa.. vi. 'You'd bleedin' walk that! You're the fastest crimper in the west!'

'I ain't sure. I don't like the bugger.'

'All the more reason to take his money. Pay off the council. Get your badge and tie and all that,' she said.

'I suppose I should.'

'That's more like it, love. Now, come on and we'll get the ladder out and nail up that sign again. Mother might think she's brown bread, but Mother's ain't, not while I'm a bleedin' woman of Cornwall.'

On her way back to Plymouth bus station, Cheel popped into Peak Outdoors in the Armada Centre, where she bought a small and compact tent, a sleeping bag and a survival kit and some Kendal mint cake, and a Swiss army knife, making sure first off that it would all fit into her rucksack.

She paid the assistant, and jogged effortlessly to the awaiting bus, flashed her ticket, and got the ride back to Wadebridge, and then on to Tredogend.

By the end of the afternoon, the old chapel was looking bright and white and sparkling, and the remarkably rapid progress was all in the can for the opening edition of *Huge! in Cornwall*. Just a day and a half until that opening, and it was right bang-on schedule.

Huge!, back from his village ramble, sat and watched Inga working hard at interviewing hopefuls for staffing the Emporium. She was very beautiful, he mused, but there was something a little different about her that he couldn't quite put his finger on…

Oggy was on the phone to the little widower, Mr Digory Hicks.

'So, can I pick you up and go grab that freezer from the lay-by? I'll have to find some other way of getting rid of it,' he said.

'I knew it would come back to haunt you,' said Digory.

'Very bloody funny. That Constable Carew says I'll be prostituted and fined otherwise,' he said.

'Prosecute you means. But don't worry,' said Digory. 'Trelawney needs a new water trough, that old one's as leaky as a basket. I'll use it for that.'

'Proper,' said Oggy. 'Dreckly boy.'

'Dreckly. Facebook me when you leave dear.'

Emma and the kids arrived back at Fisherman's Cottage after their day on the beach, and after settling the kids down in front of the telly, she took a walk through Tredogend up to the old chapel. She was astonished at the progress there.

Huge! was standing outside next to Nigel the director and a pretty blonde lady.

'I thought I'd come and say hi, Huge!' she said. 'But I can see you're rather busy.'

'Oh darling, no. Not at all,' he smarmed. 'Let me show you around.'

He took her around the glorious Emporium that was taking shape in front of their very eyes.

'My God,' said Emma, gazing up and around the transformed interior. 'That's amazing Huge!. You're so clever.'

She pecked him on the cheek.

'Thank you darling,' he said. 'Look, I shouldn't be too late tonight, but as you can see…'

'Oh, okay. It's just that the children haven't seen you,' she said. 'They want to tell you about the surfing.'

'How was it on the beach? Did you manage to find anything out?'

'Oh…no,' said Emma, with some hesitation. 'I, I didn't see him there. I don't think he was working today.'

She smiled and blew him a little kiss, and turned back towards Fisherman's Cottage, and thought how hard he was working and how clever he was, her old Huge!. She felt a bit embarrassed about what had passed between her and Mervin earlier in the day, and not a little guilty too, in a very sweet sort of way.

Huge! meanwhile, checked his watch and glanced over at Inga. Just half an hour, he thought.

Little Digory Hicks was waiting impatiently by the paddock when Oggy arrived as dusk approached. He got into the passenger seat and shook his head.

'You never Facebooked me,' he said.

'Assholes to Facebook, it's dreckly and I'm here, ain't I?'

'You gotta get with it, Oggy. 'Tis the future dear.'

'I ain't got time for that sort of bollocks. Now, have you had any action on the old cow front?' enquired Oggy, changing the subject.

'Trelawney have turned his nose up to oysters, so I been trying celery. That's supposed to help,' said Digory.

'This won't take us long. Then you can come home and play 'em some Barry White and dim the yard lamps a bit.'

'Very funny.'

They pulled out of the yard and Oggy drove off up the lane towards the lay-by to retrieve the old freezer.

Nigel was busy ticking things off on his list. He stared intently down at his clipboard and flicked page after page over, alternatively sucking the end of his bic or tapping it between his upper and lower front teeth.

'I think you're done for the day Huge!,' he said. 'Might as well pop off and see your lovely missus and kids. You've been full on. Nice to give them a bit of time.'

Huge and Inga exchanged a glance. He twitched a wink at her, and went and lurked around in the doorway, and pretended to look at notices.

Nigel peeped over the top of his glasses thoughtfully.

'Inga,' he said. 'We need to settle down and plan. Finish off in here and we'll get Tom and have a pow-wow.' He looked up. 'Oh, you're still here. Anything else Huge!?'

'Oh,' said the chef. 'Not really, just checking out the roster for the week.'

'I've got that here Huge!,' said Nigel, and he waved his sheet. 'All done.'

'Yea, yea, yea, yea. Good. Right. Okay. Night then.'

Shit, he thought, his rather sordid plans scuppered, he trudged crestfallen out of the old chapel and home to Fisherman's Cottage and the lovely family he barely deserved.

*

Cheel had been back from Plymouth for about half an hour when Vi told her that Mother had inexplicably taken to her bed, once again gripped by visions of the imminent arrival of the grim reaper.

The young girl crept quietly up into the old lady's bedroom, for fear she would wake her. Mother heard her come in and opened one eye and smiled feebly.

'What's on, Nan?' said Cheel.

'Come and sit here, my bird,' said Mother, and grasped her hand. She studied Cheel intently with her narrow slanted eyes. She squeezed her hand. Tightly. Cheel did not flinch.

'I shan't be here much longer,' said Mother.

'You keep saying that, Nan.'

'You have got it, you know that, don't you?'

'Got what, Nan?'

'The gift,' said Mother. 'The touch.'

Cheel looked at her in puzzlement.

'Listen,' said Mother. ''Tis in the water. Special water, mark you.'

'What? Where does it come from?'

''Tis from a holy well, high up on the moor. Digory knows,' said Mother.

'Digory?'

'He is the bringer of the water,' said Mother, and she closed her eyes and leaned back, and drifted back into her deep, dark pretend sleep.

The car trundled slowly up through the darkening country lanes.

'So,' said Digory. 'What's news down the shop? There was nothing put online.'

'I can tell you all you needs to know. Matey is opening his bloody place the day after tomorrow, I can't work me new oven, and all me pasties have burned, and now Mother have taken to her bed again. We don't need no computer to tell us that.'

'Dying?'

'Yes, dying, yes.'

'Again?'

'Yes again.'

'Apart from that?'

'Oh, fantastic,' he said, with a hint of fatalism, and then added. 'Oh, but I'll tell you what, I'm going down fighting boy. I'm going to win that bloody pasty crimping competition if it's the last thing I do. Oggy Sloggett, fastest crimper in the west, *and* all on the telly too! I'll bloody show 'em!'

'That's the way boy!' said Digory. 'The more crimper you are, the harder they fall.'

'Zackly…' said Oggy. 'Say it again. The crimpier you what…?'

Huge! breezed into the beautifully bijoued kitchen to find Emma staring into her mug of tea. The dishes were piled in the sink, and the slate floor was covered in wet sand from the beach. A beach towel hung limply over the arm of the sofa. She looked up.

'Any luck with a new cleaner, darling?' he asked.

'You're home,' she said. 'Quinn, Jules, Goujon, Daddy's home! Go in and see them darling. They're off to bed soon.'

Huge! went into the living room where his kids sat together on the sofa in their jim jams. The two eldest were watching the telly. Little Goujon was reading *The Concise British Flora* by the Reverend Keeble Martin, and trying to distinguish the dizzying multitude of white umbelliferous plants.

'Hi Dad,' they muttered in unison.

'Hey guys,' said Huge! chummily. 'Good surf?'

'Yes,' said Quenelle.

'Shush,' said Julienne. 'This is good.'

Little Goujon flipped a page. It was hard to tell the difference between hedge parsley and sea parsley.

'So who took you surfing?'

'Bread. He's cool,' said Quenelle. 'Not as cool as Mervin though.'

'No,' said Julienne. 'He's *really* cool.'

'He brought us pasties today.'

'They were delicious.'

'Mummy helped him make them.'

'They made them together.'

'Yummy,' said Quenelle.

'Yummy!' said Julienne.

'Yummy Mummy,' sneered Huge!.

'There it is, Digory,' said Oggy, and he pointed at his old freezer in the lay-by. 'Come on. Let's get it in and then I can get back home and sort Mother out.'

He trundled into the lay by, and they both got out and hands in pockets, walked over to the big old white box and stood there looking at it.

'Right Digory,' he said. 'I'll take this base end with the motor. You grab the top end, it's lighter.'

The two old friends grabbed an end each, and began to lift.

Inga settled into bed and with the bedside lamp on, sat up and read *Marie Claire* and ate a pasty. When she had finished this one, she opened up her new copy of *Tittle*

Tattle, a celeb and features magazine from the local newsagents, and she began to read a rather gratuitously saucy story about an ambitious young thing and her egotistical, shagnasty boss. Then she began to eat another pasty.

A barn owl screeched in alarm as it ghosted out of a thorn bush, just above the heads of the two men in the lay-by.

'Look out!' shouted Digory. He ducked and his knee gave way and he slipped and twisted and dropped his end of the freezer, and fell sideways into the brambles that bordered the lay by. Oggy couldn't fall anywhere, for he too was twisted around by the downward momentum, and he tumbled and stumbled to his knees. Both his hands were pinned to the lay-by by the freezer.

'Aaargh! Me bloody fingers!' he squealed, his digits well and truly trapped between the heavy motor end of the white goods and the gritty, gravely tarmac.

'Quick Dig',' implored Oggy. 'Quick, for God's sake. Aaaargh!'

Digory tugged and ripped himself free of the blackthorned and brambly hedge and rushed to tilt the freezer to one side and free his mate's fingers. Agonised, Oggy sat back on the ground and took in a deep breath and sighed, and shook his hands in front of him to try and get the circulation back.

'Shit,' he said. 'I can't move 'em, I can't hardly feel 'em Digory'.

Digory held Oggy's fingers out in the palm of his hand. 'Sorry, that owl properly frightened me and me knee gived way. Can you straighten this one?' he asked.

'Oww! No, and that's me main crimping finger…'

'No good, boy,' said Digory. 'This one's busted, and this one might be too I think. They're all swelled up and bruised. What a bloody mess.'

'There goes me hundred quid and me new tie and badge,' said Oggy, face contorted with agony.

'Isn't life queer?' pondered Digory. 'It never pours, doesn't it?'

'What?'

'Well, you know, the rain and that, sunshine on the righteous I mean…'

Oggy shook his head and licked his wounds.

'I never saw the forecast, Digory,' he said.

Inga slipped out of bed, popped her jeans and top on, and shimmied down the stairs. She quietly lifted the latch, and went off down the street just a little way to the warmly inviting lights and delights of Dead Dog Wong's mock-Tudor Chinese take-away. She went in and read the menu. Dead Dog was sitting behind the counter, which was unadorned except for a poster of a red dragon with a Cornish flag in its fiery mouth. He was watching a cookery programme on his overloud TV, one with super sweary inebriate celeb chef Larry Ramsbottom on an expletive ridden tour of the Dordogne, demonstrating to the 'effin frogs that they had no idea at all what real good food was until they'd tried tripe and onions, chitterlings and boiled windpipe.

'We nearly close now. What you want?' asked Dead Dog.

'I'd like a pasty please,' said Inga.

'Chilli beef Szechuan pasty, or house speciality sweet and sour chicken and special fried rice pasty?'

'Yes please,' she said.

*

Cheel, up in her bedroom above Mother's pasty shop, sat on her bed. She had completed all her sit-ups and press-ups and now, with a booklet at her feet, repeated the words of her oath over and over in parrot fashion.

'On my honour and the honour of my country, I swear to wrestle without treachery or brutality…'

After a while she stopped, for she could hear Vi and Uncle Clar downstairs making a fuss of her father. She listened at her spot on the floorboard with the carpet rolled back, as her Mum Vi mummified Oggy's hands with two packs of Bird's Eye frozen peas wrapped in brown parcel tape.

'Come here darlin',' she heard Vi say. 'Oooh, that looks sore.'

'Mind that one there. Ooouch!'

'Careful love. You'll have to get them bandaged properly by Dr Hoskin in the morning. You might have to have an X-ray in Bodmin.'

'Bugger Bodmin. I'll be all right. How's Mother?'

'Still with us, love.'

'Could have done with that hundred quid…'

Cheel sat up on the floor, and recalled her conversation with her Nan. 'You got it', she'd said to her. 'The touch. The gift. Special water,' the words were going around and around in her head. She wondered just exactly what Mother had meant.

Emma tucked little Goujon into his bed and switched off his bedside light.

'Night darling,' she said. She went back down into the kitchen to find her husband brooding.

'So he wasn't there? Mr Whippy?' said Huge! quietly.

'No, no..he…' Emma spluttered. 'Look, he was, all right. I just couldn't find anything out, okay? I'm embarrassed, that's all.'

'Embarrassed?'

'About the pasty thing. This secret, whatever, you know.'

Huge! got up and went to the door. 'Seems you might have a few secrets yourself, Emma. That's very sad,' he said, shaking his head. 'I need to go for a walk.'

Oggy and Vi both turned together to see Cheel standing in the doorway, silhouetted by the hallway light, her figure wiry and slim. Her face was in shadow.

'Father,' she said. 'I'll do it for you. Nan told me I got it. The touch. I'll win that competition, get you the hundred quid.'

'But you hate that bloke,' said Vi.

'It don't matter Mum. We need the money, I have to engage with the enemy some time, let it be now,' and at that she turned, and closed the door behind her.

'Hellfire bloody corner,' said Oggy. 'She's some maid.'

'That's the cockney in her, darlin',' laughed Vi. 'Cup of tea?'

Huge! skulked up the road, like a dirty old dog in the night, and sniffed around at the front of the Guillemot B&B where Inga was staying. He quietly opened the garden gate and crept across the lawn to just below her bedroom window. The light was still on. He picked up a small pebble and tossed it up against the windowpane.

Inga was reading *Glamour*, and had just polished off what was probably the most disgusting pasty ever imagined, chilli beef Szechuan with soggy noodles, limp bean sprouts and a single, bullet-like water chestnut, when she heard the knock against the glass.

She ignored it and turned a page, halfway through a thought-provoking article about a young professional woman who had developed an insatiable appetite for sex and food, both separately and simultaneously, and in no particular order of preference. She reached out and grabbed the sweet and sour pasty and bit into it, so intrigued by the contents of the article that she failed to register that it was at least as repulsive as the aberation she'd just finished.

Another pebble hit the window. She heard Huge! outside in the fuchsias.

'Ingrid!'

'I'm busy,' she muttered quietly to herself, through a sticky sweet mouthful of glutinous red sauce, a tinned pineapple chunk and a battered lump of bruised and abused battery chicken, all wrapped in pastry that was not exactly crimped, more cringed.

Within two minutes, all trace of Dead Dog's house speciality was gone and so too, to her blessed relief, was Huge!.

Krno and the Romanian illegals had awoken at the coming of dusk, and in readiness for their first night shift had trudged across the dark from the bungalow, and over to the pasty factory in the vast looming shape of the hangar next door. By the faint light of the half moon, they could make out the pyramid tops of the conifers that hemmed them in.

Krno could see lots of small shapes whizzing haphazardly around in the air. He had not seen so many bats since he had left his own little village in Romania many years ago, and he wondered where on earth their colony could be.

It was closer to home than he imagined. In the right hand corner of the rear of the hangar was a hole, virtually impossible to see. From inside too, screened by a sheet of boarding that covered the metal rafters, it was hard to tell it was there; a hole just about large enough for a small person to squeeze through.

And from that hole, one after another after another, the bats flew out into the night air in search of delicious, fluffy, juicy moths. It was the breeding season, and they were hungry. The lesser horseshoe bats just loved to live in large breeding colonies, and where better than in the shelter of an old hangar?

Especially now, when it was warmed by the heat of three gigantic pasty ovens.

Especially when they were a rare and declining species.

Chapter Thirteen
The Wisht List

wisht – *Cornish dialect for appearing or feeling poorly or unwell. Probably derived from the expression 'washed out', or looking pale or sickly; thus a sickly child becomes a wisht cheel. May also be used to describe other things/situations that are not so good e.g. that builder's done a wisht job on my roof.*

It was a bright, bright, sunshiny morning for the opening of the Huge! Pasty Emporium. He, of course, had done very little himself, just spouted a few wisecracks and pulled some faces here and there to camera, still very irritated by the absence of a bonk with Inga the previous night, scratched by fuchsias, and outraged that his wife apparently had the gall to actually enjoy another man's company.

The custard tarts had been frantically putting the final touches to the interior all through the night. Huge! had been around on an inspection tour with Nigel and Inga, to make sure that the place was ready for 'The plague of the great unwashed, Nige, the tsunami of pond life and hoi poloi. You know, our faithful couch potato viewers…'

Nigel was grateful that no one had overheard the gratuitously offensive remarks; they would not have been great for the first lot of ratings.

After all, he had worked hard for ZeeTV to get the slots for the opening night. First up was a recorded, hour long documentary style coverage of all the building and DIY work to convert the old chapel, and then little pieces about Tredogend itself, and the community down there, flagging up lots of 'interesting and colourful local characters'. Nigel hoped they'd continue to crop up, time and again, as the series progressed, to ensure a sort of combination of a Victorian freak show with a 21st century cookery programme.

This was to be followed at eight in the evening by a half hour of *Coronation Street*, and then that in turn would be followed by a live broadcast from the Huge! Pasty Emporium of the world's first ever pasty crimping championships.

The custard tarts had done a marvellous job to the interior, considering the time available, it had to be said. Tredogend Methodist chapel had been converted into a massive state of the art demonstration kitchen. Above and along the entire width of the chapel was a gigantic tilted mirror, upon which punters seated in row upon row of pews could watch continuous live demonstrations of the art of the pasty maker.

In the centre was a ten-legged kitchen table, where it was planned that the quaintly mop-capped, rosy-cheeked and smiley, kindly old lady army would work, gossiping and chattering, floury fingered, and make pasties to entertain an entranced public, and where Huge! would occasionally demonstrate his own pasty making skills on camera.

At the serving area to the right side of the counter were the tills and the bagging section, and the original Treleaven pasty oven purloined from Mother's, cleaned and polished almost beyond recognition. Above it was a massive black and white photographic portrait from the early 1950s, of a Cornish woman with high cheekbones and a determined mouth, a woman with rather narrow, slanted eyes, lifting a tray of pasties from the same

Treleaven oven. A woman who looked suspiciously like Mother herself.

Next to the portrait was a text. *'Have you seen this oven before? Yes, it's an old Treleaven family heirloom! This photo was taken in 1951, and the oven was already old back then! Now it's here, still cooking our pasties to this very day.'*

All around the walls of the Pasty Emporium, between alternate chapel windows, there was a great collection of heritage photographs, some dating back to the late 1800s, on display. To the left of the counter, on the opposite side to the Trelawney oven, was a vast plasma screen that ran a loop telling of the history and geography of the pasty, and a demonstration of how to make one, and even instructions on how to eat one.

Along the front of the counter stood printed hessian sacks of locally ground strong flour, from the Rilla Mill Waterwheel Company, a mill recently restored by escapee city broker, Petroc Forbes and his partner Jo 'Tinky' Brown.

There were branded baskets of swedes and onions, and sacks of potatoes, all sourced from Jasper Fanshawe's organic farm (bought with 2008's bonus) down on the Roseland. They were all opened, allowing the vegetables to look as if they had spilled out naturally onto the restored and sawdusted floor. It was not immediately noticeable that they were all held in position by blobs of (organic) Blu-Tac.

The few ingredients that the artisan pasty makers would actually need to demonstrate with were kept in a room at the back of the Emporium. There was no need for anyone to touch what was out on display at all, for that was all arranged far too prettily.

And behind that back room, there was a hastily constructed windowless lean-to. It was there to where the lorry had delivered the two thousand pasties early that morning from the secret pasty factory at the edge of Davidstow moor. Tray upon tray upon tray of them, kept warm in preparation to transfer to the Treleaven pasty oven, ready for the customers. Customers who could buy Huge! pasties for ten pounds each, fooled into thinking they had been made on the premises by cheery artisans in the World's First Pasty Emporium, not in a secret Dickensian sweatshop up on the moors by Eastern European slave labour.

A magnificent deception.

Huge! looked around and rubbed his hands and nodded his head at the blinding success of his master plan so far. Inga followed him around, taking notes on her iPad.

'Where were you,' he hissed.

'Asleep Huge!. It's too dangerous there, I told you.'

He huffed and shook his head. Back to business. 'One detail, Inga,' he said. 'Jasper's swedes look a bit too clean for organic ones. Can you get somebody to take them out to a gateway somewhere and roll them in the shit and mud a bit?'

'Yea okay, but they're not Jasper's,' she said. 'All his stuff is too expensive. I just sourced some of his bags and sacks, that's all. He says he's happy if they're seen on telly. The veg is all from ValuCheap.'

'What about the flour? Not that shit from Rilla Mill, is it?'

'God no. Same deal.'

'Brilliant! Brilliant,' he said. 'That's much more like it. I must give you a little treat darling.'

'I'm okay for a bit. I've had one already today. Maybe at lunch I could manage another.'

'I don't mean a bloody pasty,' he snapped.

*

The surgery was packed with the usual selection of patients who to Dr Hoskin seemed divided between the medi-phobics who hated seeing him until they were at least at death's door and it was all too late, and then the hypocondriacs with nothing else to do except clog up his waiting room, pitifully whingeing about imaginary ailments that they had heard about on the telly or read about online.

'Oggy Sloggett. Dr Hoskin, please. Oggy Sloggett to Dr Hoskin.'

Dr Hoskin peeled off the layers of parcel tape from his mummified hands, and handed Oggy back the now defrosted peas and looked at his fingers, one by one. He told Oggy that he thought that probably only one was broken and one just dislocated, but that to be sure he should have them X-rayed in Bodmin. The nurse would clean up and bandage the others, which seemed to be just grazed and swollen.

Was there anything else, Doctor Hoskin asked, and Oggy remembered the root cause of his woes, his asteroids. The medical term is 'haemorrhoids', Dr Hoskin said. Whatever the name, the subsequent examination had not been an overly pleasurable experience for either man.

'So, pull your slacks and pants up again Mr Sloggett,' said the doctor, and flopped the latex gloves into a bin.

'What are they like then doctor? Them hasterhoids?'

'Haemorrhoids. Well…' he hesitated. 'They are a little inflamed, but you can get cream. Any chemist, or ValuCheaps,' said the doctor.

'Rhodda's or Tregenna's?'

'No, no, Mr Sloggett' he said. 'Proper haemorrhoid cream, like ointment, is what you require. I know it's organic, but the clotted thing is an old wife's tale.'

'Oh...'

'Now while I've got you here, I think maybe we should give you a bit of a check-up, an MOT so to speak. It's just that you are rather red in the face.'

Whilst Oggy assured him that he'd always had that flushed appearance, chiefly because he was ginger, the good doctor proceeded to take his blood pressure and a sample of blood, and he peered deeply into lots of unpleasant nooks and crannies that had not been inspected for years, and asked him about what he ate, and how regular he was and what his stools were like, and if he smoked or if he had ever smoked, or if he took drugs or had ever taken drugs, or if he drank and if so how many units a week and what, and how much exercise he took. Oh, and could he give a sample in the bottle, not here, behind the screen please and take it to nurse. By the end of it all Oggy was so exhausted that any exercise at all was quite out of the question.

Emma and the children didn't go to the beach. It would have felt awkward to be near Mervin after what had passed between them the previous day. In a way she was relieved that it was launch day for the Emporium, and that she and the kids would be expected to float around as part of the grand illusion of Huge!'s happy family all being part of the community. She got the kids togged up in their surfer's hoodys, and put on a nice nautical pink and navy striped top herself, and hand in hand they all walked up to Daddy's new Emporium.

Down at Mother's, Oggy rocked back in his chair from the kitchen table, like he'd been told not to as a boy.

His fingers were in a varied selection of splints and bandages and plasters, and his countenance decidedly downcast. He had told Vi that Dr Hoskin had told him there was nothing else he could do about them, unless he went along to Bodmin to be X-rated. He figured that they would all eventually mend as long as he kept them more or less straight.

'So what about the rest of ya? He's very thorough, Dr Hoskins,' said Vi.

'Thorough! Thorough!! He's bloody thorough all right. Hellfire, he been everywhere, all over me like a bloody rash he been. I goes in with a broke little finger and comes out with me asteroids in flames, high cholostemy levels and I got blood pressure, and now I can't even pick me nose nor scratch me ass…'

'Course you got blood pressure, you silly old sod.'

'…and I ain't allowed to drink or smoke or take no drugs…'

'You never have anyway. Might loosen you up a bit if you did.'

'Yea, well, I'm loose enough by all accounts.'

Cheel walked in with a bowl full of pastry and slammed it on the table. 'Mum's right, father. You needs to loosen up. Take a chill pill,' she said.

'Here we go. Another quack in the family. What's the matter with her upstairs then, Doctor Cheel? A serious case of terminal termination I should think.'

'Nan says she isn't well enough to come down, and that she'll do another bowl-full like this sat up in bed and it'll probably be her last,' she said.

'Anything else?' asked Oggy.

'She says she got flour and marg all over her sheets, she needs more special water and can she have some lard. Oh, and she says the pantry's a funny place,' said Cheel, and shrugged.

'Special water my ass.'

'You're lucky she'll make pastry sat up in bed, father!'

'Right darlin',' said Vi, ignoring him. 'You need to get plenty of practice for tonight. So Uncle Clar and me will put the pasties together, and you can season and concentrate on the crimp, ok?'

'Right on Mum.'

'Shall I switch the oven on ready for you? According to the doctor everything is knackered, but I can still just about do that one-fingered,' volunteered Oggy.

Vi and Cheel looked up at him, but neither of them said a single word, which Oggy sensibly took as a no.

When they had completed the first batch, and laid them out row upon row on the trays, Vi and Cheel carried them out to the oven and slid them in. Cheel checked the clock and the timer, and then the temperature, and switched it on, and she and her Mum went back into the kitchen.

'Shall we have a cup of tay before we do the next lot?' asked Uncle Clar.

'Lovely, Uncle Clar,' said Vi.

'What about you Oggy?'

'Have you got a straw?' he said.

A large crowd was gathering outside the old chapel, all anticipating the grand opening of the World's First Pasty Emporium. Before all the kitchen and shop staff had arrived, Huge! had got the old Treleaven oven filled up with the mass produced pasties from the factory, and now with everyone at their stations, he gave the staff their pre-opening, inspirational pep talk. Cameras rolling of course.

'Well ladies and gentlemen, it's just a matter of minutes before we open the old chapel doors to all those wonderful folk outside. I just want to thank you all for working so hard to get this project up and running. It's been brilliant! So, everyone to their positions, get peeling and slicing and dicing and rolling and crimping, and let's show them how we make pasties here in Tredogend! Ladies, open the doors!'

Outside, the cameras were craned up into an elevated spot above the crowd, and there was a massive cheer and waving of hands in the air as the old key was turned in the lock and the masses poured into the chapel, where the lights flashed and music blared in an excited, over the top frenzy.

Vast projections of Huge! imparting the secrets of pasty wisdom lit up the wall spaces that had not already been taken up with the huge old sepia photos or TV screens, and a giant glittered pasty hung as a disco ball down from the centre of the ceiling and revolved slowly, casting out reflected shards of light onto the scene below.

Nigel sidled up behind Huge! with a cameraman and sound man in tow.

'Okay Huge!,' he said. 'Now, you've got to talk to some of these as they come in. Let's grab one. You choose.'

'Oh, I'd rather not,' he hissed. 'Look at them all, for Christ's sake.'

'Any Huge!, just go up to somebody,' said the director.

Huge! tutted. 'Well, let's try womble woman there, and the shrivelled shrew,' he muttered, and dragged Nigel and the crew over towards a short, plump lady with more than a hint of a small moustache, and a hairy mole on her cheek. She had a crumpled face and hat, and was dowager-humped in a long tweed coat that reached down to her purple swollen ankles. She was matroning her inoffensively beiged and rather bewildered looking husband, who was clearly in need of constant care.

Huge! stepped over to the couple. 'Hi,' he said. 'How lovely to see you here today. What do you think of my makeover of the old chapel?'

'Last time I was in here, dear, was for Doreen's funeral.'

'Doreen?' said Huge!.

'Packed it was. More than there is in here today. Oh, hello Edith.'

'How are you, dear?' said Edith, who had wandered into shot.

'Oh, so so. Me hubby's a bit wisht. Waterworks again.'

'Dear of him,' said Edith. The beige shrew grinned inanely. The camera rolled on. 'All right then, Morley?' she enquired kindly.

Huge!, very much on the outside of the conversation, was beginning to feel rather surplus to requirements.

'He won't know you, Edith. Doctor Hoskin's put him on warfarin now,' confided womble woman.

'Oh dear, rats too? It never rains, does it. They say they're everywhere,' said Edith. 'Never more than six feet away.'

'I dearly love Doctor Hoskin though. Wouldn't have any of they others.'

'Ain't keen on that new one. Looks a little bit…you know…to me.'

'Excuse me ladies,' said Huge! politely. 'Can I interrupt and ask what you think of our new open kitchen? Would that be ok?'

'Yes dear. That's right where Doreen was laid, where that meat cabinet is. I sat over there with Pearl and Les, right by the swedes. He's gone along now too, poor old Les, very sad,' she said.

'Yes, yes…' said Huge!.

'Pearl haven't been so good lately neither. She got nerves, mind.'

'Nerves?'

'Yes, terrible nerves. She still sees Les sat in the front room, stroking Mr Marmalade on his lap.'

Huge! had had quite enough and turned to Nigel.

'Look, I've got bloody nerves now Nige, for God's sake! Who's Mr fucking Marmalade when he's at home?' he hissed.

'Probably a cat, Huge!. Like a ginger Tom maybe?' whispered Nigel.

'Her father was the same mind. He ended up with that agoraphobia…' said the womble lady.

'I wish she had sodding agoraphobia,' snapped Huge! to Nigel.

'Calm, Huge!' said Nigel. 'You have to engage. Take it easy.'

'Well, that's two minutes of my life I'll never have again,' he said in exasperation, as they moved off through the crowd.

'What about him?' asked Nigel.

'His hair's…all wrong.'

'What?'

'He's cut it himself with a knife and bloody fork, Nige. Have you seen a hairdresser anywhere here?'

'No, that's true. Her there then?'

'Oh for fuck's sake Nige, no! It's a cookery programme, not wildlife on one.'

'Her then, with the blonde hair? With her back to us.'

'Please. She's got an ass like a police horse, Nigel.'

The woman turned. She was eating a pasty.

It was Inga.

They gave up on the idea, and instead the crew filmed at the counter, where a seemingly never-ending queue of punters lined up to have their complimentary opening day Huge! pasties popped into their Huge! pasty bags by Huge! himself.

And as he popped them in, Nigel made it Huge!'s rather unpalatable duty to kiss and flirt with all the tooty, fruity old ladies, as high as kites on Bristol Cream and HRT, who brandished their stale biscuit handbags, widdle-whiffed and stuffed stiff full of used paper tissues and water tablets and bags of icky, sticky, fluffy sweets and treats, and slyed-away, hideaway butter pats and sugar sachets and mini cartons of long life milk liberated on mysterious coach trips all the way down at Hamburger Hill.

Some had teeth, some had some teeth, some had had some teeth and now had dentures; there were lewd old ladies and rude old ladies, some straight laced and smooth faced old ladies, some quite hairy and frankly rather scary old ladies; there were stubbly ones and bubbly ones, and musty ones, dusty ones and downright crusty ones, and widows and spinsters, pink and blue rinsers, and even a mincer who'd minced slyly in under the radar. He got an accidental peck as well.

And of course, Huge! kissed all the *young* ladies too.

Especially the blonde ones.

Down at Mother's Pasty Shop, Oggy flipped the sign, one fingered, from 'closed' to 'open', and sat on his stool and waited for his first customer.

And waited.

And waited.

Emma and the kids walked into the Emporium and were overwhelmed by all that they saw. Emma was also overwhelmed with irritation at the attractive blonde lady still at Huge!'s side, a lady who seemed to be very familiar with him.

They were ushered by Nigel and the crew right to the front of the queue where, being a consummate actress, she gave Huge! a big kiss of congratulation, and he made a Huge! fuss of her while Inga quickly made herself scarce elsewhere.

'Darling, my god. Look what you've done. It's fantastic! And the old oven, it's beautiful. It's just like that one in the old pasty shop down the road,' she said.

'Ya, isn't it?' said Huge! .

Nigel sidled up to her.

'Hi Em, isn't it great?' he said. 'Thanks for signing that deed, by the way.'

'Deed?' she said.

'Darling,' interrupted Huge! ever so quickly. 'Here you are, one each for you and the kids.'

He handed her four Huge! bags, each with his own face on it, and each with a pasty in it, and then picked up one himself, and they all smiled for the camera. They peeled the pasty bags back to reveal the top halves of the pasties, secretly baked up in the outlet on the Davidstow moors by Krno and the boys the previous night, and bit into them.

Huge! let out a long, rapturous 'mmmm' as he chewed away, and Emma nodded in agreement, narrowing her eyes and added her own long 'mmmm', in perfect harmony with his. Huge! held his pasty out for a close up, and the lens zoomed in on the steaming mass of pastry, potato, swede, onion and skirt beef.

'Wow!' said Huge! . 'Now *that* really is the taste of Cornwall.'

Quenelle looked down at his pasty, and nudged Julienne. They both wrinkled their noses and stuck their tongues out as far as they could in a classic child's 'yeeuch!' gesture. Little Goujon held his pasty up to his Dad.

'They're not as nice as we usually have, Daddy,' he said.

'Whoa!' called Huge!.

'Cut!' called Nigel.

Huge! bent over to his youngest.

'What do you mean darling?' he said.

'They're just not as nice as those we get from that other shop. There's little black hard bits,' he said. Huge! picked a little black hard bit from the boy's pasty, popped it into his fleshy mouth and ate it.

'That'll be milled black peppercorn, darling,' he said.

'Yeeuch, Dad,' said Goujon. Quenelle gagged.

'Nasty,' said Julienne, and shoved hers into Emma hands. 'I don't want it Mummy.'

'Don't worry,' said Nigel. 'We can cut that bit. Now I just want to do a few cut-in expressions Huge!, so we can add them into the edit as we go along. Let's have surprise for starters...'

Huge! opened his mouth and raised his eyebrows, and looked more bemused or confused than surprised.

'A bit more with the mouth...'

He opened his mouth a bit more, and now looked like a confused or bemused wide-mouthed toad.

'Good. Now, looking interested and nodding a bit.'

Huge! did all this, and then he did 'amazed', 'puzzled', 'curious', 'jolly' and 'satisfied'.

'Ok Huge!, great. Now can you give me "earnest", you know, sort of "genuine", um, sort of engaging in a caring sort of way. Do you get me?'

'No.'

'Well, sincere, you know?'

'Oh right, okay. How about this?' Huge! pulled an expression. 'Or this?'

'I'm not sure. What do you think Tom?' asked Nigel.

'Not really doing it, Nige.'

'Tom? What's wrong with it?' demanded Huge!.

'Well, it's sort of ...constipated if I'm honest...not in a bad way though.'

'Constipated? Sod off Tom. Inga?'

'No.'

'No what?'

'Just no,' she said, shaking her head. 'Tom's right.'

'No, never mind Huge!, you can't do it all,' said Nigel. 'Just a quick bit of heritage, and then you're just about done until the crimping competition.'

'Sure Nige, and will you remind me to tell those bloody bloodsuckers to use ground white pepper, not black. It's little details like that can spoil all this. There was no black pepper used in the one they're using as a template.'

'No problem Huge!. Ok, let's start over here, shall we?' said Nigel.

Although Digory had been in for his Cornish Giant with the pastry 'D' on it, Oggy had all but given up on selling any more pasties that day, and climbed down off his stool and went back into the kitchen, where Cheel was being put through her paces by Vi and Uncle Clar, and was crimping the pastry on dummy pasties with the speed of light.

Ten seconds. Faster even than Oggy himself.

Proper job.

*

Huge! faced the lens from in front of Oggy's old Treleaven pasty oven, standing in a happy family bunch with Emma and the kids.

'So, it's with such pride that I reveal my own family's local Cornish connection in this, the great pasty makeover. The oven behind me is an old family heirloom, much prized and made by the Treleaven family early in the previous century and handed down to us so that we can still use it today.'

He stroked the front of the door and the handle. It was Emma's turn to look puzzled.

'Emma's family have entrusted the Treleaven pasty oven to our project and quest, and we thank them and I know that this old piece is going to do us proud.'

Huge! was almost a little tearful. Emma looked on with incredulity.

'The Treleaven oven still baking pasties in my family after all these years. You can't buy that, can you?' he sniffed.

It was the expression of sincerity that Nigel had been searching for from Huge! earlier, and lasted from the start of the piece right through to the end. Nigel cut the take.

'What's all that about, Hugo?' demanded Emma.

'All what, darling?'

'All that family heirloom claptrap.'

'Oh just a bit of fluff for the TV darling. Underlining our local credentials and all that,' he said.

'We haven't bloody got any, Hugo!'

'Well, not as such. But we just put it out there and if half the punters swallow it, job done.'

'It was your maiden name Em, wasn't it? Treleaven?' asked Nigel.

'Be quiet Nigel. This is between man and wife…' said Huge! .

'What are you on about, Nigel?' said Emma.

'The deed poll business,' said Nigel.

'Deed poll? What deed poll?'

'Over to you, Huge!,' said Nigel.

Chapter Fourteen
The Fastest Crimper in the West

She said, I know thee now,
I knew thee all along,
I knew thee in the dark,
And I did it for a lark...

'Lamorna' – Cornish traditional song

The Beast of Bodmin, Constable 696 Carthew Carew, had hung up old sparky for the day, on the hook behind his living room door, and he was lying prostrate across his sofa with his legs dangling limply over the arm and his feet almost touching the floor, and was thumbing excitedly through the latest book in his collection, *A Huge! Life*, an autobiography of Huge!'s fascinating life in kitchens. There were lots of photos, which suited Carew in a number of ways.

He was hardly paying any attention at all to the episode of *Corrie*. It had been sandwiched between the new *Huge! in Cornwall* programme about the conversion of the old chapel in Tredogend, and the following one, a live broadcast special of Huge!'s competition, 'The Fastest Crimper in the West – Live!' He could hardly believe that as well as being here in his own living room, Huge! was so close by in Tredogend. In the flesh!

The constable remembered vividly the outbreak of graffiti there a day or so before, a crime that he had still not cracked, and despite the wisdom of his colleagues in the control room, he still wondered whether Dead Dog

Wong did in fact have anything to do with it after all. Whatever, he determined to solve the mystery, for that would be certain to lead to his meeting his TV hero, super celebrity chef Huge! himself.

With *Corrie* finished, Carew sat up and put the interesting book down and readied himself for the exciting highlight of the evening's viewing. He watched and listened as an over excited voice whipped the live audience into a kind of wild, whooping, clapping frenzy over the rather unexceptional one hundred pounds cash prize, and the camera panned across the self-conscious competitors lined up around the Huge! kitchen table in the Emporium.

Carew watched intently as Huge! went from one to the other around the table and spoke to them all in turn.

'And where are you from, my love?'

'Padstow.'

There was a little good natured booing and some laughter from the audience.

'Padstein, eh? I hope you haven't been getting any help from my old chum Rick…'

Some folk tittered, and he moved quickly along to the next.

'And what do you think you would do with the hundred pounds if you won it?'

'Well, I…'

'Yes, I know, it's a lot of money isn't it? And do you know what, in addition we've decided to add in a day's free tuition here at the Huge! Pasty Emporium in Tredogend. A day's tuition in, yes you've guessed it, pasty making….'

Egged on by Nigel and Inga's waving of hands, there was a massive cheer and applause from the live audience.

'…where I'm going to show the lucky winner how to make gourmet pasties the likes of which the world has never seen…'

The audience made a collective 'Whoooo!' noise.

'So, my darling,' said Huge! to a very pregnant thirty-something lady with knacker's yard teeth and a rather equine face. 'What's your name?'

'Sharon. Sharon Smith.'

'And where are you from?'

'Stenalees, Huge!.'

'And why are you here today, Sharon?'

'I've always wanted this Huge!,' she said, a little tearfully. 'It's been a real journey. My partner and kids are out there supporting me tonight.'

The camera panned in on them and they waved and cheered. 'A journey? Really?' asked Huge!. 'Has it been emotional for you all?'

'No, I mean I had to come up from Stenalees. Traffic's hellish, and we had to come in the back of his van, with all his tools and fibre glass stuff and that.'

'Aww, there they are,' said Huge!, ignoring her and waving out to her family. 'What's he called, your partner?'

'He's called Bill. Bill Bottallick.'

'Where did you meet him, Sharon?'

'Down by the Eden Project. It was an online thing, so…'

'How romantic! In the tropical dome?'

'Not exactly, no.'

'Where then? Do tell,' he teased.

'Well, in his van, you know, down this lane thing.'

'And you got how many kids? Six?' he asked. 'So this'll be number seven!'

'Yea, this is little Eden,' she said, looking down and smoothing her tummy.

'Do you think you'll win?'

'I'm going to give it my best shot, Huge!.'

'Thank you, thank you so much and good luck,' said Huge!, moving swiftly on. 'I hope you can get close enough to the table, it's quite a dome you've got there!'

Cheel stood stiffly. She felt uncomfortable. She dreaded the celebrity chef's attentions. But they were inevitably coming her way. Next.

'Now then, we have a very young competitor in our midst. What's your name my darling?'

'Cheel Sloggett,' she said sullenly, eyes fixed downcast on the table in front of her.

'Gosh, you've got a lot of earrings and things haven't you. Must be a nightmare going through the airport,' he joked.

'I never been to no airport,' she said. 'Except Davidstow.'

'Davidstow? That's a new one on me, my love. Now then, what do you think of our extra special bonus prize tonight? A day baking pasties with me, Huge!, in my Huge! cookery school?'

Cheel looked up and glared right at the celebrity chef, and smiled a joyless, cold as ice smile.

'You can't teach me nothing about pasties,' she said.

Oggy and Uncle Clar and Vi were watching the live broadcast at home in the lounge, whilst Mother watched upstairs in her bedroom on her own little set.

'That's it, Cheel! You bloody tell him!' Oggy shouted at the screen.

'Calm down, darlin',' said Vi. 'He can't hear you.'

'Coming down here with his fancy ways telling we how to make pasties,' he grumbled. He jumped up and shouted through the artexed ceiling, 'Are you listening to this Mother? Or are you still snuffing it up there?'

Mother gave two bangs on the floor above to confirm that she was indeed alive and listening.

'She's sounding stronger,' said Uncle Clar.

'When it suits, Uncle Clar,' said Vi.

'Hark now, hark,' hissed Oggy.

Huge! placed a fatherly arm around the reluctant Cheel's shoulder. She grimaced as he asked, 'And what would you do with all that prize money?'

'Give it to me father to pay some bills,' she replied.

'Give it to her father to pay some bills,' repeated Oggy. 'That dear little maid.'

'She's a good 'un darlin',' said Vi.

Mother thumped the floor above them in affirmation of Cheel's generosity.

'All right, Mother! You'll crack the ceiling! We bloody heard,' shouted Oggy, and then whispered. 'I prefers it when she's at death's door, missus.'

'Now, now...'

'Give it to father to pay some bills. The dear little soul,' he sniffed, and Vi looked across at Oggy, staring transfixed at the screen, and believed that she saw something very close to a tear in the corner of his eye.

Huge! positioned himself at the head of the table.

'So then, pasty crimpers. I invite you all to roll up your sleeves and get yourselves ready for the crimping countdown...'

They all turned up their sleeves, and revealed a selection of forearms, some fleshy pink, some more muscular ...

'The first competitor to crimp ten pasties will be the winner. Ten, nine, eight…'

Some were thin, some flabby, some dark skinned and some light…

'…seven, six, five…'

Some were smooth, some a little hairy…

'…four, three, two…'

Some had bangles on their wrists, and one a nice watch…

'…one, GO!'

And one had a tattoo.

WOK.

And the fingers of the hand at the end of that forearm attacked the pastry with such mesmeric speed and precision that on screen they appeared as just a blur.

Cheel's fingers.

Oggy and Vi and Uncle Clar screamed at the telly in front of them.

'Go on Cheel!'

'You can do it babe!'

'Go on, go on, go on!!'

'Yeesss! She done it!'

There was a banging from the floor upstairs.

'All right Mother, we can see, we can see!' shouted Oggy. 'Stop yer banging or you'll bring down me bloody artex!'

They watched as Cheel stepped back from the table, and clasped her hands behind her back, and an air horn blasted out amidst the rapturous applause and cheers and whooping. No one else had even come close to crimping five pasties, let alone ten.

Huge! strode over and grasped her wrist and lifted her arm aloft and waved it in triumph.

Mother leaned out of her bed and banged and shouted at the floor. 'She got it, that maid! She got the touch! Mark my words!' But no one heard, for below her all was bedlam, and Vi and Oggy and Uncle Clar danced and kicked a frenzied wild conga around and around the room, and sang 'Happy Days are Here Again' at the tops of their joyous voices.

But happy days were not here again, for back at his semi, Constable 696 Carthew Carew was also highly charged with emotion and excitement at the TV spectacular. He was jumping up and down on his sofa in sheer unadulterated disbelief, for he could see the triumphant arm that was being waved aloft by his hero.

He heard Huge! shout 'And the winner is...*Cheel Sloggett from Tredogend!*' and he saw the audience go ballistic.

He studied the screen closely, and all he could focus on was the word tattooed on the girl's forearm.

He grinned as the camera zoomed into Cheel's less than ecstatic face, and she stared right down the lens and into his living room.

Carew got as close as he could to the screen, and stared right back.

'WOK...' he laughed manically. 'I know 'ee now. Gotcha!'

Chapter Fifteen
The Robber's Retreat

And away, and away, and away,
To those caves in yonder mountains,
Where the robbers retreat…

'The Cadgwith Anthem' – *Cornish Traditional*

The following morning, the mood in Mother's was transformed. The ebullient and overjoyed Oggy was singing aloud like he hadn't done in ages. He jigged a lively polka to his own raucous, bawdy, jolly-rodgering overture of 'The Drunken Sailor', with all his rollicking, bollicking accompaniments to the *'Hooray, up she rises, ear-lie in the morning!'* bit.

He encored and entranced his captive family audience with a lewdly ribald medley of 'Blow the Man Down', 'The Whores of Baltimore', 'Bobby Shaftoe' and 'Friggin in the Riggin', and all was right in his world as hornpipingly hot, he danced like a firecracker around the kitchen table and clacked two tablespoons together as castanets, and then beat out an ear-shattering rhythm on the table with a pair of rolling pins.

Cheel had handed him the prize when she'd got home the previous night, and he'd gratefully trousered the five twenty pound notes in preparation for a little sojourn into Bodmin with his mate Digory to pay first his council tax at the council office, and then on to Trefoyle's gentleman's outfitters for his new choir badge and tie, and finally another attempt to get some trousers, in Save the Children this time.

Pasty production was still foremost on the agenda. Oggy carried a catering pack of flour, two tubs each of marg and lard up to Mother's bedroom as best he could, and dumped it down on the floor next to her bed. Then he went down to fetch the plastic water container from the back of the premises, and brought it up for her. He passed her a chopping board.

'And how are you ear-lie this morning, Mother?' he sang cheerily.

'Struggling,' she replied, sitting up in bed and not looking at him at all. 'Pass me my rolling pin boy, and me water.'

'She done well last night, that Cheel.'

'She got the touch. She's special. You need to know that,' she said, and held up the container. 'And tell your mate that I needs more of this.'

Up at the chapel too, there was an undeniable air of triumph at the previous day's opening extravaganza. The team sat around the big table and planned ahead.

'Right, the Emporium's open again and trading and we've got hordes of visitors again today. What a success!'

'We've got to keep them coming Nige,' said Huge!.

'Okay Huge!,' said Nigel. 'Well, the highways department are putting up all the brown tourist signs today. Three up at the main Tredogend turning signpost and two large ones at the North Cornwall direction signs, on the A30 and A38.'

'Brown signs?' said Inga, already chewing on a breakfast pasty.

'Yup, you know the ones, with the English Heritage rose on them,' said Nigel.

'Great Nige. What do they say?' asked Huge!.

'Cornish Pasty Heritage Site, with a pasty symbol on it.'

'Oh, and my name?'

'Yea, don't panic Huge!, your name is on there too.'

'With the exclamati…'

'Yea, with the exclamation mark, of course Huge!. And we've negotiated to get your face and name on the pasty shop window at Paddington Station, instead of that stupid inanely grinning pirate. It's gonna be Huge! at the gateway to the West Country.'

'Wow,' said Inga, through a mouthful of beef and potato and onion, not really concentrating on the briefing. 'God, that's hot.' She fanned her lips with her spare hand.

Huge! glanced at her and gently shook his head in apparent disapproval.

'Nige,' he said. 'Have we considered contacting UNESCO and making this a world heritage site?'

A world heritage site for the pasty or for you, wondered Nigel, never any more surprised at the sheer astounding grandeur of Huge!'s ambitions.

'Uhh, no. Not quite yet, Huge!,' he said. But, well, you know…'

Vi and Uncle Clar got on with all the pasty making in the kitchen, whilst Oggy did all that he could with his squash-buckled fingers, which wasn't much but at least he was singing joyfully. Until, that is, there was a loud banging at the tinkling shop door, and Oggy looked out and saw Constable 696 Carew's heavy prehistoric brow peering in again. The singing stopped.

'Hell, not again' muttered Oggy as he walked out towards the door. 'What the bloody hell does he want so early in the bloody morning?'

Carew banged again.

'They ain't ready yet. Give us a couple of hours,' shouted Oggy through the glass.

'It's not about that. Open the door,' said Carew.

'What do you want? I got blood pressure!'

'What's that got to do with the price of fish? Open up!'

'I got high cholostemy too, mind...'

'Just open the door.'

Cheel was upstairs and sitting on her bed, legs crossed, and chanting to herself from her booklet.

'...and in token of my sincerity I offer my hand to my opponent, in the words of my forefathers...'

She stopped as she heard the shouting and the shop door rattle and tinkle open below, and the policeman being let in. She listened, her ear at the floorboard.

'Right, mister,' sneered Carew. 'Do you know a Miss Cheel Sloggett?'

Cheel jumped down from her bed like a cat. She hurriedly pulled on and laced up her walking boots. She grabbed her rucksack, and shoved in her tent and her waterproofs, then her mobile and some Kendal mint cake and a bottle of water, two cans of spray paint and a map of Bodmin Moor, and she dropped in her maneless My Little Pony into a side pocket, with its gaudy pink head poking out.

But there was something missing, she thought. Damn. Her iPad. It was down behind the shop counter. No matter, she had her mobile, and that would have to do. Maybe, just maybe she thought, the time for cyber wars had now passed. Maybe the time for direct action had just dawned.

Stealthily, she crept from her bedroom, along the landing to the rear of the building, and lifted the sash window at the end. She lowered herself out onto a galvanised shed roof, and then catlike sprung down into the yard and out of the back gate, and away.

By the time her father had come to the foot of the stairs and shouted up to her, and then blundered up and into her bedroom to get her to come down and speak to the officer, Cheel was gone like a long dog.

Away to the moors.

'So what's she supposed to have done, darlin'?' asked Vi.

'Something about a tattoo on the maid's arm, Carew said. Saw her on telly last night he did,' said Oggy.

'We'll ask her when she gets back,' said Vi.

Mother pushed the door open, and stood staring into the kitchen.

'Well I'm damned, you're looking well for a woman who died three times yesterday Mother. Feeling better are we?' asked Oggy.

Mother ignored him.

'She won't be around for a while yet, so I've come down to help,' she said.

'That's all I bloody need. Me fingers is busted, I got blood pressure and high cholostemy, me asshole's on fire and now you'm back.'

'Shhh now, Oggy. What do you mean Mother?' said Uncle Clar.

'I seen her leave. She was packed.'

'Packed?'

'With a rucksack and stuff. Loaded right up. She've gone.'

There was a faint rumble from behind the pantry door. Mother twitched.

'I told you,' she said nervously. 'Something funny's going on.'

*

Nigel was drawing their production meeting to a close.

'Okay,' he said. 'Anything else?'

'Yup,' said Huge!. 'Had a brilliant, *another,* brilliant idea Nige.'

'What's that Huge!? Not the UNESCO thing…'

'No, no. I've just one word to say to you, Nige,' he said, and he rocked back in his chair, looked from left to right and licked his lower lip. 'Huge!Fest.'

' Huge!Fest? That's two words, isn't it Tom?'

'Well, it depends I guess on how…'

'Shut up Tom, it's one word and it'll be a festival of all things pasty *and* all things Huge!, all right?. We get a load of stalls flogging Cornish grub, but with the Huge! marquee right in the middle. No, hold that, marquees are too small. Too village fête! We'll have the Huge! big top, all bright and stripey, stuffed full with demos, competitions like last night's, music, lights, all the lot. There'll be bands, fairground stuff, bunting, streamers, and we can get a giant pasty-shaped balloon flying high up above it all, with Huge! written all over it, and we'll get a couple of celeb chefs down on the lash and butter 'em up a bit and get 'em to do some cooking and swear at the punters and stuff for a laugh. That fat piss artist who can hardly string two words together, what's he called again…'

'Larry Ramsbottom?'

'Yeah him. Can't cook for toffee. He'd be good value! And that shagnasty frog, that oh-so-sophisticated, smooth-talking, egotistical twot, what's he called?' asked Huge!.

'Is it Huge!?' chirped Tom, who attempted a laugh, but it was without doubt a tumbleweed moment for him. Even so, Inga threw him a glance. She found it quite amusing.

'Serious now Tom,' said Nigel. 'You mean Marcel St Jacques Buffon, Huge!?'

'Whatever, him. Get him down to rattle a few cages. Let's big it up Nige! Huge!Fest baby! Let's make Woodstock look like some shite picnic,' said Huge!. 'And no one thought that was funny, Tom.'

'Are you on it, Inga?' asked Nigel.

She was busy on her iPad.

'Yea, okay. I'll need to go back up to town. Just booking my ticket right now. Okay, done. Could somebody get me to Bodmin station?'

'I'll get you a cab…' said Nigel.

'No,' said Huge!. 'It's ok, Nige. I'm going that way Inga…'

'Oh, just one thing Huge!,' said Nigel. 'The black pepper. You've got to remind the guys up at the outlet to use ground white.'

Huge nodded back at Nigel, and he and Inga left the meeting and stepped out onto the street, where the one-legged gull above seemed to laugh as it shat polka dot all over Huge!'s flowery Boden blouse, and yet managed to miss Inga, the area of outstanding natural beauty, completely.

It took Cheel just over an hour to jog cross-country up as far as Dordigor Farm. She was hoping to see her father's mate Uncle Digory, but the DigsCab wasn't there and she deduced that he wasn't at home, rather out on a job.

She wandered around the jerry built, tumbledown outbuildings. Trelawney, Pam and Brenda gave her a fleeting glance of extreme indifference as she nosed her way into a low shed. The quad bike was parked at the rear on the dry, earthy, straw-strewn floor, all dusty and rusty and seemingly quite forgotten, hidden behind some bales. She heaved them up by the twine and threw them out of the doorway, and on inspection discovered to her delight that the key was still in the quad's ignition. Cheel sat astride and turned it, and the engine purred into life. She manoeuvred it into the light at the entrance to the shed.

Cheel felt troubled. She knew that Digory would have lent her the quad with no qualms at all, but he was not there to ask.

She looked towards his house. 'Sorry Uncle Digory,' she said to herself. 'I'm only borrowing it. But needs must. You'll understand, I know you will.'

She revved the quad, and screeched out of the yard and out through the gates of Dordigor Farm and away.

Dapper little Digory Hicks had been on another Newquay airport run in the DigsCab, wearing his gilet with the 'DigsCabs' logo, and was pondering the next concert appearance of the Tredogend Fisherman's Choir and not really paying attention to the road at all, when like a bat out of hell, a quad came screaming around the corner towards him. The rider leaned right over to one side and swerved around the taxi and off, up and away and along the lane towards the moors, leaving a cloud of dust in its wake.

When he pulled into his yard at Dordigor Farm and saw the scattered bales, he feared the worst, and jumped out and rushed to the back of his shed, and saw that his old quad was gone.

Digory ran indoors, and picked up the phone and immediately dialled the constabulary.

'Hello. Police? I'd like to report a stolen vehicle.'

'Yes. What sort of a vehicle sir?'

'A quad bike dear.'

'A quad bike. Now sir, am I right in thinking that a vehicle such as this might have four wheels?'

'Yes dear, that's correct.'

'I thought as much, we usually find that,' said the operative. 'Now sir, what might your date of birth be?'

Cheel waited next to the Tredogend junction, just off the main A30, tucked in behind a large road sign. When the busy streams of traffic had cleared in both directions, she emerged slowly on the quad, then throttled back to cross to the track on the opposite side of the main road. Cheel looked back at the 'Tredogend 7 miles' sign, and noticed that something was different, for beneath it was a new one.

A brown one.

Emblazoned with the English Heritage rose.

The Cornish Pasty Heritage Site.

Huge!.

Mervin was sitting outside the surf shack when the text came through. He read it aloud to himself.

'M, had to clear out and go to ground. Don't worry about me. Let them know I'm okay. I'll keep in touch. Sis x.'

He texted her back, 'Where u then?'

The reply came quickly.

'On the moor x.'

'Where on the moor?' he asked.

Another 'x' was all she sent.

Digory was still engaged with the constabulary operative on the other end of the phone in Exeter. It had been some minutes now.

'Now sir, do you have a chassis number?'

'A what?' said Digory.

'Chassis number sir. It's a number on the chassis. It'll be on the registration document. You do have a registration document, sir? It is an offence not to have one, I should tell you,' said the operative. 'There is a fine…'

'Oh, I don't want no fine, my dear. Hold the line,' said Digory.

'Where can she have gone?' said Vi.

Uncle Clar shook his head. Mother too.

Oggy walked in with the morning's post and slapped the letters onto the table.

'More bastard bills,' he said. 'Water rates. Thirty quid. Bang goes me bloody badge and tie and trousers.'

'What's that other one?' asked Vi.

'For Cheel,' said Oggy.

'Might as well open it for her,' said Mother. 'Might be important for the maid.'

Oggy slid one of his bandaged fingers into the envelope and ripped it open. He stared down and studied it. It was headed with the crest of the Cornish Wrestling Association.

'Go on then, darlin', what's it say?'

He read it aloud:

*'Dear Ms Sloggett…*Ms Sloggett, I say…

*Congratulations on your selection for the Ladies Elite Cornish Wrestling Team, and further we would like to confirm your appointment as team captain…*team captain, our maid… *for the forthcoming tournament in Brittany in October.*

We wish you every success in the featherweight division, and have every confidence that you will prove to be a worthy ambassador...there now, ambassador she is... *for our sport and for the county.*

Kind Regards

Terry Polkinghorne (Hon Sec)...Hon Sec, I don't know what one of them is, but it sounds important to me.'

Oggy stood open-mouthed, the letter at his side.

'I never knowed it. Rasslin? Mother, did you know?'

'No, I never.'

'Off to Brittany she is, in October. Captain of the ladies elite whatever that is,' said Oggy.

'All the top girls,' said Vi.

'Ain't no Sloggett been abroad before, Mother,' said Oggy proudly.

'I went to Plymouth, 1968,' said Uncle Clar.

'But not proper abroad Uncle Clar. I know they talks funny in Plymouth, but our maid is breaking new ground, she is,' said Oggy.

'Told you,' said Mother. 'Thing is, where is she now?'

Digory, meanwhile, was a full forty minutes into his reporting of the theft.

'Right sir, that seems to be everything. Now let me give you a crime reference number. Oh, what was your name again?'

'Digory dear.'

'Mr Digory dear?'

'No, no, it's Hicks. Digory Hicks. Mr,' he sighed.

The operative was typing.

'Dig, as in grave, and ory as in...ory. Digory, there we go. And Hicks, with an H. Oh. It doesn't like that, the computer. What's the matter here then, let me get me screen up. Damn, it's gone. Let's try again, now it was one of those quads, wasn't it? How many wheels?'

Cheel rode the quad right into the shell of the abandoned control tower in the middle of Davidstow aerodrome. She jumped off and pitched her survival tent inside the high, crumbling reinforced concrete walls that would offer some protection from the wind, and above all, meant that she could not be seen by the outside world.

She made the inside of the tent comfy, and sat inside and settled herself, and repeated the words of the wrestler's oath to herself, over and again.

'On my honour and the honour of my country, I swear to wrestle without treachery or brutality and in token of my sincerity I offer my hand to my opponent, in the words of my forefathers "Gwary whek yu gwary tek".'

And when satisfied that she had finally memorised it by heart, she took out the Ordnance Survey map of North Cornwall, and marked it in places with a pencil, and began to plan her night manoeuvres.

It had been a busy day in Tredogend, with more tourists than anyone had ever seen before, all drawn by the lure of the TV celebrity chef, but Mother's Pasty shop had been eerily quiet. The Sloggetts all sat around the kitchen table drinking tay. Oggy was talking to Digory on the telephone.

'How many times did you have to tell him?... Three?...Do you think he's all there, Digory? ...Well, that's bloody computers for you, I told you so...Yes, you're right, he must be as thick as two short bricks, he must...'

There was a tinkling of the shop door bell, and Oggy jumped to his feet

'Must go Dig, customer at the counter. See you dreckly,' he said, but sat down again quickly when Mervin popped his head around the door.

'Hello babe,' said Vi.

'All right Mum? Got a message from Cheel, she says she's okay and not to worry.'

'Where is she? France?'

'No, not yet. She's up on the moor somewhere. I don't know where.'

'The moor?' said Mother.

'Don't know where?' blared Oggy. 'Don't know where!?'

'Chill out father. Like, she's cool with it,' said Mervin.

'Chill out? Cool? She'll be bloody chilled out and cool up there all right. What's she been doing to run off like that?' he raged. 'Is she in the shit boy?'

'I don't know, father. She never said. But if you ask me, it's the moors that should be afraid, not her.'

Mother looked at Oggy and nodded in agreement with her grandson.

'He knows,' she said, and left the kitchen.

Chapter Sixteen
Enter the Dragon

'Good play is fair play.' – *a part of the Cornish Wrestler's Oath, to be sworn by all wrestlers prior to any wresting taking place; this passage is normally spoken in the Cornish language.*

Dawn began to break across the dear old county, first up faintly illuminating the vast expanses of the Bodmin Moors. Up at Davidstow, even in the midst of the dense bottle-green forestry plantation, shafts of misty golden light broke through and began to project coniferous shadows upon the walls of the old aeroplane hangar.

One after another after another, the little bats skittered and squeaked their way through the cool morning air, and fat-full of moths and unwary early morning flies and gnats, they flapped back in through their secret hole and into the beamed rafters of their roost, where they wrapped their wings around themselves and hung upside down by their pointy little claws, right above the plastic storage vats of sliced potatoes and onion and swede.

The quiet of early morn was broken by the hum of a lorry's engine, and the hiss of its brakes as it pulled to a halt outside the front of the hangar.

The hangar door opened, and Krno stepped out cautiously from its brightly lit interior and went to the cab and shook hands with the driver, a Lithuanian who had been in the country less than a fortnight. He beckoned to his mate, who manoeuvred over a decrepitly rusty fork-lift truck, upon the front of which was stacked a teetering pallet of plastic baker's trays, each full of pasties.

One pallet followed another, wobbling over to the rear of the unmarked lorry until it had been filled, the fabric sides flapped down and secured, and the door closed, and then off the driver weaved his way down the near deserted early morning lanes to Tredogend, to deliver his illicit cargo to the lean–to shed at the rear of the Huge! Emporium.

The huddled figures of the Romanian illegals slunk like spectres out of the door, their sad, sunken eyes unused to the natural light that was now streaming in. Rumped-up like winnards and dour-draped black in donkey jackets and hoodies, they hunched wearily to their sleeping bags in the unloved, unlovely and unfurnished mausoleum of a bungalow, where all ten of them slumbered uneasily through their miserable, colourless daylight hours.

The Lithuanian lorry driver had been doing this run for a couple of days now, and thus far had met nothing on the road at all, except a hare lolloping around near the wind farm at Delabole and a freshly squashed cock pheasant down by Slaughter's Bridge, so when a quad came hurtling up the road from the direction of Tredogend, straddled by a helmetless dark rider who swerved the machine around his lorry with such reckless abandon for her own safety, it did rather keep him on his mettle.

And although he had begun to master the rudiments of the English language, he did not quite get the gist of 'Shift out of my road, emmet!'

The highways men were surprised to find that their new brown signs had been vandalised so quickly this time.

There had been many instances before, but this time it seemed that the signs had barely been erected before the English roses were defaced by the familiar sprayed on black discs and white crosses of the St Piran's tags. No sooner had one been reported on the A30, then one came up on the A38, both on the North Cornwall turnings, followed by three more at the three Tredogend turnings on the B3745. It was, as they say, a spate.

But these were different. For across the Cornish Pasty Heritage Site logo and the pasty symbol, something quite new had been sprayed.

WOK.

'Mum,' called Quenelle. 'There's a lady at the door.'

Emma peeped out a side window, and went around and opened the sea-gem green door with its shiny brass mermaid knocker.

'Hi?' said Emma.

'Oh, hello,' said Vi. 'I saw your card in the beach shop window. Always used to put notices up in the post office for people, but they closed that.'

'What a shame. So sad for a small community.'

'Well, yeah. But he was a miserable old so and so to be honest. Fingerless gloves and all that. No one used to use it any more…'

'I'm sorry,' said Emma. 'Look, come in. The thing is, we've been let down by the cleaner, and I need someone to help out. Only a couple of hours a week.'

'That's fine,' said Vi. 'I was going to say I can help out for a bit until you find someone permanent. Is that any good?'

'Oh yes, please. When do you think you could start?'

'I can do a couple of hours now if you like. Same again next week.'

'Perfect,' said Emma. 'Really good. Sorry...I recognise you now, you're the lady from the pasty shop, aren't you?'

The ladies smiled and shook hands, and Vi grabbed the hoover and mop and bucket, and the polish and duster and bathroom and kitchen sprays, and began to spruce through Fisherman's Cottage as she cleaned through Mother's daily. As clean as a pin.

Huge! and the crew from *Huge! in Cornwall* were surprised to find another batch of black and white symbols sprayed across the front of the Pasty Emporium in Tredogend when they arrived to open up and start the day. Constable 696 Carthew Carew insisted that the whole building be taped off and treated with forensic care as if it were the scene of a serious crime, for this was the second such incident in a matter of days, and said that no one should go near lest they contaminate possible evidence.

His control room, however, managed to calm him down and persuade him that a gruesome double murder in Plymouth and a messy GBH at a stag do down in Newquay were rather more pressing engagements for the force's scenes of crime officers than some criminal damage; albeit there seemed to be a spate of it.

Huge! and Nigel had said that they would rather not wait until Thursday week for the forensics, for they still had all the arrangements to complete for the coming weekend's Huge!Fest. It was a tall order even for Nigel, but he had turned things around for Huge! before and was determined to do it again. He got the custard tarts scrubbing off the spray paint and restoring the outside of the pasty Emporium to its former pristine condition.

By nine o'clock it was open and up and running, and the mop-capped and aproned ruddy faced ladies were flogging by the dozen the pasties that had been so shadily and secretly baked the previous night.

'Brilliant Nige,' enthused Huge!. 'Now look, there's all sorts of enquiries coming in from all over. We *have* to step up production. I need some quality time with Em and the kids this avvy, and we need to tell the bloody Adams family to pull their fingers out, so tell them to crawl out of their coffins and work through the days if they have to, the daylight won't hurt them, that's all a myth. Oh, and tell them to stop grinding black pepper into the pasties. It doesn't look right and it tastes funny!'

'I thought you were going to do that.'

'Not my job. The other thing is, if we're getting vandalism, we should get some security cover.'

'Okay, I'm on it.'

The floor of the abandoned control tower was surprisingly comfortable, for the broken lumps of concrete and bits of rusty twisted metal had been quilted over by a thick layer of sphagnum moss, and Cheel had managed a reasonable sleep following her night's spraying extravaganza.

She checked her mobile, and read a message from her brother.

Bronzed and blonded, Mervin was rolling one up outside the surf shack when his mobile played its hippy dippy ring tone. It was Cheel.

'What's on, sis?' he asked.

'When did the police go to see father?' she enquired.

'This morning again, still looking for you he said. Father told him you was back down at Falmouth with friends. He rang me and asked if I knew anything.'

'You never told him, did you?'

'Course not. Did you do all them Cornish tags?'

'Yes.'

'How did you manage to get round all those in one night?' he asked.

There was a silence at the other end.

'And Digory's had his quad bike pinched too. Did you....oh no, say you haven't Cheel....Cheel?'

Cheel shook her mobile. The signal had always been good up on the moors. She checked the screen. Her battery was dead.

Cheel shoved it into her rucksack, which she slipped onto her back. She peeped cautiously out of the shell of the old tower. There was nothing around except a scattering of tattered moorland sheep, and a few scrawny piebald ponies. She popped a lump of Kendal mint cake in her mouth, and set off to explore the terrain, across the flat of the vast old aerodrome towards the crumbling runway that ran through the darkly foreboding forestry plantation, and Crowdy Marsh and Lowermoor beyond. Surely, she thought, even up here in the back of beyond there must be somewhere I can get a re-charge.

Oggy was on his stool behind the counter at Mother's reading the *North Cornwall Advertiser* when his little mate Digory Hicks, as dapper as ever, stepped through the tinkling doorway to collect his daily Cornish Giant. He was carrying a plastic jerry can of water. He saw that there were pasties galore in the window, and in the oven, and on the counter and he could hear even more being made in the kitchen behind; but there seemed to be no other customers. Trade had been far from brisk for days, and so when Digory's opening gambit of 'My God, they're some bloody busy in that place up the road dear,' fell upon less than enthusiastic ears, he maybe should not have been altogether surprised.

'That bugger's killing us, and I can't do nothing,' said Oggy. 'What's on with you?'

'Mother's special water dear,' said Digory, and put the jerry can on the counter. He reached into his pocket and showed Oggy a scrap of paper with a rather long number scrawled on it.

'CR5011349/12. What's that?' asked Oggy.

'The reference number for me quad. The police said I'll need that,' said Digory.

'What for?'

'I don't know.'

'They are bloody useless. That Carew's been around here again this morning looking for our Cheel. I don't know where she's to, and he don't believe me. What can I do?'

'He's as pig ignorant as a pig he is,' said Digory. 'What's Vi say?'

'She's gone out too. Don't know where.'

'Anyway, I see you got yourself an iPad, dear. That's good.'

Oggy held up his hand and examined it. ''Tis just a normal bandage,' he said.

'No, that thing there on your shelf.'

'Oh no, that's Cheel's.'

'Well you might as well have a go on it while she's away. You can't do nothing else sat here. Give it here and I'll show you,' said Digory.

Oggy passed him the tablet, and his mate touched the screen, and it sprang into life. 'There look,' he said. 'There's your mate the chef's website and his Facebook and blog and all the lot...'

'Twitter and twatter?'

'Yes, all that too. Now look, here's the keyboard.

You can reply to all his old nonsense one fingered,' said Digory. 'Which finger is best for you to use?'

'It'll be the middle one.'

'I thought it might be! Proper job dear,' chuckled Digory. 'What could be better?'

Cheel edged across the dry-cracked margins of the twiggy, pine-coned forestry floor. She kept her profile low, and moved along a line between the sterile rows of conifers and the relic of the wartime runway, and she listened nervously as the hushed echo of her own footsteps rebounded back to her from the solid barrier of trees; a snap here, a crack there.

Half a mile along, over to her left and out along a rough side-track, Cheel was intrigued to see a somewhat denser wall of high leylandii, and she took the track and walked to its end where there was a gap in the trees just wide enough for a vehicle to go through.

Within the confines of the leylandii enclosure she was amazed to see a vast old aircraft hangar and a bungalow standing alongside. Nervously she slipped across and stood on tiptoes to try and see in through the high windows of the prefabricated wartime building, but to no avail.

She checked behind her. All was deadly quiet. Curious, for she was a Sloggett, Cheel crept around to the rear of the hangar, and climbed up the wall by means of the web of metal girders that formed its exoskeleton, all the way up to a hole in the top right hand corner, a hole just about large enough for her to squeeze through. She peered in, and was astonished to see spread out below her what appeared to be a fully equipped pasty factory.

She looked behind again. There was no one around. She listened intently. There was no sound save the breeze in the treetops.

Cheel took off her rucksack and lowered it in, then headfirst eased herself in through the small hole by holding on to a rusted girder, from which she swung down like a monkey to the floor. She crouched and gazed around with incredulity at the factory set up around her, the piles of vegetables, the freezers, the sinks and sacks and work surfaces and ovens, and all this in a rusting, abandoned hangar, apparently now the Marie Celeste of the pasty world.

Cheel reached into her rucksack and took out her mobile and charger. She plugged it into a socket at the rear of one of the work areas. 'Charging' flashed up on the small screen. Relieved that there was a current, she sat in silence and waited for it to re-charge.

Inga swooshed into ZeeTV and went about the arrangements for the following Saturday's Huge!Fest down at Tredogend. The first episode of *Huge! in Cornwall* and the live follow-up had been such a ratings success that it seemed that all the other celebrity chefs fancied a piece of Huge!'s action.

Inga had no problem in securing the appearance of morbidly obese, super-sweary lush Larry Ramsbottom. His star had rather fallen recently, subject as he was to an investigation by broadcasting complaints for his overemphasis on extolling the delights of spotted dick. She swore to herself that she'd got a pungent blast of extra strength export lager down the line when she listened to his profane Anglo Saxon slurrings from his TV kitchen. 'You tell Huge! that I'll come on his poxy show, love,' he said. 'He'll need summat to get his ratings up, the bloody great fairy. But make sure there's plenty for me to sup…'

On the other hand, when she called Marcel St Jacques Buffon, his vocal notes were bouqueted with a smooth Gallic charm and warm sensuality and, perhaps more pleasingly, just the merest hint, nay soupçon, of fresh fruitiness. This contrasted with the velvety chocolate smoothness of the finish, a finish that lingered a little longer than it should have.

Mmmm, she thought.

To complete the line-up, Inga contacted *The Foodie Times* as to the availability of the aptly named food critic A.J. Grill, whose acerbic column was generously laced with spitefully poisonous cocktails of adjectives, words that he had learned to use as stiletto daggers whilst being bullied at Webbington School and then at Oxford.

Inga had been very clever, for it was a deliciously toxic mix of equally detestable chefs and critic who could hardly countenance the sight of one another, and was thus surely the basis for an eventful half hour of TV.

She chomped away at the first of three pasties she had purchased at Paddington on her arrival earlier that morning, from under the gleaming new Huge! sign at the new pasty shop in the station. They were okay, but not quite to the standard of those she loved the most, from Mother's down in Tredogend, though of course she could never say so. There was just a little something missing from Huge!'s pasties that Inga, now quite the connoisseur, couldn't put her finger on.

And then there were those tiny black pieces of milled peppercorns that they kept putting in.

They weren't even crunchy, they were oddly soft and squidgy.

Not right somehow.

Even so, she kept on eating, and her mouth was still half full of pasty when the lady answered her phone in her workshop office over in Bristol.

'Hi, Cameron Hot Air Balloons, can I help you?'

'Oh hi,' said Inga, swallowing. 'Yes please. Look, I know this is an unusual request, but my friends tell me that you can make balloons in just about any shape. I'm after one shaped like a giant Cornish pasty. The only thing is it's for this Saturday...'

Cheel had been in the hangar for around half an hour when she heard the lock click on the outside of the building. She ducked down to open a unit door beneath the work surface, slid its bolt across then quickly grabbed her rucksack, bent and nimbly squeezed herself into the tiny cupboard space, and jammed the door shut behind her.

She heard echoey footsteps come across the floor towards where, hardly daring to breathe, she lay on the inside of the cupboard. It was so tightly cramped that she had no option other than to lay motionless. She could make out the shadow of legs just inches away from her through the slight gap between the two cupboard doors. She heard the person take something from off the top of the work surface above her.

She heard a muffled whisper. That person was talking to himself.

'Someone left mobile. Is charged now,' the voice said.

Cheel heard a car door shut and someone else called out, this time from further away.

'Hi! Oh, hi,' it said. 'I'm Nigel from ZeeTV. Do you remember me?'

'Yes, remember you,' said the voice closest to her.

'Hiii. Sorry, what was your name again?' asked Nigel.

'My name Krno.'

'Krno, yes, of course. Look Krno, couple of things from Huge!. We've just opened up at Paddington, sort of a gateway to Cornwall outlet, and we have orders from the supermarkets too. Tesco, Morrisons, you know. Then on Saturday we've got this one-off, a festival. The upshot is we need to step up production quite a bit,' said Nigel, a little nervously.

'Can't do no mores. Shifts no long enough,' reasoned Krno. 'It not possible.'

'Well Huge! says you'll need to work longer hours. He needs double, treble pasties, more. Maybe even work in the daytime.'

'No work in daytime.'

'Three times as many pasties at least. And he says to stop using milled black pepper. It's not right.'

'No use black pepper, use white,' snapped Krno. 'We make at night, but you tell him more pasties is more monies. You tell him zat.'

Cheel heard the car door close again, and the vehicle being driven away.

'Bloody black peppers, my ass,' she heard Krno mutter.

His shadow again darkened the front of the cupboard in which she was hiding. He slid the bolt shut across the front of the two cupboard doors behind which she lay, trapping her within. She heard his echoey footsteps walk off to the other side of the factory and then out, and she heard him lock fast the pasty factory door.

Cheel stayed in the cupboard, cramped and contorted, for some minutes before she convinced herself that the silence meant that the coast was clear.

It gave her time to take in the conversation that she had heard. That this factory was supplying mass produced pasties to masquerade as Huge!'s apparently homemade, handmade ones. That he was intent on expanding the scam beyond all belief. That for sure, this was the death knell for Mother's Pasties, and for the Sloggett family tradition.

She had to get hold of her mobile and call Mervin, and alert the family.

Cheel eased her shoulder and put outward pressure on the cupboard doors. They did not move an iota, and try, try as she might, she was so restricted by the contorted way in which she was squashed in, she was unable to push and force them open. They simply would not budge.

Emma, Quenelle, Julienne and Goujon had spent another lovely day down on the beach at Porzeath, and were walking back across the sand carrying all their beach paraphernalia, when little Goujon spotted Mervin's locks tousling amongst some belly boards at the front of the shack. He ran over to him.

'Hey, what's on lil' dude?' said Mervin.

'We been surfing again Mervin. It's rocking out there,' he said.

Emma waved over, and so did the others. 'Hi,' she called.

'Hi. You okay?' called Mervin.

He saw her nod and coyly smile a lovely, sweet smile.

'Come on Goujon,' she called, hand held out. 'You can see Mervin tomorrow.'

Goujon ran back to his Mum, and Mervin waved as Emma and the kids walked off hand in hand towards the road. He sat down on the bench by the driftwood shack and waxed the faithful board that Bunty had sculpted for him back last year. He looked back to the grassy knoll at the top of the beach and watched Emma and her three children pass the ice cream hut and the hair braiders and bead stringers and the Galleon Café, and as they crossed the sand-blown road to the small playground beyond, he swore he saw Emma take a glance back.

His hippy-dippy ring tone rang.

'Hey sis, that you? Cheel?' he said.

There was a pause before the reply.

'Zis last number re-dial. Who vas zis?' said a man.

'Who am I speaking to?'

'Who you?' said the man.

'I don't know who you are mate, but this is my sister's phone,' he said.

The man hung up.

Emma and the children walked into the beautifully bijoued Fisherman's cottage to find Huge! with his feet up on the sofa, snoring like a Gloucester Old Spot and dribbling out of the side of his mouth. There was a half empty coffee mug on the floor next to him, all the cushions were scattered around, there were crumbs and buttery marmite smears on the chopping board, and there was a piece of toast face down on the rug. He awoke with a start when Quenelle threw his sandy, drippy wetsuit over him and ran upstairs to be the first in the shower. He pushed it off onto the floor, and sat upright still half asleep, and kicked over his coffee mug.

'Oh,' said Emma. 'Thanks a bunch. Twenty quid for the cleaner. That makes sense.'

'Yeah, well, it's my twenty quid. Don't worry about it. I'm not.'

'I just spoke with Nigel. He told me that you were having quality time with me and the children this afternoon. Sorry, I didn't notice you around on the beach.'

'For God's sake Em, can't I have just a little bit of "me" time? I've been blogging a new recipe, you know? Why is it always all about you and the kids? Get over yourself.'

'It'd just be nice once in a while, that's all.'

'I wouldn't want to put Mr Whippy's nose out of joint.'

'Whatever.'

Little Goujon ran in from the garden.

'Are we going to go surfing with Mervin tomorrow, Mummy?'

'I'm sure Mummy would love that, darling,' said Huge!. He got to his feet and picked up the keys to the beast cruiser.

'Oh right, and now you're going out, are you?'

'I've got to fetch someone from the station, all right?'

'Someone. That wouldn't be the blonde artistic director now, would it?'

'This is ridiculous!'

'You're ridiculous!'

Huge! brushed past her and out of their idyllic seaside paradise, jumped into the beast cruiser and roared off to Bodmin Parkway.

Back in the cupboard Cheel had managed, Houdini-like, to twist and contort her small frame around at last, so that the palm of her right hand was on the inside of where the bolt had been drawn across. She applied as much pressure as she could possibly muster, and began to feel some relief as she heard the cracking and splintering of the wood around the screws that held the bolt plate in place. One gave, then another and then quickly a third, and with a sharp bang of her hand the last one went, and she was able to burst the cupboard doors open.

Cheel got to her feet and looked around the interior. It was not as light as she had expected. She must have been trapped inside the cupboard for hours, she thought, for it seemed to be dusky outside.

She looked up on the work surface, and saw the straggling lead and jack of her charger, but no mobile.

A key clicked in the lock of the main door. Cheel swivelled quickly around, and this time she froze. She stared as the men drearily drudged in, at first oblivious of her presence. The man at the front, his black hoody pulled up over his head, switched the lights on and they flickered into life with an electronic buzz. He was followed by a shorter man in a long, black leather coat, and another in a trilby with a rook's feather standing proud of the hat band. Others followed, a couple in donkey jackets and cheap baseball caps, and one in an old dark suit and wearing a beret. To a man, they looked dishevelled and beaten, their eyes dark and skin wisht and pale.

It was Krno who saw Cheel standing at the back of the factory.

'Vat's zis?' he said.

Cheel said nothing.

'How you get in? You steal from us?'

'I just want my phone,' she said quietly.

Krno had it in his hand. 'Come and get it,' he said.

The others gathered around him. He waved it for her to see, and smirked mockingly. Cheel fixed him with her eyes, and slowly advanced across the floor, and as she walked she whispered to herself. 'On my honour and the honour of my country, I swear to …'

Footstep by footstep, Cheel got closer and closer.

'…wrestle without treachery or brutality and in token of my sincerity…'

The men watched in silence as she approached.

'…I offer my hand to my opponent…'

She stood looking up at Krno, and held out the palm of her hand.

'Gwary whek yu gwary tek.'

'Vat zis mean's?' he asked with a mocking shake of his head.

'Give me my fucking phone,' she said, hand still outstretched. 'Please.'

He turned to the others and they laughed. Cheel could see that Krno was not going to place the mobile in her hand. She slowly reached out for it. He snatched it away and lunged at her.

She grabbed him by his lapels and using his own momentum, pulled him towards her. In a flash, she turned and arched her back, and at the same precise moment hook-kicked her heel behind his calf and flipped him up and over herself, and as he came flying down backwards in a perfect arc, not knowing where he was, she slammed him hard down crash on his back on the factory floor.

He lay motionless, moaning, severely winded.

Cheel took a step back, and as she eyeballed each of them in turn, the other men did likewise. Krno looked up trembling from the hangar floor, still wheezing and gasping for breath.

She bent down and retrieved her mobile, dusted it off, and shoved it into her rucksack.

'Thank you gentlemen,' said Cheel. 'That's all I wanted.'

They parted as the Red Sea, and with a small bow of her head, she walked to the open door.

'I'll see you dreckly,' she said quietly, and ran like a rabbit out of the factory, weaving and skittering through the coniferous plantation rows in the gathering gloom, back to the safety of her hiding place on the moor.

Chapter Seventeen
The Beast of Bodmin

The Beast of Bodmin – *though considered by many to be a modern myth, is highly likely to exist. Many big cats, notably pumas and leopards, were released into the wilds in lieu of the Dangerous Animals Act being passed, and are likely to have bred up in the vastness of the moors. There have been many sightings.*

Mervin had been alarmed when, in previous texted conversations with Cheel, she had once or twice mentioned the word 'contaminate' in relation to her intentions towards Huge!'s pasties. He reflected that such ventures normally involved substances like weedkiller or rat poison, or bleach, lead or mercury, or maybe she had envisaged spiking them with razor blades or nails, or road kill, or even lacing them with whatever she could find on the grass around the dead benches.

Whatever she had meant, 'contaminate' inferred something dangerous, at best highly unpleasant and at worse something deadly to whomever was the unfortunate recipient. Surely, he mused, a terrorist outrage of such serious proportions would be beyond even the most desperate Cornish insurgent, certainly his own little sister, however great the provocation she perceived from the massed, goose-stepping ranks of the Essex Regiment of the English junta's undeclared, insidious war of cultural and economic repression.

He was quietly pleased, then, with the dastardly cleverness and sheer cunning of her plan, which if pulled off successfully would do more to damage Huge! and the forces of cultural genocide than anything else he could possibly imagine.

Cheel's plan was in fact so devious as to be certain to turn the entire indigenous Cornish population against the chef, even those who had thus far sat on the fence. It was something so repellant that anyone with any understanding whatsoever of the Cornish or of the pasty would instantly cast him out of the dear old county for all eternity.

It was a plan involving something so terrible that it is impossible for a Cornishman or a Woman of Kernow to even contemplate speaking the word…

It was the vegetable that dare not speak its name.

The carrot.

Carrot. Mervin took an hour off work and got himself into Bodmin and got her four sacks of the deadly orange veg from ValuCheaps. He understood perfectly their purpose. But what he did not understand was why on earth she would need a boogie board and wetsuit up on the moors too? Mine is not to reason why, he thought, not in the presence of genius.

And so it was the following day that when Emma and the kids came down for a surf at Porzeath, and she sent little Goujon running over to Mervin to ask if he'd like to come and take a surf with him and Quenelle and Julienne and Mummy too, Mervin had smiled and said, 'No thanks little surf dude, you enjoy it.' He had for the time being a more important job to do, peeling and slicing carrots, and he wouldn't be able to surf until he'd done all four sacks.

He sat at the surf shack all that morning, first peeling then slicing the carrots so thinly that they were slightly opaque, a sort of pale orange. A very similar hue of pale orange to swede; in fact so similar that one could barely tell the difference. Until of course, you tasted a piece.

Mervin dragged the sacks of prepared carrot back to his ice cream van home in the dunes, and left them and the wet suit and the boogie board outside the back for his sister as arranged, and when he awoke the following day he was pleased to see that everything had disappeared and that Cheel had come in the small hours as she had said she would, and spirited them away. He had not even heard the quad approach.

Oggy had come downstairs to the kitchen. He'd put the kettle on and while it boiled he jabbed a bandaged finger at the screen and peered at the Huge! blog on Cheel's iPad.

'*...so, hey, I've decided to properly re-invent the pasty with some exquisite new Huge! recipes. So first up, a take on that old festive favourite, the bird in a bird in a bird in a bird in a bird, how about a pasty in a pasty in a pasty in a pasty? Just like a Russian doll, first up we make a mini pasty, which we place inside a cocktail pasty, which itself goes inside a standard sized pasty and that in turn inside a giant pasty – shall we call it The Cornish Giant? The name just came to me as I was inventing this and...*'

Oggy growled to himself, and there was a faint rumbling noise from within the pantry.

'Cornish Giant? You cheating bollocks, that's our name,' he said. 'Right!'

He lifted his splinted middle finger, and began to slowly craft a carefully considered online response.

*

Cheel had remained awake since arriving back at her small tent just before dawn, the quad still laden with the four sacks of prepared carrots, boogie board and the wet suit. As the early light spread pink across the horizon beyond Rough Tor, she crept out across the dank and dewy open moors to the cover of the forestry plantation and the old hangar. After a half hour's walk, she settled herself into some undergrowth, and trained a small pair of binoculars on the building; she waited for the end of the night shift.

There was a cloud of bats whizzing and zipping around the hangar, and occasionally Cheel heard a sonar squeak as one flew out and around to where she hid, somehow managing to negotiate the mesh of branches and twigs at a breathtakingly batty breakneck speed.

She waited.

Sure enough, after a while she saw headlamps approach and watched three lorries pull up. She saw the men from inside the building load tray upon tray upon tray of what she was certain must have been pasties into them. When the lorries had been fully loaded, Krno gave the drivers a wave of his hand and they departed. He locked the doors behind him, and trudged after his friends back into the sad and dilapidated bungalow next door to sleep the day away.

Cheel waited and watched for another ten minutes, just to be certain. Belt and braces.

All was quiet and still.

She made her way back through the trees and across the bleak, flat Davidstow moor to her tent in the confines of the crumbling shell of the aerodrome's old control tower.

It was eight a.m. She pulled herself into her sleeping bag, and planned her next move.

*

When Carthew Carew had checked his messages, he had been thrilled to have got one from Inga at the ZeeTV production office, hoping that he would be able to help out with security at the forthcoming Huge!Fest down by the harbour at Tredogend. He had e-mailed them straight back to confirm his availability, and wrote that yes, of course he remembered her well from the WOK spraying incident.

Who wouldn't have remembered such a lovely lady? He stopped short of messaging that she was the most stunning piece of crump that he'd seen on his beat for years, and that she was so superior to all the local dogs it defied all logic. That might, he thought, just be a little over the top and jeopardise his chances of meeting his hero, Huge!.

As luck would have it, he said it was perfect as he was on a spot of annual leave, and would be delighted to help out as he admired Huge!'s work so much, and often did private security work to supplement his meagre police salary and would do so on a very competitive basis this time. He hoped that he might meet Huge! himself as part of the deal, and Inga confirmed that this would, of course, be possible.

So it was that the day before Huge!Fest, Carthew Carew turned up for security duty down by the harbour in Tredogend still wearing his police shirt and epaulettes, now partly hidden by a bright green reflective tabard that had 'Old Sparky Festival Security' emblazoned across the back, along with a cartoon of an electric cattle prod with arms and legs, and with a smiley face and red hooter rather like Mr Punch.

With old sparky side-piped down the leg of his trousers, a small canister of mace in his pocket and his massive cruel hands and bad attitude, he was armed to the teeth. If he had later to provide close-up protection for such a high profile celeb as Huge!, he was not going to be found wanting.

Carew strode in through the fenced off harbour side area, which had been set aside for the Huge!Fest by sections of interlinked aluminium fencing, and he pulled his mirror shades down over his Neanderthal brow, his gigantic frame casting a long, rather ugly shadow over the site, and he looked around for his contact Inga.

He was a truly terrifying, if slightly ludicrous, sight.

Around the old kitchen table at Mother's, Oggy, Vi, Uncle Clar and a rejuvenated Mother were making and baking. Oggy had put the first batch into the new oven that he seemed to have at last mastered. All they needed now were customers. Since the opening of the Emporium up the road, they had barely sold anything, and although they could keep a stock of pasties a day after the day of baking and just about get away with it, any longer and they had to throw out.

Dapper little Digory Hicks wasn't displeased with this, for it saved him buying expensive feed for Bovril the boar and his Gloucester Old Spot sows, and they were growing fat and healthy on pasty swill, all quite against the rules of course. He came down every day to collect his own fresh Cornish Giant pasty with the pastry D on it, and to take away anything not previously sold by Mothers in the back of the DigsCab. There had been a lot lately, and he could tell that the pasty-fed pigs were happy by their jovial grunting.

'Come in Digory boy,' shouted Oggy on hearing the tap on the back door. Digory walked through into the kitchen to find the cottage industry in full swing.

'Pull up a chair and shut home the door,' said Mother, and squared up some dishes and a rolling pin and made him a space.

'He's all right standing Mother, don't fuss,' said Oggy.

'How's yer hand dear?' asked Digory.

'Getting better.'

'And yer other ailments?'

Oggy threw Mother a glance. 'Don't ask,' he said.

'Tay?' asked Mother.

'Proper, Mother,' said Digory.

She switched the kettle on. 'Pop in the pantry and get us the tea bags, there's a love, and mind what you're doing in there,' she said.

Oggy shook his head in despair, and Uncle Clar enquired whether or not there might be a biscuit. Digory emerged with a handful of tea bags, and closed the door behind him. There was a low rumble from behind him, and the door gently shook.

'What was that?' he asked.

It was Mother's turn to shake her head.

'Never you mind,' said Oggy. 'What's on?'

'Only matey's pasty festival tomorrow. Everybody's going on about it. Haven't you had an invitation?'

'No. How much?'

'Three hundred quid a stall.'

'I couldn't afford three quid, let alone three hundred.'

'Did you get your letter from Jeff?'

'No.'

'Come yesterday. We're singing there at one. Full uniform.'

'I ain't got no uniform. I can't afford that neither,' said Oggy with a sad little shake of his head. 'I'm afraid my singing days might be over.'

Digory looked with pity on his old mate, but Vi gave him a sly smile and a wink, then looked down and sprinkled some flour and rolled some pastry. 'He'll just have to wait until times is easier Digory, that's all,' she said.

'Oh, yes, and before I forget dears, I hear that the council's doing health and hygiene spot checks around all the cafes and restaurants. They was down Padstow yesterday, Tintagel today,' said Digory.

'Don't you worry, Digory,' said Mother. 'They won't find nothing here to jaw about. This place is spotless. Always has been.'

'Come on Dig, I got something to ask you,' said Oggy.

The two old pals went out to the counter, where from beneath Oggy conspiratorially produced Cheel's iPad and showed Digory the Huge! blog and the pasty in a pasty in a pasty in a pasty recipe, the one that Huge! was now calling the Cornish Giant.

'What the hell is that all about?' asked Digory. 'Your's is called the Cornish Giant, always has been.'

'Never mind. I'm fighting back. Look, I'm doing a reply,' said Oggy.

Digory studied the text. 'Yes, that's proper. It's quite short too, that's just the way to do it.'

'Short? I been typing since breakfast!' he gasped. 'Anyway, see where that little thumbs-up thing is, that's 'likes', right?'

'Yes…'

'Is there anywhere on here you can do a 'hates'?'

'No,' said Digory with a shake of his head.

'Pity,' said Oggy. 'Never mind. Now look, you was always top of the class for spelling, wasn't you?'

'Yes…'

'Boss always used to give you silver stars, didn't he?'

'And gold, yes…'

'Yes, and gold. So, is shithead all one word, or is it two? I don't want nobody to think I'm ignorant, that's all.'

'No, we must keep standards up dear. I think it can be either.'

'Proper job,' said Oggy. 'Right then, ready?'

Digory nodded, and Oggy held his splinted index finger aloft, then pressed the send button. 'There, gone. Now, grab your pasty. It's the only bugger I'm gonna sell today that's for sure, then we'll load up all the others for Bovril and his fat trolloping sows. I shall look forward to tasting one of them this winter; pasty-flavoured suckling pig, now that *is* something new.'

They went to the back of Mother's and loaded up the DigsCab, and Oggy gave his mate a wave as he set off back to Dordigor Farm, and then he went back to the kitchen to continue his futile task of pasty production.

Because that was what he did.

At the harbour, the bunting and streamers were strung out all around and fluttering jolly in the sea breeze, and along the harbour side a row of whelk stalls and oyster shuckers, mussel men, smokeries and lobster stalls, crab and crayfish jowders, gigantic pans of paella and mackerel and sardine barbies were all setting up under a varied selection of awnings and tarpaulins and tents. Then, in the row opposite, were all the pasty makers of the county with their stalls, the Philps, Penrose, Tregorrans, Barnecutts and Polkinghorne pasty dynasties, and Rock Bakery, Cornish Made, Aunt Avice, Pasty Presto, Looe Pasty Co., Mevagissey and Mousehole and St Just and St Ives Pasty shops. All were there.

But not Mother's.

Then, rising gaudy and grand above all around it, in its primary coloured majestic splendour, covering the entirety of the harbour car park and dominating the whole of the festival site, came the big top. The Huge! big top.

With the legend 'Huge!' all over it, of course.

And vans came, and lorries too, and boats moored up at the harbour wall, and boxes and bags on sack trucks and trailers were distributed all around in preparation for the big day to come.

Huge!Fest had arrived!

It was eerily silent inside the secret pasty factory, save for the occasional high-frequency bat squeak. They hung in sleepy rows at the rear, hooked by their sharp claws onto the metal girders that served as rafters, upside down as bats do, way up above the plastic vats full of prepared ingredients.

All had returned to roost now, for it was mid-morning, and like the Romanians in the bungalow next door they were nocturnal creatures, but in their case by nature rather than by necessity. They had been catching juicy, fat moths all night long. Some were very full. Uncomfortably so.

There were no toilet facilities for the bats at all, but to be honest they were not unduly bothered or at all toilet trained, and they simply squeezed out their little black mousey droppings from where they hung.

Down, down into the ingredients far below.

Like gritty little pieces of milled black peppercorn.

There was plotting afoot down in the production office of the World's First Pasty Emporium at the old chapel.

Inga, Nigel and Huge! and Tom and others in the team gathered around a table and planned.

'So Huge! I think everything is in hand for tomorrow. We'll keep things running as usual here in the Emporium, hand in hand with the fest. We've got treble the amount of pasties being made up at the factory…'

'Shhh,' hissed Huge!. He glanced over his shoulder with just a hint of paranoia.

'Sorry,' whispered Nigel. 'We'll leave a camera team here in the Emporium just as a fill in and for a bit of background to the main event, where we've two lots of crew, one for you in and around the Huge! Big Top, and one for all the rest and outside stuff, all the stalls and goings on and the custard tarts running around and keeping the punters happy…'

'Yea, yea, yea…'

'…and then the main event, the "pasty off" between you and Larry and Marcel, judged by some local luminary or other…'

'One of the Cornish? What do they know about pasties? They're not chefs.'

'…and Inga's got the services of A.J. Grill from the *Foodie Times* to judge it with him.'

'Grill! Grill! Please no!' spluttered Huge!. 'I hate him. I used to bully the stammering little turd at Webbington. He hates me!'

'*And* he hates Marcel and, more especially, deeply despises Larry too. You're all in the same boat. Anyway, don't worry; it will all be taken care of on the day.'

'Used to gob in his gravy and shove his head down the bog,' muttered Huge!. 'Can't we offer him…'

'Please leave it to me, Huge!. Now, the brilliantly clever Inga has pulled off another coup for us…'

Inga wiped a pasty crumb from the corner of her mouth, put her mid-morning pasty on its small dish, and smiled. Huge! couldn't quite put his finger on it, but she looked a bit different. Still delicious, but different. There seemed to be, well, more of her somehow.

'...she's had a mega, massive pasty-shaped hot air balloon made up for us, with "World Pasty Champion" emblazoned right across it. When you win the pasty-off we're gonna get you into it and fly you up high above the fest and Tredogend.'

'Will the balloon have 'Huge!' on it too?'

'Don't panic Huge!, yes, of course...'

'In really big letters?'

'Yea. *Really* big.'

'How can we do that if, say, Marcel or Larry were to win?' asked Tom.

'Tom,' said Huge!. 'We're all grownups here. I think we all know that ain't gonna happen.'

'Oh...'

'Just one thing though,' said Huge!. He glanced over his shoulder through the glass door behind them. 'What the hell is that?'

Inga and Nigel both looked up as well. Carthew Carew, the Beast of Bodmin, grinned alarmingly through at them, like something from entirely another age, and made a small wave with his large hand.

'Ah, now, he's our security for the fest. Normally a police officer. He's very keen,' said Inga.

Huge! turned around and looked again. 'Keen? Keen! That's not the word I'd use. All that's missing is the bloody bolt in his neck,' he hissed.

'He's really desperate to meet you,' said Inga. 'He's such a fan.'

'I mean Nige, please...' said Huge!.

'Get it over and done with Huge!. Go say hello. He's here to help, and he's going to be around all weekend.'

Carew leered in so close to the glass that his fetid breath began to steam it up, whilst his heavy brow and forehead rested against the top of the doorframe itself, such was his extreme size. His excitement knew no bounds; Huge! was just a few feet away, and when Inga got up and came over to the door and opened it for him to come in and meet his celebrity chef hero, it was almost too much.

He strode in and marched up to Huge! and extended his vast paw for shaking. Huge! reciprocated with his own flabby hand, and immediately wished he never had. Huge! was by no means a small man, but even he had to look up at Carthew Carew, and as he did so his hand was enveloped in a vice-like handshake.

'What an honour to meet you at last, chef,' he said with a studied reverence.

'Aaah, aagh, yes, yes, me too.'

'I always watches your programmes.'

'Do you? Aaagh, would you mind...'

'And I got all your DVDs, chef.'

Huge!'s eyes were watering and he was breaking into a cold sweat, and his hand was becoming quite numb. 'Yes? Really? Do you think you could...'

'And all your books. And tea towels. And an apron with your face on it!'

Inga reached over and gently loosened Carew's grip with her elegant fingers.

'Careful now, Carthew. We need Huge!'s fingers and hands for cooking, don't we?' she said kindly.

Huge! danced around the table in a considerable amount of pain, and shook and wrung his hand and fingers to allow the blood to circulate back and the numbness to subside.

'And I got one of your kitchen knife sets too, and, and, and a fridge magnet...' gabbled Carew, quite overwhelmed.

'Well thank you Carthew,' said Nigel. 'Huge! is thrilled to have you on board the team for this important weekend,' and he led Carew by the elbow towards the door. 'It's great to know we're gonna be so safe.'

Carew turned and smiled manically, and brandished his electric cattle prod, and gave it a little buzz.

'Look Huge!, I got old sparky!' he said in an ecstatic tone. Nigel ushered him out. 'I always keeps him side-piped down me leg. And I got a can of mace too!'

'Lovely. Thank you so much,' said Nigel appreciatively. 'Let me bring Tom out and he can show you around the site, and you can meet all the rest of the team.'

Huge! stared at Inga with incredulity.

'Old sparky! Old bloody sparky! Well, what could possibly go wrong?' he said.

'He's all we could get locally, Huge!. He's got experience.'

'At what? Rendition? Electro-convulsive therapy? For heaven's sake!'

Inga stood up, and for just the briefest moment glared at the ungrateful chef. She popped the last morsel of pasty into her mouth. Huge! scanned her up and down. That was it. That was exactly it. That *was* what was different. She was definitely carrying a bit of timber.

'Can I ask you something Ingrid?' said Huge!.

'It's Inga!' she replied, irritated. 'What?'

'Yea, yea, Inga. You're not, you know, are you? Because...'

'Not what? Oh, please,' she said and stomped out the door, not exactly slamming it, but not being gentle with it either.

Huge! sighed and shook his head knowingly.

'Pasties,' he said.

It took Cheel some time to get the sacks of carrot close enough to the old hangar for convenience, but still far enough away in the forestry plantation that the quad's engine did not disturb the nocturnal Romanian workforce, asleep in their deeply creepy and decrepit bungalow.

From there she dragged the sacks one by one around to the rear of the hangar, where she climbed up to the hole, and with ropes and a pulley set up a system to haul the sacks up the side and then into the building itself.

At first alarmed by the occasional bat squeak, Cheel became fascinated by the furry little creatures that hung down in ranks from the girders. She made it her business not to disturb them; first she manoeuvred the sacks of beautifully sliced carrots across, and then from above lowered them down to rest next to two large vats of sliced and prepared swede. One at a time she lifted them and tipped them in, until all her sacks were empty.

She dipped down into the vat with a large stainless steel ladle, and stirred the carrots and swedes together, and grinned as she could see that it was virtually impossible to tell the difference between the two orangey coloured vegetables.

Satisfied, she climbed up the girders like a monkey, stroked a particularly cute bat on his little snub nose, then popped out through the hole and around the back of the hangar and off through the forestry, back to the quad, and from there back to Cheel HQ in her tent hidden in the remnants of the control tower. Phase one of her plan had been completed with military precision. She knew that now she had to rest up before attempting phase two.

Carthew Carew, determined to impress, raised his hand to stop the land rover and trailer as it came to the festival entrance gate. He went around to the driver's side and leaned over.

'Yes?' he said.

'I've got a hot air balloon and a burner for you.'

'Right, I've heard that one before. Let's see it, and don't try nothing,' said Carew.

Somewhat taken aback by the security man's brusquely aggressive manner, the driver got out and peeled back the tarpaulin on the trailer. There was the folded up balloon, a sack of ropes, a large basket and a shiny metal burner, and a large gas canister.

Inga waltzed over.

'Hi, you must be from Cameron's. I'm Inga, come right over here.'

Carew went to the next vehicle in the queue, an old style Renault van with a giant fibreglass pasty on the roof and 'Pasties' sign written in bold italics on the side.

'Yes?' he said.

'I…I've come for the Huge!Fest.'

'Oh really? What are you selling then? Let's have a gander in the back, shall we?' he said.

It was to be a long day ahead.

'I likes a nice cup of tay before bed, maid, don't you?' said Oggy. He propped and plumped up Vi's pillow for her.

'Lovely darlin',' said Vi.

'I ain't fussed that he never invited us along, are you? We couldn't afford that sort of money. I should think there'll be plenty of people around in the town tomorrow anyway, and they all got to walk right past us to get down to the harbour. They might come in and buy.'

'They might, but the old chapel's going to be open as well, darlin',' she cautioned.

'What can we do? Just got to keep buggering on as we know best. Digory's pigs are enjoying them anyway. He said he'll let us have one of them for the freezer. We might have to live on that all winter.'

'Don't get fed up love. Here you are,' she said, and passed him a carrier bag she had been hiding.

Oggy put his tay down and reached in and pulled out a pair of grey flannels, and held them up.

'They ain't slacks, are they?' he asked suspiciously.

'No they're trousers. Try them on, you silly old sod.'

Oggy jumped out of bed and pulled them on. They fitted perfectly.

'Proper job,' he said grinning.

'Save the Children. Go on, look in the bag, you ain't finished yet,' insisted Vi.

Oggy dipped his hand in and pulled out a choir badge and tie.

'Bloody brand new. Ansom. Thank 'ee maid,' he said. 'Where'd you get the money for all this?'

'Never you mind,' she said. 'I'll sew it on in the morning. Come on, drink your Rosie Lee. We got an early start if you're going to go and sing and show 'em how it should be done.'

Cheel struggled in the dark to shrug and tug herself into the wetsuit, and when she'd finished she strapped the boogie board to the back of the quad. She shoved some canisters of spray paint into her rucksack, and got astride and kick-started the machine.

Cheel Sloggett planned to be the first visitor to Huge!Fest. The thing was, as yet she had no ticket.

Chapter Eighteen
Roots

'Hossed up like a pox doctor's clerk'. – *a compliment upon a person's smart appearance, or their wearing of new apparel.*

Carthew Carew's night patrol of the festival site had been disappointingly uneventful for him. He'd spent hours prowling the perimeter fence, off the leash like a rabid Doberman, slavering and growling at every breeze-rustled crisp bag and at every polystyrene fish and chip box that tumble-weeded across the deserted harbour side. He reflected on his regret that Huge! had not wanted him to stay at Fisherman's Cottage on close protection duties for him and his family, and found it hard to understand why. He would have to do better if he was to fully ingratiate himself.

Carew was grateful when he was able to lift the boredom by enticing a feral moggy over with a cold chip, and zap it (gently) with old sparky. That certainly broke the silence for a moment or so. Carew had never seen a cat run up a vertical wall before, and he'd quite enjoyed it.

But the unfortunate cat had been his only company, and by four in the morning Carew had had quite enough and dragged a chair across the gravel to the site entrance where, canister of mace in his hand and old sparky side-piped and trousered down his leg, he closed his eyes.

Indeed, at four in the morning, this was probably okay. For despite his fearsome guard dogging of the perimeter of the site, unbeknown to him the latest insurgent outrage had already been committed.

Cheel had taken the quad to Tredogend Point, a half mile over at the opposite end of the bay. She'd paddled her way SBS style across the inky black, diesel oily sea on the boogie board and climbed up a salt-rusted ladder onto the harbour side. Only a yowling cat screeching in agony broke the silence, a noise followed quickly by a kind of primitive laughter that in some respects almost sounded human, but not quite. Under cover of night, keeping as low as she could, Cheel moved through the quiet, empty stalls in search of her target.

When Mervin awoke that day, he was surprised to discover the boogie board and wetsuit already returned, propped against the side of his ice cream van home, and next to them the words 'all done cheers bruv x', written by a finger in the damp sand.

Mervin would also have been surprised to find that back home in Mother's, there had been pasty baking activity at the kitchen table for hours already, and Vi, Mother and Uncle Clar were hard at it, on Oggy's theory that everyone on their way to the Huge!Fest had to pass right by their door and was likely to come in and buy. One lot was in the oven baking, and the next batch close to finishing.

Vi had sent her husband upstairs to try on the various bits of his new choir uniform. Oggy had put it all on, and shuffled back down and stepped through the door and stood there awkwardly, awaiting inspection.

'Oh, here he is, look Mother,' said Vi. 'Come here and let me do your hair properly.'

With a lick of her palm, she smoothed his ginger strands across, and pulled his tie straight for him, and fiddled with the knot and generally made him a little more symmetrical and presentable. She brushed down the smart new badge. 'How's them slacks? Sorry, trousers, darlin'?'

'All right,' said Oggy, and bent his knees. 'Proper job. Not too tight like them others. They was casterising me, they was.'

Vi stepped back. 'What do you reckon, Mother?'

Mother looked up from her rolling pin. 'Hossed up like a pox doctor's clerk.'

'Mother!' protested Vi.

'Proper job, boy,' said Mother. 'Reminds me of your father, and Granfer.'

'I kept Granfer's old badge in me drawer, Mother.'

'Roots. Never forget 'em. You look very smart, boy.'

'Thank you, Mother. And don't call me boy.' said Oggy. 'What shall I do now? We ain't singing until one,'

'Man the counter darlin', we're all right, ain't we Uncle Clar? Mother?'

'Lovely Vi, yes. Was there more tay?' said Uncle Clar, busily seasoning.

So Oggy wedged himself rather self-consciously in behind the shop counter, sat on his stool behind the screen, and blazered and badged with his new tie and flannels (not slacks), he smartly waited for their first customer to tinkle the shop bell. And as it had been since the opening of the Emporium up the road, he waited, and waited, and waited; and as he waited, he reflected that his hunch had been right, that the ever increasing crowds of people had to walk right past his door to go down to the harbour side and queue to get into the festival of pasties. The trouble was, that was *exactly* what they did.

*

Huge!'s stock of pasties had arrived and been dropped off at the lean to at the rear of the Emporium at five thirty that morning. The usual staff were all arriving for the start of the day, and in the office the team was preparing for the festival. Nigel was briefing everyone.

'So Tom. What about Facebook and stuff? How's that all going?' asked Nigel.

'Yea, all good. Thousands of likes and some really nice comments,' he said scrolling down his screen. 'Lovely stuff coming in from…oh hang on. Oh, this one's not so good.'

'What?' said Huge!.

'Just some nutter I guess.'

'But what? How could anyone say anything bad?' said Huge!. 'It must be a mistake.'

Tom kept looking. 'No, I don't think so. It's from motherspasties or something. Hang on, it says *"Your pasties is bollocks you shithead"*. Is shithead all one word Nige?'

'I'm not sure,' said Nigel. 'I think it can be either.'

'Oh right. Well anyway, whoever posted this has put it as one,' said Tom. 'He's spelt bollocks right.'

'Yea well, that's altogether easier,' said Nigel. 'Although I've seen it spelt with an 'x' on the end.'

'Oh yea,' said Tom. 'I never thought of that.'

'Excuse me interrupting,' said Huge!. 'But I'm being cyber bullied by some rabid troll and all you can do is sit there and do a bloody spellcheck! For god's sake, it could be Hannibal Lecter out there.'

Nigel was not convinced. 'Steady on Huge!, I've seen worse.'

'It's a troll!' insisted Huge!. 'I want him punished. People love me! How can he say that about me?'

'Leave it with me Huge!.' said Nigel.

'It's a hate crime! I'm shaking. Look at me Tom, bloody shaking.'

'He *is* shaking Nige,' said Tom.

'I'm a victim here, Nige. You and Barney have a duty of care you know.'

'I'll speak to Carew, Huge!, all right?' said Nigel. 'Now, moving on. We're a bit short on pasties. I don't know why. We'll have to make do, that's all,' he said.

Huge!'s demeanor changed in a flash. 'Short? Why?' he demanded.

'Don't know, but it's too late now. So listen, at nine the Huge!Fest gates open, and cameras roll. Huge!, it would be nice to get some shots of you welcoming the punters in with a merry quip or two. Kiss a few old dears and that. Can we make it a family thing? Can you get Emma and the kids up?'

'Uhh, I'm not sure. Little Goujon has a head cold and…'

'Well let's try. Now, A. J. Grill, Marcel and Larry are due in at midday. We're bringing the chefs in on a trawler, in fact on two trawlers because they bloody hate one another so much…'

'I can see why,' said Huge!. 'They're both tossers.'

'Whatever. So's Grill, but he's arriving by car. So, you'll do some cooking with Larry and Marcel, separately of course, and then at four we have the grand gourmet pasty making competition, which you will win…'

'How do we know I'm going to win? Can't we get Helga or someone to be, you know, nice to him? Just to make certain?'

'What did you say?!' she demanded.

'Easy now, Inga,' said Nigel. 'Cash, Huge!. A nice wedge of twenties always helps to oil the wheels.'

'What then?'

'Then the balloon goes up, so to speak Huge!. And the balloon bears the legend which says, Inga?'

'World Pasty Champion!'

'And…?'

'Yes, yes, yes, *and* your name. Once that's been done, Huge!, we go to closing credits and you can do what you like. Now, have we got all we're going to get from you know where?'

'The factory?'

'Shhh! Tom, for God's sake. Loose lips and all that.'

'Sorry. Everything we're gonna get, by the looks of it,' said Tom.

'Okay. And do we have all the local organic ingredients on show as usual, for in here and down at the fest?' asked Nigel.

'Yep.'

'And do they all look muddy and misshapen?' asked Nigel.

'What, the locals?'

'No, the vegetables Huge!'

'Same bloody thing if you ask me, Nige!' guffawed the chef.

'Well, that's it then. Quick coffee and a snack and we're away.'

Nigel poured himself and Huge! a mug, and each grabbed a sandwich. Everyone else milled around and helped themselves. Inga grabbed a pasty and sat down and began to nibble away. Huge! sly-eyed her from the corner of the room. She certainly seemed to be taking up the whole of the seat these days.

'What's the matter with little Goujon then?' asked Nigel.

'Oh, some bug or another. Quenelle and Julienne both went down with it last week.'

'Kids. They soon get over these things, don't they. How's Em?'

'She's good,' lied the chef.

'Would be nice if you could get her…'

Their conversation was suddenly halted by a terrible gagging noise. They turned and saw Inga bent double with her hand over her mouth. She had bitten into the pasty.

'Oh my God!' she said.

'Inga! What is it?' said Nigel running over. 'Are you all right?'

She retched and spat the remnants of the mouthful into her hand.

'That's disgusting,' she said.

'What? Not black pepper again?'

She looked up and held out the orange-slithered contents of the palm of her hand. There was a momentary deathly hush.

'Carrot,' she said. 'I hate bloody carrot!'

Huge! rushed over and grabbed the partially chewed pieces from her hand, and examined them. He removed two slithers and held them up to the light, one swede, one carrot. It was hard to distinguish, but there *was* a difference.

'Oh my God! She's right, Nigel, and she's the bloody pasty expert so she should know. It's carrot all right,' confirmed Huge!.

'What do you mean, *expert*?' demanded Inga with some indignation.

'That means they could all be contaminated. The whole batch.'

'Pasty *expert* Huge!? I don't believe you fucking said that,' persisted Inga.

'What can we do? I could be ruined,' said Huge!, steadfastly ignoring her protestations. 'Half of Cornwall is coming today. If anyone gets carrot in their pasty I'll be done for. It'll be culinary *hari kari*!'

'Pasty *expert*! Cheeky bastard.'

'Can't we go through them all and take the carrot bits out?' said Tom.

'Take the carrot bits out? Take the carrot bits out!? Are you on bloody day release?'

'Calm Huge!,' said Nigel.

'Well come on, what's going on with those neck-puncturing nincompoops up there? First up, they've not sent us enough of the sodding things, and now we find out they've all been stuffed with the one ingredient that the Cornish would lynch you for!'

A huge shadow appeared in the doorway. Carthew Carew, part time chief of security and officer of the law lurched into the room, totally oblivious to any tension.

'Any chance of a coffee?' he asked. Everyone pretended not to notice him, and he walked over to the pot and started to pour himself a mug.

'Well Nige,' raged Huge!. 'What do you suggest? Ingrid? You others? Come on, earn your money. Let's have some ideas. It's nearly time to open!'

Carew grabbed a pasty. He hadn't had any breakfast and bit off a huge chunk.

'Wow!' he said. 'Carrot! Who'd have thought of that? Huge!, you're a genius!'

Huge! turned on the giant man. 'That's just it, you knuckle-scraping knuckle-headed buffoon. I didn't put them in! That's why we can't sell them, all right? Oh dear, I'm not getting through, am I? Get him out of my sight someone, please.'

But everyone has a moment in their life, a moment of clarity, that life changing moment of sheer unadulterated brilliance. It was now that Carthew Carew, security guard, slaughter man, policeman, Neanderthal psychopath, Huge! obsessive, and beastly Beast of Bodmin experienced his.

'You could buy up all of his pasties from the shop down the road,' he said.

All around him were momentarily dumbstruck.

Open mouthed, Huge! gripped Nigel's arm. 'Say that again,' he said quietly, not even daring to look at Carew.

'You could buy all of Sloggett's down the road and pass them off as yours. From Mother's. He'll have plenty. He hardly sells any these days. He'll be only too pleased.'

Huge!, still with his back to Carew, looked at Nigel. 'He's got it. My God, fucking Lurch has got it!' he turned on his heel. 'Genius...what was your name?'

'Carthew. Carthew Carew.'

'Carew, Carew, Carew. Magnificent. Look, you know those morons down there, don't you? Get on down and buy them all, and we'll bang 'em out as Huge! celebrity gourmet pasties for a tenner. As many as you can get, do you hear?'

'All of them?'

'Yes, everything. Everything! And threaten him with being done for cyber bullying if he says no. He's bloody trolling me on Facebook. Called me a shithead, can you believe that? If you scare him enough, you'll get them for a quid each. Cheap as chips! Quick Carew, take as many people as you need.'

Carew (still carrying the carrot infested pasty which he rather liked) was despatched with as many helpers as he could gather, and Nigel, Inga and Huge! took a deep collective breath.

'Thank Christ I thought of that. Could have ruined me. Good job you can't stop eating pasties, Inga,' said Huge!. 'We'd never have known, would we?'

'Yea, well,' said Inga unsmilingly. 'Like you say, I'm an *expert*.'

Oggy's neck was getting stiff as he watched all the people pass to and fro his shop front. He had unloaded the first batch onto trays in the window, and now the second batch were done, and the third waiting to go in. He had that deep down feeling that his hunch about passing custom had probably been a miscalculation after all, and that maybe he should stop Vi and Mother and Uncle Clar from making any more.

Bored, he flicked on Cheel's iPad, and had a taste of Huge!'s latest genius online recipe that had already been given thousands of 'likes'. Why this should be was not entirely clear. Surely to create a deconstructed pasty was to remove the very raison d'etre of the thing. A pasty had to be constructed, or it couldn't be a pasty. Or could it?

A photo had been posted of a Cornish blue plate with a short crust crescent of crimped pastry curved along its inner edge. The skirt beef was presented three ways, carpaccio, slow roasted and corned, and with the rest of the ingredients appeared to have been artistically arranged on the plate by one of the more avant-garde artists of the Newlyn School, with a smeared puree of swede, a pasty shaped quenelle of crushed potato, Penhavern clotted cream and caramelised Marazion onion, and some strategically placed droplets of Cornish beurre blanc, with a sprinkled sand of Cornish sea salt and white pepper seasoning.

I'd like to see you take that down a tin mine for your crib, or out on a trawler when it's blowing a gale, or out harvesting in the fields, Oggy thought. The very idea of such a dish gave him chronic indigestion.

'De-restricted pasty my ass,' he muttered sourly to himself, and reached for the iPad.

But before he had the chance to express his carefully measured and considered response online, the door tinkled for the first time that morning. It was Carthew Carew, and Oggy's heart sank.

'Look,' said Oggy. 'I told you. I don't know where she is. She's away. You know kids.'

'Hang on there, Sloggett,' said Carew. He put his half-finished pasty down on the counter. 'What you writing on Facebook, eh?'

'Nothing,' said Oggy, and he quickly slid the iPad beneath the counter and out of sight.

'You need to watch what you're doing, pal. First dogging, now trolling. You could get into serious trouble.'

'Trolling?'

'You know what I mean. Cyber bullying, you nasty piece of work! Saying bad stuff about Huge!.'

'Cider what?'

'Look,' said Carew under his breath. 'I'm off-duty and doing you a favour here. I need all your pasties for the festival. How much are they?'

'Mother's Traditionals are two quid.'

'Right. A quid each I'll give ya, and then we'll say no more about the troll thing. How many have you got?'

'There's hundreds. Over a thousand.'

'I need more than that.'

'I can't…'

'Yes you can, unless you want to be done in Bodmin Magistrates. They takes a dim view of trolls. You could end up in Dartmoor. I needs two thousand all told.'

'Now?'

'Yes, right away.'

'That means I'll have to bake off another thousand,' said Oggy.

'Well you better get on with it, hadn't you?' sneered Carew. 'Don't forget. Dartmoor's a cold old place in the winter.'

Shaking, Oggy went back into the kitchen, where Vi and Uncle Clar and Mother looked up. They had overheard the conversation.

'Sorry,' he said.

'What *did* you put on Facebook?' said Vi.

'Nothing much,' said Oggy. 'Digory helped with the spelling.'

'I'm sure he did. Come on then,' Vi said, putting a brave face on things. 'At least we'll be selling some pasties again for a change. We got until dinnertime and he'll buy the bleedin' lot, *and* Mother's Pasties will be there at the pasty festival after all.'

Heads down, they went at it like navvies. Beef chopped, veg sliced, pastry rolled and pasties stuffed and seasoned and crimped in a swirling, whirling cloud of flour and white pepper and steam from the ever boiling kettle that sustained them with the sweet tay of life. By one o'clock, all their ingredients were gone and they could make no more.

Oggy picked up the final two trays of pasties himself and carried them out the door and waddled off down the street towards Huge!Fest, right past the queue of eager punters and right up to the gate.

Carew was waiting there, swinging old sparky behind his back, and passed Oggy an envelope in exchange for the final batch of Mother's pasties, and two of his helpers came up and took the trays away.

'Right, that's it,' said Carew. 'Off you go.'

'Oh,' said Oggy. 'And I brought you a couple of our signs, with 'Mother's' on them, and some of our bags. I thought you...'

Carew snatched them with his monster hand, and with a leering sneer stepped over to a wheelie bin by the entrance, lifted the lid and dumped them in, and slammed it shut.

'Oi,' protested Oggy. 'What's on?'

'These are Huge! pasties now, mister. He's the chef, not you! You got your money, now sling yer hook before I zap ya.'

'Hang on a minute. I'm coming in anyway to sing with the choir!'

'We'll see about that. You stand there at the side and wait, you're holding up the queue. Next! Thank you madam...'

A runner was despatched, and after some minutes Oggy was relieved when Jeff the choirmaster emerged from the throng with a pasty, half-wrapped in a Huge! pasty bag. He was eating it as if there was no tomorrow.

'Hello Oggy. Have you tried one of these? They are bloody lovely, here, have a bite,' he said.

Oggy reached out and took a bite of what was unmistakeably one of his own, baked that very morning.

'Of course it's bloody lovely. I made it this morning! What's going on?' Oggy said.

Carew strode over.'What up with you now?' he said.

'That's one of my pasties.'

'Well that ain't what it says on the bag now, is it?'

'He's a bloody cheat!' shouted Oggy. 'These are my pasties in his bags! Mine!'

People in the queue began to laugh.

'Don't you dare say nothing about Chef, he's brilliant and famous, a genius celebrity, which is more than you'll ever be, you ginger nutter. Now move on, you're holding people up. Unless you want me to tell all them people behind what you gets up to in lay-bys at night!' said Carew. 'Oh, and stay off-line, troll!'

'I'm coming in to sing. Tell him Jeff,' protested Oggy.

Jeff stood back and looked him up and down, and not without pity, shook his head. Oggy stopped and looked down himself. He looked down at his flour dusted blazer and his new tie and badge, all pastry ingrained and margarine and lard smeared, and his flannels splattered in skirt beef blood and whitened with potato starch.

'Sorry Oggy,' said Jeff. 'But even your slacks…'

'They're flannels,' he said quietly. 'They was new for today…'

Oggy sighed a heavy sigh, turned and began the slow walk of shame, back along the queue and away from the festival up the street to Mother's, his head bowed, shoulders drooped and covered from head to toe in the detritus of pasty making.

What neither man had remembered was that when Carthew Carew had come to Mother's earlier, he had left his own half-finished, disgusting, carrot infested pasty behind on the corner of the counter, quite out of sight of anyone, and there it sat for the rest of the day. Even when Vi and Mother and Uncle Clar performed their thorough daily deep clean-up, they missed it completely.

There it sat, abandoned and forgotten, cold and lonely, congealed and full of sliced slivers of carrot masquerading as swede, and full of nasty, gritty bits of milled black pepper.

Or was that, in fact, nasty, gritty, shitty little bits of bat poo?

Chapter Nineteen
A Certain Lack of Grace.

Good food,
Good meat,
Good God,
Let's eat.

A Cornish Grace - traditional

Two Padstow trawlers moored alongside the harbour wall at Tredogend, delivering their precious cargo of rival celebrity chefs hired in for the day's live broadcast from Huge!Fest. First up the gangplank was super-sweary, corpulent inebriate Larry Ramsbottom.

Larry had thrown up over the gunwales all the way from Padstow, not because of seasickness, but rather because of the ridiculous number of cans of wife beater lager he had swigged back in the buffet car on the train down to Bodmin Parkway.

Larry's celebrity was based on being a northern man of the people, on being a drunk, on extreme and advanced profanity, and on his absolute refusal to dabble in any of the fine and delicate arts of international or classical cuisine. Rather, he cooked straight down to earth, no nonsense British 'grub'. The finest 'grub' in the world, according to him.

Nowt like a steak and kidney pud, battered cod and chips and mushy peas, ham in parsley sauce with mash and broad beans, good old British bangers and roast beef or pork or lamb with all the trimmings, and of course the full English. Nowt like it, he'd say. And as for our puddings, the Euro-faggots (and there were nowt wrong wi' a good faggot) had nowt that could answer a broadside of jam roly poly, treacle tart, apple pie or bread and butter pudding all with lashings of custard and never, ever, that thin, watery foreign muck, crème Anglaise.

Huge! waited at the top of the gangplank to glad hand him into Tredogend.

'Nige,' he whispered nervously. 'He's even fatter than before.'

'Shush Huge!, he'll hear you. He's had a lot on his plate.'

'I should think he's bloody eaten most of it!'

'*Don't,* Huge!.'

'Well look at him, for God's sake. Has he been given the freedom of Melton Mowbray or what?'

'What was that Huge!? Your round is it? About time! Get 'em in you tight bastard!' shouted Larry from the deck.

A little titter ran around the assembled crowd. Larry stepped off the trawler, which began to rock violently from side to side, and then he teetered on the edge of the gangplank, as a hippopotamus might.

'Nothing wrong with his hearing then,' said Nigel.

'Oh my God,' hissed Huge! secretively. 'The loathsome oaf's going to fall in the harbour and make a bloody tsunami! We're done for. Cornwall's ruined.'

Larry tumbled over a mooring rope and sprawled across the top of the harbour wall flat on his face.

'Hi Larry! Welcome to Huge!Fest. How ya doing, man?'

'Fuck me, Huge!, I went down like a sack of shit, lad,' he slurred, stumbling unsteadily to his feet and dusting himself down and looking around at the people. 'Eeeh, it's a shithole here, in't it?'

The gathered crowd laughed aloud. Good old Larry.

'Come on Larry,' said Huge!, magnanimously placing an arm around the old super-lush's shoulder. 'Let's get you into the Huge! big top and pour you a glass of vino. Red or white? I've got a nice Tempranillo, and a Sauvignon Blanc to die for.'

'Fuck off, what do you think I am, made of soft southern poof pastry? Get me a beer, you flouncy treacle tart!'

Huge! had to smile engagingly at the laughing audience as he helped Larry along. They were all well versed in his over the top vulgarianisms from the so successful programme, *Cookin' Effin' Grub with Larry Ramsbottom*, where weekly he pulled in various desperate soap stars and abused them terribly whilst they messed up their pitiful efforts at cooking.

'So, 'ow are ya, Huge!? Last time we met you couldn't boil a fuckin' egg!'

'He doesn't mean it, we're mates really, aren't we Larry?' laughed Huge! to the faces in the crowd. 'Old mates. I know him, it's all right, so…'

'Fuck off,' hiccupped Larry. 'You've always been a tosser. Where's your missus? I've only come down here to give her a portion of spotted dick, she's effin' gorgeous her, unlike you, you floppy-haired ponce.'

Nigel was a little alarmed. It was a live broadcast, and although Larry was expected to deliver a modicum of controversy, this had been a rather full-on entrée of gritty northern profundity, even for him. Particularly as it was only just lunchtime, and the watershed still a fairly distant prospect.

'Ladies and gentlemen, more, much, much more I'm sure, from him later,' said Huge!. 'Can you give it up, please, for Mr Larry Ramsbottom!'

The crowd was in raptures, and clapped and shouted and cheered and screamed, and waved their autograph books at him from behind the ropes.

'You can all fuck off,' shouted loathsome Larry. 'I'm not signing owt. I'm gagging for a pint!'

Man of the people.

And the crowd cheered even louder.

Oggy stomped into his front room to find Uncle Clar snoring asleep in his chair, and Vi and Mother exhausted by the day's exertions and gawping at Huge!Fest on the box.

'It's all to hell missus. He's only selling our bloody pasties and pretending they're his,' said Oggy, whose sadness had turned to anger as he'd stomped back home from Huge!Fest.

'What?' said Vi, not even turning. 'We're watching the festival. Come and sit down darlin', there's loads we know. Just seen Pearl and Mrs Tregupter, ain't we Mother?'

Mother nodded and pointed at the screen.

'He's putting them in his own bags, he is, the bloody fake,' said Oggy.

'And we saw Digory's back. Looked some smart in his blazer he did.'

'Oh never mind,' said Oggy.

'I thought you was singing with the choir?' said Vi, her attention still fixed to the screen. 'Look, Mother. There's Renee.'

'Where?' said Mother. She leaned forward.

'There look, scratching her nose.'

'She's picking it,' said Mother. 'She's always picking it. She won't like that. Not on telly.'

'I was going to sing, but Jeff didn't want me. Look at me, maid,' said Oggy. 'I'm bloody lagged in pasty, ain't I?'

Vi didn't look up. 'Look, there's that Ron Price. What's he doing in a Cornish kilt? He ain't lived here five minutes.'

'We see 'em come, we see 'em go,' said Mother.

'What was that darlin'?' asked Vi, and turned from the telly, but Oggy had already left the room.

He sat at the kitchen table alone. He opened the brown envelope, and counted his wodge. Ten, twenty, thirty, forty...Two grand for two thousand pasties, it was all there. He fanned the notes out and laid them on the table, and he stared at them and shook his head sadly. He tucked them back in and sealed the gummed edge of the envelope, and left it on the table.

Huge! escorted Larry into the big top and over to the podium, where Inga waited for him with a four pack, having already cracked one open for him.

'Cheers luv,' he said. 'Nowt like a swig of wife beater. What's your name then gorgeous?'

'Hi. It's Inga. Nice to meet you Larry.' She held out her hand, and as she did so dropped her notes, and bent down in front of his grotesquely bloated belly to pick them up. Her long blonde hair tumbled forward over her face.

'While you're down there, luv, very kind all the same!'

'All part of the service, Larry,' laughed Huge!.

Inga got to her feet. 'All part of your service maybe, asshole,' she said, and stormed off and out of the big top.

'Wooo!' said Larry. 'Nice one Huge!. I suppose a shag's right out of the question then, eh?'

'Sorry, Larry,' said Huge!, not really meaning it.

Larry swilled down his can of wife beater in one, belched riotously, and then cracked open another, and toasted Huge! with the can.

'In yer hole, lad,' he said. 'So, where's she gone now, your fat lezzer mate?'

'Oh, *is* she really fat?' said Huge! with uncertainty. 'To fetch Marcel I think.'

'God bloody save us from that garlic-stinking bastard frog. The only good thing that ever came out of France is fucking Tourettes!'

Inga was waiting for Marcel St Jacques Buffon as he stepped elegantly from the top of the trawler's gangplank onto the harbour side, and Huge! huffed and puffed his way over through the throng of punters, and was just in time to meet him with a hearty handshake and a manly double kiss to each cheek.

'Marcel, so good of you to come. Welcome to Huge!Fest, Chef.'

'Bonjour et merci, Uge!,' he said, and waved to the cheering crowd. 'Bonjour, toutes le monde.'

'How was your crossing, Marcel?' asked Huge! jovially.

'Ah, okay, but at least I was not, as you say, Moby Dick, not like some others I could mention,' he laughed.

Huge! chortled. The crowd laughed. Inga giggled. He was charming indeed, and handsome. Very handsome. But Marcel was not as one might have expected from the Gauloise district of Paris or the Saucisson district of Toulouse. No, Marcel was from Port Talbot. But fair play, he did have a tidy French accent and could throw a magnificent Gallic shrug.

'Ah,' said Marcel holding Inga's outstretched hand. 'Enchantée, Mademoiselle. Ooo is this, Uge!?'

'Oh, sorry Marcel. This is Ingrid, my assistant.'

'Inga,' said Inga. 'Artistic director.'

Marcel gave her fingers the lightest of kisses, and dipped his head politely.

'You're a very lucky man, Chef,' he said.

Not any more he isn't, thought Inga.

'Let's go to the Huge! big top and meet your old friend Larry, Marcel.'

'I 'ave been looking forward to it, Uge!. I just 'ope he doesn't throw up on me, that's all.'

Cheel had set off on the borrowed quad, down around forgotten lanes and footpaths and bridleways. At the old Camelford Road station, near to the site of the Arthurian battleground at Slaughter's Bridge, she joined the old Southern railway line. She bumped along past the gaping depths of the slate quarry at Delabole and down on to where the tunnel was barricaded at Trelill, and then the rest of the way cross-country, out to Tredogend Point. She hid herself in some rhododendron bushes, and waited with binoculars in hand, looking across the mouth of Tredogend harbour to where the Huge!Fest was in full swing. She whiled away the time by repeating in parrot fashion to herself the Cornish wrestler's oath, over and over again. It had taken her some time, but now she had it absolutely off pat.

'Shall we have another cup, Vi?' asked Uncle Clar, just come round from his nap.

'Not for a minute, Uncle Clar. We're watching these chefs making pasties.'

They watched the little screen as the three chefs made up their pasties and put them to bake. Huge! was holding forth close-up to camera.

'So today we're also honoured to have with us here at Huge!Fest two VIP guests. First up, the head of the Parish Council here in Tredogend, Mr Ron Price, who is also chairman of the RNLI, treasurer of the Local History Society, secretary of the Round Table, president of the Chamber of Commerce, vice chair of the Tredogend Social Club and I believe Ron, a Cornish bard,' he said. 'Come on over Ron. Ladies and gentlemen, Ron is going to help our food critic judge our pasties today to see who is the *World Pasty Making Champion!*'

Inga escorted Ron Price across to the podium in the centre of the big top. He was wearing his Cornish tartan kilt, short black jacket with pewter buttons each embossed with the fifteen Cornish gold bezants, and cream knee-length socks.

'Well, look at you, very smart Reg,' said Huge!. 'What do you think of today's Huge!Fest? Having a good time?'

'Praper jab, Huge!,' said Ron. 'It be ansom, it be, ooh arr, ooh arr.'

'Lovely Reg. Ooh arr! It be ansom, me dear. Good to hear the accent. Praper Cornish that be,' said Huge!. 'Now, tell me, which part of Cornwall is that accent from? Not Bodmin, is it?'

'No.'

'No right, I bet it's Redruth,' said Huge!. ' Hang on, wait, say ansom' again for me.'

'Aaansom.'

'Yea, I got it Reg. You're from the other side of the hill, a Camborne man. Am I right?'

'Uhh, no Huge!. It's Camberley, actually. And it's not Reg it's Ron.'

Huge! erupted with forced laughter. 'Camberley!!' he blathered. 'Yea, right Reg. Camberley!'

'No, no,' he said. 'It actually *is* Camberley.'

'Oh, right. Anyway, you've lived here a long time now, Reg?' said Huge! hurriedly.

'Oh yes, Huge!. I've lived here in St Dogend for five, no, nearly six months now. Margaret and I love it.'

'Tredogend I think you mean Reg. And, being a Cornishman now, you're going to help A.J. judge our pasty competition for us?'

'Yes. My Margaret makes the best homemade pasty in St Dogend.'

'Is she Cornish too?'

'Well, she liked *Poldark* when it was on.'

'That's good enough for us Reg. And what will you be looking for from the winner?'

'Oh fresh ingredients. Nice mashed potato, minced beef, but it must be lean Huge!, and some diced carrot. Maybe even some peas. And the crinkling must be right of course…'

Oggy had stepped back into the living room at Mother's, where Vi and Mother were sitting open mouthed, and he stared at the screen with incredulity.

'Crinkling?' said Vi.

'I ain't voting for him again,' said Mother. 'I liked his kilt, too.'

'Bollocks,' growled Oggy. 'That's what it all is.'

The chefs lined up and under the scrutiny of the cameras and two judges, they made up their pasties, and placed them upon tin baking trays. With the attention all on the cursing Larry and cool as a cucumber Marcel, Huge! made his switch. He shoved his own less than commendable effort into the drawer beneath his preparation area, and retrieved the Mother's Traditional left in there for him by Tom earlier, and with a sly glance around popped that out on the tray instead. The three pasties were carried over to the Treleaven oven and slid in to bake.

Huge! patted the old oven on the side.

'Come on then, old girl,' he implored. He looked with sincerity down the lens. 'Do your best for us. It's for the honour of the county.'

Whilst they baked, the choir stood up on the podium, and Huge!, Marcel and a propped-up and pissed-up Larry took centre stage as they sang their way through a short repertoire, finishing with the 'Flurrie Dance', with Huge! taking the solo lead. Never before had the Tredogend Fishermen's Choir been on national TV.

And Oggy Sloggett had not been there.

At the pasty-off, Huge! stood between bladdered, beery-belching Larry and suave sophisticat Marcel, each with a plate in front of him with his fresh baked pasty at the ready for the judges. Each celebrity super-chef was filmed in close-up as he cut his pasty in half, and then took each half over for judgement, firstly to Ron Price the Pooh Bah of Tredogend, and then to A.J. Grill, the sniffy, snotty, snobby food critic of *Foodie Times*. A.J. Grill, Hawtryesque in demeanour and young fogeyed in Harris Tweed and brogues, a pinch-lipped, detestable little tit, pokey-nosed in pince nez specs.

'What will you be looking for A.J.?' he was asked from off camera.

'I expect a s-symmetry of form and of taste on the dish. An even crimp, I think, beautifully sh-sharded and translucent potato and swede, onion cooked to perfection, and the skirt beef in evenly sized pieces, nicely pink in the middle, and the natural jus that flows from that combination should be as a river of savoury delight. Of course, p-perfect seasoning will be required. In short, I want to taste *Cornwall*.'

'Ron?'

'Yea, what he said,' said Ron, quite lost.

Marcel was first up with his effort. He placed it on the judge's table.

'Judges? Ron?'

'Very nice. Praper jab.' Clearly, Ron could not tell one end of a pasty from another.

'Thank you Ron. A.J.?'

The food critic held his half pasty aloft and sneered, and examined it with evident suspicion. With a rather pained expression, he tasted it and shrugged his shoulders.

'I am,' he said. 'Indifferent to this offering.'

'*Qu'est-ce que c'est?*'

'I am offended by its p-pretensions of grandeur, m-my dear.'

'Eh?'

'For me, Marcel, this p-pasty rather misses the point. The pasty is artisan. I find this a little too refined, if you will, it's p-p-preciousness demeans it, it is too self-consciously Michelin. It simply will not do, Marcel. Your p-pastry is excellent as one might expect, but it is filo, not short crust. Your beef is perfectly cooked, but not, I suspect skirt. Marcel, one suspects t-t-topside. Is one right?'

'It is my own twist, A.J.,' said Marcel.

'Quite, and there we have it. For my taste, I fear, this is a t-twist too far.' said A.J. 'This *is* a t-twisted pasty,'

Marcel leaned forward and whispered with his valley boyo's lilt discreetly into A.J.'s ear that he was now banned indefinitely from all his restaurants, and that he rather wished that the gourmet pasty had bloody choked him, and better luck with the next one which he had heard on good authority had been spiked with nails and ground glass and served with a garni of hemlock leaves and slug pellets.

It was *de rigcur* for food critics to be assailed with dishes of occasional deliberate 'unpleasantry', shall we say. A.J. pushed the dish back towards the chef who picked it up and, with a Welsh Gallic shrug and sniff, he carried it back to his place at the table, where Larry was grinning triumphantly from ear to ear.

'I told thee that were a pile of shite, lad,' hc said. 'Now then, let's show ya how it should be done, by a proper British chef cooking proper British grub.'

He carried his forward. The judges tasted.

'Ron?'

'Very nice. Praper jab again.'

A.J. stiffened, and put the pasty down as if he had takcn a mouthful of arsenic.

'If I may say, Ronald, you are rather wide of the m-mark with your assessment here. But no matter, for it is evident that you are no gourmand, no connoisseur. You are, my dear, of the people and thus entirely free of the somewhat s-suffocating sh-shackles of good taste. This is a pastry case of m-mere m-mush. There is no delineation betwixt meat or vegetable, the jus has long since evaporated into the ether and the seasoning is non-existent. It is a dog of a pasty. A dirty dog....'

'Now fucking hang on pal...' bridled Larry. Nigel craned the cameras and mikes in closer. This was beginning to look like good TV.

'Quite frankly, my dear, you have s-served me a dish of disappointment...' st-stammered A.J..

'I know what I'd like to do with the dish!'

'It's a very nasty pasty, Larry.'

'Cheeky sod. What the f-f-f-fuck do you know about g-g-g-grub?' demanded the bloated and rather tanked-up celebrity chef, squaring up to A.J. and m-mocking his rather unfortunate affliction.

'Precisely, Larry, precisely. I know nothing of what you so eloquently term as 'g-grub',' he said, and held up Larry's effort to the camera. 'And if this is, indeed, 'grub', then I am rather pleased that my f-finely-honed taste buds have not been polluted by it before, and remain confident with my assessment that you possess the c-culinary prowess of a troglodyte. You are, sir, a philistine. You couldn't cook a can of beans.'

'And you don't know owt about owt! You just scrounge round from one bloody posh restaurant to the next, stuffing yer plumby, public school gob for fuck all. You're banned from my gaff!'

'You should be so lucky, m-my dear. I wouldn't be seen dead in your e-coli and c-cockroach infested transport cafe! G-grub indeed.'

Larry went in up close and personal for a nose to nose confrontation, his own like a swollen strawberry squashed up against A.J.'s rather more pointy, pokey one, only his grossly distended belly intervened and gut barged the slightly built food critic backwards and knocked him flying across the kitchen and clanging into a pile of pots and pans. Tom dashed in and helped him up, whilst others restrained Larry from commiting further brutalist outrage, and escorted him back into position and sat him down, and cracked him open a can of wife beater which he swilled down, followed rapidly by another.

It was Huges!'s turn. He took his two pasty halves forward and put them in front of the judges.

'Ron?'

There was no reply, for it was so delicious that Ron could not put it down.

'A.J.?'

Visibly taken aback after the first taste, he reverentially placed his half pasty back on his dish.

'They do say one should save the best until last, my dears,' he opined. 'I am utterly in thrall of this astounding creation. It is p-paradise in pastry, a nirvana of n-nourishment. The skirt beef melts in one's mouth, a veritable meringue of meat, and the jus dances a wild fandango, nay flurrie dance, upon one's tongue, and the perfect balance of vegetables and seasoning is testament to an instinctive prowess, a genius.'

He took another mouthful, then another, and went on. 'It teases me, it beguiles me, it seduces me; it leaves me both s-satiated and enraptured. There is magic abroad on this platter. What sorcery, what necromancy is this? This p-pasty has been sprinkled by stardust, created not I suspect by a mere chef, but by a Cornish shaman. It is the rocky shore, the granite tors, the…'

He bit off another huge chunk and wolfed it down.

'All right, all right, don't overdo it A.J..' whispered Nigel from off shot.

'It's the s-sweeping moors, the rolling wave….' he said, frantically st-stuffing the pasty into his mealy mouth and chomping as if there were no tomorrow.

'That's fine, no more. You've had your money, haven't you?'

'Frankly, m-my dear, I am moved to tears…' said A.J. Grill, and he pinned the winning rosette on the scant remains of the pasty he was supposed to have merely tasted. He gave Huge! his vellum victor's scroll, and publically forgave him for all the bullying he had presided over back in their schooldays; the taunting of his girly lisp, the gobbing in his gravy and shoving his head down the bog to flush away his stammer, all forgiven. He stood back and applauded Huge!, and then quite overwhelmed by the emotion of the moment, he stepped forward and embraced him as a conquering hero. He kissed Huge! on both cheeks.

'Oh for God's sake, pull yourself together man, it's embarrassing,' hissed Huge!. 'It's just a fucking pasty!'

Inga nudged Tom. 'And *he* didn't even bloody make it,' she said.

Out at Tredogend Point amidst the rhododendrons, Cheel could hear the announcements over the PA system and the applause that followed. A minute or so later, her ears were assailed by an even more rapturous clapping and whooping and cheering that clattered across the water, and told her that Huge! had won the competition and been anointed by A.J. Grill as the bona fida World Pasty Champion.

'More tay, Uncle Clar?' asked Vi.

Uncle Clar was leaning right forward, his nose almost touching the screen, and studied the close-up of the winning pasty.

'Not for a minute, Vi,' he said. 'Look at this.'

The Sloggetts all gathered close up to the telly, heads bobbing a little, squinting, jostling very slightly. Curious.

Uncle Clar pointed.

'Not much of that one left, is there Uncle Clar?' said Vi.

'No, Vi, and I'll tell you why. See that join right there on the crimp? That's one of ours! That one with the rosette on it! First prize it says. I remember that join, I did that one this morning. That's one of my pasties.'

Mother focused. 'It is too, you can just make it out, that's exactly how you join them, Uncle Clar.'

'I told you he was using our pasties for his own,' said Oggy.

'Don't bleedin' blame us,' said Vi. 'It was you who wanted to sell them all to him in the first place!'

'Now he's World Champ with our pasty...'

'What were you thinking of?'

Before Oggy had a chance to defend himself, there came a sharp knock at the shop door. 'We're shut!' he called out. The knock came again.

'Shut!' he snapped. 'Are you bloody deaf?'

Again came the knock. This time more incessant, and continuous, and louder and louder. Oggy raged out of the room and went to the door. He could see a man and a woman standing there.

'We're sold out!' he shouted.

The woman reached inside her jacket and held forth an identity card in a plastic case on a white nylon string. She pressed it to the glass. Oggy moved forward and examined it.

'Bridgett Hook, Cornwall County Health and Hygiene, and Tony Wright, Food Standards Authority. Can you let us in please? Spot inspection.'

Chapter Twenty
An Inspector Calls

proper – *vernacular Cornish denoting anything or anyone that is good, fine, upstanding, deserving of merit or praiseworthy. A 'proper job' is an affirmation of satisfaction with a state of affairs, similar to the popular 'right on'.*

Huge! undertook a quick change of outfit, and ditched his apron quickly in favour of a Cornish kilt, just like Ron's. He was now, after all, a Cornish icon. He was Huge! in Cornwall. The Huge! big top emptied as everyone piled out after the man himself to see the next stage of the extravaganza, the balloon going up.

Marcel stood on the podium next to Inga. She was holding the remains of the rosetted winning pasty.

'That was, as you say, a fix?' he enquired.

'Try it,' she said.

Marcel bit into the winning pasty. 'Oh *mon Dieu*, A.J. is right, it is magnificent,' he said. 'Truly superb. Delicious!'

Inga nodded. 'Pity it's not one of Huge!'s,' she said.

'Eh? You mean that's not the one he made on camera?'

Inga raised her eyebrows. They heard a noise from beneath the table, rather like a pig grunting. It was Larry on his back, drunk.

'Come on, let's get out of 'ere,' said Marcel.

'Only if you give me a little bite,' said Inga.

'Oh,' said Marcel. 'I think we can arrange something…'

*

From a safe distance away out on Tredogend Point, Cheel watched the giant pasty shaped balloon being inflated. It was still lying flat when Huge! was helped into the basket alongside the pilot, who was operating the noisy stainless steel gas burner. The deafening roar of the burner increased in bursts. Cheel could see Huge! looking over the side.

The balloon slowly took shape, until all at once it seemed to inflate very quickly and suddenly wobbled up into the air. The anchor ropes that held it down tensed and then, except for one long one, all were cast away by the crew and the giant pasty floated gracefully towards the sky and hung high up above the Huge!Fest.

Huge! had not been prepared for what was such a rapid and thrilling ascent over the harbour side site, and felt totally exhilarated.

Neither had Huge! been prepared for laughter from the crowd, and he wondered what it was all about. First up, he feared they might have been looking up and trying to peep beneath his ridiculous kilt. Then he thought that they may have been laughing at Marcel, who he could see running off out of the main gate towards the town, hand in hand with Inga, or at A.J. still enraptured in tears of ecstasy, or at fat Larry as pissed as a fart under the table.

Then he realised that they were all pointing up at the balloon itself. He leaned out of the basket and turned to look up, but couldn't see what was up there above his head.

But Cheel *could* see all right. She could see her giant St Piran's tag, and she could see her massive black letters sprawled right across the balloon – the legend 'WOK!', all but obliterating those offending words, 'World Pasty Champion – Huge!'.

And it could not only be seen by her and all the thousands below at the Huge!Fest and across all of Tredogend, it could be seen live by millions across the country.

WOK.

As Huge! made his slow descent from above to the ecstatic cheers of the crowd, it was not just the balloon that was a little deflated, but Huge! himself. But all this soon turned to disappointment and then into an incandescent fury as he pondered the day's mishaps, and on touchdown the kilted chef leapt out of the basket in a manner that could hardly be described as graceful and stood there fuming, and looked around desperately for someone to blame.

His old friend, the one-legged gull, was on a fly past. It did a brief reccy above and circled around, then swooped and pooped polka dot all over his new Cornish kilt. Huge! looked up. The gull flew away. For a moment he stood motionless, and took a deep breath.

'Oi, Huge!,' shouted an amusing wag from the crowd. 'That's good luck, that is mate!'

His balloon had been vandalised, his name all but obliterated and he'd been denied his rightful moment of global culinary triumph by some hooligan or other armed with a can of spray paint, and there'd very nearly been a carrot catastrophe with the pasties and now Inga was off shagging that disgusting bloody frog. Oh, and he'd been shat upon by his stalking gull. He tore off and shoved through the crowds in his vile temper, back to the Huge! big top, and blustered in to find Nigel talking with a soundman.

'What the hell is going on, Nige? What is this WOK thing? Is it the sodding Triads or what?' he raged.

'No, no, I don't…'

'Of course it's not, you fool. That was a bloody joke, just like I look like a bloody joke, floating up there like Slimcea man in a fucking dress with some garbage scrawled all over the balloon!'

'Don't you mean Nimble man? It was Nimble, wasn't it Nige? The bread ad?' asked Tom helpfully.

'Something must have happened. Someone with a grudge,' said Nigel, deep in thought.

'Good ad that. What song was it they used again? *'Would you like to fly in my beautiful balloon?'* sang Tom. 'I'm sure that was it.'

'A grudge? A grudge! Who could possibly…oh, you're having a laugh, Nige. I get it!' Huge! shouted. 'Very funny!'

'Oh no, I know what it was,' said Tom, and he began to sing. *'She flies like a bird in the sky-yi-yii, she flies like a bird and I wish that she were mine…'*

'Shut up Tom!' shouted Huge! and Nigel together.

Carthew Carew had wandered into the tent. He didn't like to see Huge! so upset. It upset him.

'I know what it is,' he muttered. 'It's the work of Cornish insurgents.'

'See Nige. Lurch here's got it all worked out,' ranted Huge! still in his sarcastic pomp. 'Give me strength man, insurgents my ass! Why insurgents? Just look out there at those crowds! I embrace them with my charismatic caress and sprinkle a little bit of stardust into their miserable, dull, joyless lives, don't you bloody get it? Everyone here loves me!'

Inga walked in, alone and rather dishevelled.

'Oh, here she is, my esteemed assistant…'

'Artistic director!'

'Whatever. Where've you been? Having a bunk up in a lay-by with Marcel d'Amore?'

'Certainly not! I just put him in a cab for Newquay Airport. He's off to Marseilles to do a new series,' she said.

'Bloody Welsh fake!'

'Fake? Really? You'd know all about that, wouldn't you?' retorted Inga.

Beneath the table, something stirred; an unpleasant squelching noise, rather like the sound that a Wellington boot might make squidging out of a bog.

'Jesus, what was that?' said Nigel.

Everyone was on edge. Carthew Carew, concerned for Huge!'s safety and highly trained in matters of security, sprang into action. He assessed the situation, and with his arms outstretched, held everyone back. He drew his electronic cattle prod, as a hussar might his cutlass, and jabbed it beneath the table into the source of the noise, and into what he believed could be a Cornish jihadist, or even a Triad armed with a wok or a pair of sharpened chopsticks.

The appalling castrato-screeching stream of Anglo-Saxon profanities far surpassed any of loathsome Larry's previous utterances, amplified as they were by nearly three thousand volts of electricity zapped into his nether regions by old sparky. He jerked bolt upright and cracked his fat head on the underside of the table.

'Oh for heaven's sake, it's Ramsbottom,' said Huge!. 'Larry, come on out. You've done your bit, turned up, got assholed and sworn at a few people! It's all over now, time to go home, all right?'

'That's a fine way to treat your guests, you shifty ponce,' he blathered, crawling out on all fours.

Huge! bent to the grotesquely rotund chef. 'Oi! Don't you get it? In your own words, time to fuck off lardie!' he said.

Larry stumbled, then jolted to his feet and knocked the table over, and threw up all over Huge!'s shoes.

'Oh that's disgustin', I can taste the bloody bile lad, any chance of another beer to clear the old palate?'

'Oh for God's sake, get rid of him Olga!'

'It's Inga!'

'Yea, yea,' said Huge!. 'Just try not to shag him on your way to the station, all right?'

Oggy was a bit on edge too. He and Vi and Mother and Uncle Clar had kept exchanging knowing glances. The cups of tay they'd offered the hair-netted and latex-gloved inspectors had been politely, yet coldly, declined. They had been through Mother's with a fine-toothed comb.

After three hours, the lady had popped her head around the living room door.

'Mr Sloggett,' she said gravely. 'Could we have a word?'

Oggy went out into his own kitchen and sat nervously at the old table opposite the two grim-faced inspectors. He was astonished when the lady's face cracked into a broad smile.

'Well, thank you Mr Sloggett. We've no recommendations at all. Your establishment has passed the inspection with flying colours. It's a shame that we didn't have any of your products to sample and analyse, but as you say, they are so popular that you sold out. Clearly you and your family are very aware of public health requirements, and as such you are a credit to your profession. Congratulations.'

She handed him a certificate.

'A cistificate. Proper job,' he said. 'I'll frame that.'

'We'll be on our way then. Thank you again,' she said, and they shook hands, and went out through the kitchen door and out into the shop.

'Here,' said Oggy. 'Let me get the door for you.'

Oggy, smiling, held the tinkling door open for Ms Hook, and she turned as she left. She looked over Oggy's shoulder at her colleague, Tony Wright. He was standing at the corner of the counter, on the customer's side. He was holding up a half-eaten pasty. The one left there earlier that morning by Carthew Carew.

'What's up Tony?' asked Ms Hook.

'What's this?' he said.

'Never seen it before in me life,' said Oggy.

'Mr Sloggett, we need to take this for analysis,' he said. He pulled on a latex glove and dropped the pasty into a plastic bag, and he held it up to the light and examined it through squinted eyes.

'Carrot, Mr Sloggett? That's very unusual. And bits of black pepper too, by the look of it.'

'We don't put stuff like that in our pasties! It's not one of mine, we sold out.'

'Sign here please. For the pasty.'

'But I told you...'

'Just on the line there. Thank you.' He placed the plastic bag with the half eaten pasty into his case.

'Okay Tony? Well spotted,' said Ms Hook. 'Oh, Mr Sloggett, could you let me have the certificate back, please?'

She snatched it from him, opened her briefcase and dropped it in. 'We'll be in touch,' she said. 'Sooner rather than later, of course.'

Chapter Twenty One
The Rain Softly Falling

And the rain softly falling,
And the Oggy Man's no More.
I can't hear him calling,
Like he used to before.

'The Oggy Man' *by Cyril Tawney.*

Nigel had had to take control. He convened a meeting at the Emporium, and he, Huge!, Inga, Tom and the others involved in the production sat around and had a wash-up of the previous day's events.

'The thing is Huge!,' he said. 'Now you've calmed down a little, no matter what happened yesterday at the Fest, it was a massive…'

'You mean Huge!,' interrupted Huge!.

'Yes, sorry Huge!, *huge* success. There were one or two glitches, but it was a one off. You simply can't legislate for all the 'what ifs' that might or might not happen. Millions were watching, advertising revenues are astonishing, and the Emporium is going from strength to strength. Barney is thrilled. *Huge! in Cornwall* is a brand. It's been that quick.'

'That's all well and good Nige, but the wheel nearly came off yesterday because the sodding drac pack messed up. Not half enough pasties, and the ones we did get were rammed with bloody carrot. Carrot! It defies belief. I save them from deportation to a life in the gulag and they do this to me. Fangs a fucking bunch lads!' sneered Huge!.

'I don't know what happened there. They never did that before.'

'And we have to move on,' said Inga impatiently.

'Maybe a step forward is to diversify, with speciality pasties?' suggested Tom.

'You mean gourmet?' asked Nigel.

'Or fusion,' said Inga.

'Any ideas guys? There's no wrong ones,' said Nigel.

Nigel had obviously misunderstood the concept of 'the pasty'. There were numerous wrong pasties already. There was a plague of wrong pasties of biblical proportions. All over the dear old county like a rash.

'Chilli chicken tikka bolognaise pasty?' called out someone. Wrong.

'Paella and pasta pasty?' Alliterative, but wrong.

'Sushi and bush meat pasty?' Clearly ridiculous.

'I've already put up a deconstructed one, and a pasty in a pasty...'

'In a pasty in a pasty, yea, I think we got that Huge!,' said Nigel. 'Any others?'

'What about something mentally scientific, a la Professor Herman Bratwurst, or whatever he's called? A lab pasty,' suggested Tom helpfully.

'Yea, all sparklers and dry ice and stuff. With stem cell skirt beef and genetically engineered veg, and maybe a synthetic Cornish tartan pastry? We could put a musical pressure pad beneath it so that it plays Trelawney as you pick it up!' said Huge!.

'No, no, too gimmicky' said Nigel.

Huge rolled his eyes. 'Really Nige?' he said.

'We need to do something more like that Danish guy does. Ants and slugs and woodlice and worms, jellyfish and seaweed and stuff. He's got Michelin stars coming out of his ears,' said Nigel.

'Eh?' Huge! appeared confused.

'Foraged, Huge!.'

'That's the ticket, Nige. A foraged pasty! How brilliant of me. And it'll be so cheap!'

'What would you put in it?' asked Tom.

'Oh who bloody cares? Any old weeds and insects as long as they're 'free and organic man'. I'll work it out and we'll just chuck a load of flavourings in there and Bob's yer uncle and Fanny's yer aunt,' said Huge!.

'Who'll make them? You?'

'God no, Nige. Come on! I won't have time apart from making the odd one for camera. I'll be too busy being filmed out there gathering and foraging and banging up the old profile, won't I? It's for all our benefits. In my Hunter wellies and my Barbour International I thought? With the kilt? I can see it now. And one of those canvas and leathery bags slung across me probably. What do you reckon Inga?'

'Yea. Good luck with that,' she said dryly, without even looking up.

'Look Inga, try and display just a little bit of enthusiasm, will you?' said Huge!. 'It's you that's gonna have to go up there and tell those sodding post-commie Rumalien vamps how to make a foraged pasty. They'll be used to eating shite like that back home. Can't be that hard, it's not rocket salad, is it?'

'Science,' she said dispassionately.

'Exactly,' said Huge!. 'It was meant to be a joke Inga.'

'Really? Thanks for telling me.'

'But what about large scale production of the traditional ones?' said Nigel, interjecting. 'They seem to be struggling enough with that.'

'Oh don't you worry Nige. I've thought about that. What they need up there is a bit of persuasion, a gang master, someone to crack the bloody whip. They respond to that sort of thing. They like all that, eastern Europeans,' said Huge!.

'But who...?'

Huge! looked over his shoulder to where man mountain Carthew Carew stood leaning against the doorframe, nose buried inside his new signed copy of *My Huge! Cornwall.*

'No,' said Nigel. 'Tell me you're not serious.'

'He's big, he's strong and he'll do what he's told. He's a copper too, so he can threaten them all with deportation to boot. What's not to like?'

Nigel was speechless.

'Carew,' called Huge!, and the giant man lurched in. 'Carew, put the book thing down a minute, before you hurt yourself. I've got a little job for you, up on the moors. Inga will explain. You might need your proddy thing.'

Oggy stood outside Mother's with his mouth agape as the health and hygiene people ran the barrier tape forth and back, and back and forth across his shop doorway and window, making a yellow and black striped macramé of the frontage, rather giving the impression that there was something dangerously toxic within. One of them hammered up a closure notice on the doorframe:

'By Order Cornwall Council – These premises are closed pending further investigation by Cornwall Council (Health and Hygiene Department) and the Food Standards Authority.'

Oggy was desperate. 'But when can I open again? 'Tis me living, come on,' he implored them.

'Sorry boss,' said a man. 'We're just doing what the department tells us.'

Oggy went back inside to where Vi and Mother and Uncle Clar were standing ashen faced, looking out of the shop window.

'Well?' said Mother.

'They've closed us. I can't believe it…' said Oggy.

'They said we was spotless!' said Vi.

'After all these years,' said Mother.

'It was that pasty. Someone left it there.'

'Did you tell 'em that, darlin'?'

'Tell 'em, yes I told them. No, it wasn't one of ours I said. But they never believed me.'

'What'll we live on? We was hardly keeping our heads above water anyway.'

'Well, we got that two thousand. We'll just have to try and make that last until they let us open again.'

A car pulled up outside, and the two people from the previous day's inspection, Ms Bridgett Hook of the council and Mr Tony Wright of the FSA, got out, picked their way through the spider's web of tape and came into the shop through the tinkling door.

'What's this all about?' said Oggy.

She handed him a piece of paper. He squinted at it. Vi and Mother and Uncle Clar stood at the back, unable to speak.

'You can read it at your leisure later, Mr Sloggett. It's just to say that initial analysis from our laboratory in Esher indicates some faecal matter in the sample.'

'So, what? Are we in the clear then?' said Oggy, visibly cheering. 'Thank the lord for that.'

'Faecal matter. Excrement, Mr Sloggett.'

'See Mother, Vi. We're okay. The lady says it's excellent.'

'No, Mr Sloggett. *Excrement.*'

'What? Shi..'

'Yes Mr Sloggett.'

'Well who done that? It wasn't me.'

'Not human, Mr Sloggett.' She pointed at the second paragraph of the preliminary report.

Oggy read it aloud. ' *"Though it is too early to be specific, indications are that the foodstuffs examined contain traces of bat faces".* ' Bat faces? Bat faces!'

'Bat *faeces,* Mr Sloggett. Basically, we believe there may be bat droppings in your pasty. It is a very serious charge, I'm afraid.'

'I keep telling you that wasn't one of my pasties. It must of been left there or something. I don't put bat faces in mine, only the best skirt beef.'

She pulled a form out from her briefcase, and placed it on the shop counter.

'That's as maybe, Mr Sloggett. In the meantime, I have to issue you with one of these,' she said ominously.

'What's that?'

'A fixed penalty notice, for failing to keep your product under cover and on an appropriate dish, or within a prescribed cabinet. My colleague tells me there was a fly on your pasty when he first saw it yesterday.'

She handed it to Oggy.

'Oh my God! Two thousand quid? Two thousand quid! How can I pay two thousand quid just like that. I ain't got that amount in me account. I ain't got nothing in me account!'

The telephone rang.

'Do you want to just get that, Mr Sloggett?' said Ms Hook.

Oggy breathed deeply and answered.

'Good morning, this is Business Solutions for You calling, how are you today? My name is Colin. Am I speaking with Mr Oggy?'

'Oggy,' interrupted Uncle Clar.

'Hello, is that Mr Oggy? Today we can offer...' said Colin.

'Oggy,' persisted Uncle Clar.

'Yes, Uncle Clar, what is it now?' said Oggy. He hung the receiver up.

'Wasn't there two thousand in that brown envelope on the table in the kitchen, or did I dream it?'

The telephone rang again. Oggy looked straight at Ms Hook, then shut his eyes and shook his head. 'No, Uncle Clar,' he said. 'You never dreamt it.'

It was a mild and drizzly day, the thick mists sheeted in from the Atlantic and swirled around the streets and cottages and houses, seeping into every pore of Tredogend's skin, and it felt as if the town was suffocating beneath a grey, damp blanket. Despite the weather, Emma, Quenelle, Julienne and little Goujon braved the elements and made their way to Porzeath, and across the vastness of the beach to the surf shack, where Mervin was huddled with his locks piled high into the hood of an oilskin, sipping on a mug of coffee. She stood in the doorway, the kids in front of her.

Mervin smiled a wide, dimpled smile.

'Suits?' said he.

'Suits,' said she.

'Thing is,' said Mervin. 'It don't look a good day, but you got to look through the mist and drizzle and see what it's like out there. Can you hear the rollers? They come in sets. This surf is the best, guys.'

The kids ran over and grabbed the wet suits from the hanger rail and pulled them on.

Mervin looked at Emma. 'So, you wanna go and see what it's like?'

She nodded. The kids cheered. Mervin picked out a wetsuit and handed it to her, and went and waited outside while she changed, and when she emerged from the criss-crossed planks of the driftwood shack, out into the light and onto the sand, she saw her children standing all in a row hand in hand with him, and she smiled inside.

They grabbed their boards, and jogged off across the wet sand towards the rolling waves.

Huge! stepped up to the front door of the B&B and knocked. The landlady answered, and he saw Inga looking over her shoulder, eating a pasty. 'It's okay, it's for me,' she said. The landlady turned and went back into the dark passage. Inga waited for her to go. Huge! stood there in the clinging wet.

'What?' she said.

'Can I...?'

'No,' she said.

'Could we...?'

'Absolutely not.'

'Not even if...'

'No, not even if nothing. Next question?'

'When were you, you know, going to the moors?'

'Going to the moors with a schitzo psycho to see a clutch of vampires? Oh, later if that's okay.'

'Yes, it's...'

'Anything else?' she said.

Before he could reply, she had slammed the door in his face and in a stonking rage Huge! stomped down the path and back towards Fisherman's Cottage; hell hath no fury like a celebrity chef scorned.

'Fat Dutch lezzer!' he cursed. 'Who the fuck does she think she is? You'd be nothing Ingrid, bloody nowhere without me!'

He bulldozed his way through the crowds of day-trippers in the street, flung his gate open and rattled in through his front door.

'Oh Huge!,' called a lady down the pea gravel and sea-shelled path. 'Any chance of an autograph love?'

He slammed the door behind him, and leaned back heavily against it.

'No there fucking isn't!' he shouted to no one in particular. 'Em! Emma! Are you in? Emmm?'

He stepped into the kitchen. It was very quiet.

There was a note on the table. He picked it up. It read simply 'gone to beach.'

No 'Love Em'. No x's. No nothing.

Oggy was flopped on his stool like a damp dishrag, bored behind the counter of the closed shop. He stared out, framed dejected by the window, as the day's visitors passed by. Some stopped and read the notice pinned up by the council. Some ran their hands along the tangle of plastic barrier tape. Others peered into the shop and at Oggy himself, and he could see and hear them pointing in and giggling and laughing at him just sitting there like a stuffed exhibit on his plinth.

A little boy ran up to the windowpane and squashed his nose and then his whole face, mouth agape, against the glass and he gurneyed and writhed them around and around in a grotesque distortion, eyes crossed and tongue wiggling slimy like a lugworm. His Mum called to him, and held out her hand and he ran back to her, having provoked no reaction at all from the strange, staring man within.

Some were eating pasties from the Emporium up the road, others licked ice creams or gobbled fudge from small, white sweetie bags, and one or two dipped fish and chips into ketchup, while other braver souls tackled Dead Dog's oriental pasties. Occasionally gulls would glide down and skitter squarreling and flapping across the road in pursuit of a chip or a discarded piece of a pasty.

Vi brought him a cup of tay, which he let go cold. Uncle Clar brought him a Garibaldi on a plate. He didn't like them at the best of times. Then Mother popped her head around the door and asked are you all right boy, and he did not even reply to that most extreme of provocations.

Oggy stared at Cheel's iPad, sitting abandoned on the counter shelf in front of him. Without really knowing why, he pressed the on-button, just as Digory had shown him and the screen flickered into life with a nauseating little tune.

Digory had told him all about Google and how you could find anything, anybody, anywhere in the world with it. We'll see, he thought, and middle-fingered he tentatively typed the words 'Business Solutions for You' into the long space at the screen's top. He scrolled down through the list that appeared, and fixed on one and hit on it.

In a flash, the screen exploded into life.

And there he was, a young man in a cerise turban, sitting in a tropical park with palms and parrots, and smiling the widest, cheeriest smile that he had ever seen, and beneath it the Bollywood dancing words jiggled across the screen, 'Colin has the Business Solutions for You!'

Oggy held the iPad up close and squinted at the image.

'It don't look much like Delabole to me, Colin,' he huffed.

Huge! screwed up the note and threw it at the wall.

'Gone to the beach! Gone to the bloody beach!' he screamed. 'Oh yes we all know why you're at the sodding beach, don't we Emma? Mr fucking Whippy, that's why, the maple syrup squirting little turd!'

In frustration and fury, he looked around for something else to sling at the wall, and picked up his own personalised copy of *Huge in Cornwall* from the table. He was about to chuck it when he saw his own cheesy smile beaming out from the cover, and just in time was able to put it down again gently on the table and smooth out the creases on the sleeve.

Huge! sat at the table and began to shake and hyperventilate, and spoke to his own gleaming image in an attempt to compose himself.

'Come on now Huge!,' he said. 'Calm, easy now. Remember who you are. Let's keep it together.'

He practised his deep breathing technique and began to remember who he was. He was Huge!. Huge! the celebrity chef extaordinaire. *Huge! in Cornwall!* Huge! all over! He slowly lifted the book and began to look square into his own hypnotising eyes that pierced out from the cover.

'You're better than all this, Huge!,' he said reassuringly to his own image. 'So, so much better. Now think, what can we do? What *can* we do?'

A smile began to slowly form on his face. 'Oh yes. Yes, you beauty Huge!. That's it! Genius, that's it!'

He grabbed the telephone and began to dial a number.

'Yes?' came the answer.

'Carew? Is that you?'

'Chef? No, it's never you. I don't believe it. What an honour, oh my God,' said Carew, rather grovellingly.

'Yea, yea, yea. Look, listen to me. Are you on your way up to the moors yet?'

'No chef, I was going to go later if that's all…'

'Yes, that's all good…'

'I can go now, if you like Chef…'

'No you dunderhead, listen to me. I need you to do something for me first.'

'Anything chef.'

'Do you have a tow hitch?'

'Yes.'

'Do you know a local scrap yard? With a crusher?'

'Yes chef, Jack Shrapnell in Bodmin.'

'Excellent. Can you deal with him candidly? Discreetly?'

'Eh?'

'Sorry, they were quite hard words weren't they? Does he owe you any favours?'

'Oh right,' said Carew. 'Do you want me to…'

'I just want you to listen to me, you numbskull. This is what I want you to do.'

Huge! related his nasty, vicious plan to the ever-eager-to-please Constable 696 Carthew Carew, the beastly Beast of Bodmin, who took it all down in his notebook at the other end of the line.

'When shall I do it?' asked Carew.

'Now,' he said. 'Do it now, Carthew. Do it now!'

Huge! hung up and laughed to himself. The beast had been released.

'Crushed nuts, eh Mr Whippy?' he chuckled. 'I'll give you more than crushed nuts.'

*

Oggy was still staring at Colin in the cerise turban on the iPad screen when he heard Uncle Clar answer the phone in the room next door.

'I'm not sure if he's in Mr Gregory,' he said. 'Oh yes, you're in luck. He's just here.'

He covered the handset with his palm and whispered. 'Mr Gregory. From the bank. Would like to talk to you.'

'Thank you, Uncle Clar,' said Oggy, momentarily out of his trance.

Vi stood at the doorway and listened.

'I know that Mr Gregory. Is it four months? I thought just the three…No, they closed me this morning….No other form of income, no….Foreclose? What do you mean?….Up for sale?….What, today? You don't waste no time do you?….Thank you. Bye.'

He put the phone down, and when Vi asked him who it was, he told her it was only that Colin again, and just stared straight ahead.

'I can't believe how warm it was,' said Emma.

'I can't believe you stood up. First go too!' said Mervin.

'You were cool Mum!' said little Goujon, jumping up and down.

'Yea, Mum. You're a natural!' said Julienne.

'Surf dude, Mum!' shouted Quenelle.

'There you go,' said Mervin. 'Does that tell you something, or what?'

'You know,' she said. 'I think it does. Could I make us a coffee? Would that be okay?'

'Sure,' said Mervin.

'Sugar?' she said. 'No, I know what you're gonna say…'

'Sweet enough?' he said.

Emma nodded.

'Sweet enough.'

Inga folded the quickly scrawled foraged pasty recipe inside her jacket, picked up her bag, and walked out of her room in the B&B and off up the road to the Pasty Emporium. There was the thriving busy buzz of activity, and the thronging customers just kept on coming to buy their Huge! world champion pasties.

'Is he here today?'

'Oh, we love him. He's the best thing on telly.'

'Oh, we think he's marvellous. So talented, will he be in later?'

'Does he really make all these pasties?'

Inga made her way out through to the back, picked one up and bit into it. Not bad, still using milled black peppercorns, but at least there was no carrot today she thought.

A dark shadow loomed up behind her. It belonged to Carthew Carew.

'You're early,' said Inga. 'I'm not ready yet. I've got to…'

'I got another job to do for Chef first. He wants me to do something important for him, see? So I'll be back in a bit and then we'll go up there and kick ass.'

'Do what?' said Inga.

'You heard. Just be ready.'

Inga watched and brimmed with trepidation as the gigantic brute turned and strode out of the office

The now scattered bits of cloud broke up to reveal blue sky behind. The sun was beginning to break through, enough blue to make a sailor's shirt.

'Sun's out Mummy. Can we go and build dams?' asked Quenelle.

'Yes darling,' said Emma. 'Where will you be?'

'In the stream over by the rocks, by Tristram pool.'

'Okay, off you go. You too Goujon, put your book down darling and save it until you get home,' she said. 'Don't go in the sea. I'll come and find you later.'

Little Goujon closed his book and placed it on a table, and the three happy children ran out of the shack and skipped off across the sand.

'They love it,' said Mervin. 'Happy.'

'Me too,' said Emma. She got to her feet and walked over to him. 'Mervin…' she began.

She stopped in her tracks as his mobile rang, and nervously he shoved it to his ear. It was his Mum, Vi, clearly in a state of some anxiety, and whenever she got anxious, her accent reverted right back to her Plaistow roots.

She gabbled to him about the shop and the inspectors and the cistificate, and she gabbled to him about the bleedin' pasty that had been left in there by some geezer and that it had been full of, would you believe it, bat poo and even more disgustin', carrot? Yes, bat poo, have you ever heard anyfink like it? Where had that come from? Anyway they've bleedin' closed us down. Yes, only put tape up all over the front and a sign and shut us down and given your father a fine! For starters! How much? Oh, only four bleedin' monkeys, that's all. A bleedin' Archer, Mervin! Two grand! If he gets done in court for the bat poo it'll be another ten or twenty grand, Oh, I don't know how much, and now he's just sat on his bleedin' stool staring out into space and the bank have rung and are going to foreclose and re-possess the old shop and it's daylight bleedin' robbery, and we don't know what to do.

And where's Cheel to? She seems to have disappeared off the face of the bleedin' earth!

Carthew Carew bumped across the sandy track in his pick up truck, out through the marram-grassed dunes that backed down to the rear of Porzeath beach. He drove up over a steep rise and stopped for a moment or two at the brow, and he looked out over the golden sands and the breakers beyond, before he dipped down once again into a dry and sandy valley, sheltered on all sides and quite hidden from view. He had never seen the ice cream van before, and had no idea at all of its existence up here in the dunes.

He reversed up to it and hitched one end of a rope around his tow bar, and the other around the van's bumper. He checked that it was all secured properly, then jumped in and sat in the driver's seat and released its handbrake. A small, handstitched felt pasty was hanging from the mirror and he unhooked and necklassed it for a souvenir before he clambered out again.

As he strode away from the van, he wafted an irritating lone bee away with his hand and stepped back into his own cab. He began to drive off. The rope tensed and shuddered, and for a moment the pick up stopped in its tracks. Carew revved hard and slipped the clutch in and out, and it lurched and juddered and began to shake.

Carew had not seen the beehive that was standing on the driftwood decking screwed on to the front of the van, and it began to rock back and forth on its plinth, and the bees became irritated, very irritated, and as the pick up slowly began to inch forwards the hive wobbled, then fell over completely.

My, the ninety thousand Cornish bees were cross. Very cross indeed. They decided to investigate.

The Beast of Bodmin opened his window, leaned out and peered back at the van. The wheels now appeared to be jammed in soft sand. No matter, for he had a plank in the back and so he hopped out, grabbed it, and wedged it under the ice cream van's wheels to give then some purchase and grip.

At first he was quite oblivious to the angrily buzzing swarm, but *not* for long. The first bee stung him right in the neck, the second on the side of his nose, and then he got one on each ear. Slapping himself around the head and yelping like a frenzied madman, he frantically fled the stinging winged attack and as more throbbing, pulsating stings were embedded in him, he dived back into his cab and wound the window winder up as fast he could.

Bee after bee after bee fizzed and buzzed into the cab with him, and more bees still hit the outside of the window and windscreen as they desperately endeavoured to inject their nasty stings into the beastly Carew with the supreme act of self sacrifice.

Swishing and swatting madly to fight off and squash as many of the furious little insects as he could, Carew revved the pick up and it moved forward across the plank that made the platform for the ice cream van's wheels. He began to tow Mervin's home away, leaving the wrecked remains of his driftwood deck and potted fig tree and swarm of angry bees behind, trailing some fairy lights and old nets and bunting with him as he went.

He bounced up across the dunes at breakneck speed, van in tow, bits falling off at regular intervals, a mirror here, a number plate there. Finally, the giant illuminated swirly ice cream on the roof, complete with its flake and raspberry sauce, shook and toppled over as the twin loudspeakers kicked in and blared out '*Jack and Jill went up the hill to fetch a pale of water*'.

But Carew had no tutti frutti or raspberry ripple to sell at all, and vacated the dunes the way he had come and got back on the road, his head, neck and face swollen furious in an angry red by the stings of Cornish bees. But Huge! would be happy and that, after all, was what *really* mattered.

At the surf shack, Emma looked at Mervin as he popped the phone in his pocket.

'Was that your mum?' she asked.

'Yeah,' said Mervin. 'Things aren't good at home. But listen…'

'What?' she said.

He turned his head towards the dunes.

'I'm sure I could hear 'Jack and Jill…'

Chapter Twenty Two
The Fairy Ring

I knowed her old father, old man,
I knowed her old father, old man,
I knowed her old man, he blowed in the band.
Going up Camborne Hill, coming down.

'Camborne Hill' – *traditional Cornish song*

Cheel was in her tent when Mervin called and told her all the sorry tales, of the van he had made his home in now gone who knows where, of his beehive and pot plants and lights, and the pasty left on the counter and the health inspectors. Of course, that last bit did all made sense now. All those little bats hanging asleep over the vats of ingredients. Doubtless, it had been one of the pasties made up in the factory in the old hangar, one of the ones that she had ensured would be contaminated with carrot. But *who* on earth would want to pinch his old van? Mervin had no idea.

'Look, just go home and tell them I'm all right brother,' she said.

'What if they ask…'

'Leave it to me.'

'And me van…'

'I'll deal with it,' she said.

The phone went dead.

Carew arrived to pick up Inga at the Emporium. He was running late, having pulled over outside of Tredogend to squeeze out some of the bee stings. She looked at him with some alarm, for he looked a fright.

'What on earth happened to you?' she said. 'And what the hell is that?'

'An ice cream van. Long story, shut up and get in,' he said. 'I got to get it crushed in Jack Shrapnells.'

'Crushed? Why? It looks like somebody's been living in it."

'Just get in,' ordered Carew. 'We'll do the van, then we'll deal with the pasties.'

'You're losing it,' said Inga.

Carew leant across and dragged her into the cab. 'Come on!' he said. 'We got no time to waste. Chef wants it done!'

He squealed his tyres, and with the van in tow, they sped off out of Tredogend to Bodmin.

It took them half an hour to get to the Walker Lines Industrial estate, and they drove in beneath the metal sign 'Jack Shrapnel Scrap Dealer' towing Mervin's ice cream van behind them. A small dark skinned man with faded tattoos in inky blue on his hands and neck, who Inga took to be Shrapnel himself, emerged from a caravan and came over to Carew's window and peeped in. He nodded to Inga and spoke to Carew.

'Who have you been fighting?' he asked.

'Bees,' said Carew.

Shrapnel laughed. 'Good for the bees,' he said.

'It ain't bloody funny. Now, are you going to crush this for me, or what? Remember that little conversation we had?'

'Yea, don't worry about it. Put it over there by the conveyor belt. I got half a dozen to do dreckly.'

'I don't want this getting out mind.'

'Want what getting out?' laughed Shrapnel, shrugging his shoulders.

'About the ice cream van...'

'Yea I realise that,' sneered the scrapper. 'Like I said, what's to get out?'

'Well, you make sure...'

'Over by the belt,' said Shrapnel, and turned and walked back to his caravan.

Huge! was being interviewed by Jerry Parsons on Radio 5 Live, to promote his new ghastly ghost written glossy, *My Huge! Cornwall.*

'So Huge!, you're well known for having this big, this huge personality. How does this fit with your new life down in Cornwall?'

'I, we, have been totally accepted by the community of Tredogend. It's back to my roots really, producing good, honest artisan food from local ingredients. Low food miles, all that sort of thing, and then giving it all a gourmet twist to run alongside the more traditional recipe.'

'What, like chilli chicken tikka masala pasty, a bit of fusion?'

'Not *that* much fusion, Jerry! But certainly to take the pasty forward into the twenty first century, sex it up a bit, you know...'

'Sex the pasty up? What do the locals think?'

'Oh, they love being sexed up Jerry!'

'Now, now Huge!. So, how on earth do you sex up a pasty?'

'Well, in all seriousness, we're working on a foraged pasty at the minute. One whose ingredients one can find for free, within walking distance of where it'll be prepared and baked.'

'So I guess it's eco-friendly too?'

'All very green Jerry.'

'Wow. And how on earth do you find time to make and bake all these *and* run the Emporium, *and* run gigs like Huge!Fest, *and* be a devoted family man?'

'Well, you know. It's not all roses at times, but one struggles on Jerry,' he said.

'Not all roses? Well, you look to me like a man who has his life/work balance just about perfect, Huge!, good on ya.'

'It's not without its downside, Jerry, I can tell you.'

Jerry Parsons sniffed a story. 'How do you mean?'

'Well, I don't want to make too much of it,' sniffed Huge!. 'But I've been stalked by an internet troll. It's been terribly upsetting for Emma and the kids. He's said some awful, vile things that I couldn't repeat on air.'

'Oh my goodness. Do you know who it is?'

'Oh, just someone with a grudge, I can't really say. It wouldn't be right. Another pasty maker, as it happens.'

'That's ridiculous.'

'Well, it's human nature unfortunately, isn't it? Here I am setting up a project to take the pasty out to the world, and the little guy with the pasty shop down the road, Mother's I think it's called, doesn't like it,' said Huge!. 'Oh, sorry Jerry. I guess I shouldn't have said the name. The food standards people are closing him down anyway, as it happens, so I, I, I'm sorry, you don't want to hear…'

'No Huge!, are you okay?'

'It's a lonely journey at times, Jerry.'

'It sounds terrible what you've been through.'

'Jerry, I'm a survivor, a troll survivor,' croaked Huge!. 'I guess it's a badge of honour.'

'Huge!, thank you for being so candid with us here on the Jerry Parson's Show today, and good luck with your venture and the rest of your series.'

'Aaagh!' Inga screamed at Carthew Carew's car radio. 'Turn that bastard off! Where's the button?'

She leaned forward and reached out for the off button.

Carew slapped her hand away. 'Oi!' he said. 'These are my controls. Hands off, I'm listening to Huge!, all right?'

'Don't you touch me.'

'Well don't you touch my radio.'

'I don't even like your radio.'

'Well then it's good that you don't have to touch it.'

Inga slumped back in her seat and huffed and folded her arms, and concentrated on looking away from him and out of the passenger window, out across the empty moorland expanses, to Rough Tor, and then across Davidstow to the old aerodrome. As they turned off to the right, along an old concreted runway, the car began to bump and scrape on the potholed and crumbled surface.

The fir trees of the forestry plantation gathered darkly in around them until, maybe a mile or so along the way, Carew took a turning into a narrow gap between some tall leylandii. She was a little bemused to see such a sad and miserable bungalow within the darkly overbearing quad of trees, and the old hangar-come-factory where the Emporium's pasties were being made.

The car jarred to a halt, and Carew got out and stretched and flexed his raw-boned frame. Inga sat and watched him as he scowled and stalked menacingly around the premises. She got out herself and, a little apprehensive, stood by the car and watched as he marched up to the door of the bungalow and rapped on it, hard and continuously, with the butt end of old sparky.

Cheel watched from the dark safety of her patch of undergrowth beneath the firs. She could see the little felt pasty that hung around Carew's neck on a string; she had stitched it herself and given it to her brother when he had moved into his new home in the ice cream van. And she *definitely* recognised the man who answered the door. It was the man she had floored in the factory days before.

Flat on her stomach, Cheel crawled forward through the brittle, desiccated needles that carpeted the lifeless forestry floor, to close behind a bleached tree stump vantage point from where she could peep between its antler-branches and take in all the action.

One by one, other scrawny, grey-faced men emerged, hunched and dishevelled, from the bungalow, and stood alongside the first man.

'Right,' she heard Carew say. 'Huge! has sent me up here to sort you lot out. What's going on? What's with the carrots?'

Krno pulled himself up straight.

'Carrot? What carrot?' he said indignantly.

'The carrots in Huge!'s pasties, that's what, pal,' said Carew.

'We don't use no stinking carrot. It not traditional fool. You sink we stupid?'

'Yea, I do, as a matter of fact,' he said, and took a step forward. 'You lot need to shake it up.'

'Who you? Why don't he come tell us?'

'He's too busy for the likes of you,' sneered Carew. 'He's a celebrity. A star. He's important. You're nothing, get it? I've come to tell you that you need to work days too, and I'm going to make sure you do.'

'Can't work days. Police,' said Krno.

'I am the police, all right?' said Carew, and he tapped the numbers on the epaulettes of his shirt. 'You work days, or I'll have you kicked out the country as quick as you can say knife.'

'You can go to hell!'

Carew took one great stride forward and quick as a flash, poked Krno with the electric cattle prod and jolted him with three thousand volts, and he fell uncontrollably twitching to the ground.

'What are you doing?!' screamed Inga.

'You shut up,' he snapped. 'Right. Anyone else want a little kiss from old sparky? Get into work, you scabs.'

One of Krno's friends stepped forward.

'Come on then, bring it on if you want to join him,' said Carew, smiling.

The man took another step.

Carew zapped Krno again. Again he twitched, violently.

'Anyone else want some?' he challenged, and glared at each of the cowed, wretched men, who stood aghast: motionless and silent, sullen and defeated.

Carew was quite taken by surprise by a voice that came from behind him. It was a voice that didn't sound of Eastern European origin at all. It was a voice that sounded Cornish.

'Yeah, me,' it said, softly. 'I want some.'

He spun around. So too Inga.

At first they did not see the slight figure of a girl standing diminutively behind them on the concrete. She had short black hair, the spikey ends dyed golden. She wore a white t-shirt decorated with a sprayed St Piran tag. Her arms and neck were tattooed all over, and on her right forearm Carew could read the three large letters.

'WOK,' he growled menacingly through his twisted lips. 'I been looking for you.'

'I been looking for you, too,' said Cheel. She pointed at the little felt pasty dangling from his neck and fixed him with a cold stare.

'Where's the van?'

'It's going in the crusher,' said Carew. 'You wanna join it?'

She removed her rucksack and placed it on the ground. She removed her shoes. She removed her nose stud and her earrings and the ring from her lip, and put them in her pocket. She moved towards him, and as she moved, she repeated the words.

'On my honour and the honour of my country, I swear to wrestle without treachery or brutality...'

Carew looked her up and down. 'Oh right,' he laughed. 'And what's all that bullshit about?'

'...and in token of my sincerity I offer my hand to my opponent...'

Cheel outstretched her hand towards Carew.

'...in the words of my forefathers...'

Carew started to laugh out loud. Krno looked over to him from where he lay on the ground.

'I vouldn't laugh if I vas you,' he said.

'I've told you. You can shut up now,' he said, and zapped him again, and he twitched back down to the ground.

'...Gwary whek yu gwary tek..'

'It's no good asking your Romanian mates for help, luv. You're gonna get some,' he sneered, and held up the buzzing prod in front of his face and spoke to it. 'Looky here old sparky, another customer! What a busy boy you are today.'

Carew lunged clumsy and ham fisted at her. Lightning fast, Cheel danced to one side and slapped the cattle prod out of his hand, and it clattered to the ground. Nimbly, she hopped to his right, and using his own clumsy momentum she grabbed his fluorescent tabard and pulled him forwards at speed, and hooked her foot behind his leg and spun him around, twisted him upside down, and made a back for him so he was looking right up at the sky and totally disorientated. Then, with all the finely honed skills she had practised all through the year, she flipped him as high into the air as she could, and holding him by the wrist, brought him down in an arc and slammed him on his back onto the concrete below with an almighty whoomph.

Done. Winded. Nineteen stone of ugliness in a helpless, wheezing, gasping heap on the floor, and the cowed men from the factory rushed across to finish the job off.

'Stand back!' shouted Cheel, as she mantled over the cowering Carew. She snatched the felt pasty from around his neck, and put it around her own.

'So,' she said. 'Where's the van?'

'Shrapnel's. Bodmin,' he bleated.

Cheel dusted her hands together and stepped back. She looked at the gang of Romanians.

'All yours, boys,' she said and in seconds she heard the hiss of mace and the coughing and screaming of the Beast of Bodmin as the Romanians cackled and swarmed all over him like a flock of starving hungry black-feathered vultures.

Cheel returned to her rucksack and took out her earrings and studs and reinserted them all. Inga walked over and reverentially held out her hand. They both smiled shyly.

'Hi, I'm Inga,' she said. 'I enjoyed that.'

Cheel shook it gently.

'Cheel,' she said. 'Woman of Kernow.'

'Come on,' said Inga. 'Jump in and I can take you to the van. But we'll have to hurry.'

Even while they nailed up the 'For Sale' sign, Oggy just stared out.

'What's on Father?' asked Mervin. He peered deep into his father's eyes. There seemed to be nothing in there, blank like a goat's. 'Father?'

'He been like it all day, Mervin, I'm terrible worried,' said Mother.

'Ain't moved, darlin',' said Vi.

'Ain't drunk his tay. He'll make himself wisht, he will,' said Uncle Clar.

'Well, he can't stay here, he'll fall off the stool and hurt himself,' said Mervin, logically enough. 'We're gonna have to take him through and sit him in the kitchen.'

'How are we gonna do that? He's a big old unit, your father,' said Vi.

'No probs Mum,' said Mervin. 'We got a sack truck.'

Together they manhandled Oggy's dead weight sideways onto the sack truck, holding him upright at all times, and Mervin lashed him securely on with rope. They tilted him backwards, and wheeled him back and into the kitchen, where they untied him and together eased him into an old Windsor chair at the head of the table.

And Oggy just stared silently ahead.

*

The pick up screeched into Shrapnel's scrap yard, scattering gravel and billowing up a dirty cloud of dust.

'There it is,' shouted Inga. 'He's put it on the conveyor belt. Shit!'

She slammed the brakes on and in a flash, Cheel had leapt out of the cab and up onto the slowly moving belt in front of Mervin's ice cream van screaming 'Stop!' at the top of her voice.

The jaws of the pneumatic crusher slowly opened in front of her, and she could see Jack Shrapnel on the other side of the belt with his ear protectors on and his gnarly hand on the operating lever, and she vaulted down and grabbed his hand with her own and shoved the lever back to the stop position.

The conveyor belt shuddered to a halt, with the front bumper of the van just an inch from the gaping metallic jaws, saved by the skin of its teeth.

'What's on!' shouted Shrapnel in surprise. 'What do 'ee think you're doing?'

'Sorry,' said Cheel. 'But 'tis me brother's. That's his home.'

Shrapnel gave her a look.

'I knows you. Sloggett's maid, ain't 'ee?' he growled. 'I sings with yer father.'

Inga ran over. 'You remember me from this morning, Mr Shrapnel? With Carew? There's been a big mistake.'

'Look, Miss. I don't know who *you* be, but he told me this wasn't to get out. This gotta be crushed.'

'How much?' said Inga. Shrapnel scowled.

'I ain't got nothing,' Cheel hissed to Inga.

'I have,' said Inga. 'How much?'

'Well,' said Shrapnel. 'Couple of hundred should get it off the belt and seal me lips.'

'Here,' said Inga, and passed him a handful of twenties. 'Now get it down please, and we'll take it away. No questions asked.'

Jack Shrapnel trousered the wodge and nodded.

'No questions,' he said, and put the conveyor belt in reverse and pointed at Cheel.

'And tell father I expects one of they pasties of his, do you hear?'

They towed Mervin's ice cream van back up to the factory on the old Davidstow aerodrome, and pulled up outside and got out; relieved, Cheel and Inga strolled side by side along the crumbling runway that ran through the plantation.

'So why would Carew do this to Merv?' asked Cheel.

'Huge! got him to do it.'

'Beats me,' said Cheel and shook her head.

'Beats me too,' said Inga. She touched Cheel's neck. 'I like that one. What sort of bird is that? Not a swallow, is it?'

'No,' chuckled Cheel. 'It's a chough. Our national bird.'

'Oh,' said Inga. 'Have you got many tattoos?'

'Only all over,' she said, and shushed her finger to her lips. 'I spent nearly all me student loan on 'em,' she confided. 'Don't tell father; he'll have a heart attack or something worse. What were you up here for anyway?'

'Huge! wants me to give this new recipe to these poor devils. A foraged pasty. I honestly never knew they lived like this.'

'Let me see,' said Cheel. She read the recipe.

'What do you think?'

'I think there's one or two improvements we could make,' grinned Cheel. 'How do you fancy doing a bit of baking?'

Inga smiled and nodded.

Together they walked through the gap in the leylandii to where Krno stood alone outside the hangar door. He bowed his head slightly to Cheel.

'Sank you,' he said.

'Where's Carew?'

He raised his eyebrows. 'It has been done,' he said. He held out the palm of his hand, and Inga reached out and picked an object from it.

'What's that?' asked Cheel.

Inga looked at her.

'A silver number six,' she said, rather puzzled, and then she turned it over with her finger and thumb. 'Or a nine…'

'Where's your mates gone to?' Cheel asked him.

'Zey be back dracly. A little job is necessary,' said Krno, rather ominously. 'Zen we have to leave.'

'I can help you, but before you do, would you do me and Cornwall one massive favour?' she asked. 'Bake me one more batch of pasties for Huge!. Just the same as you always have.'

Krno nodded and for the first time smiled. 'For "wok", is no problem,' he said.

Digory had not heard from Cheel for ages, though he knew she'd done a vanishing act, and when she made her contrite confession to him that it was she who had borrowed his quad without first asking, he was instantly forgiving, but naturally curious as to why she'd needed to do it.

She explained the circumstances fully, and he said that he understood and he'd have done the same, dear. He told her that he'd be happy to let her have some of his organic pork, and to help her find the other things she needed, and when she'd turned up at Dordigor Farm on his quad and offered him the driver's seat, he'd politely declined, and he rode pillion behind her up along and through the lanes to the moors on a fairground death ride of terrifyingly fast proportions.

Less than a mile from the forestry plantation, at the edge of the old aerodrome, at Digory's behest they stopped and dismounted on a patch of squelchy grass that had been closely cropped by moorland sheep.

'Now,' said Digory, still in truth shaking like a leaf from the white-knuckle ride. 'This is where we used to find them.' He shuffled around and peered down at the ground for some minutes. 'Nope, can't see any.'

'When did you last see 'em, Uncle Digory?'

'Nineteen sixty eight, no, I tell a lie. Sixty nine dear,' said Digory.

'What?'

'We was having a party in one of the Nissen huts, me and yer father. Got all the bloody freaks from Boscastle and Tintagel and Port Isaac and Porzeath up here, we did, as well as all the girls and boys from Tredogend. Had bands and everything, went on for days, least it felt like it,' he said. 'Shroomfest we called it.'

'Not Father surely!'

'Yes, your father was a proper heller in his day.'

'Digory!'

'We was all young once, Cheel. Look, here's one.'

He bent and plucked a small toadstool from the ground, an insignificant little thing, beigy, fleshy coloured with a tell-tale nipple on the top of the umbrella.

'That's the boy, this is what you want. Now let's see what we can find. Oh look, here's more…'

'Wow,' she said. 'They must have a proper name I suppose? Latin and stuff?'

Digory nodded. 'Magicus mushroomus, dear,' he said, laughed, and popped one in his mouth. 'Shroom tay, shroom quiche, chicken and shroom pie. Proper job! Mustn't use too many though.'

Cheel grinned. 'Mustn't you?' she said mischievously.

They cropped the little toadstools from the fairy ring until they had filled a ValuCheaps carrier bag, and Cheel proudly held it aloft.

'Right, Uncle Digory, just one more thing,' she said. 'Mother's told me all about the holy well, the special water. I need some.'

Digory looked sheepish. 'Told you did she? St David's Well?' he said. ''Tis a bit of a trek over the moor. Other side of Davidstow Church. You'll need me to draw you a map.'

The inside of the hangar factory was a hive of activity, as the Romanians ran to and fro to complete their final batch of pasties, this time without carrot, but very definitely still with the bat droppings, or ground black peppercorns as everyone thought they were.

Inga stood close to Cheel at a table, and they worked the pastry, their fingers cold from the bowl of special water that they flicked and dripped into the mix. Then Cheel, with a rolling pin in her hand, helped her roll out a circle of pastry, and together they practised the refined art of crimping. Inga felt thrilled and privileged to be having a one to one with the fastest crimper in the west. Slowly, but surely, the two girls began to concoct their pasties. One was an organic pork pasty, full of Gloucester old spot, rice and apple and a single, one-off special ingredient for Inga to take to Nigel. The other was a foraged pasty, not exactly to Huge!'s recipe, but to their own altogether more imaginative, more creative, more excitingly mind-blowing one. One for Huge! himself.

'Oh,' said Cheel, as if it were an afterthought. 'Uncle Digory, did you remember that Ketamine?'

Hubble, bubble, toil and trouble.

Chapter Twenty Three
The Pantry

The other night, I had a dream,
The funniest dream of all...

'Little Lize' – *Traditional Cornish Song.*

One by one in the early morning light, the little bats flapped back in through the hole in the rear of the old hangar on the moor, as they had done since the end of the last war, stuffed full of delicious moths and exhausted from flying all night long. It was dark in the hangar again, as it always used to be. Silent, save the occasional sonar squeak.

On the work surface below, a single pasty had been left; just one pasty from the batch destined to be the last ever baked there.

And in the unloved, unlovely bungalow next door, there was nothing save a damp smell and an old torn sleeping bag.

All gone.

Cheel and Inga knelt at the holy well. It was roughly constructed of granite, and in the shape of a small, rounded beehive. The inside was padded with moss and maidenhair ferns that dripped with clear, fresh water. Special water. Cheel opened a package and produced the two pasties, which she placed on a flat stone at the hearth of the well. She held Inga's hand, and together they looked up to the skies.

'Blessed by the sweet, sacred waters of St Piran, I invoke ye ancient spirits of Kernow past, Kernow present and Kernow future by the gift of these pasties, that our people might rise again! Gwary whek yu gwary tek!' she called.

Somewhere way off in the distance a curlew shrilled its warbling, haunted cry, and a little breeze fluttered across the two girls, and then was gone again as quickly as it had come. The moor was silent.

'Gwary wh….what does that *mean*?' asked Inga.

Cheel looked her right in the eye.

'Fuck knows,' she said. 'Come on, let's go!'

Vi came downstairs to where Oggy was still sitting bolt upright in the chair, as he had been all night long. She boiled the kettle and made tay. She poured him a mug full, and slid it in front of him, and he moved his eyes for the first time in nearly a day, and set them on her.

'Thank 'ee,' he said.

'Tea and reflection, darlin',' she said, and squeezed his hand.

He huddled over the mug, and blew into the steam. He slurped noisily.

'That's it then maid,' he said quietly.

'What?'

'Time we moved on, anyway. Been here long enough.'

'What do you mean?'

'We'll go somewhere else. Somewhere far, far away,' he said.

'My gawd darlin'. We're too old to be let into Australia, though the kids might come, that could help us. America I suppose, Canada maybe? New Zealand's beautiful.'

He looked up, puzzled. 'I was thinking Bodmin,' he said.

The telephone rang. Oggy answered.

'Is that Mother's please?' said a voice.

'It was,' said Oggy.

'Good morning please. Am I speaking with Mr Oggy?' said a deep sub continental voice.

'Who's that?'

'My name is Colin.'

'You don't sound like the Colin I speaks to. Are you the one in the photo on that interweb, in that nice pink hat thing in the park with parrots?'

'Oh no, that's not me Mr Oggy. That would be a model.'

'What, he's called Colin too?'

'We're all called Colin here at Business Solutions for You, Mr Oggy.'

'What, isn't that confusing? Do you all wear different coloured hats then?'

'No, no, Mr Oggy. We all have our real names too, sir,' he said.

'Funny old place, Deli. What's the weather like up there today, foggy?'

'Oh no, it's a beautiful day here today Mr Oggy. Thirty eight degrees, bright sunshine, and no monsoon warnings.'

'That's nice. I might have to move up there if it's like that then, Colin. 'Tis pissing with rain here, four mile down the road. Any houses for sale?'

'Oh Mr Oggy,' said Colin. 'We would love to have you here in India sir. It would be our pleasure.'

'India? What, you ain't up Delabole?'

'Oh no, please Mr Oggy,' said Colin cheerfully. 'Delhi, India. Now, Business Solutions for You has another offer. This time 4% plus twenty two pence per transaction on debit cards and...'

'How much for a little place where you lives then? A little bungalow for me and Vi with a room for Uncle Clar and a shed out the back for Mother?' asked Oggy.

'Oh for Christ's sake darlin', buck up! I ain't going to India, Australia, Delhi or Deli or bleedin' Bodmin. We ain't leavin'!' shouted Vi

'Look missus, the sign's up, read it,' he said. His face was a furious crimson and angry tendrils of ginger hung down over his eyes, and he dropped the receiver.

''Tis all over! We're out on our ears. I never want to see another pasty again in me life.'

'What?'

'You heard!' he blared, and jumped to his feet. 'Get Mervin. I'm going to sell off every bloody bit of this place, every shelf, every light bulb, every tap, everything before them buggers get their thieving diddy-co fingers on it all. 'Tis all going! Mother was right, there's something funny in that pantry, so we'll start with them flagstones in there, shall we? We'll get good money for them! Out of me way missus! Where's me crowbar?'

And the telephone hung swinging under the counter, and a faint voice could be heard saying 'My utmost apologies Mr Oggy, sir. Would 3.98% be more suitable? I will be speaking to my supervisor Mr Oggy, and will be getting right back to you...'

Up at the Emporium, the customers flooded in and the mop capped ladies were making and baking and selling, and the day's stock of pasties were beginning to roll out as usual, skirt beef, sliced swede and potato and onion, all seasoned with salt and white pepper, and milled black peppercorns, or tiny bat turds if you prefer.

Huge! and Nigel were briefing in the office behind.

'Looks like Peter Cushing's mob came up trumps last night then? Good old Carew,' chuckled Huge!. 'He must have sparked some life into 'em.'

'Yep,' said Nigel. 'Still using black pepper though. Must be a cultural thing.'

'Did Inga the minga get back unscathed? They like virgins, don't they? Still I don't suppose that'll affect *her* much.'

'No, no. She's back.'

'Yea, I thought they'd soon let her go,' said Huge!. Inga walked in carrying two pasties on a plate. 'Oh,' said Huge!. 'Hi Inga.'

'Hi Huge!.' she said.

'Wow, is that the foraged pasty?' asked Nigel.

'Yea, that one is,' she said, and pointed at the one on the left of the plate. 'I think you'll love it Huge!. It's *so* right on. I'm loving it, it's got local provenance, it's green, it's delicious, and hey, it's cheap. Ticks all the boxes. Really, I think it's a winner Huge!. You've really got something special here.'

'Can I try it?'

'Well,' said Inga. 'You could, but you know what I thought, where better to try it out than right at the place where all the ingredients were foraged? We could take a trip up there Huge!. Then if that works, we can use that as the theme for the next programme. What do you reckon?'

She flashed her eyes at him.

'A trip up there?' said Huge!, a little surprised. What a turn up for the books, he thought. She may be a little bit of a bloater at the mo, but hey!

'Nige?' she said.

'Brilliant. Sounds good to me Inga. You should do it, Huge!, you really should,' said Nigel.

'I didn't want you to feel left out Nigel. There's one for you too. Organic pork, apple and wild rice,' said Inga.

'Wow,' said Nigel. 'See you both later Huge!.'

'Oh,' said Huge!. 'For sure. I'll get the beast cruiser Inga. Let's go.'

After the previous day's cold shoulder, Huge! had not expected such a quick turnaround in Inga's affections, though of course he was never in doubt that eventually she would overcome whatever ridiculous little notion or misgiving she'd had and come round submissively to his charismatic charm.

The beast-cruiser took them up through St Breward and onto the open moor, and across to Delphy Bridge, where he manoeuvered the grotesquely oversized vehicle across the hummocky grass and along the side of the De Lank river, to their hidden spot behind a thicket of wind-crippled blackthorn bushes.

In a flash he'd pulled his shirt off, and then his trousers and boxers, as usual forgetting his socks. He turned to the delicious Inga, who was holding the delicious pasty, and reached across and tried to slobber her a kiss with his fat fleshy lips.

'Whoa tiger, not yet,' she said hurriedly. 'Have the pasty first and tell me what you think. I worked very hard on it. Please.'

He took it from her. 'If you think you can wait that long darling,' he said.

He bit into it. It was delicious.

'Wow,' he said. 'And the pastry Ingrid. The crimping. Where did you learn to do that? It's all brilliant!'

He dusted some crumbs from his tum, and he took another mouthful, then another, then another, and she watched intently as he finished off the whole extra special pasty. He was chomping away so greedily with his mealy, fleshy mouth that he did not notice the quad bike and little trailer that pulled up behind them.

'Oooh,' he said. 'Oooh my head's spinning a bit. I'm, I'm…'

'An asshole? Yes you are,' said Inga coldly. He didn't hear.

'Wow, what colours,' said Huge. He leaned back in his seat and closed his eyes. 'God I'm full. Wow, dizzy…'

His mouth dropped open and his head rolled back.

He was quite oblivious to Cheel, who had opened the rear door and got into the back and was looking over the top of the headrest.

'Cheel,' said Inga over her shoulder. 'Do you think we might have put too many mushrooms in his pasty?'

'Possibly,' said Cheel. 'Well, probably.'

The naughty girls giggled, and as they looked on, Huge!, naked apart from his socks, slowly but surely spiralled off into his own horrifying world; a nightmarish trip into a psychedelic, Technicolour kaleidoscopic of Cornish hell.

A Cornwall where, dressed in just his socks and unable to run fast or to cry out, he was chased and stung by an angry swarm of little black and yellow striped Cornish bees into a Cornish meadow where, breathless, he was charged by a rampaging, blaring, bellowing, wild St Piran's Cross bull, that buffeted and jostled and trampled him down to the shitty grass and gored him with his sharpened longhorns.

A Cornwall where it rained carrots from an orange sky, and where a flock of one-legged gulls swooped down and screeched and squarrelled and splattered around his head and pecked spiteful at his eyes, and where bats swirled down and around and in and out of his floppy hair and scratched at his face with their razor claws and bit vicious into his bloodied neck.

A Cornwall where an army of vindictive and evil little piskies and knockers and Buccas pulled and pinched at him and tweaked and tripped him, bundled him up and carried him off aloft up over Hamburger Hill, where coachloads of mysterious, mystery tripping blue rinsers overtook them on the dual carriageway and pointed and laughed at him all trussed up, and mockingly shouted and waved 'Hiii Huge! We love you, we do!'

A Cornwall where Inga and Nigel and his lovely Emma, hand in hand with Mervin, stood waving with Quenelle and Julienne and little Goujon along the verge of the A30, and screeched with helpless, hysterical abandon as he huffed and puffed past them stark bollock naked, and flabbered panting and wheezing, pathetically trying to protect his modesty with a Little Pixie pasty bag, pursued relentlessly by the brutish PC 696 Carthew Carew who galloped along, blue light-flashing, bareback on the snarling, slavering Beast of Bodmin, and poked and prodded his bare, flesh-pale ass with all three thousand volts of a smoking old sparky, all the way up to the English border.

A Cornwall where at the border the Cornish giant Anthony Payne bid him a fond fare-thee-well, and brandished his good and trusty sword as a baton and conducted a vast, vampire male voice choir and silver band ensemble from the darkest, deepest bowels of Cornish hell, performing 'Trelawney' at the very top tenor of their terrifying banshee voices.

It was not what you might call a good trip.

Just think Newquay.

Just think Friday night and hens and stags.

Just think August.

Cheel and Inga watched Huge!'s face twitch and contort with each new layer of terror on his magically-mushroomed mental mystery tour trip. Slowly, they shoved him across and out of the driver's seat, and Cheel got to work on him with her spray paints, and an indelible felt tip pen for the finer details.

By the time she was nearing the end, Huge! actually looked rather good; a little tribal, maybe, but nonetheless arty. He was a cultural fusion, sort of Samoa meets Scredda. Inga was impressed.

'Wow Cheel. He looks annoyingly cool like that,' she said.

'Just the finishing touch to go,' said Cheel. She flopped back his fringe, popped the top off her thick nibbed felt tip and leaned forward. She held the fringe back with her left hand and began to write across his forehead. She turned and grinned at Inga.

'Sometimes, only one word will do.'

Inga nodded. 'He certainly is,' she said.

The girls reflected that the decorated Huge! would have made an interesting installation down at the Tate St Ives, but it was too late for all that now. They were planning to head in completely the opposite direction; coincidentally, in the very same direction that his own terrifying nightmare trip was taking him.

Cheel backed the trailer around, and they hoisted him aboard with a harness and a wire pulley and hook, just like the carcass of an unfortunate ruminant. Inga jumped up on the back of the quad and put her arms around Cheel, and off they sped with Huge! trussed and loaded up, laid out and quite oblivious to it all in the trailer, towards the badland border country in the lush rolling hills just the other side of Lanson.

Nigel had been relieved to be rid of Huge! and Inga. There had been noticeable tensions for some days now, and clearly there were some issues that they needed to resolve, and it was better left to the two of them. He sat at the table with Tom, and looked at the pasty she'd had baked for him.

'Well Tom, we might as well try this while we wait for his hugeness,' he said.

Tom watched as Nigel bit into it. He seemed to enjoy it, and nodded his approval, and passed it to his subordinate for a bite. It made Tom feel quite peckish for more, but Nigel pulled rank, snatched it back and finished the pasty off himself.

'It's good,' Nigel said. 'Inga's done a great job. You can *really* taste the pig, if you know what I mean. Oh, there's a hard bit. What's that I wonder…'

He poked out his tongue, and with his thumb and forefinger picked off a small silver object. The secret, surprise ingredient.

'That shouldn't be in there.' He held it up. 'What is it, a number six?' he said.

'Or a number nine…' said Tom.

Nigel hadn't been able to raise anyone at the factory to answer his call, but Inga was most helpful when he rang her as to the whereabouts of Carthew Carew and the Romanians. She told him that Carew had been rather cruel to them with his electric prod. There had been a bit of an altercation she said, and they'd all set upon him at once, and his clothes had been ripped and torn.

It had all looked very nasty. She had no idea what had happened to Carew, and now the Romanian guys had all disappeared into thin air too. Like a puff of smoke.

She said that, now that he asked, she remembered Carew's number from the epaulettes of his police shirt. It was 696. Maybe the 9 had been upside down, she joked, because he really wasn't a very nice person at all. Quite demonic, in fact, and 666 would certainly have been a little more apt.

And as for Huge!, hadn't he gone back to see them in the Emporium down in Tredogend? He'd seemed to be very pleased with the foraged pasty, and wanted to tell them all about it.

Nigel put the phone down. He looked a bit wisht.

'What's the matter?' said Tom. Nigel put the silver number 9 down on the table.

'You know I said that pasty tasted of pig?' he said.

'Oh my god,' said Tom, clutching his hand over his mouth. 'It's Carew. I feel sick!'

'Get your coat! We're out of here.'

The dapper little widower Mr Digory Hicks had been busy at Cheel's instigation. Ms Bridgett Hook and Mr Tony Wright, Cornwall Council health and hygiene inspector and Food Standards Authority Inspector respectively, pulled up outside the 'Huge! in Cornwall' Pasty Emporium in Tredogend, a town fast becoming a happy hunting ground for them. More especially so now, since they'd had a tip-off that very morning that something in there might be of interest to them. How thrilled they were to discover that this time the tiny little bat droppings were in *all* the pasties they checked. They were closing so many establishments that they were very nearly running out of yellow and black striped hazard tape and closure signs.

And this time it was all being filmed. It was good TV after all.

Digory had then agreed to accompany Miss Daphne Masters of the Cornwall Wildlife Trust up to the old Davidstow aerodrome to see the unusual colony of lesser horseshoe bats. She didn't know that part of the county terribly well, and it only made sense for her to go with him, as he had such an extensive knowledge of the highways and byways thereabouts. They swapped wildlife stories all the way there, and she had to admit that she would never have found the location without his help.

She had never seen such a large roost before, and was keen to go back with Mr Hicks at dusk, after dark, and at dawn as well to see all the activity. He seemed to be very keen too. Miss Masters (spinster) told Mr Hicks (widower) that she would have to alert the authorities about their find, as this habitat was clearly one of special scientific interest, and it would have to be made a protected site and the dear little bats properly looked after.

Miss Masters said she would also have to alert the council's health and hygiene authority, for judging by the one single pasty left on the side, the whole building was being used as some kind of massive pasty production unit. Apparently, she whispered, by those TV people down at Tredogend who it turned out had just been pretending to make their own pasties in the Emporium.

Oh dear, said Mr Hicks. *No* dear, surely not. Wouldn't you think they'd know better, and him being such a famous celebrity chef and all that. We see them come, we see them go, don't we just? Would you care for a cream tea down at Tredogend, Miss Masters dear?

Digory had enquired. It would be a perfect end to an enjoyable day, she said.

Oggy was trying to prise up the valuable slate slabs from the pantry floor, swinging his crowbar with manic abandon, sweating and swearing and cursing on his hands and knees in a futile and desperate attempt to get them up, sell them and get his hands on a bit of cash from the local architectural salvage merchant up Deli.

Vi, Mervin, Uncle Clar and Mother had tried to stop him and persuade him that all was not yet lost, but he had barricaded himself in there by shoving the new freezer up against the inside of the door. From outside, the digging and grunting was becoming increasingly frantic, and they began to worry for his very sanity.

Cheel and Inga got to a lay-by on the A30, just past Lanson, where Cornwall ends and England begins. Together the girls tipped the still comatose and beautifully tagged and decorated Huge! out of the trailer, and dragged him along and pulled him up into a sitting position to rest against the Devon side of the sign that above his head read, with a certain irony, 'Welcome to Cornwall.'

They draped a St Piran's flag over him and left him for the buzzards, and were it not for the appearance of a text from Mervin, Cheel would have felt quite elated.

She read it aloud. '*Come quick - father not well.*'

Cheel burst into the kitchen and found her family distraught.

'He's shut himself in darlin',' said her Mum tearfully. 'He's tearing it all up. Don't know what to do with him.'

Mother looked at Cheel. 'She'll know what to do, won't you my ansom bird?'

Cheel nodded. 'You're coming in too, Nan,' she said.

'I can't,' she said. 'You know why.'

'You got to,' said Cheel, and held out her hand. Mother took it.

With Mervin, Uncle Clar and Vi's help, Cheel slowly shoved the door open. Oggy was in there on all fours. He'd prised up a load of the floor slates, and piled them up in a corner.

Cheel led Mother nervously in. Vi and Mervin and Uncle Clar peered in from outside.

'What the hell are you doing, Father?' she asked.

'We're selling up. Going away. To Delhi or somewhere, any-bloody-where.'

'No we ain't. I've sorted it father. We shan't see him again; he's gone.'

'It's gotta go, all of it, I ain't leaving nothing,' he said.

'All of it? All of it, father? Oh bloody genius, yea. Let's rip the lot down and sell it. You've done the floor, let's get rid of the walls too shall we!'

Cheel grabbed the crowbar from her father and plunged it into wall, and ripped it towards herself in a downward motion that began to pull the sheet of hardboard away.

'Stop Cheel!' shouted Mervin.

'What are you doing?! Stop!' shouted Vi.

'Oh my lovely, you mustn't be so rough,' said Uncle Clar.

'No, no, no, father says it all gotta go, so it all gotta go!'

Dust fell from behind the panel in clouds as she wrenched and twisted, and there was a deep rumbling noise as the panel finally toppled away from the wall and fell outwards, and crashed onto the floor in one sheet. Oggy lay there coughing and spluttering, and Cheel stood back and wiped her eyes and sneezed.

Mother, transfixed and with her arms at her side, stepped slowly past Cheel and stared at the plaster wall that had been hidden behind the panel since before anyone could remember.

Oggy stumbled to his feet. 'Come on Mervin. Give me a hand to move this bloody freezer then I can get the rest of these slates up!'

'Shut up a minute, boy,' said Mother. 'Look. Look at this.'

She stepped closer to the wall and blew some more dust away, and then lightly wiped it with her fingertips. She picked up a dry cloth and cleaned a patch.

'Oh my God,' said Cheel slowly.

'I been telling you there's been something funny in here for years, boy,' said Mother.

Oggy said nothing, just gawped.

Mother grasped Cheel's hand. They both stared at the wall. 'I been worried about you, my ansom.'

'I been all right, Nan.'

'I know you have,' she said, and squeezed it tight.

Across the old plaster wall was an exquisitely crafted panoramic mural of old Tredogend. At the top, overlooking and dominating the town, the castle itself had been painted, in far better repair than in the present day, with flags flying and helmeted soldiers with pikes and muskets patrolling the ramparts. Beneath the castle, floating on a calm blue sea just out from what was undoubtedly the lion-head of Tredogend Point, a square rigger lay at anchor, and away from that small rowing boats were being pulled ashore, laden with sacks of what looked very much like potatoes, and they were being unloaded by men, women and children at the quay.

Across the middle of the composition the fields and meadows at the edge of the town were depicted, much the same shape as they remained to the day. There were vegetables growing in neatly cultivated strips; the lush green tops of onions and swedes growing side by side in the ground. There were hessian sacks, some upright and others tipped on their side with vegetables tumbled out across the ground. A gardener stood overlooking his crop, holding a basket full of produce that he had gathered. There was a busy beehive, and terracotta pots, spades and forks and hoes and rakes scattered all around.

To the right of the mural, the artist had painted a meadow bordered with a may blossomed hedge and wind-bent trees, while swallows and gulls dipped and glided above in the vivid blue of a summer sky. Shaggy St Piran's longhorn cattle, black with white crosses on their backs and fringes lanked down over their eyes, grazed on lush green grass, attended by a stick-wielding husbandsman smocked in stitch-patterned canvas, in conversation with a drover who seemed about to drive them off to market.

To the left of the meadows and vegetable plantation was a tall, narrow, three-storey building near the old harbour, built of timber and plaster. It had a kitchen, and around the big old table four rosy-cheeked ladies in mop caps and aprons peeled and sliced potato, swede and onion, and chopped meat. One was rolling out pastry circles with a rolling pin, and in front of her sat a tray of perfectly crimped pasties.

Beside her, overseeing the whole affair, a ruff-collared gentleman was depicted, a larger figure than all the others, he had a ginger moustache and goatee and was wearing a cocked hat, his ruddy, cheery face a picture of happiness and contentment as he sampled their delicious wares. One hand was outstretched in the direction of the sailing ship, and in the other he held up a pasty. A ginger gentleman, and clearly lord and master of all he surveyed.

Beneath the colourful panorama of the mural, Mother and Cheel read aloud the beautifully hand-scripted words.

'*Potato importer of Tredogend. Pafty fhoppe 1628. Women of Kernow pafty making – Squire and Mrf Sloggett and their maidf.*'

'There you go, WOK, 1628. What do you reckon, father?' said Cheel. 'Are you glad you never artexed *that* over?'

Cheel looked across at her brother.

'All right Merv'?' she said. 'Close your eyes and hold your hand out.'

'What?' he said.

She pressed the little felt hand stitched pasty into his palm and sang quietly to him, '*Jack and Jill went up the hill to fetch a pale of water.*'

'No way! You haven't. Where was it?'

'Towed it back earlier,' she said, and winked her sassy eye. 'Louspeaker still works too.'

Vi picked Oggy to his feet and together they stood behind Cheel and Mother, a hand on each of their shoulders.

'Squire, eh Cheel? Looks exactly like me too, don't he?' he said proudly, with just the faintest trace of a smile on his lips.

Cheel had to agree, and nodded to her father.

'You was right all along, Mother,' he continued. 'There *was* something funny in the pantry, I never doubted you for a minute.'

'Why are you slowing down?' said Nigel.

'It's a thirty. I've got seven points,' said Tom as he checked his mirror.

'What are you worried about? We've probably eaten the only copper in the area, remember? Put your bloody foot down!'

The car sped along the lush valley lanes, and Tom and Nigel's heads bumped the inside of the car as it bounced over an ancient humpback bridge.

'That's it. That was the Tamar. We must be over the border. Look, by the lay-by, there's the sign…'

'Someone's dumped a sack of shit next to it. By the Mrs Baggit bin there…'

The car pulled over into the lay-by, and the two men craned their necks, and leaned and peered out. Slumped against the 'Welcome to Cornwall' sign was the semi-naked Huge!, sprayed and body-painted from head to toe, with a one-legged seagull standing on his head.

'Oh my God,' said Tom. 'I'd recognise that floppy hair cut anywhere…'

They stopped and got out, and the gull flew up screeching and squawking with what sounded very much like laughter. They dragged the still tripping Huge! into the back of the car, lay him down and slammed the door.

'Welcome to Cornwall?' said Nigel, looking at the sign. 'You most certainly bloody are!'

They screeched out of the lay-by and high-tailed it back across the border and into England, back to what they knew best, and they left the dear old county far, far behind.

Chapter Twenty Four
A Proper Job

Dancing here, prancing there,
Jigging, jogging everywhere,
Up and down and round the town,
Hurrah! For the Cornish Floral Dance.

'The Floral Dance' *by Kate Moss*

It was in the dead of night that Cheel had stood by the harbour side at Tredogend, and watched as the Padstow trawler had come in and spirited Krno and the Romanians away as contraband, out over the silver moonlit sea, across to France and from there, who knows? Maybe they'd be back again next year, maybe somewhere else. She waved them off, until the trawler had turned the corner of the bay and chugged off into the churning darkness of the westerly heave.

The following day she jumped on the quad and made her way up to Dordigor Farm to finally return it intact to Digory, and screeched into the yard to find the dapper little chap splashing water from a hose into some plastic jerry cans. She thanked him and handed him the keys.

'Haven't seen you since I went up to the well,' she said. 'Took us hours to find it right up there, Uncle Digory. Never knew such a place existed.'

Digory screwed a cap on one can and started to fill another.

'I nearly forgot myself. Haven't been up there in years,' he said.

'How's that? What about when you gets Mother's special water for her pastry?'

Digory looked sheepish.

'Uncle Digory?'

He sloshed the hose out of the jerry can, chucked it down and strolled over to the yard tap and turned it off. Cheel watched him as he walked back and screwed the top on the second can, and then lifted one in each hand.

'You won't tell Mother, will you?' he said quietly.

'What? No, but how long since you got it from the well?'

'Last time when you was just a little maid.'

'No! All that time.'

'Will you take them to her now, or shall I bring 'em dreckly?' he said.

Cheel nodded and smiled. 'Dreckly,' she said. ' 'Tis still special water.'

Oggy had been persuaded by representatives of the Cornish Studies Faculty at Falmouth University that he was the owner of an historic building, in a remarkable state of preservation, and testament to a proud Cornish lineage and heritage. Historians revealed that Squire Thomas Gabriel Sloggett had been a sea captain, who had taken Puritans and Quakers and other non-conformists across to the New World, and in return brought back potatoes to North Cornwall, where he had set up plantations and became a merchant for the magical and exotic new vegetable. Undoubtedly, it was his potatoes that were the missing link in the story of the evolution of the food that today we still call the pasty.

The historians had been astounded to discover that up on nearby Dordigor Farm there was still a plantation of potatoes, and though it was now untended and quite overgrown by nettles and brambles and Japanese knotweed, it held the remnants of the original tubers shipped home all those years ago; ancestral potatoes of the 'Great Spud of Tredogend', if you will. Even more astounding up there were Mr Hicks' St Piran's longhorn cattle, a breed long suspected extinct. From the mural on the pantry wall, it was evident that the skirt beef and the potatoes used in those original pasties were what Mr Hicks was still producing up on his smallholding to supply Mother's pasty shop. The link was complete.

It took the builders less than a week to remove all Oggy's improvements to the outside of Mother's, and several expensive skip loads of pebbledash and cladding and artex later, the Stuart façade (c1610) of the old shop was revealed for the first time anyone could ever remember, and restoration of the ancient timber frame and plasterwork build began. Mother Sloggett's Original Cornish Pasty Shop was re-born, and four hundred years of uninterrupted pasty production continued unabated.

They retrieved the old Treleaven oven from the chapel and put it back in its rightful home, and gave it pride of place behind their counter, and daily they filled their shop window with Mother's gloriously delicious pasties. They overwhelmed the street with the heady, bewitching aroma of their pasties and created queues of desperate, starving customers so long that they stretched all the way down the street to the harbour front.

'Mother's Pasties! Come on in and get a Taste of the Past!' said the notice in the window.

But Mother's was no longer just a pasty shop, for when they had bought their Little Piskys or their

Mother's Traditionals or Cornish Giant pasties, still sold in their own charmingly illustrated bags, they were funnelled out past the secret inner sanctum of the working kitchen and out to the entrance of the newly discovered 'pasty pantry'.

The pasty pantry, where the now famous pasty mural had become the dear old county's major tourist hotspot, overtaking Land's End, St Michael's Mount, the Eden Project, Trago and Par Market.

The pasty pantry, internationally renowned as perhaps one of the most important artefacts of it's kind, competing as it now did with the hieroglyphics of the Valley of the Kings, the cave paintings of Les Eyzies, the Bayeux Tapestry and even the ceiling of the Sistine chapel. At least, this is what Oggy thought, and although some historians were a little more sceptical of its overall significance, there was no doubting which of these was most important to the patriotic Cornish.

Oggy tilted his trilby hat to a jaunty angle in front of the three-sided dressing-table mirror. It was not as high in the crown as the one his ancestor Squire Thomas was wearing in the mural, but it was not far off. He lifted the net curtain and pulled it across from the window to his throat and grasped it behind his head, and then folded and bunched it up high around his neck, imitating the potato merchant's ruff. He lifted and smoothed his chin. He had not shaved it for several days, and there were a few orangey sprouts beginning to make a show. He admired the triptych of reflected images, which he thought reminded him of someone regal. There were, he decided, definite similarities.

He replaced the curtain and went downstairs to the shop counter. The telephone rang. He picked it up.

'Good morning,' said the voice. 'My name is Colin from Business Solutions for You. May I speak to Mr Oggy please?'

''Tis *you*, Colin!' said Oggy, catching his own reflection admiringly in the shop window and adjusting the brim again. 'By gar, I've spoke to that many Colins I never thought I should hear from you again. How is it in Delhi boy?'

'Very well, thank you, Mr Oggy. Now today I am bringing a new offer for you. 3.75% plus fifteen pence per transaction on all debit and credit cards, wireless terminal, full back-up within twenty four hours.'

'That sounds good to me Colin. It's time I got with it. When can I get it all put in?' he said, and tweaked the hatband. 'I got that much cash coming out me ears these days, I don't know what to do with it all.'

'Tomorrow at the latest, Mr Oggy.'

'Right on.'

'Proper job,' said Colin happily. 'And I am very pleased Mr Oggy, as this will get me my bonus, so thanking you and you have a great day now.'

'Speak to you soon,' said Mr Oggy, and hung up the receiver, and skipped singing through the door back into the kitchen, ducking just a little lest he disturb the hat.

'What have you got on your 'ead?' asked Vi.

'What? I've had this for years,' he said.

'It looks very nice now Vi,' said Uncle Clar. Mother said nothing. Oggy kept his chin down.

'And what's them wispy bits on yer chin?'

'What whippy bits?'

'You looks like a Nanny goat, boy.'

'More like a Billy goat if you don't mind, Mother, so look out I don't butt you up the ass,' he said. 'And don't call me boy.'

'We should all dress up like them geezers on the picture,' said Vi. 'That'll get the customers in. Cheel says she got still mates in dance and drama; they'd love to come and do a performance she said. *Pasty*, the musical. What about that?'

'Bollocks to dance and drama,' he chuckled. 'Like the maid said, 'tis too shallow and superstitial.'

'Superficial!' shouted Cheel from the hallway. 'Right Mum, Nan, Uncle Clar, I gotta go. Ready father?'

'Yes,' said Oggy. 'Vi, did you do me a flask, or no?'

'You're only taking her to Plymouth, darlin'.'

'Zackly, you never know what'll happen when you crosses that bridge. Nothing but whores and rogues the other side of the Tamar.'

'Come on father, or I shall miss the boat.'

'You be careful, now,' said Uncle Clar.

'They're the same as us over in Brittany, Uncle Clar. Celts!'

'Well gawd help ya then, darlin'!' called Vi.

'Bye!'

'Cheers and gone!' called Cheel.

'Byeee! Good luck!'

And as father and daughter left their little village for Plymouth and the Brittany ferry across to Roscoff, Oggy reflected that it was the first time he was going to cross into England for nigh on twenty years, and more than this, that Cheel was destined to be the first Sloggett of Tredogend to have gone abroad since his ancestor had brought back the 'Great Spud of Tredogend' from Virginia four hundred years ago.

What was the world coming to?

The Treleaven oven was not the only thing that they had retrieved from the deserted pasty emporium in the chapel. On a table towards the back, Cheel had seen something sparkling, and had gone over and retrieved the silver number nine that she and Inga had planted in the Gloucester Old Spot pork pasty, and she'd slipped it into her pocket and ever since had carried it everywhere she went for luck.

Oggy drove Cheel up the hill and out of Tredogend, and through the narrow country lanes down past St Kew and St Mabyn and Pencarrow, and on into Bodmin, where he turned left at the clock tower, and along down past the turning for the gaol and the old station, and then turned right and found himself snarled up in the pedestrian friendly zone of Fore Street.

'Where are you going now, father?'

'Why, up here.'

'You should have turned left for Plymouth down by the church.'

'Hellfire! Too late now. Just like yer mother, always tells me when we gone past the turning! That's no use to man nor beast.'

'I just can't wait 'till you got to drive in Plymouth,' sighed Cheel. 'Deep joy.'

'Where'd I go now then? I always gets lost in Bodmin.'

'Keep yer hands on the wheel. Why don't you stop and ask someone?'

'Here,' snapped Oggy. 'You bloody ask.' He swerved and pulled over on his left outside the vast old Bodmin United Methodist chapel, now metamorphosed into one of Witherton's ghastly gastro pubs. A lone figure clad in a dark suit and tie stood in the doorway, hands clasped across his front. Cheel wound down her window.

'Excuse me,' she called. The tall doorman walked over and leaned to the car, and she immediately recognised the heavy, Hammer House of Horror Neanderthal brow and all the other features that would have excited anthropologists and doubtless inspired Mary Shelley. When ex-constable 696 Carthew Carew (recently 'retired') clocked who it was that had called to him, he stepped away in trepidation, and tripped across the kerb and fell sprawling backwards onto the pavement.

Cheel jumped out of the car, and stood over the quaking, shaking man.

'No,' he cried. 'Please, not again…'

She offered him her hand, and slowly, guardedly, he took it, and she pulled him to his feet and stared up at him. She reached inside her pocket and took out a small silvery number. She held it up for him to see.

'Thing is,' she said. 'Can't tell if it's a nine or a six, can you?'

'It's a nine,' he said.

She pressed the number into his palm.

'Good,' she said. 'All our little secret, Carthew. Now, how do we get back on the Plymouth road? Tell me father or we shall never get out of the county.'

Carew went around the car, tugged an imaginary forelock and bent reverentially to Oggy's window.

'Morning, Mr Sloggett, sir. Nice to see you. How's business these days? Good, I hope. Now, if you just go up here along Fore Street and hang a right and go back around the system…'

Oggy Sloggett, due to past experience, was rather dumbfounded by Carew's display of reverence, but did exactly that. He turned left at St Petroc's Church and drove off out of Bodmin, past Parkway Station and along the Glynn Valley, then past Trago and Dobwalls and on towards Liskeard. From time to time, through the corner of his eye, he glimpsed his slip of a daughter and he remembered what Mother had said, 'She got it, she has. Mark my words.'

They travelled in silence. He was puzzled and he was curious and, quite forgetting she was sitting beside him, he wondered aloud to himself.

'What was up with Carew, then? Why's he being so helpful?'

Cheel looked straight ahead. 'Gwary whek yu gwary tek, father.'

'Yes, he is,' said Oggy. 'That's exactly what I thought.'

Mervin put his feet up on the decking outside the ice cream van, making the most of the unseasonal October sun, and drifted off into a little daytime nap, bees busily and contentedly buzzing around him. He awoke to find a small child standing there right in front of him.

'Hi Mervin,' said Goujon. 'This is for you.'

Mervin sat up, and took the bag from the little boy. He opened it, and took out a pasty. It had the letter 'M' written in pastry on the side.

'Wow, little surf dude. Where'd you get this?' he asked.

'We baked it, didn't we Mum?' he said.

Emma and Julienne and Quenelle crept around from behind the shack.

'Hi,' said Emma. 'Yes we did. It's for you Mervin. A little something to say, you know...'

'How have you been?' asked Mervin. He bit into the pasty. 'Ain't seen you for months.'

'Okay, you know,' she said. 'Kids, why don't you go off and play on the beach?'

The children scampered across the all but deserted sands with buckets and spades, off to dig and dam and divert and channel their favourite stream.

Emma gazed out at the crashing surf. 'Hugo and I have separated. Long story, but the kids and I will be happier here. There's more for them, just look at it all, I love it so much,' she sighed. 'I'm so sorry for what he did to you. Your van and all that.'

'Never mind, I got it back didn't I?' said Mervin. 'Anyway, where will you live? Have you got yourselves an old ice cream van yet?'

'Hot dog you mean?' she laughed. 'No, I think we can rent the same cottage long term.'

'That's nice,' said Mervin.

'Well, it's a bit small but…'

'No, I mean *this* is nice,' he said, and held up the pasty. 'This might just have the magic touch. Made with love.'

'I think it might be,' said Emma, and smiled into his eyes. 'Proper job.'

Cheel looked back over the stern at the long, bubbling wake of the Quiberon as it steamed out past Plymouth breakwater at the commencement of the channel crossing. A couple of gulls dipped and chattered overhead and followed the ferry as the land behind her shrank slowly away into the distance.

She heard a voice behind her.

'Cheeeel!'

She turned. Inga stood framed in the doorway of the viewing deck. Cheel ran over and they kissed each cheek and hugged one another.

'So what are you doing?' Cheel asked excitedly.

'Well,' said Inga. 'I got a text from Marcel to say that he was filming an episode down in Provence, and he asked if I'd be up to being his researcher. So I thought I'd take my time and travel down through, I don't know how yet, but…'

'Cool.'

'Yea, well. So what about you? Oh, your wrestling. My God, is that now?'

'Saturday.'

'Saturday,' said Inga. 'Where?'

'Concarneau.'

Inga held Cheel's hand. 'Can I come? Let me come. I'll shout for you when you win. Cheeeeld!! Like that!'

'What about Marcel?'

Inga wrinkled her nose. 'Naah,' she said. 'Change is as good as a rest, isn't it?'

'Proper job,' said Cheel.

It was Saturday night. Oggy and Digory leaned against Trelawney's rickety stockade fence. The bull chewed silage, fringe dangling across his face. Pam and Brenda stood rump to rump, staring as one directly at him.

'Mind yer new blazer on that nail there, dear. Them pallets are full of them,' said Digory. Oggy looked down and leaned gently back.

'When did you find out then?' he asked.

'Daphne saw it first. She knows all about animals. Said they was both looking pretty perky, and Trelawney there was looking all puffed up and full of himself.'

'Well, I s'pose you would do, wouldn't you?'

'Her son's a vet, he said Brenda's having twins,' said Digory.

'Daphne's a very nice lady. She'll do you the world of good Digory.'

They made for the car, and Trelawney craned his neck and lifted his head, and with the steam spouting from his ringed nostrils, he let go three blaring bellows that rattled around the yard.

'See what it's done for him?' said Oggy. 'If we can sing out like that tonight we'll be all right!'

The old chapel in Tredogend was packed to its restored and made-over rafters for the Tredogend Fishermen's Choir autumn concert. There were still no fishermen amongst them, but they lived and sang on in hope. The choir marched smartly down either side of the pews, tenors to the right, and baritones and basses to the left, and they lined up in their ranks. For most of them, it was the first performance they had ever given where they were actually outnumbered by an audience.

Jeff stood in front of them all, then swivelled on his heels and began to introduce the choir and its repertoire. Lavinia lounged stunning in a swirling cobalt-blue ball gown and dangly diamante earrings like chandeliers, Cleopatra-eyed, rouge cheeked and lips cherry glossed, and the beautified nails on her builder's fingers polished and delicately poised above the awaiting ivories.

Vi sat proudly between Mother and Uncle Clar. Next to them Miss Daphne Masters, spinster and companion to Mr Digory Hicks, and then Mervin who, with Emma at the other end, sandwiched Quenelle, Julienne and little Goujon. When Jeff raised his hands, they joined the rest of the audience on their feet in rapturous applause of the choir's re-appearance in their old village chapel.

They listened to the words with an intensity they had never held before.

'And no one will ever move me away from this land,
  Until the lord calls me to sit at his hand.
  For this is my Eden, and I'm not alone.
  For this is my Cornwall, and this is my home.'

Oggy looked out at the audience, and as he looked out, he could see his family, and he thought of his own father and granfer singing in that chapel, and in his mind's eye he saw his ancestor in the mural, all ruff-collared and goateed and cocked hat, four hundred years ago.

He looked at Mother, and swore that he could just make out the slightest glisten of a tear in the corner of her eye. He looked at Vi, the wife he loved very much, who winked at him in affirmation of the very same.

He looked for Uncle Clar, but his place on the pew was empty. His eyes drifted above the heads of the good folk of Tredogend right to the back of the chapel, where in an alcove by the kitchen the jovial old boy stood at a trestle table with a cup and saucer in hand, slurping tay and nibbling on a nice biscuit.

He looked at Miss Daphne Masters, spinster, and peeped across to Digory his old mate. He thought of Trelawney and Pam and Brenda and the pitter-patter of tiny hooves.

He looked at Mervin, all loved up and with somebody else's kids. She seemed very nice, but he wished that the boy'd get a decent haircut and a proper job.

He looked out and thought of that dear maid Cheel, all the way over in France.

Huge! burst into the glass walled office of ZeeTV, a pretty young secretary carrying his papers in tow, and dashed around the table to an empty space.

'Hi Nige, Tom. Hi Barney,' he said.

Barney looked up at him in puzzlement. 'What's that mark on your forehead, Huge!?'

Huge! tugged down his fringe. 'Nothing,' he said. 'Just a bit of felt tip I can't seem to wash off.'

'Let's see it,' laughed Barney. 'Have you been on a stag do or something?'

Reluctantly, Huge! pulled back his fringe for the big reveal.

'I can't really make it out,' said Barney. 'Only the 'T' at the end, what did it say?'

Huge! glanced at the young secretary. 'I...I can't really remember,' he said, a little embarrassed. She giggled.

Nigel sighed. 'So, anyway, what is it Huge!?'

Huge! grinned a wide, floppy, foppish grin all over his face. He glanced, nodding, from one to the other and then back again, the tip of his tongue wetting his lower lip.

'Huge!?' said Barney.

'You want me to smack ma pitch up?'

Nigel leaned back in his chair. 'Well I suppose...'

'Oh, come on noo, McNige,' oozed Huge! in *Braveheart* mode. He slammed a tartan package, shaped like a fat, squashed sausage, down hard on the boardroom table. 'You take the high road and I'll take the low road to the wee, camber-tossing, tasty tartan totty up there in bonnie Jockland! Och aye, the noo, Donald, where's your troosers? That's the story, Balla-bloody-morey, Nige!'

Again he eyeballed each man in turn.

'Come on doon to Brigadoon!' he chirped with a wink. 'It's time to sex up the haggis boys!'

He patted the package.

'Gentlemen,' he said, in a rubbish Rab C Nesbit, 'See you Jimmy,' Glaswegian accent. ' I give you...*the shaggis*!'

'Wow...' said Nigel, after having taken some seconds to draw breath. 'Well, I...'

Barney got to his feet and made for the door. 'So,' he said. 'I'll leave that one with you Nige.'

'Ladies and gentlemen,' announced Jeff the choirmaster. 'Thank you for coming to our Annual Autumn Concert, back here at last in our dear old chapel. Before we all finish off together, as is traditional, by a community singing of Trelawney, I have an announcement about a very, very special, surprise guest.'

The audience stared at him, intrigued, so too the members of the choir.

'All the way back from France, the Inter Celtic Ladies Featherweight Champion, and victorious captain of the Cornish Ladies rasslin team. Please give a massive round of applause for our very own Cheel Sloggett!'

There was an audible intake of breath as the double doors at the rear burst open, and carried proudly aloft by all of her teammates, Cheel Sloggett was paraded above their heads into the wildly thronging, clapping, cheering chapel to the mighty strains of Trelawney, with the great silver trophy firmly and triumphantly held in the grip of her little hands.

They lofted her to the front where the excited Sloggetts herded ecstatically around her, and Oggy came down from the choir and grabbed his daughter and gingerly lifted her, trophy and all, up onto his shoulders for the first time since she was a little maid, and the tears streamed down his face and Mother's too, and Uncle Clar and Mervin's and Vi's, for they *could* cry, the Sloggetts.

Mother wiped her eyes, and blew her nose in a tissue. 'I told you, boy,' she said. 'She got it, she has.'

Oggy studied his Mother. She reached out and squeezed his hand.

'Proper job, Mother,' he said, quietly. 'And don't call me boy, eh?'

She leaned forward and kissed him on his cheek.

'Sorry boy,' she whispered.

And so the great feast began, and they sang and they whooped and cheered, these people of Cornwall, and passed around Mother's pasties and jam and cream splits to the strains of Trelawney, and the cider and beer and tay flowed like a golden river, and they danced that Cheel way up high on their broad shoulders, around and around and around, the queen of her people, the queen of her land.

A woman of Kernow.

The End

About The Author

Jon Cleave is the author and illustrator of seven children's books of the adventures of 'Gully the Mischievous and Wicked Cornish Seagull', first published in 2005. He is the bass singer and MC of the award winning Cornish sea shanty group The Fisherman's Friends, and as such has extensively toured the UK and performed amongst other places at the Queen's Jubilee River Flotilla, the Festival Hall and Albert Hall and on the Pyramid stage at Glastonbury Festival, as well as numerous occasions on TV and radio. The group's incredible story is soon to be told in a movie. He has an acting credit for his lead role in the movie short 'Black Car Home'. A Cornishman through and through, Jon lives in Port Isaac with his wife of over thirty years Caroline, and their three sons Jacob, George and Theo.